SUCH
A GOOD
MOM

ALSO BY JULIA SPIRO

Full

Someone Else's Secret

SUCH A GOOD MOM

A NOVEL

JULIA SPIRO

MINOTAUR
BOOKS
NEW YORK

First published in the United States by Minotaur Books, an imprint of St. Martin's Publishing Group

SUCH A GOOD MOM. Copyright © 2025 by Julia Spiro. All rights reserved. Printed in the United States of America. For information, address St. Martin's Publishing Group, 120 Broadway, New York, NY 10271.

www.minotaurbooks.com

Designed by Omar Chapa

The Library of Congress Cataloging-in-Publication Data is available upon request.

ISBN 978-1-250-32417-7 (hardcover)
ISBN 978-1-250-32418-4 (ebook)

Our books may be purchased in bulk for promotional, educational, or business use. Please contact your local bookseller or the Macmillan Corporate and Premium Sales Department at 1-800-221-7945, extension 5442, or by email at MacmillanSpecialMarkets@macmillan.com.

First Edition: 2025

10 9 8 7 6 5 4 3 2 1

For Caroline Davey Hannah, and for all childcare givers.
Thank you for being the village.

SUCH A GOOD MOM

PROLOGUE

Like most New England summertime destinations, Martha's Vineyard was no stranger to tragedy, though it often hid deep in the island's underbelly, safely tucked away from tourists, rarely disrupting their cycle of lobster rolls and blue-sky beach days. But real islanders—the ones who raised children there, the ones who buried parents there, the ones who weathered hurricanes there, the ones whose darkest secrets existed within the lush ninety-six square miles of that Massachusetts island—knew far too well that tragedy was, actually, everywhere on the island, all the time, waiting to strike.

Winter on the Vineyard showed no mercy for locals. Beaches once bathed in warm sunshine, festooned with sandcastles and ice-cream-cone drippings, stood frozen and barren from November through March. Occasionally, during that long winter, the sun would appear, and moods would temporarily lift, but only briefly. While summer residents were back home in Greenwich and Wellesley and on the Upper East Side, island locals were struggling to find housing, to secure childcare, to prepare for the onslaught of another season of demand. Addiction of all kinds quickly became a familiar old acquaintance to most residents, knocking at their doors during those lonely, cold months, offering an escape from the brutality of the off season. Every winter, the island braced itself for inevitable losses: to drugs, to alcohol, to depression.

But the island wasn't immune to hardship during the summer, either. Summer, in particular, was ripe for tragedy, and violence, and pain. Deceptive and misleading, the island felt impossibly safe to summer visitors and seasonal residents during its peak season—a wholesome, bucolic snow globe of white picket fences in Edgartown and roadside farmstands in Chilmark. How could anything bad happen in such a beautiful place? How could anyone feel pain and suffering on an island where the sunset was so vivid, painted in bright hues of apricot and coral, that it seemed to be pouring right out of the sky and into the sea? Serious crimes couldn't happen here, summer folks assumed, not in a place that didn't have a single traffic light on the entire island. A trip to the island was, to visitors, a potent reminder that there were places in the world impervious to danger, places where happiness was the norm, places where humankind was *good*.

In the summer, guards were let down. People relaxed. People got careless. They became sloppy, forgetful, a little too much at ease. One more drink? One more swim? *Why not, we're on vacation*. And in turn, locals needed to let loose during the summer, too—if they were ever lucky enough to have an opportunity to do so. Locals spent those months breaking their backs working double shifts, barely making enough to get by, so when a chance to have some fun presented itself to them, they sure as hell took it, and they took it hard. Accidents happened.

It made sense, then, that on a perfect day in late June, when the body of a young woman was found on the shores of Norton Point Beach, residents weren't particularly shocked. Already that summer, islanders had suffered a fatal car accident, a drowning off the infamous *Jaws* bridge, and an overdose. These tragedies hit the island like tidal waves, delivering swift and powerful blows of pain and sadness, but then pulling back just as fast as they'd arrived. Because islanders weren't allowed to grieve during the summer. June, July, and August were the most important months of the year, when residents were laser-focused on one thing: work. This numbness to pain was an act of self-preservation that islanders had developed over time, enabling them to forge onward whenever tragedy struck, despite their hearts shattering silently inside.

This time, at first, it seemed like all those other senseless and terrible accidents: a young person partied too hard, went for a swim, perhaps with a lover, but was caught by the riptide, or got a cramp, or was simply too intoxicated to swim and drowned. The island would cry and mourn, but then it would be forced to move on, for it would have to usher in the next round of hotel guests, of house tenants, and of dinner reservations, all with a smile.

But this time was different. Once the initial shock wore off, and funeral arrangements had been made, and people stopped bringing flowers to the makeshift seaside shrine, the island began to realize that this was, in fact, nothing like all the other tragic accidents. Once the island learned who this person was, who she knew, and *what* she knew, the island realized that this wasn't an accident at all.

This was murder.

CHAPTER 1

Brynn Nelson seemed to be nursing the worst hangover of her life. The kind involving six dirty vodka martinis, a pack of Parliament Lights, smudged eyeliner, a tank top strap slipping down a shoulder, dim lights at a crowded dive bar. It was early morning now, and her head throbbed, her stomach churned, and her body ached.

But she wasn't hungover. It had been months since she'd even tasted a dirty martini—almost a year. And she hadn't smoked a cigarette in almost ten years, when she was in her early twenties, living in a shoebox apartment in the West Village. She *yearned* for that shoebox apartment now, a world away from the island of Martha's Vineyard, where she lived today. She longed for the freedom to drink martinis with abandon and smoke cigarettes with a stranger, knowing that she'd never be able to do that again. Not really.

Brynn only *felt* hungover, because she was a first-time mother to a three-month-old who refused to sleep. She was exhausted, and this was now how she felt all the time. A hangover seemed like a luxury in comparison to the way she felt now.

That morning had started for Brynn like any other since Lucas was born: with a headache and a sense of dread. She'd spent most of the night wide awake, either feeding Lucas every hour and a half, which he demanded almost down to the minute with a glass-shattering wail, or pumping in the dark stillness of the kitchen, and then carefully transferring the milk into freezer bags and labeling them with the date and time, and finally stuffing her face with blueberry muffins and cookies—whatever carbs she could find—then putting on a fresh change of clothes, as her shirt became drenched in sweat every hour throughout the night, and her underwear still became speckled with blood, even though she'd had a C-section. No one had warned her about the sweat, or the blood.

Last week, Brynn thought she'd successfully implemented the sleep-training technique from a virtual sleep coach for which she'd shelled out four hundred dollars. She'd found the coach on Instagram while she was pumping at three in the morning and immediately purchased the "Magic Sleep Package" in a moment of sheer desperation. The package included a half-hour phone call with the sleep coach and an emailed brochure with a personalized plan. But really, in its most distilled form, the plan simply gave Brynn permission to let Lucas cry. For one torturous week, she followed the instructions. And at the end of the week, it really *was* like magic: she and her husband, Ross, had enjoyed an entire night of peace and quiet, when Lucas hardly moved during a glorious nine-hour slumber. But that had turned out to be a fluke, and now he woke throughout the evening in a relentless pattern, screaming and crying at such an acute, guttural pitch that Brynn thought her eardrums might actually burst.

Brynn had tried other things, too, in addition to the expensive sleep coach. She still kept notes on her phone documenting his sleep stretches and feeding times throughout the night. She'd read every parenting book, she followed all the advice-giving social media accounts, she bought all the baby gear and gadgets out there, she had the pediatrician on speed dial. She'd even reluctantly joined a local support group for new moms through Martha's Vineyard Community Services, which she knew had been a huge help to many island parents before her.

Lucas had cried a raspy cry the entire meeting. And the more he cried, the more anxious Brynn got. She could feel her own body temperature rising, her muscles tensing.

"He's just fussy," she had said to the group while bouncing Lucas in her arms. No one asked for an explanation. The other parents just looked at her with a mix of what she discerned as pity and confusion.

"Brynn," the group leader had said, as her own toddler sucked away with ease at her breast beneath her cocoon sweater, "he's a *baby*. When he cries, he's trying to *communicate* with you. You're his mother. You just need to listen to him." Brynn had nodded. She'd heard this advice before—that babies cry to tell us something. Usually, that they're hungry, or tired, or need a diaper change. The problem was, whenever Brynn addressed these potential needs, Lucas still wasn't satisfied, and his relentless wail continued no matter what kind of comfort she offered him. She tried to listen closely, as though something might suddenly click, and she'd innately understand him, the way she thought a mother was supposed to understand her child. She shut her eyes and tuned out everything else around her. But Lucas's cries only stabbed away at her eardrums, tightening her chest, and filling her with panic. The truth was, all she really heard when Lucas screamed was the disappearance of herself, and the suffocating feeling that she was forever lost. Each time he opened his mouth to howl, she swore that she could feel a piece of herself being erased. Sometimes, she felt like she'd do anything to silence him for just a moment, to have a few seconds for herself. To *breathe.* "I'll try that," she had responded to the group leader. Brynn never returned to the support group again.

Now, it was just past seven in the morning, and she'd already fed Lucas, changed him, and put him down for a nap. The daytime schedule the sleep coach had given her was a far cry from the reality of how Lucas's day unfolded. "Try to sleep when he sleeps," the coach had advised, as so many others had, as well. Brynn wanted to, and sometimes she did, but she found it difficult to mentally unplug enough to fall asleep. She had too many worries constantly jogging through her mind: Did she put the next pediatrician appointment in her calendar? Did she move the laundry into the dryer? What was she going to make for dinner? Did she wash the bottles from last night? Did she rub the vitamin E oil on her scar? Was her car-insurance payment due or did she already pay it? Did she respond to the email from her literary agent asking—for the *third* time that month—when the new chapters of her next book would be ready? Quieting these thoughts was impossible. It was easier, instead, to stay awake and distract herself during Lucas's naps with Instagram or Bravo or by cleaning the house.

The other baby she needed to take care of—her third book—she'd all but abandoned, and the guilt ate away at her constantly. Brynn had already published two romance novels, which had sold well enough to give her financial independence and a respected name in that genre, but with that success came responsibility—and *deadlines*. She'd secured a third book deal halfway through her pregnancy, thinking she'd zip through her first draft before Lucas was born. But she'd gotten side-tracked. She'd fallen into nesting mode, something she never thought she'd do. Every day there had been a project for the baby that somehow consumed Brynn's time—the crib needed to be assembled, curtains had to be put up, clothes had to be laundered with skin-sensitive baby detergent. There was always *something,* and then suddenly, Lucas was born.

But she'd told herself that she would have plenty of time to write during the newborn phase. "All they do is sleep and eat at first," everyone had said. She didn't need to send Lucas to daycare or hire any childcare, she thought, because she could just work from home with him, and that's what she'd always wanted, anyway. And nearby, she had her mother-in-law, Margaux, who was a true baby whisperer and was always ready to help. Brynn would have all the time in the world for writing, she thought. And yet, now, there somehow wasn't time for anything. The concept of *free time* no longer existed in Brynn's world. If she had any time for herself, she had to use it to address her own basic hygiene or chores.

And even if Brynn *did* have time to write, she didn't have the creative brain capacity that she used to have. During the few attempts she'd made at writing, she was embarrassed by what she produced: generic characters, flat storylines, and—worst of all—sex scenes as dull as watching paint dry. These days, her writing was the opposite of romantic. It was downright depressing.

She used to be able to write the most vivid and electric sex scenes in five minutes on a Post-it. Creativity was never something she had to *work* for. But now she couldn't conjure up a steamy lovemaking scene no matter how hard she tried. It didn't help that her own sex life was nonexistent. How could she describe a kiss when she hadn't even had one herself in months? At least not a good one, anyway. Did she even remember what it was like to have an orgasm?

Maybe it was just the sleep deprivation that was causing her to lose her literary edge, or maybe, she thought, it was something more. She felt as if she'd had to remove the part of her brain that maintained her intellectualism, curiosity, and creativity so she could replace it with a deep knowledge of baby choking hazards, the risk of SIDS, the difference between swaddles and sleep sacks, the multitude of baby bottle styles. It was as though her brain couldn't handle being both a mother and a writer. *One or the other,* it told her, though she refused to accept it, and she continued to try to do both. The result was that she couldn't really do either.

"Good morning, honey," her husband Ross said as he bounded into the kitchen, bright-eyed and well rested. Brynn had just sat down on one of the kitchen stools to pump. The plastic flanges were tucked into her nursing bra, the kind with little slits to hold the flanges steady. Her nipples engorged and retracted with the pump's pulses, and she immediately started dripping milk into the bottles. She'd bought one of the portable pumps that she could carry around like a purse. It had been advertised to her as one that would allow her to be mobile while pumping. But it only ended up making her feel trapped. Anytime she tried to do anything while pumping, she'd forget that she was hooked up to the machine, or that the tubes from the flanges to the machine were only two feet long, so she'd accidentally disconnect them and cause everything to go haywire. The only thing she could do while she pumped was sit there and count the minutes, watching the milk drip down into the bottles until she reached her capacity.

The first time that Ross had seen her pumping, his eyes had widened with bewilderment and horror.

"Whoa," he had said, cringing. "Does that hurt?" He'd watched Brynn's nipples expand inside the clear plastic flanges as if she were some kind of animal in a lab.

"No," she said. "It sort of feels good. Or at least, I feel better when it's done."

She stared out the window now as though the world outside was a foreign land that she'd never know again, full of freedom and sunshine and youthful people without any responsibilities.

Brynn had elbowed Ross a little past midnight, sometime after feeding Lucas. She had been furious at the sight of Ross in his deep sleep, and she had wanted him to be awake with her, if only for a moment. But the nudge hadn't even stirred him.

He kissed her forehead now, so lightly that she barely felt his lips on her skin. He was obliviously happy as he went to make coffee. "How was the little man last night?" he asked.

"He was . . . he was fine." The stupidity of the question confounded and enraged her. It was both infuriating and miraculous that Brynn's fatigue was not shared by Ross, even though they slept in the same bed and were subjected to the exact same cries from their son, who slept in the bassinet right next to them.

It was as though Ross existed in another realm entirely, one where he only *watched* the changes happening around him since becoming a father, but he and his own life continued as before, relatively unchanged. Sometimes, Brynn felt like she and Lucas were animals in an observation room, with Ross waving to them from the other side of the glass while she cried out for help. It didn't make sense that Ross was *right there* with her and yet he wasn't there at all. He didn't share even a shred of Brynn's suffering. The only disappointment he ever seemed to show was in *her* disappointment with everything. And Brynn had started to hate him for it.

Yet she didn't have the energy to tell Ross how she really felt, or that the night hadn't been *fine*. It had been a disaster. *All* the nights were disasters.

"That's great," Ross said. Somewhere in the past few months, their conversations had devolved into meaningless, robotic words—*great, good, okay*.

It hadn't always been like this. Everything changed when Lucas was born. Well, not really. What had *actually* changed, Brynn knew, was her. From the moment Lucas was born, Brynn had not become the soft, maternal, joyful mother she'd expected to become, the mother that Ross had told her he knew she'd be, the one she thought he wanted her to be. Instead, she had transformed into a stranger, as if she were playing a role, pretending. When she held Lucas for the first time, her entire body shaking, her eyelids fluttering and her throat burning for water, she did not look at him with the adoring eyes of a devoted mother. She'd looked at him with bewilderment, fear, and resentment. The resentment wasn't for him, exactly, but for everyone around her expecting her to feel anything different. Brynn had been in labor for almost forty hours, become violently ill with a high fever and nausea, then had an emergency C-section when Lucas's heartbeat started to drop and he turned sideways, throughout which she continued to vomit bile into a plastic bag held by a nurse, with the bright lights of the operating table blinding her eyes, her arms held down. And from the instant that Lucas was lifted from the swamps of her stomach, her guts pushed aside to create an exit for him, and then presented to her covered in white, creamy film, screaming with the anguish of someone who had indeed just been ripped from their home, Brynn was tasked with taking care of him, and not of herself.

So, while Brynn and everything in her life had permanently changed, the only thing that had really changed for Ross was the disposition of his wife.

"What's your day look like?" he asked her. The question was a mockery. He knew *exactly* what her day looked like, because it was the same each day: try to survive. Brynn felt Ross's eyes quickly glance over her bathrobe-clad body, with her gigantic, veiny breasts exposed. Was this his way of asking her if she was going to shower today? Or if this would be the day when he'd come home to a happy wife, who would greet him with a T-bone steak for dinner and a blowjob for dessert? Ross didn't have to say it; Brynn could feel his disappointment in her all the time. His sadness was loud and physical, hanging heavy in his sighs, in the shrugs of his shoulders, in his slow and steady hand on her shoulder when he returned home from work to still find her on the couch, still in her bathrobe, another pizza ordered for dinner, another hamper of laundry to do. She perceived it to be the sadness of someone whose partner had turned out to be someone else entirely. A letdown.

But what Brynn wished Ross understood was that she didn't *want* to be this way. She *wanted* to be his happy wife. She *wanted* to be a happy mom. She *wanted* to get back to her writing. She just didn't know how. She didn't know if it was possible.

"You're looking at it," she said. "I mean, we'll get some fresh air, go to the playground to see everyone. Lucas has a doctor's appointment in the afternoon. And I'm going to try to do some more writing if I can. I made some progress yesterday." It was a lie, of course. She hadn't made progress on her book yesterday. She hadn't made progress in months.

"That's great. Great." He tightened the lid of his thermos. "Well, I love you. Try to have a good day today, okay? It's so nice out." He kissed her forehead again and headed for the door. "I have to play a round of golf tonight at the club after work. Clients. But it should be quick."

"*Again?*" Last night, Ross had been out late with his father and brother, courting potential clients for a big job in Katama. Brynn couldn't remember what time Ross had come home, but she knew that it was during one of the rare, brief windows when she had been sleeping. He'd briefly woken her up by accident and she'd been furious.

"Last night was Katama," he responded, somewhat defensively. "Tonight is the North Water Street job."

"Okay," Brynn said. She couldn't argue with him when it was work. But there was always a round of golf. Always a client dinner. Ross worked for his father, Henry, who was considered the island's foremost builder and developer. If a home was being built by Nelson & Sons, it was going to be spectacular, with no expense spared. Still, Brynn had naively assumed that Ross's hours could be flexible since he was the boss's son. But it was the opposite. Ross put pressure on himself to work the hardest, to be the most available, to always say yes to his father no matter what the request. And having a new baby didn't mean anything to Henry in terms of Ross's work schedule. Paternity leave wasn't something Henry even knew existed. Henry valued family above all else, but his view of it was traditional. As far as he was concerned, Brynn's role was to take care of Lucas, just as Ross's mother, Margaux, had done with Ross and his brother, Sawyer.

Before Ross left, he turned back toward her and gave her a funny look, one Brynn hadn't seen in years. He smiled and his eyes locked with hers.

"Brynn," he said, "I . . . I need to tell you something."

What does he need now? Brynn thought to herself, already annoyed. *Did he invite his friends over this weekend? Did he say yes to the guys' fishing trip to the Bahamas, even though the two of us had discussed it already together and decided no? In what way is he going to make my life harder today?*

"I . . ." he started to say. He paused. "You're such a good mom."

Brynn almost laughed. "Really? That's what you wanted to tell me?"

"Yes," Ross said, serious. "I should tell you more."

"Well, thanks," Brynn said. "I don't feel that way."

"You are. You're an amazing mom."

Brynn started to remove the flanges from her bra; she was done pumping.

"I want to be here more," Ross continued. "For you, for Lucas. I do. I know it's been hard. But I promise it won't be like this forever. Things . . . things will change soon."

Brynn carefully poured her new milk into freezer storage bags and labeled them with a marker. She knew that Ross had to go, but there was so much she wanted to say in return. She'd been waiting for a moment like this—a moment of connection. She hadn't realized how much she needed to hear those words of affirmation from Ross until she heard them.

"I wish you and I could switch places and I could just hang out here with the little man all day," Ross added before Brynn could say anything.

Almost instantly, the affection Brynn had felt for Ross a moment ago disappeared and was replaced with rage. She knew that Ross didn't mean to insult her, but the implication that she just *hung out* with Lucas all day was hurtful. Except that when Ross did take care of Lucas—so that Brynn could shower, or work out, or cook dinner, or go to Cronig's for groceries—his only job *was* to hang out with Lucas. He didn't worry about prepping dinner or getting on the preschool wait lists or signing Lucas up for swim lessons. He wasn't on hold with Lowe's for forty-five minutes trying to track down a lost order of the filter to go on the fan above the kitchen stove while also wiggling Lucas out of a spit-up-covered onesie. He wasn't debating whether Lucas was ready to go up a size in diapers or not, and what to do with the leftover ones they hadn't used. He wasn't photographing the mysterious bump on the inside of Lucas's left ear and then searching the ends of the internet to find out what it was while waiting for a call back from the pediatrician. These tiny, sometimes stupid, but entirely necessary things that demanded Brynn's time and mental capacity prevented her from just *hanging out* with Lucas all day. Rather, taking care of him often felt like another job on her to-do list, even though she felt terrible admitting that.

Ross kissed Brynn on the cheek, and then he was gone. Brynn squinted as she watched him go; she knew him well enough to know that something was on his mind that he wasn't telling her.

Almost the moment Ross got into his car, Lucas's cries pierced through the monitor. Brynn hurried to her room and threw on some stretchy shorts and an oversize tank top. She sniffed the nursing sports bra she wore yesterday and decided that she could wear it today, too. She threw her hair up in a bun, slathered on some tinted moisturizer and deodorant, and somehow remembered to take her birth control pills, which she'd just started back on last week, though they only seemed to ridicule her in their complete uselessness to her. She looked at herself in the mirror—just once, briefly—and tried hard not to cry. She didn't even recognize herself. Her face was gray and sunken, marred by exhaustion, and the shape of her body had shifted into something unfamiliar, something she didn't like. She wanted to celebrate her new body for all that it had accomplished, but the truth was that she hated her new stretch marks and wider hips, her elongated and cracked nipples, her displaced abdominal muscles and the pain she felt whenever she squatted.

Her phone buzzed with a text from her friend Ginny Bloch, asking if she'd see her at the playground that morning. *Yes,* Brynn thought to herself, and typed it out. *Where else would I go?* The West Tisbury playground, just a five-minute drive or a fifteen-minute stroller walk from home, had become Brynn's go-to for when she needed to get out of the house. Now that it was summer, and school was out, the same group of parents always showed up there in the mornings. In the past few months, seeing them had become a comfort that Brynn needed each day. Lucas was still too little to do anything there but sleep and eat in Brynn's arms, so the playground was more for her than it was for him. Something about being there, and being around other moms with their kids, made Brynn feel a kind of validation as a mother that she needed.

She found comfort in the other mothers not because she related to them, though. On the contrary, Brynn felt like a fraud among them, even among her own friends. None of the other moms seemed to be struggling. They somehow all looked like they'd slept and showered. They cooed over their babies, inhaling the sticky scent of their heads as if it were a revitalizing smelling salt. They didn't hate their husbands (well, most of them didn't, or at least they didn't say so). Brynn had been to some of their houses, and they were all clean and tidy. She'd come to the conclusion, with absolute certainty, that her experience of motherhood was more difficult than theirs because of some innate deficit of hers. Everyone else at the playground was meant to be a mom, she thought, but not her.

That's exactly why she went, though. Because being around these other moms—the ones who had their shit together—gave Brynn proof that she was at least attempting to have some semblance of normalcy in her life as a mom. It gave her the façade of belonging. Temporarily, it made her feel okay. And she thought that if she kept going through the motions of doing all the nice, happy things she was *supposed* to do as a mother—like go to the playground and hang out with other moms—she just might trick herself into actually enjoying motherhood. She might trick herself into being happy.

She might even, somehow, turn herself into a good mom, instead of the bad one she was sure she was.

CHAPTER 2

It took Brynn nearly half an hour to get out of the house, even though she hustled the whole time. She changed Lucas, fed him, then restocked Lucas's diaper bag with the essentials: diapers and wipes, a pacifier, a bottle of breast milk in a mini cooler bag in case she didn't want to nurse at the playground, wipes to clean the bottle nipple in case she dropped it, alcohol-free hand-sanitizing wipes, a travel sound machine, a portable fan, an extra outfit for him, burp cloths, a few rattly toys, and an extra shirt for her in case of spit-ups. Then she had to change him again before they left.

Once she was outside, she instantly had to pee, but it was too late. It had taken so much effort from her to get out the door that she was not about to turn back now. She was thirsty, too, and regretted not grabbing a seltzer for herself from the fridge. But her own needs were an afterthought.

Brynn spotted Ginny as soon as she approached the playground. Ginny was unmissable, with long legs, dark skin, curly black hair, and a big toothy smile. She was also pregnant. Very, *very* pregnant, due in just two weeks. Brynn watched Ginny as she handed her eighteen-month-old daughter, Olivia, a pouch of applesauce, while she simultaneously called out to her four-year-old son, Sam, to be careful going down the slide.

"Hey!" Ginny yelled to Brynn. "Look who it is, Olivia! It's your buddy Lucas." Olivia sucked the applesauce pouch down and stared.

"More," she demanded, and Ginny handed her another. Then Olivia waddled off.

Lucas was now asleep, his brow furrowed in a look of discontent, even though he was peacefully snoozing. Brynn pushed the stroller up next to where Ginny sat. She took out the sound machine and turned it to an ocean-wave setting.

"I got you an iced coffee from 7a," Ginny said, handing her the drink, with the perfect amount of half-and-half, just the way Brynn liked it. The act was so kind and so *necessary* that Brynn nearly cried. "And a jalapeño biscuit breakfast sandwich."

"Thank you," Brynn said. She shook her head. "You know, I actually mean it when I say that *I don't know how you do it,* Ginny. Seriously. Just the logistics of buying breakfast with two little kids. I can barely do anything with one." Brynn really did mean it, and she often wondered how Ginny completed errands like that with such ease. Did she leave both kids in the car while she went into the café to get the food? Did she let them both come in with her and run around while she waited in line, hoping that they wouldn't bolt into the busy parking lot? Brynn had no idea how all these other moms juggled everyday things like that, but she never asked.

"Nothing was going to stop me from getting a sausage, egg, and cheese today," Ginny said. She leaned back, putting her hands on her stomach. "I actually had two of them. And now I feel like I'm going to explode."

"One for you, one for baby," Brynn said, eyeing Ginny's belly. "How are you feeling?"

"Ready to *not* be pregnant," Ginny said. "It's funny. You know I love kids and I love babies, but I fucking *hate* being pregnant, I really do."

Brynn had known Ginny for a long time, before either of them had kids. Ginny had always wanted a big family. *I want the chaos of a big family,* she'd told Brynn long ago. *I want the messiness of it all.* Brynn had never understood this. The thought of *wanting* chaos in life made Brynn feel claustrophobic and out of control. But maybe if Brynn had the support system that Ginny had, she'd want that, too. Ginny's mother *and* sister lived on the island, nearby, and had the time, energy, and resources to help Ginny out with the kids all the time, so she basically had two free nannies available around the clock. She also had a husband who let Ginny make all the decisions when it came to childcare and preschool, whereas Ross had an opinion on everything.

Brynn's parents had moved off-island to Falmouth years ago, so she only had her mother-in-law nearby to help her. And while Brynn was grateful to have her, it wasn't the same. Brynn was mostly on her own.

They watched Sam climb up the slide. Brynn appreciated that she and Ginny could just sit in silence sometimes. They were both exhausted, though it didn't need to be said. In addition to having two kids, Ginny was a freelance reporter for both of the island's newspapers, as well as several nationally distributed magazines. Her husband, Trey, was one of the island's few public defenders, so he was even busier.

"How's the writing going?" Ginny asked. Brynn could usually be honest with Ginny about their careers. Though they were different types of writers, they'd always shared the same level of ambition.

"It's *not* going." Brynn sighed.

"You know, you had a baby, like, *yesterday,*" Ginny reminded her. "Why don't you just put work on hold for a while, enjoy the summer with Lucas?"

"I can't," Brynn said. "I have a deadline. I somehow thought that I'd be able to get a lot of writing done during the newborn days. I was such an idiot. And now, if I take a break, I feel like I'll never start again. You know?"

"Yeah." Ginny watched Olivia push a toy dump truck around on the grass in front of them. "But trust me, you will. I know it feels like you'll never get your old energy or drive back, but you will. Eventually. For now, you're still in the eye of the storm."

Brynn nodded, but she wasn't so sure. She'd seen the way Ginny had thrown herself into a routine after having Sam and Olivia, and it wasn't something she herself seemed capable of: the way Ginny had returned to the gym as soon as her doctor cleared her, the way she brought both kids with her to run errands as if it were no big deal, the way she locked in babysitters early on so that she and her husband could have regular date nights. Ginny even found the time to read both *The New York Times* and *The Wall Street Journal* every morning! Brynn only scrolled Instagram while sitting on the toilet these days, her eyes glazed over. She could practically feel her brain cells evaporating with each passing day.

But there was something else that separated Brynn from Ginny, and the other playground moms, too. Something that felt more sinister to Brynn. Even when Ginny complained to Brynn about her struggles of motherhood—the kids' sleep regressions, the difficulty of potty training, the tantrums, the fights with her husband—there was always an unspoken implication that Ginny nevertheless *loved* being a mother, and that she *loved* her children.

It was this understanding of unconditional love that entitled Ginny to lament her exhaustion and frustrations. Even the sharpest anger toward her kids on a given day could be excused by the unwavering fact that motherhood was, to her, a sacrifice she was always *willing* to make. Happily.

Brynn's truth was that she *wasn't* necessarily willing to make the same sacrifice. She thought she would be willing, but now that she was a mom, she wasn't sure she *could,* even if she wanted to. Whenever she opened up to Ginny about her difficulties with Lucas, Ginny assumed that Brynn also felt the same unconditional love for her child that she felt. She assumed that Brynn loved Lucas above all else. Because that was what mothers were supposed to feel. But Brynn knew, deep down, that she didn't feel that way. For her, it wasn't just a bad day, or a rough night, or a tough fight. It was all of it. It was her decision to become a mother in the first place. It was the way she'd been swallowed up by her own life, unable to claw herself out. It was how she often regretted becoming a mother.

Brynn and Ginny appeared to be in sync, on the surface of things, but Brynn knew she existed somewhere else—a darker place, a lonelier place. She didn't want to drag Ginny—or anyone else—down there with her, so she kept it hidden.

"What about you?" Brynn asked. "How's the story going?"

Ginny paused and gave Brynn a quizzical stare, like she'd been caught in a lie.

"Oh," she said, "right. The motherhood story. Good, actually." Ginny had been writing a piece on the specific challenges of motherhood on an island—how hard it was to find year-round childcare, or baby supplies, or access to certain pediatric healthcare. It was the kind of article Brynn wished someone would finally write. It was a conversation that *needed* to be had on the island. "There's just so much to cover," Ginny added. "This island is like a microcosm of our country, really."

Before Brynn could respond, they both heard voices from the parking lot.

"Hi ladies!" Their friends Annie Adams and Marcus Haywood were walking toward them. Marcus cradled his six-month-old, Liam, while Annie pushed a double stroller, containing her twin toddlers, Stella and Benji, who were both gnawing on bright pieces of fruit leather, staining their lips red.

"So much for a relaxing morning," Ginny said, though Brynn knew that she was joking. Annie and Marcus were their close friends, but any time spent with them was sure to be full of chatter. The two of them loved to *talk*. Whatever the island gossip was, they knew it before anyone else, and they were quick to share it, too. They spent nearly all their time together, so much so that strangers often thought they were a couple. Marcus was always fast to correct that assumption.

"I'm married," he would tell people, flatly, "to a *man*."

Annie was a gossip magnet—it followed her everywhere—since she was the island's preeminent wedding planner. She knew before anyone else who was getting married, who was splitting up, who was behind on their Big Sky rental bill, and which mother-in-law was trying to elbow out another one for the prime wedding weekend at the Edgartown Yacht Club. But Annie never spilled anything about her clients. That is, unless they treated her staff poorly or tried to shirk their bills. Annie and Brynn had grown up together on the Vineyard, but both had fled the island after high school, with Annie winding up in Los Angeles and only returning years later when her dad got sick. Today, the two of them shared an understanding that while they might have become legging-clad, stroller-pushing island moms, they once had big lives in big cities. They saw each other's former selves, and that was something for which Brynn was always grateful.

Marcus was a respected Wampanoag tribal member, born and raised on the island, and a math teacher at the high school, revered for his ability to connect with even the most math-averse students. He often told Brynn and their friends that they were his *only* outlet to talk about everyday parent life, especially during the summer, his precious time off from school. His husband ran a successful caretaking company and was always on call, 24/7, especially in the summer. Brynn knew that Marcus yearned for more family time together. After all, they'd spent five agonizing years going through the adoption process before finally bringing Liam home four months ago. But Marcus did have his mother to help him. She lived just down the road from him and came over daily to help cook and clean.

"So," Annie said once she took Stella and Benji out of the stroller and let them run to the slide with Sam. She looked toward Ginny and Brynn. "Did you guys hear?" She sat down and stirred her thermos of iced coffee with a metal straw. Brynn knew that sometimes Annie liked to gossip to deflect attention away from herself. If anyone ever asked Annie how she and her husband were doing, she'd say *Great!* and that would be that. Everything had to be fine, all the time. But Brynn knew better. "About the girl?" Annie continued. "The dead body?" Annie looked at them all like they hadn't heard her. *"Hello?"*

Marcus sat on the grass in front of them, and gently put Liam on the ground for some tummy time. "Brynn, what did Ross say about it?" he asked.

"Ross?" Brynn looked at Ginny to see if she was equally lost, but Ginny cast her eyes downward. "What are you guys talking about? A dead body?"

"Yes. A body was found at Norton Point," Annie said, leaning in. "It was a girl, a woman." She paused. "Cecelia was her name. Cecelia Buckley."

"The paper said that she worked at the Oyster Watcha Club," Marcus added. "Did you know her, Brynn?" It wasn't a surprise that Marcus would ask Brynn if she knew Cecelia. All of Brynn's friends knew that Brynn and the Nelson family spent a lot of time at the club. It was where Margaux had thrown Brynn's baby shower, and where she and Ross had hosted their wedding rehearsal dinner. And Ross was there almost every night. Of course Brynn knew Cecelia Buckley. All the Nelsons did.

Brynn's throat tightened.

Cecelia Buckley was dead.

She tried to process it.

Cecelia Buckley was dead.

It didn't make sense. Brynn had just seen her a few days ago when she, Lucas, and Ross had met Henry and Margaux at the club for Sunday brunch.

"The usuals for you all?" Cecelia had asked them when they had sat down. She'd worked at the club for the past three summers, and because the Nelsons were always there, they'd all gotten to know her. Brynn knew that Cecelia wanted to be a veterinarian, and that she spent her summers working around the clock at the club to save money for school. Cecelia had told her that she'd earned a scholarship to attend Middlebury, and that she was from somewhere in Pennsylvania. She'd also told her that she had been dating Jacob Hammers, a young Edgartown police officer and the son of the police chief.

"I did know her, yes," Brynn said. "She'd worked there for a few years." She cleared her throat. "She . . . Henry especially loved her. They were close."

"What do you mean *close*?" Marcus asked.

"Not like *that*," Brynn said. "Margaux loved her, too. We all did. Everyone at the club did. She was just a hard worker, smart, always took great care of the members."

Brynn didn't tell them that Henry's fondness for Cecelia was in fact somewhat like *that*. It wasn't romantic, not at all, but it was . . . noticeable. A little strange, even. Henry thought of her like a daughter. She was his point person at the club, the place where he felt most important and the most at home. Cecelia knew exactly how he liked his gin martini, how he took his after-dinner coffee, what time he finished his daily round of golf, which David McCullough book he was reading, and of course what Margaux's favorite wine was and how she only liked the tuna tartare with *no* green onions. Henry often asked Cecelia to sit with him in the library or on the porch overlooking the golf course as he finished his last drink. He would ask her about school and her ambitions. None of this was secret. The club manager, Mauricio, was aware of it, and he ran a very tight ship, never allowing staff members to cross inappropriate lines with members or vice versa. Even *Margaux* was aware, and didn't care. But now, the relationship between Cecelia and Henry somehow made Brynn queasy. Now, it somehow felt wrong.

Lucas woke from his nap just then, blinking his eyes and releasing a groan. The June sun had intensified since the early morning. Brynn felt the back of Lucas's neck. It was slightly sticky. She needed to feed him.

"Hold on," Brynn said, still in disbelief. She took out the bottle she'd packed. "What do you mean she's *dead*? What *happened*?"

"Trey learned about it first thing this morning," Ginny said. This made sense; Ginny's husband was always aware of the island's criminal activities. Most of the time, he had to clean up the mess. He practically lived at the courthouse. But this was the first time that Ginny had spoken since Annie and Marcus had arrived. She hadn't even mentioned Cecelia to Brynn before that. How come everyone else had heard about this but Brynn hadn't? Ross and his family were usually some of the first people to know about anything related to the club.

"And my niece Halle is one of the beach patrollers at Norton this summer," Marcus said, "so all the twentysomethings are talking about it." Norton Point Beach was one of the island's most popular beaches in the summer, because it was one of the only ones that you could drive your car onto. In the summer, employees of the preservation organization that owned the beach patrolled it to make sure that dogs were kept on leashes and that cars didn't drive over the endangered piping plovers' nesting areas.

"I guess a guy shore fishing for stripers found her last night on the beach. She'd been in the water," Annie said. "Seems like a drowning."

"Honestly, the way kids drink these days, maybe there was a beach party, and she drank too much, went for a swim, and just drowned?" Marcus suggested. "Sorry to sound so callous. But it's happened here so many times. And Halle told me the popular drink these days with kids is called *fire water*. It's literally just tequila and water. Not even ice. Can you imagine? *Blugh*."

"Yeah, but supposedly there's no sign of a party having happened out there on Norton that night. I mean, it's so hard to drive all the way out there anyway, no one goes there late at night anymore except for fishermen," Annie added. "And I heard that, like, none of her friends were with her last night. So, I guess they're not ruling out any kind of foul play."

Brynn began to feed Lucas, who stared up at her, his tiny body sinking into her arms. Her friends kept talking, guessing about what had happened, who was involved, what clues there might be. But Brynn couldn't hear. It turned to white noise.

She tried to imagine what Cecelia could have been doing before her death. Brynn knew *facts* about her, she realized, but that didn't mean that she actually knew her. She had no idea who her parents were, or what kind of parents they'd been, or whether Cecelia had even been close with them or not. Brynn had a vague recollection of Cecelia telling her once that she had a brother, but she wasn't sure. She wondered if her parents had already been informed. Had they cried, or screamed, or sat in silent shock? Would they be looking for someone to blame? But she did know that she had a boyfriend. And he wasn't just any guy on the island.

"Her boyfriend is a cop," Brynn said, thinking out loud. "Jacob Hammers. And his dad is the chief."

Jacob's dad, Pete Hammers, the longtime and revered Edgartown chief of police, was close friends with Henry. They were proudly cut from the same cloth—self-described "washashores" who arrived on the island with nothing and rose to be prestigious leaders in the community. Brynn hadn't ever really interacted with Jacob herself, though she'd seen him at barbecues and at hockey games. He played in the same winter men's hockey league as Ross.

"Oh, interesting," said Annie. "I wonder where *he* was last night."

"It's always the boyfriend, right?" asked Marcus. "Ginny, what do you know? You always know everything."

"Nothing," Ginny said. "They still don't know if it was just an accident."

This wouldn't be the first time that Ginny was withholding confidential information that Trey had given her or that she'd heard on the local news circuit. And Brynn could understand why Ginny would be secretive about this one. The police chief's son's girlfriend found *dead*! Brynn was certain that this case was going to be kept far away from the scrutiny of the public eye. Or as far away as it could, in a small community like this one where secrets never stayed secret for long.

"Ugh," groaned Annie, breaking the conversation away from the news about Cecelia. She was looking at her phone. "This fucking bride is going to be the end of me." Annie was supposed to be taking it *easy* this summer so she could spend more time with the twins, but she'd begrudgingly agreed to plan the wedding of a well-known Edgartown socialite, Joanna O'Callahan. "*Shit,*" she said.

"What happened?" asked Marcus.

Annie let out a frustrated sigh, and frantically started typing into her phone. "We were supposed to have the welcome dinner for this wedding at Oyster Watcha—*this* weekend. But I just got an email from the manager saying that it's going to be closed. Out of respect for Cecelia. So the staff can mourn." She continued to type. "Great. Now I have to find a whole other venue. Hold on, I need to call this guy." Annie dialed. "Go figure. It keeps going straight to voicemail."

"Is it Mauricio you're calling?" asked Brynn. "The club manager?"

Annie nodded. "You'd think this would be an important time to be reachable. So annoying."

While Annie called her assistant next, Brynn's phone vibrated. She was certain that Ross would be calling her now that he'd heard about Cecelia. *I can't believe it . . . so terrible,* he'd say. *She was a good kid. My dad's really broken up. . . .* Or maybe Ross already had the full story; maybe he'd tell her that he'd heard that the staff at the club had all gone out partying together and Cecelia never made it back. Maybe she'd gone swimming. Maybe she'd taken pills. Maybe she'd drunk too much.

But instead, it was a text from him:

Trust me. Please. I can explain everything. You'll understand soon.

CHAPTER 3

Brynn hastily said goodbye to her friends, muttering something about Lucas having a pediatrician appointment. She called Ross as soon as she got in the car. But he didn't answer. She called again. And again. No answer. She called the Nelson & Sons office, but all she got was the receptionist Loretta's voicemail.

Brynn had a sour taste in her mouth, and she started to feel bile rising up in her throat. Maybe Ross's text to her had nothing to do with Cecelia at all. It was possible he still didn't know. After all, he was busy with work, and the news about Cecelia had only broken early that morning. Maybe he was only texting her to apologize for forgetting to take the trash out, as he'd promised he would the night before. Or maybe he'd made some outlandish charge to their credit card—another set of golf clubs?—and wanted to explain. Maybe the text was just bad timing. Or maybe he and Mauricio were together at the club. Maybe Mauricio had called him to help relay the news to Cecelia's family. That wouldn't be so strange, would it? Maybe that was why they both were unreachable right now.

Except that none of those possibilities really made sense.

Brynn's mind reeled. Did Ross know something about Cecelia's death? Was he involved in some way? Had they been having an affair?

She called Ross's brother Sawyer next. He probably knew where Ross was, since he worked for Henry, too.

"One sec, Brynn," Sawyer said when he answered, on the second ring. He was driving, too, and she could hear him rolling up the windows of his vintage Bronco. The engine roared like a fire; it was a distinct sound that she'd known since Sawyer bought the car, more than fifteen years ago, when they were both teenagers. Back then, Sawyer wasn't just Ross's brother to Brynn. Back then, it was the other way around. Back then, Sawyer was the one that Brynn thought she'd end up with.

"Sawyer," Brynn said, "did you hear about Cecelia?"

"I just heard," he said. "I can't believe it."

She could hear Sawyer take a sip of his coffee. She waited for him to say more.

"Well, what do we know?" she asked. "Have you . . . have you talked to Ross? Where is he?" She was yelling.

"Yeah, he's at the office with my dad," Sawyer said. "Brynn, is everything okay? You sound really panicked."

Sawyer had always been a glass-half-full kind of guy. At times, this was endearing. His positivity reminded Brynn not to take things so seriously. But sometimes it drove her mad. Sometimes, he was *too* laid-back. *Everything will work out,* he'd always say. And she didn't agree. She'd learned from an early age that sometimes things *didn't* work out, and that was that.

Even though Ross and Sawyer were born just eighteen months apart and practically raised like twins, they were opposites in pretty much every way—and always had been. Ross had darker hair, olive skin, and the same compact frame, height, and square shoulders as Margaux. Sawyer was built just like Henry—towering at almost six foot five, lean, and fair-skinned, with a wave of blond hair always peeking out of his backward baseball cap. But the brothers were opposites in how they carried themselves, too. Ross was clean-cut, well groomed, on time, organized, polite, in control, *reliable*. Sawyer, on the other hand, came and went like the wind, always misplacing his wallet or his shoes or his keys, never on time, one of his legs constantly bouncing during the rare times he sat down, always scruffy and unshaven, slightly dirty.

Once in a while, only when Ross really annoyed her and she could barely stand the sight of him, Brynn imagined what life would be like if she'd ended up with Sawyer instead of with Ross. She never *used* to imagine this. Before Lucas, Brynn had hardly even *thought* about Sawyer romantically—at least not since they were teenagers. She looked at Sawyer now like a little brother, even though they were the same age. He hadn't grown up, and she had.

But when Ross was physically and emotionally distant, as he so often was lately, Brynn allowed herself to imagine what this alternate life might be like. With Sawyer, she thought, life would be full of laughter. He'd crack jokes, he'd give her back massages, he would blast music in the kitchen for impromptu family dance parties. He'd tell her that she was beautiful. The only thing Ross told her lately was when he'd be home, and it was always late. Ross didn't *see* Brynn anymore. But she felt like Sawyer did.

"I don't know," Brynn said. "I'm just trying to reach Ross and he's not answering."

"My dad's pretty bent out of shape over this," Sawyer said. "He's real sad. I'm sure Ross is getting an earful right now."

"Right," Brynn said. She felt silly for jumping so quickly to such wild conclusions. Ross's text meant nothing. He was a notoriously bad texter anyway, and she knew this better than anyone. He was just busy consoling his dad and trying to take things off of his plate at work.

"Well, I'm headed to our Fuller Street job now," Sawyer said. "It's turned into a big mess with the new septic system."

Brynn didn't know how Sawyer was able to return to work as if someone they'd known for several years hadn't just suddenly been found dead. But Sawyer never really seemed to think too hard about anything.

"Wait," Brynn said. "Did you guys see Cecelia last night at dinner? Was anything off?"

"Yeah, we saw her, like normal," Sawyer said. "Everything seemed fine, like it always does. And then we all left around . . . I don't know, ten? That's when young people just start their nights. You remember."

"Right," Brynn said.

When she hung up, she turned the car around and began to drive toward the Nelson & Sons office in Edgartown instead of home. If Ross wasn't going to answer the phone, then she was going to go see him. As much as she tried to reason with herself, something didn't feel right about Ross's text, or the way she'd learned about Cecelia after everyone else. Something felt wrong.

As she drove, she tried to remember last night, but it was hazy. *Everything* had been hazy since Lucas was born. What time had Ross come home? Had she felt the rustle of the bedsheets when he climbed into bed next to her? Had she been in Lucas's room when he got home, half asleep in the glider chair, feeding him for the millionth time that night? Or had he come home earlier, and she just couldn't remember? She had a vague recollection of Ross still not being home when she gave Lucas his dream feed, the feeding around ten o'clock that she always hoped would finally be the one to get him through the night. But she wasn't sure.

Still, even when Ross enraged her, she never felt that she couldn't *trust* him. It wasn't in his nature to lie, and certainly not to her.

She couldn't stop her mind from picturing Cecelia's thin frame and long, thick hair, her narrow hips and bony knees. Brynn's own body was bloated, her flesh pliable like soft dough. Characters in her books worried about husbands with wandering eyes, or wives having torrid affairs. She had friends who'd dealt with it. But her and Ross? She'd never even imagined it.

She called again; nothing.

The only other time Brynn had gotten truly angry over Ross being unreachable was a few weeks ago when an angry-looking rash had suddenly appeared on Lucas's back. Brynn had raced to the pediatrician and called Ross frantically on the way, but he didn't answer.

"You have a *son* now, Ross!" she'd yelled at him when he finally called her back later that day. By that time, she'd returned home with Lucas, and she was exhausted from having spent three sweaty, stressful hours in the hospital only to be told that the best she could do was monitor Lucas's symptoms and hope it didn't get worse.

"I'm sorry, Bee," he had said. "We were digging the foundation and hit some stuff, it turned into a whole situation, I couldn't be checking my phone."

"I need to know that we're your priority," she had told him. "Not work, but us. Your *family*."

"You *are*. You and Lucas are all that matters to me," he had assured her.

She had believed him then.

But now, she wasn't so sure anymore. Now, she wasn't sure she had *ever* been Ross's priority.

CHAPTER 4

Brynn glanced at the reflection of the baby mirror above Lucas's car seat. He'd fallen asleep, and now she'd have to keep driving to let him get a full nap. Instead of turning onto upper Main Street to go downtown, she made her way to Katama Road, toward the left fork to South Beach and the turnoff to Norton Point. Though it was still early summer, Norton was already a zoo on most nice days because of its soft sand and big waves. At the very end of it, where the land became Chappaquiddick, the beach narrowed into a mesmerizing spit of sand reaching out into the sea. This was where Cecelia was found. The tip of the island. The beginning or the end, depending on how you looked at it.

Today, the entrance to Norton was closed off, and several police cars were parked in the lot. Brynn drove by slowly, hoping to see something, though she wasn't sure what. The air was still and quiet, as if the ocean itself were in mourning. But when she turned right to continue onto the other side of South Beach, a sense of normalcy returned. Cars were lined up on the sides of the road and families schlepped boogie boards and coolers up the dunes to find a spot for themselves.

Sometimes, when Brynn drove around Edgartown, she felt like a visitor. Her whole life, she'd been an up-island girl. She didn't spend her summers sunbathing at South Beach in a Lilly Pulitzer bikini or sneaking into the back door at the Wharf Pub wearing white jeans and seersucker blouses. She'd spent it in jean cutoff shorts, searching for treasures on Lucy Vincent Beach, years before it became too crowded, or having bonfires with friends on Quansoo Beach, to which someone always had a key and at least one bottle of vodka. Some Edgartown kids, like Ross and Sawyer, had never even set foot on Quansoo, or many of the up-island beaches where Brynn roamed as a child. That was a foreign world to them, just as this was to her, even though she was a Nelson now.

She never thought she'd marry someone whose family was the embodiment of Edgartown itself. When she and Ross decided to buy their house in West Tisbury, the threshold between down-island and up-island, it was a compromise. And the only reason Ross had agreed was because he wanted to flip the house and sell it for a profit someday. He'd always planned to raise his family in Edgartown. It was what was *expected*. Edgartown was the Nelsons' home.

Brynn swung back through town, past the Stop & Shop and Donaroma's, toward the Nelson & Sons office. Henry had bought the office building in the 1970s for next to nothing. It had once been a simple but beautiful colonial-style home, and Henry restored it into a pristine structure lined with lush hydrangeas and a tidy pea-stone driveway.

"Ugh," she said as she looked at her reflection, once she'd pulled in and parked. She redid her bun, sniffing her armpit in the process, trying to recall the last time she showered. The day before yesterday? Whenever Margaux was over last. She rubbed some hand lotion she kept in her car onto her palms, and then onto her cheeks, trying to brighten her face.

She freed Lucas's car seat and lugged him and his diaper bag with her into the office. The chill of the air-conditioning hit her as she walked in, and Lucas stirred. Loretta was now back at her desk, with a takeout bag from Among the Flowers on it. Brynn felt a pinch of embarrassment; Loretta hadn't answered the phone because she'd gone out for lunch. That was all.

"Well, what do we have here!" Loretta exclaimed. Loretta hardly looked at Brynn at all, which Brynn was used to at this point. She instead immediately locked her gaze on Lucas. Lucas had this effect on almost everybody; it was like he hypnotized them. Brynn could be on fire, screaming for help, and no one would notice her if Lucas was there. She didn't mind, though. Right now, she didn't want any attention on herself.

"Can I?" Loretta asked, reaching for Lucas to pick him up. Loretta had five grandchildren herself, though all were off-island now, and Brynn knew how much she missed them. She lived for Lucas's visits to the office.

"Of course," Brynn said.

Lucas blinked and yawned as Loretta rocked him in her arms.

"You are just perfect, aren't you?"

"So," Brynn said. "Is Ross here? We were running errands nearby, and I just thought we'd pop in and say hi."

"He's in Henry's office. Poor guys have been in there all morning. Henry's quite sad. So terrible what happened to that girl," she said.

Brynn tried to act calm. How could *Loretta* have already talked to Henry and Ross about Cecelia, but Ross hadn't thought to call her yet? It wasn't every day that someone they personally knew and cared about was found mysteriously *dead*. And this was a small island community—last week Ross called Brynn during the day just to tell her that he'd seen one of the moms from the birthing class they took buying a pack of cigarettes at the Edgartown Depot. As a couple, they shared their lives and observations with each other this way; to have not acknowledged *this* to each other yet felt purposeful and strange.

Loretta handed Lucas back to Brynn. "But I'm sure this will make their day. How could anyone be sad around this little bundle of joy?"

Brynn knocked on the office door. She couldn't make out what they were actually saying, but she could hear Ross and Henry talking. Then, the room went silent and Ross swung the door open. Henry sat at his desk, jotting down notes on his notepad, something he always had with him. Ross's face was pale. But he lit up when he saw Brynn and Lucas, as though he had pushed a button somewhere inside of him telling him what to do: *smile.*

"Hi, honey," he said. "This is a surprise."

"Brynn. And my grandson!" Henry rose from his desk. It was obvious that Henry was sad, even though he was glad to see Lucas. He was hunched over, and his face drooped down in distress. He looked like he hadn't slept the night before. He took Lucas from Brynn's arms to hold him.

Even though Henry was tall and lanky, like Sawyer, with a commanding presence and a firm handshake, there was a softness to him, too, that Brynn had always loved. He was easy to talk to, easy to laugh with, just easy to be around. Brynn knew that Henry had another side to him that only his sons really saw—the mentor, the tough negotiator, the demanding boss who wanted things done yesterday even if they were assigned today. But Brynn didn't see this side herself, she only heard about it from Ross. The Henry she and Lucas got was sweet and supportive, albeit old-fashioned and stubborn.

Brynn waited. She waited for Ross to acknowledge his text to her. Finally, she couldn't take it anymore.

"Can we talk?" she asked Ross. "I got your text."

"I can't right now," Ross said. "Just . . . just trust me."

"Is this about Cecelia?" Brynn whispered.

"What? No," Ross said. "It's . . . I'll explain at home."

"So sad about Cecelia, isn't it?" Henry chimed in. His eyes were wet, staring adoringly at Lucas. "It's just really unthinkable."

Brynn felt like the floor beneath her feet was shifting. The air in the office felt thick with secrets, as if she had entered the room midconversation and wasn't meant to be there.

"I know you two were close," she said to Henry, being careful not to say something that might upset him or be taken the wrong way. "I know how much you cared about her. I'm just so sorry."

Henry rocked Lucas. "We're setting up a fund," he continued. "The club is. For whatever the family needs. They're flying in today. We're putting them up at a member's home at Seven Gates, someone who's away in Jackson Hole. While everything gets sorted out."

The family. She wondered if Cecelia's family would be looking at the club to take responsibility. For exposing their daughter to a culture of excess and debauchery, tucked neatly away beneath a façade of good manners, cobblestone driveways, and freshly pressed polo shirts.

"She had big plans, you know," Henry continued. "She was like you, Brynn. Smart. Ambitious."

That was the first time Brynn had ever heard Henry describe her— Brynn—that way. It was the first time she'd ever heard him describe her in *any* way, really. Henry and Margaux had never acknowledged her career as a writer with much admiration. She always felt that they were embarrassed that she wrote romance novels, not the kind of books that they discussed in the library of the Oyster Watcha Club. She once heard Henry tell someone that Ross's wife wrote "chick lit," and even though she'd used the term herself before, proudly, with the self-awareness that her mostly female readers were the most voracious and discerning readers in the world, she knew that Henry hadn't been using the term positively.

"And I heard that the club is closed, to mourn her. Right?" Brynn asked.

Henry looked up. "Not exactly," he said. "It's closed because Mauricio has gone missing. No one can reach him."

"Wait, *what*?" Brynn felt her stomach twist. Mauricio had two teenage sons and a wife who worked at the Edgartown Public Library. He'd been at the club for almost two decades. "What do you mean no one can find him?"

"We don't know," said Ross. "Just that suddenly no one can get ahold of him. Even his wife doesn't know where he is. So, obviously, people are worried. Or suspicious. Or both."

"Oh my God," said Brynn. This must have been what Ross had tried to tell her but couldn't over text. It was too sensitive.

"But Pete tells me that they're going to find him. This is their priority," Henry said.

Brynn wondered if Pete had already questioned his own son about last night. Where was *he*, anyway?

"Well, we should go," Brynn said. "Lucas has his pediatrician appointment soon."

"I'll walk you out." Ross followed her out the office door, after she said goodbye to Henry and let him give Lucas one last kiss.

On the front steps of the office, Brynn suddenly burst into tears. She couldn't hold it in anymore.

"Brynn, come here," Ross said. He took Lucas in his car seat and set him on the ground. He wrapped his arms around her. "I . . . We should talk."

"Can you come with us to the pediatrician appointment?" She didn't know why she felt so helpless, so in need of Ross to just take care of her and tell her that everything would be okay.

"I . . . Brynn, I wish I could, but there's something really important I need to deal with here. I can't explain it here right now. But I wanted to tell you because . . ."

"Because *what,* Ross?" Brynn snapped. She wiped her eyes. Her whole body felt so tired, so burned out. "I can't do this."

"Do what?" Ross asked.

"This!" she said, pointing to Lucas. "I can't be a mother! It's too much. It's too hard." Brynn hadn't planned to have this outburst, especially not right now, not with the news of Cecelia's death, not with whatever Ross was trying to tell her. But she couldn't contain herself; she was in too much pain. She was too tired. She was too overwhelmed. She'd reached her breaking point on today of all days. Her words made her feel sick with guilt. But in that moment, they felt like the truth, and she had to say them out loud.

She knew what Ross must be thinking: that she was a disappointment. *Again*. That he'd married someone who wasn't equipped to be a mother. That she was nothing like his own beloved mother. She'd let him down. She'd let everyone down.

"Listen, Brynn," Ross said, holding her shoulders. "You are doing an amazing job. And I'm going to do better. I haven't been there for you. Or for Lucas. And I'm sorry. I really am."

Brynn nodded. "I knew that this would be hard," she said, "but I just didn't know it would be *this* hard. I don't feel like myself. I'm not happy. I should feel happy right now, right?"

"I don't know," Ross said. "I don't know what you're supposed to feel. But I know that I *want* you to be happy. And I will do whatever I can to help you feel happy."

Brynn didn't want to cry again, so she looked away.

"You know, sometimes I miss when it was just the two of us," Ross said.

Brynn looked up at him.

"Really?"

"Of course," he said. "We had the best time. We had total freedom. It was awesome. This is awesome, too, but it's different. It's hard right now."

Brynn felt instant relief and the shame she'd been harboring started to slip away.

"But then," he said, "I look at Lucas, and I just think . . . *wow*. I'm the luckiest man in the world. I mean, look at our son. He's perfect. We made him. I just get . . . overwhelmed with love, you know? I know things are hard, but we're lucky, right? We have amazing lives. We have this perfect family."

Brynn ached with guilt. Of course she knew how lucky they were as a family. But that knowledge still couldn't change how rotten she felt inside; how alienated she felt from Ross when he looked at Lucas with so much love that his heart practically swelled out of his chest. Ross had something inside of him that she lacked, something that allowed his heart to open to his son without force, without hesitation, and without condition. From the moment Ross had met Lucas, it had been clear that he'd love him forever, with ferocity and devotion. And the clearer Ross's love for Lucas was, the more shame Brynn felt that she did not share that love. She couldn't be honest with Ross, not anymore. If she told him the truth, all of his doubts about her would be confirmed.

"We should ask my mom to help more," Ross said. "If you want, I mean. Or maybe I can do bath every night. Whatever."

Brynn nodded. What she needed was something so much bigger than Ross could give her. It wasn't just about a lack of time in the day to get things done that she needed to do—like write her book. It was about finding the person she'd lost when Lucas was born: herself.

"Pretty wild that we made him, right?" Ross said, looking down at Lucas.

"It is, it really is," she said. She opened her mouth to say more, to say how she really felt, but once again, she couldn't. She looked at Ross gazing at Lucas, and it made her heart hurt with longing—the longing that someday she might feel the same way.

And then Ross's expression changed.

Instantly, Brynn knew something was very, very wrong.

Two police cars approached. They pulled into the Nelson & Sons driveway.

Ross looked at Brynn with a sudden urgency in his eyes. His face grew serious.

"Brynn," he said. "Listen to me. I know why the police are here. I . . . There's not a lot of time. But you have to believe me. Please. This is what I wanted to tell you."

Brynn was stunned, paralyzed. She couldn't say anything. Was this a joke?

"It's my dad," Ross said, moving closer to Brynn's face, whispering. "They've come for him. It's the business. I've been trying to change things for years now. I couldn't tell you because I couldn't get you in-volved. It was too dangerous. I didn't want you to know anything and be liable. Please. I've been trying to turn him around, to turn it all around.

That's why I've been so absent. There's a lot I need to explain. And I knew that it all might come out publicly today. I wanted to warn you."

"Ross, what do you mean the *business*? What is going on? What does this have to do with Cecelia?" Brynn had picked up Lucas's car seat and her knuckles were white she was holding it so tightly.

"*Cecelia?* What? This has nothing to do with her. I . . . It must just be a coincidence with timing that they've finally nailed my dad today. Brynn, he's been doing illegal things with the business for a long time now. Bad things," Ross said. "I couldn't tell you, Brynn, but I was going to. You have to believe me."

Brynn was stunned. The Nelsons weren't perfect, but they were certainly not rulebreakers. Everything in their lives was meticulous, both at home and at work. Everyone kept lists, everyone was on time, everyone's affairs were always in order. Well, except for Sawyer, but the most trouble he ever got into was when the manager of the Lookout Tavern scolded him for lighting up a joint on the outdoor deck.

"It's all going to be fine," Ross added. "I promise."

They both watched as the Edgartown police chief, Pete Hammers, and several officers stepped out of the cruisers.

"Please, trust me," he said. "Like I said, I can explain everything." Somehow, Ross seemed calm. He seemed like he'd been expecting this and was prepared.

"Ross," Pete said. "I wish I wasn't here under these circumstances." He sighed. Ross nodded.

The door opened, and Henry came out.

"Pete, what's going on?" he asked, though Henry didn't really look surprised either.

Pete didn't say anything for a moment. He stood next to Ross on the porch. His uniform was a bright blue and looked especially crisp, as if it had just been ironed. "Ross Nelson," he said suddenly, turning toward Ross instead of Henry. "We have a warrant for your arrest." He paused. "For the murder of Cecelia Buckley."

"*What?* What are you talking about? Murder? You're here for *me*?"

Ross blurted. Brynn knew that his shock and surprise were real. She couldn't explain it, but she just knew.

"Pete, what the hell is going on here?" Henry wedged himself between Ross and Pete. "You're accusing my son of *murder*?" The two older men stared at each other as if they were waiting for the other one to break. But neither said more.

Ross leaned in toward Brynn just then and whispered.

"Brynn, listen. I didn't do this. But I think I know why this is happening. I need you to find *the orange sun*. It will tell you everything. Please. *The orange sun*. Don't talk to anyone else. Don't trust . . . anyone. Especially not my dad."

"What about Mauricio?" Henry yelled at Pete. "Don't you think that's worth looking into?" But Pete didn't acknowledge it. His face gave away nothing.

Brynn felt a tingling sensation in her feet and hands, and a heaviness in her chest. Her breaths shortened. Sometimes, Brynn tried to look at catastrophes in her life as fodder for her writing. She could turn a real-life fender bender into a fictional meet-cute, or an actual missed flight into an opening-chapter one-night stand. It was a technique she used to stay positive in her life when things went wrong. But this was different. She couldn't even process what was happening around her. It didn't seem real.

The orange sun? She stared at Ross with blank eyes, completely lost, and her mind spun. An officer came up behind Ross and placed his hands into cuffs. He didn't object.

Brynn watched, frozen, as Ross was marched down into one of the cars. Henry screamed at Pete. She could see the veins in Henry's neck and forehead bulging out. She could see spit spraying out of his mouth. His anger was visceral. But Brynn felt nothing. It was as though she were watching a movie. She had left her body and was looking down at some performance, some kind of charade.

She wondered then if everything she knew up until now had been a lie. She wrote stories for a living—of all people, shouldn't she have been able to see a twist like this coming? If Ross was guilty of something, shouldn't she have predicted it somewhere along the way? Weren't there signs? She shut her eyes for a moment, wishing that when she opened them, her world would go back to normal, and she'd realize that this had all been a bad dream. But she opened her eyes and Ross was still gone.

If Brynn hadn't been in the eye of the storm before, she was in it now.

CHAPTER 5

I have been able to laugh and see the funny side of things.

I have blamed myself unnecessarily when things went wrong.

I have been anxious or worried for no good reason.

I have felt sad or miserable.

I have felt happy.

Brynn sat in the hallway waiting area outside the pediatrician's office and stared at the sticky iPad screen with the questionnaire on it. Her hand wavered above the possible answers for each: *No, not at all. Hardly ever. Yes, sometimes. Yes, all the time.*

As crazy as it now felt, Brynn had decided to keep Lucas's pediatrician appointment that day. After the police had left and taken Ross away, she stood outside with Lucas and Loretta in a silent state of disbelief until Margaux and Sawyer both showed up a few minutes later.

"I don't understand," Margaux kept saying, despondent. "I just don't understand."

Neither did Brynn. Whatever had just happened felt like a cruel joke, a sick and elaborate prank, and yet it was actually happening.

Henry and Margaux had called their longtime local lawyer, who'd referred them to a Boston lawyer specializing in high-profile criminal defense cases. They waited for the lawyer to call them back, and when she did, they told her that there was no way Ross could have done this.

"Okay" was all the lawyer had said in response, her voice unrevealing. She told them she would catch the last flight to the island that night. Margaux got to work securing her a room at the Harbor View Hotel.

"What do we do now?" Brynn asked, once the plans for the lawyer had been arranged. "We can't just sit here."

"Well, we wait to see if he'll be granted bail," Henry said.

"I highly doubt he'll be granted bail," Sawyer said. "Sorry, but not when he's being charged with . . ." He couldn't even say it. None of them could.

"We need to find Mauricio, is what we need to do," Margaux said. "Henry, we have to *do* something."

"I don't know what else we can do, Margaux," he said. "The entire board is trying to find him. And we live on an island, for God's sake—there's only so many places he can be. But obviously there's some reason why they think Ross is . . ." Henry put his head in his hands. He couldn't finish the sentence. "There's some reason why they're not pursuing Mauricio."

Margaux wiped her eyes with a tissue. Brynn had never seen her cry before. Margaux was elegant and always put-together—she was unflappable. It seemed to Brynn that Margaux had rarely ever been in a situation that she couldn't control or make better. Brynn understood why Ross relied on his mother so much, and why his first instinct was always to call her for help or advice if Lucas was ever sick or if they needed help. She was a natural caregiver. And a natural problem solver. But in this case, she was just as helpless as Brynn felt every single day.

"I just don't see why Pete can't do something about this," Margaux said. "He knows us. He knows Ross. This is *ridiculous*."

Henry shook his head in agreement.

"This is all a massive misunderstanding," Margaux continued, her voice leveling as she regained her composure. "They're going to clear it up. And then we'll sue them. They can't just *accuse* someone of *murder* out of thin air!"

Brynn and Sawyer shared a look. They both knew that these kinds of accusations *didn't* just happen out of thin air. They happened for a reason. Even if the police were wrong, they had something compelling enough to believe that Ross could be guilty. The Nelsons just didn't know yet what that was.

Brynn told them she was going to cancel Lucas's appointment, but both Margaux and Henry had told her to keep it. They knew, as islanders, how nearly impossible it was to get a doctor's appointment on the books. Margaux offered to go with her, but Brynn said no. Margaux needed to be available for the lawyer.

But now, sitting there in the hospital hallway, she wished that she had said yes. If everyone on the island didn't know about Ross's arrest yet, they'd know soon. Any minute now. And once they did, Brynn wouldn't want to show her face anywhere, even if this *was* just a big misunderstanding.

Her hands shook, but she rushed to finish the questionnaire. It was the same test she took every time Lucas had an appointment. The questions never changed, nor did her answers. The Edinburgh Postnatal Depression Scale, its formal name, was meant to gauge potential postpartum depression in new mothers. But for a test that diagnosed something so serious, the process of it always felt simplistic and flippant to Brynn. It was her fifth time completing it, only one of those times having been at an appointment for herself rather than for Lucas.

As always, Brynn selected all the answers that she knew would deflect attention away from herself:

I have felt happy: Yes, all of the time.

I have felt sad or miserable: No, not at all.

Sometimes, when Brynn took the test, she wondered about the people who had invented it. She'd Googled it once and learned that it hadn't been updated since it was first developed almost half a century ago. She wondered if they knew that mothers would be asked these questions at their children's doctor's appointments, not at their own, or if many pediatricians wouldn't administer the test at all. (The mothers weren't their patients; the kids were. Why should the *pediatricians* be the doctors screening the mothers for postpartum depression?) She wondered if the creators of the test could ever understand Brynn's fear of anyone—especially Lucas's pediatrician—knowing the dark truth that sometimes she wished she'd never had Lucas at all. That since he was born, she'd been drowning in her own sadness and anxiety. That she desperately missed the days when she wasn't a mother. And that she felt suffocated by the permanence of becoming one.

Still, she always marked her answers to indicate that she was happy. That she was *thriving*. What was the alternative? Would they take Lucas away from her if she told them the truth about how she really felt? Would they call Ross and tell him that his wife was a bad mother? Would they tell her that she just wasn't *meant* to be a mom?

This time, in particular, Brynn made sure to make her answers as benign as possible.

She handed the iPad back to the receptionist when she was done, and searched her face for any indication that she knew who Brynn was, and what her husband had supposedly done. But the receptionist was busy; she was distracted. Brynn was just another mom coming through with a newborn.

"This way," a nurse told her, and she led Brynn and Lucas to a room.

After a few minutes, there was a knock at the door.

"Queen Bee," he said. "How *are* you?"

Dr. Smith had been Brynn's pediatrician when she was a child, too. He gave her the nickname Queen Bee before she could even talk. He was going to retire sometime in the next few years, he had told her, but he agreed to take on Lucas as a new patient just for her. He smelled of cherry lollipops—the thin, flat kind with clear cellophane wrappers.

His pockets were always filled with them to give to the kids as a reward after each appointment.

Hearing Dr. Smith ask her how she was almost made Brynn burst into tears again. She considered telling him the truth—the *entire* truth. But in just a split second, she envisioned what might happen if she did. The stakes were even higher, now. If she showed herself to be an unfit mother and had Lucas taken away from her, then he might not have *anyone.* Clearly, Dr. Smith hadn't heard the news about Ross yet; and Brynn wanted to keep it that way. Here in this room with him, Brynn was in another world, where the past few hours had never occurred.

"We're good," Brynn said.

"I didn't ask how anyone else is," he said. "I asked how *you* are."

Again, she felt the familiar tingle of oncoming tears. She fought them back.

"Really, I'm good." She cast her gaze down. "I mean, exhausted, but okay."

"Tough as nails, kiddo," he said. "Always have been." He typed into the computer and pulled up Lucas's file.

"Now this little guy," he said, "looks *very* healthy."

Brynn hoisted Lucas out of the car seat and got him onto the table for Dr. Smith to examine him. She relaxed for a moment, knowing that even just for a few seconds, Lucas was in the care of someone she trusted more than she trusted herself.

Lucas didn't object as Dr. Smith skillfully checked his ears, his heartbeat, his lungs, felt around his throat and his belly. He measured his height and his head, he checked his testicles, he checked for diaper rash, and then he placed him on the scale and took his weight. Brynn didn't want it to end. She felt so safe and free just sitting there, arms empty and weightless. She imagined what it might feel like to run.

"Yes, you are," Dr. Smith cooed to Lucas when he was done, and he held him up. "You are a healthy boy. And a *happy* boy. Look at that face!" He handed him back to Brynn and she rocked him in her arms, certain that Lucas would feel her anxiety and launch into a screamfest at any moment.

"Yes," Brynn said. "We're lucky."

"How about sleep? How's he sleeping?"

"Uh, he's waking at night to feed a few times. But that's normal, right? At this age?"

"Yes," Dr. Smith said. "But by the next visit, he should weigh enough to cut the night feeds entirely. You could even try now."

Brynn nodded. As if it were going to be that easy.

Dr. Smith typed into the computer, and they sat in silence for minute. Then he turned to her.

"And you and Dad? Everything happy on the home front?"

She wondered again if she should tell him the truth now. If she didn't, it would look incredibly strange to Dr. Smith when he inevitably found out later. But if she told him now, she'd break down and she might not ever be able to put herself back together.

"We're good," she said. "Busy, but good."

"The perfect couple," Dr. Smith said. Brynn had heard this many times before from other people.

"And when is the next book coming out?" he asked. "I told Susan that I'd find out. You know she's your biggest fan."

"Soon," Brynn said, mustering a smile. She was starting to sweat as she realized what an insane idea it had been to come to the appointment. She should be hiding at home. She should be helping Henry and Margaux try to get Ross out of jail. She should be doing *something*. But then again, she wondered, who else could do this for her? No one.

Brynn sniffed the air and detected the distinct scent of Lucas's poop. She had hoped that she wouldn't have to change him there, in front of Dr. Smith or a nurse. Even the simple task of a quick diaper change made Brynn feel like she was being put on the stand, *tested*. She'd changed hundreds of diapers at this point, and yet she still didn't know what she was doing. She fumbled with the diaper bag, finding the wipes and a diaper, trying to stay calm, though her hands were still shaking, now even more violently.

"There ya go," she murmured to Lucas as she hastily cleaned him. Her voice came out in a grainy whisper. She was grateful that he didn't put up too much of a fight this time, which he usually did. Dr. Smith only glanced over; Brynn knew deep down that he wasn't judging her. And yet she worried that at any moment, he might look at her and say, *You're doing it all wrong. You can't do this.*

"And are you taking any time for yourself? You know, alone time?" Dr. Smith asked. "Exercise? Naps?"

"When I can," Brynn said. "Ross's mom has been really helpful. She gives me some time a few days a week."

"Well, that's a nice bonus," Dr. Smith said. "A helpful mother-in-law. That doesn't always happen, you know."

And it was true. Margaux had been incredibly helpful to Brynn over the past few months. Brynn wasn't sure what she'd do without her. At first, Brynn had wished that her own mother was there to help, but her parents had moved off-island years ago, having sold their Lobsterville house for an offer they couldn't refuse. They had moved just a ferry ride away to Falmouth, where her father still worked full-time as an electrician and her mother as a librarian at the West Falmouth Public Library. Even if they did still live on-island, though, Brynn knew that she wouldn't see them that often. She had stopped relying on them a long time ago, and now she never asked for their help. Her parents led their own lives. They always had. Even when she was little, her mother and father made it clear to her that her first line of defense should always come from within.

When Brynn was eleven, she was at the beach with her parents when she got a fishhook stuck in her thumb. At first, she felt nothing, and she examined the way the hook bent into the fleshy mound of her thumb so easily, as if she were made of clay. But seconds later, blood began pouring out of her, and she ran to her parents, screaming for help.

"Brynn," her father said, "take a deep breath. You know what to do."

"You're going to have to learn what to do when you're alone," her mother said. Brynn was crying. The hook had latched into her; she couldn't see a way out unless she dragged its spiky head back through her skin the way it had gone in.

"Here," her father said, handing her his fishing pliers. "You've got to cut the tip of the hook off."

With her small, uncertain hand, Brynn cut the fishhook tip and pulled the smooth half of it out.

"See?" her mother said. "You didn't even need our help."

What Brynn wanted to tell them, but she didn't know how, was that she might not have needed their help, but she desperately wanted it. She always had.

Margaux, on the other hand, had offered her help from the start. She was always available and happy to devote her time to Lucas if Brynn needed her. She loved her grandson, and she loved her own boys more than anything in the world.

Almost every other day, Margaux came over and forced Brynn into the shower, or out for a walk, or into the bedroom for a nap.

"Why don't you treat yourself to a manicure at Spa L'eau?" Margaux would ask. "Or, even better, *I'll* treat you. It's important to do things that make us feel good about ourselves, Brynn." Despite Margaux's kindness, sometimes Brynn wondered if her mother-in-law was covertly encouraging her to take care of her *appearance,* not her well-being. For Ross's sake, not Brynn's.

Initially, Brynn resisted the help. She wasn't comfortable breast-feeding in front of Margaux, especially since the breastfeeding wasn't going well (Dr. Smith had called Lucas a *grazer,* meaning that he ate in little increments *all the time*). But after a while, Brynn gave in and just let Margaux be around as much as she could be. She was *helpful,* and Brynn needed the help. She started relying on Margaux for guidance whenever she wasn't sure what to do.

Do you think he's ready for the next nipple speed? Brynn would ask her. *Can you show me how you take his temperature, uh, rectally? I can't seem to do it.* Margaux was a *pro,* and nothing seemed to faze her. She held Lucas with a sense of warmth and calm, the kind of confidence that comes not just from experience but from a genuine love of motherhood. The kind of confidence that Brynn wasn't sure she'd ever have.

As Dr. Smith typed up a few final notes on the computer, Brynn thought about what Ross had told her to find: *the orange sun.* The most famous sunset-watching spot on the island was at Menemsha, but what clue could possibly be hiding there on that public beach? There was no store, no restaurant, no hotel or inn, no landmark on the island that had anything to do with an *orange sun.* She was stumped. She felt entirely useless.

"Okay then," Dr. Smith said, bringing Brynn back to the present. "Nurse Diana will be in to give this fellow his shots, and then you're free to go. He looks perfect, Brynn." He rested a hand on her shoulder and looked at her. "You're doing a great job."

"Thanks," Brynn said, again trying to hold back her tears. "And please tell Susan I say hi."

"Hang in there, Brynn," he added, before closing the door. "I know it's hard. But this will all pass."

If only he knew, she thought. Brynn had already felt like she was in a nightmare before. Now, she was in something she didn't even have the words to describe. She felt the tears welling up the moment he left. The hardest part of the appointment—the shots—hadn't even happened yet. She took a deep breath.

Diana knocked and entered a few moments later. Out of all the terrifying moments of early motherhood, holding Lucas while he received shots were some of the worst, and today was a bad one, with three vaccines. Brynn knew that it was necessary and good for him and that the pain was temporary, but her fear was that she wouldn't be able to soothe him, even though that was her one job. There was so much pressure on her to be *everything* to Lucas, all at once. But how could she be the one to hold him while he experienced the pain of the shots *and* be the one to comfort him, too? Sometimes she felt like it was just too much all on her and her alone.

"Here we go," Diana said, poking Lucas's thigh with the first shot. Diana was a pro—she was always the nurse for Lucas's appointments, and Brynn was grateful. But she never wanted Diana to leave when they were done. Diana possessed that distinct quality of maternal warmth that Brynn longed for. Brynn wasn't even sure whether Diana had kids or not, but she was so good with Lucas that Brynn always wanted to ask her how she did it, what the secret was, where she learned how to understand babies so well. Lucas wailed immediately once Diana gave him the first shot, and he wiggled his body, kicking his legs and flailing his arms. Brynn had to hold him tight.

"Almost done, sweetie," Brynn whispered to him. It felt so unnatural to hold him down the way she was, but she knew she had to.

Diana finished the last two quickly and then stuck a Bluey Band-Aid on Lucas's leg. He continued wailing.

Brynn opened her shirt for him to nurse right away, a trick she'd learned to get him to calm down soon after the shots. She tried to get him to latch, but he only cried harder. The chair Brynn sat on felt sticky against the backs of her thighs and she regretted wearing shorts. His screams got louder. He cried into her chest not just with pain but with anger—and anger toward *her.* Brynn could feel her body tensing, her temperature rising, and this seemed to only aggravate Lucas more. Her fear was coming true: that she—his own *mother*—was incapable of comforting him. Brynn was incapable of doing the one thing she was meant to be able to do.

Finally, Lucas's mouth clamped onto her nipple, and his cries melted into shortened breaths as he sucked away. But even then, it didn't feel like a true relief. It felt as though she and Lucas had simply struck a peace treaty with each other: he tolerated her, and she tolerated him. She exhaled, but she couldn't relax. She was already bracing herself for the next meltdown, the next obstacle, the relentless cycle of frustration.

"Take your time," Diana said before leaving. "We don't have an appointment in here till later." She gave Brynn a smile—one of sympathy—and shut the door.

Brynn finally released her tears when the nurse left. She wondered how many other mothers had cried in that same room and never told anyone. She switched Lucas to her other breast, hoping that he would nurse more, but after a few sucks, he rejected her and groaned. Many times, Brynn had been told by other moms that newborn babies feel the energy that their mothers feel. If she was anxious, Lucas would feel anxious, too. Usually, Brynn rolled her eyes at this. After all, there was only so much she could control in the way she felt. She couldn't help but feel exhausted and overwhelmed—that was just her reality. But now, she was certain that she'd been putting all her negativity onto Lucas, and he'd been suffering as a result. She'd shared with him her fear, stress, depression, and her sense that everything was falling apart. She was unable to bring her focus back to Lucas, and for that, she felt awful. None of this had anything to do with him.

Her neglected breast ached, and Brynn considered her options of waiting to pump when she got home or expressing out some milk now into the portable rubber flange that she brought with her. She decided to express the milk now, even though it would take a good ten minutes. She didn't want to go home just yet; there was somewhere she needed to go first. But she continued to cry, unable to stop herself and not really wanting to try.

Her phone had been vibrating throughout the entire appointment, but she'd ignored it. She finally looked once she had Lucas tucked back into his car seat. She had too many missed calls and texts to even process. *Shit,* she thought. *The word is out now.* She knew she'd have to hightail it to her car. She packed everything up as fast as she could and slipped out the door, waving goodbye to the receptionist and quickly saying that she'd schedule the next appointment online.

Another woman was entering the building just as Brynn was leaving. She had a newborn baby strapped to her chest, and a toddler ran in front of her. The woman held the door for Brynn, who was struggling to carry everything with just one child.

"Slow down, Nico," the woman said to her toddler. She gave Brynn a knowing smile as Brynn brushed past her.

The smile was one of commiseration, and yet it wasn't. There was *nothing* relatable about that woman to Brynn. That woman seemed effortless. Breezy. She wasn't lugging a giant diaper bag bursting with all kinds of emergency supplies. She wasn't sweating. She didn't have oily hair. She looked happy.

Brynn envied that woman and how easy her life seemed. How suited to motherhood she was, how happy her children were to have a mom like her.

CHAPTER 6

Brynn had run out of diapers in her diaper bag; she needed to get home, but it would have to wait until she went to the police station.

Ginny called her as she drove there.

"Brynn," she said, "I just heard. Oh my God. Are you okay?"

"I mean, no," Brynn said. "I don't know what I am right now. I don't know what to do."

Ginny breathed into the phone. "I'm so sorry. Do you want me to come over?"

"No, thanks, or . . . I don't know. Maybe." Brynn still hadn't processed the fact that Ross wouldn't be coming home tonight. That he might not ever come home again. "I'm going to the station now to get some answers."

"Brynn," Ginny said, "are you sure that's a good idea?"

"Why wouldn't it be? I need to know what the hell is going on."

"Right. Just be careful."

Ginny promised Brynn that she'd let Annie and Marcus know she was okay. They'd all been worried, and just as shocked as her.

As Brynn pulled into the station, she was hopeful that somehow, though she knew it was probably impossible, she might see Ross. Or at least get to talk to him somehow. Henry and Margaux had told her that Ross was still at the station, not in the jail. He would stay there until they finished questioning him, but his lawyer hadn't arrived yet. So, there was still a chance she could see him, Brynn thought. She *had* to see him. He'd been taken away too quickly, before she could even respond to what was happening. She needed *answers.* She needed to know what the orange sun was. She needed to know where to look. She needed to know what evidence the police had to justify arresting Ross for murder in the first place. She needed to know how they had gotten here, and how she was going to get them out.

She expected to see local reporters outside the station, trading information and making calls. But it was quiet. Serene, even. The sun was still high; it wouldn't set for a few more hours.

And then she saw someone standing on the station steps, smoking.

It was Jacob Hammers.

He was taking a drag on a cigarette and staring at his phone. He wore his uniform.

Brynn jumped out of the car and grabbed Lucas in his car seat.

"Hey," she said.

Jacob immediately put his phone in his pocket. He looked like he'd been caught. He took a few seconds to process who Brynn was, and when he did, he dropped his cigarette and smashed it with his foot like he was trying to squash the life out of it. But then he glared at her.

"What are you doing here?" he asked. His voice came out like a wheeze. Brynn wondered if he usually smoked.

Compared to his father, whom Brynn had seen that morning, Jacob looked like he was playing dress-up. His uniform was white and wrinkled, and the fabric looked cheap and lightweight. Sweat stains circled out from his armpits. Brynn tried to imagine what Jacob and Cecelia's relationship had been like, and whether he was capable of doing something like what Ross had been accused of.

"Ross didn't do this," Brynn said, instinctively. "I'm, I'm so sorry for your loss, but this is a big misunderstanding." Brynn had so many questions for Jacob, but she couldn't ask them, not right now, maybe not ever. But why wasn't *he* the one arrested? What was *his* alibi? Brynn was a writer; she knew that it was almost *always* the husband or boyfriend. So where was Jacob last night and why was he immediately off the hook? If he wasn't guilty, then what did he *know*? "I mean, they haven't even told us how they know she was murdered. And for all I know, *you* could have killed Cecelia," she blurted, unable to stop herself. "Or Mauricio, who I'm sure you've heard is missing. But not Ross, of all people."

Jacob didn't respond. Brynn braced herself. She knew that she shouldn't have said what she'd just said, but she was so angry, and she had no one else to talk to, no one who was telling her anything. Jacob took a deep breath and looked off toward the cemetery.

"There's a lot you don't know," he said. His voice was stronger now, but he still seemed like a little boy to Brynn. "But to be clear, I loved Cecelia and never would have hurt her."

Jacob started to walk away toward his car in the parking lot in back.

"Wait," Brynn said, walking after him. She was carrying Lucas in his car seat. She couldn't keep up. "Please, just talk to me for a second."

Jacob stopped. He looked around and then stepped closer to her. So close that she could smell the lingering scent of tobacco and see the stubble on his chin.

"If I were you," he said, "I wouldn't believe everything the *Nelsons* say. Even your husband." His voice cracked a little, and for a moment Brynn thought that he might cry.

"But what about Mauricio?" Brynn asked. "How do you explain him being missing now?"

Jacob snorted. "You don't get it."

He jumped into his car before she could ask him anything else. Brynn was left there dumbfounded.

She watched him drive away in his gray Tacoma, the same truck nearly all men on Martha's Vineyard seemed to drive. It was the same shade of gray as Ross's truck, though Ross's was much bigger and an entirely different make and model. Still, she thought, maybe Jacob had killed Cecelia and then he and Ross had been mistaken for each other on the road. Maybe Pete was covering everything up to protect his son, and Ross was just an easy target. Brynn wondered what lengths she would go to for Lucas. Would she blame someone else for something terrible he'd done? She didn't think she would. But she couldn't be sure.

She didn't want to believe that Jacob was telling her the truth—that he'd never hurt Cecelia. And yet, his sadness seemed so sincere. When she looked at him, she'd seen a heartbroken young man.

Brynn walked up the stairs and into the station, carrying Lucas with her. The station was not as quiet as the street outside. Inside, phones were ringing, printers were beeping, and people were briskly walking in and out of offices, their lips and expressions tight.

Brynn approached the receptionist, who looked up at her with a surprisingly helpful smile. The smile of someone who didn't know who Brynn was.

"Hi, I need to see Ross Nelson. He's my husband, he's . . ."

The receptionist interjected, "Oh. You can't see him."

"I know, but I just need a minute," Brynn tried to argue.

"Brynn," a voice said from down the hallway. Brynn turned and saw Pete. "Why don't you come into my office?"

Brynn walked toward Pete, who held his door open for her. She felt naked and exposed as she went, as if she were the one guilty of murder.

Pete shut the door behind her. His office was warm and cozy, full of MV Sharks memorabilia and family photos. She sat down in the chair across from his, and placed Lucas on the floor beside her.

"I can't stay long," she said, "and I'm sorry for just showing up. I really just didn't know what else to do. No one is telling me anything, and I . . . I just am so confused. I wanted to see my husband. This has to be a mistake. It absolutely has to be." She paused. "Ross was home last night. With me. With his family."

She hadn't planned to say those words. They'd just flown out of her mouth. And the moment they did, she regretted it. Not because they were a lie, but because she wasn't *sure* that they weren't a lie. She didn't have proof of anything. But somehow, she knew that Ross was innocent. Or, at least, she wanted to believe that he was. She *had* to believe that he was.

"Look, I know how hard this must be. A total shock," Pete said. He rested his hands on his desk and leaned forward. "Unfortunately, I can't tell you much. But what I can tell you is that we have some evidence that points very directly to Ross. I couldn't believe it myself. But we have to let the evidence guide us. And, in this case . . . it's pretty clear."

"What kind of evidence?" Brynn asked. It would all come out sooner or later, anyway, she knew. Why couldn't he just tell her now?

"You know I can't tell you that," he said. "We're still putting all the pieces together. But we'll know more soon." Pete stood up, signaling that their conversation was over. "I hope you'll be staying with Henry and Margaux. It's not a good idea for you and the baby to be alone right now."

Though he was right—that Brynn didn't really want to be alone right now, not at all—it was a strange thing for him to say to her. Brynn felt a ripple of fear go up her spine, as if what he'd said had been a threat.

"Yes, I won't be alone," she said. "Thank you for your time, Chief. I guess . . . I'll come back when I'm allowed to see him. When will that be?"

"Not sure right now. But my officers will keep you informed." He gestured toward the door. "And Brynn," he added, "you're going to need to come back in for questioning, you know. Tomorrow."

"Okay," she said. She swallowed. She wondered if what she had just told Pete—about Ross having been home last night with her—would be recorded.

Brynn hurried out of there as fast as she could. Many times she'd written characters who had found themselves entangled in a mystery and been frustrated by the lack of police transparency. But she'd been privileged to have never experienced that herself. It was maddening, having no power whatsoever, and being told absolutely nothing.

She felt like an idiot, having shown up there with no plan. What had she expected would happen? There was *nothing* she could do. She didn't know where to start figuring out what was really going on or who to trust. And now she had to get a lawyer.

Brynn kept her eyes ahead of her on the way out, but as she briskly walked down the hallway toward the exit, something caught her eye. In one of the conference rooms, she saw a man sitting, being questioned by a police officer. It was *Mauricio*. He wasn't missing. Not anymore.

He looked up at her, and they locked eyes just for a moment. His eyes were red, like he'd been crying. But Brynn couldn't tell if they were tears of sorrow, or tears of guilt.

Suddenly, Brynn remembered all the countless times that she'd been at the club with Ross and had seen him interact with Mauricio. Had they been secretive with each other? Once, Mauricio had asked Ross to go look at the roof outside to see if he thought it needed repairs. Brynn had seen them through the patio doors, but she couldn't hear their conversation. Maybe there had been an entire dialogue between them that day—and all the others—to which she'd been oblivious.

Because if Ross was still in jail, and now Mauricio was being questioned, too, did that mean that they'd somehow been involved in something together?

Brynn got into her car, her heart rate accelerating. She needed to breathe.

There was no one she could talk to who could give her answers. Her only hope now was to find the orange sun.

CHAPTER 7

Finally at home, Brynn fed Lucas and put him down for his first real nap of the day in his bassinet. It was almost five o'clock. She felt horrible that she'd been so neglectful of him all day, taking him with her wherever she had to go, especially after he'd gotten shots at the doctor's appointment. Usually, her actions and movements revolved around Lucas and his needs. Today, she had forced him to work around what she needed to do and where she needed to be. He fell asleep almost immediately when she put him down. According to the sleep coach's schedule that Brynn still feebly clung to, this would be his last nap of the day, and she'd try (as she always did) to get him to sleep through the night after that.

Once he was down, Brynn began searching. She rummaged through all of Ross's drawers, every single jacket and pants pocket, even inside his shoes. She ransacked the bathrooms, the musty basement, even the barn with the lawn mower and fertilizer and rakes hanging on the walls.

She was about to give up when she realized that Ross's iPad was here, and it was linked to his phone. She knew his password—and he knew hers. They always had trusted each other that way. And until now, she'd never once felt the need or want to look through his phone.

She pounded his code into the screen and anxiously waited as it opened. She looked. But after a few minutes, it became clear that she wasn't going to find anything. There was *nothing*. Not only that, but she found nothing to indicate that Ross had done *anything* wrong. There were no cryptic text messages, no suspicious photographs, no criminal emails hiding in the deleted folder. Ross's entire footprint was clean—almost too clean—and Brynn was as lost as ever.

She felt a wave of rage fill her body. She hadn't let herself be angry at Ross yet, not about this, but she suddenly was consumed with vitriol toward him. Even if Ross was innocent of what he'd been accused of, he admitted to her that he'd been hiding something from her—something big—about his father and their business. He *had* been lying to her. Whatever was going on, he'd kept her in the dark. While she had been suffering, caring for their child, drowning in her sadness, he had been keeping something out of her sight, assuming that she'd never find out.

She threw his iPad onto the floor. "Fuck you!" she yelled. "You fucking asshole!"

Part of her wished that she *had* found something incriminating against Ross: evidence of an affair with Cecelia, a blood-encrusted shoe, a suspicious credit-card charge, anything. As awful as the thought might be, Brynn felt that it would be easier in some ways if she discovered that Ross was guilty. Then there would be no conflict, nothing to debate or figure out, no mystery. She could move on.

She had started to cry—*again*—when her phone rang. She frantically answered it without even looking at who was calling.

"Honey." Brynn heard the voice of her mother. "What is going *on*? I heard on the news about the girl and then someone from the library told me they had a suspect, but I didn't think anything of it. Then when your dad got home from work, the contractor on his job had heard through the grapevine about Ross. Everyone's talking about it. What happened?"

"I don't know, Mom," Brynn said. "Everything happened so fast. It's been a really . . . confusing day." As Brynn spoke, she couldn't believe how much her entire world had changed since just that morning.

"Well, do you want me to come over there and stay with you? I don't think you should be alone right now."

"No," Brynn said, without hesitation. "This is all going to be cleared up quickly, I think. It's a big mistake." She could hear how she sounded—as if she were either lying or just dumb—but right now it was the easiest thing to do. "I'll be okay. Ross didn't do this, Mom."

"Well, he hasn't exactly *been there* for you," her mom reminded her. "I mean, maybe he had a whole other life you didn't know about."

"Mom, just because he hasn't been helping a lot with Lucas doesn't mean he's a *murderer.* Think about what you just said." To her parents, Brynn had been defending Ross for years, and she was tired of having to justify her relationship.

"I'm just saying, Ross was selfish."

"What do you mean *was* selfish, Mom? He's not *dead*!"

"No, an innocent young girl is dead. Such a terrible thing."

"I have to go," Brynn said. "I'll keep you posted, okay?"

"Honey," her mom said, her voice softening, "I'm sorry. I never say the right thing. But we're here to help. Your dad and me. If you need anything."

That's rich, Brynn thought, coming from her mom, who had hardly ever helped her with anything when she was a kid and certainly hadn't helped her as an adult. Everything had to be politicized with her mother, everything had to have a bigger *point,* nothing could ever just be as simple as Brynn wanting something because she was a human being with needs and desires.

She hung up, her anger reaching what felt like a boiling point. She needed to shower and wash her hair. She'd worked up a sweat searching through the house. With Lucas still asleep, she turned on the shower and jumped in.

Brynn regretted the occasional times she'd vented to her mother about Ross. But it was easy to complain to her mother about Ross or any of the Nelsons. Her mother had never liked the family, ever since Brynn started hanging out with Sawyer in Menemsha when they were teenagers.

"They represent the worst of the island," she had told Brynn back then. "In fact, they're even worse than the summer people. At least the summer people aren't pretending to be something they're not. But the Nelsons . . . it's like they're ashamed to be from the island. They're ashamed to live here year-round. They think they're better than us."

Brynn had wanted to snap back at her and remind her that seasonal people on this island, as annoying as they might be with their Range Rovers with Connecticut plates and their impatience and their entitlement, were what made up the island's entire economy. They might not live on the island in the winter, but they still paid taxes that built the schools and paved the roads. They donated to the hospital, to the Island Housing Trust, to Camp Jabberwocky, to Family Planning—just like locals did. They helped make the island *run,* whether Brynn's mom wanted to admit it or not. Even before she was eighteen, Brynn had enough perspective to understand that that was how the island worked. As a year-rounder, she knew that you could dislike the summer folks all you wanted, but you couldn't hate them, and you couldn't survive without them. It didn't work that way. The Nelsons weren't summer people anyway, she had wanted to shout. Just because they didn't rely on a woodstove all winter for heat or refuse to drive down-island because of traffic and gas prices didn't mean they weren't islanders. They were locals as much as Brynn's family was. Just a different kind.

Brynn was so tired that she almost fell asleep standing up in the shower. She blinked to stay awake.

It wouldn't be the first time she'd accidentally fallen asleep when she was alone with Lucas.

Just last week, she'd put Lucas down for a nap around noon and decided to sunbathe a little on the deck while he slept. She'd shut her eyes. The sun had felt so good on her skin, as if it were making her new again. She knew that there were so many other things she needed to do while Lucas napped: appointments to schedule and confirm, packages to unwrap and boxes to break down, dinner to prep. But she was just so tired. She couldn't peel herself up from her towel.

She fell asleep quickly, unknowingly. She'd only meant to shut her eyes for a few minutes and let the sun warm her face. But she was awakened by Ross screaming. *"Brynn! Brynn!"*

She opened her eyes and was instantly consumed with dread, and then fear. She was more frightened than she'd ever felt in her entire life. She'd fallen completely, deeply asleep, while alone with Lucas. She'd abandoned him.

"What happened, Brynn?" Ross asked.

They could both hear Lucas crying. Brynn sprang up and pushed past Ross. She glanced at her phone. She'd slept for *three hours.*

"Oh my God," she said. "I—I fell asleep." Her face stung and her throat was dry. Her hips ached.

"I can see that," Ross said, as he followed Brynn upstairs to Lucas. "The monitor says he woke up almost an hour ago. How did you not hear him?"

Brynn didn't respond. Lucas was writhing in his swaddle like a worm, screaming for help, hungry, wet, and now exhausted from his fruitless cries for help. She felt like the worst mother in the world. Worsened by the fact that Ross had caught her, and she had no excuse.

"What if I hadn't come home just now?" Ross asked her. Brynn still didn't answer. She was obviously sorry. What did he want her to say? She felt incapable of speaking, even if she had a sufficient response to give.

She changed Lucas's diaper. He had soaked through the swaddle. Now she'd have to wash and dry it before putting him down for the night. It was the only swaddle he liked, the only one that didn't make him wail when she put it on him. She'd ordered another one online, but it hadn't arrived yet (she reminded herself to look up the tracking; maybe it was lost at the post office). Her mind instantly spiraled with all that she had to do now, calculating the domino effect of her mistake: the laundry, the lost time, the fact that she herself had to pee but she would just have to put it on hold for now while she took care of Lucas. And where was the extra bassinet mattress pad? She knew she had one somewhere.

"Brynn?" Ross asked again. "What *happened*?"

She couldn't bring herself to look at him, though she could feel his eyes on her. He'd followed her into the room and watched as she had picked Lucas up and changed him. She sat down to nurse. Lucas started crying again.

"I don't know...I'm sorry," she'd finally said, too tired to say more. That was all there was to say, anyway. Ross wouldn't understand her if she told him that she hadn't meant to fall asleep but that she was so deeply tired that every cell of her body had made her slip into a dream state. She hadn't been able to control it. *He* should try taking care of Lucas all day, every day, she thought to herself as Lucas finally latched on. She shut her eyes. *He has no idea how fucking hard this is. He'll never know.*

"Was your monitor even on?" Ross asked. "How could you not have heard him? If you're so tired, why wouldn't you just nap right next to him instead of all the way out here?"

Brynn had a sudden, consuming desire to punch Ross in the face, or to kick him in the groin. Maybe both. If she hadn't been sitting with a baby attached to her breast, and if she hadn't been so utterly tired, she just might have done it.

Ross simply didn't understand what was required of Brynn in taking care of Lucas every day, all day. Since Lucas had been born, Ross had only spent a total of two hours alone with him, when Lucas was six weeks old and Brynn had to see her doctor to get the knot of her stitches cut off after it didn't dissolve right on its own. And even then, Brynn had prepared everything for him to make it as easy as possible. All he'd had to do then was *hang,* as he liked to call it.

"If you were so worried about Lucas," Brynn said, "why didn't you go to him? Why did you waste a minute berating me?" Her voice started to shake, and she could feel tears coming on. "Think about that, Ross. You literally had to wake me up just so I could go get *your son,* because . . . what? You can't do it yourself? Because you're afraid to step up and be a father? Well, Ross, you *are* a father. It's what we always talked about. It's what you always wanted. It's happened. And you're not even here. I need you here."

She practically spat the words out. She had so much more to say, but she was too tired, and too clouded by her anger and hurt. She knew better than to keep going. Not now. She waited, expecting Ross to apologize. How could he not? She'd finally told him how she really felt. She'd told him what he'd always wanted to hear: that she needed him.

"I literally just walked through the door and could hear him screaming," Ross said, annoyed. "I saw you outside and wasn't sure you were even okay. There wasn't time for me to do anything else."

"Well, I'm *not* okay. I'm not okay at all, Ross. And I think you know that. You've *known* that, but you can't handle it."

Brynn hadn't wanted to have this conversation. She hadn't planned to, but now they were in it, and she'd said it, and there was no going back. The truth was, Ross wasn't wrong for berating her. What if she'd kept sleeping and Lucas had rolled over and suffocated? What if he'd choked on his saliva from crying? *What if, what if, what if?* Brynn had turned the volume of the monitor all the way up, and yet she hadn't heard a thing. She'd shut him out.

Annie had once said to Brynn that she hardly even used a baby monitor at all because she just had a *sense* of when the twins were awake.

"You'll just *know* if Lucas is up. You'll hear him cry no matter what. You'll feel it," she'd said. "There have been serial killers and kidnappers who use recordings of babies crying and play them outside women's doors to lure them out. It's like, our natural instinct to help, when we hear a baby cry."

Brynn kept waiting for that natural instinct to kick in. She wanted to feel that primal urge to protect and comfort her child when he cried.

Sometimes, she convinced herself she felt it. She tried to trick herself into believing that it was working, that she had the right reaction, that she was naturally maternal. But even she couldn't convince herself of something that just wasn't real.

When Lucas cried, Brynn definitely felt *something,* but it wasn't anything good. It was fear. It was panic. She could feel her skin breaking out into hives, her heart rate quickening. She hated his cries, not because her heart ached for him or because his pain was her pain, but because his cries trapped her. His cries held her responsible for fixing something she knew nothing about, something she wasn't equipped to fix. His cries told her she wasn't doing it right. His cries told her that she was a bad mom.

Sometimes, Brynn put the monitor on mute when Lucas napped. Just for a few seconds. It was like a high, to go from the constant static of the noise machine, and his piercing cries, to the fluffy silence of being alone, in another room. Those few seconds of silence were heavenly. She could imagine she was somewhere else. But even with the monitor on, full blast, she had developed a way to tune it all out, to leave her life—if only for a few seconds. What kind of mother was capable of that? she wondered. What kind of a mother *wanted* to ignore her own son?

"I'm not okay," she said again, crying. Lucas wasn't latching right on the other breast. She felt lopsided and achy. She stood up. Lucas was still hungry, but the nursing wasn't working.

Ross stood up, too.

"I'm going to go make a bottle," he had said. "I'll be right back, and I'll take over. It's okay."

When Ross had emerged with a bottle, she handed Lucas over to him like he was something she had stolen. Ross embraced him and sat on the edge of the bed. Lucas began drinking immediately from the bottle, and she could see his little body relax, comforted by being in the arms of someone who wanted to hold him, someone who knew *how* to hold him.

"I'm going to pump." Brynn had wanted to keep talking to Ross, to tell him more about how she felt. But her breasts ached, and she needed to pump, or she'd get mastitis. She'd learned that a few weeks ago the hard way. And she had to wash the swaddle. She couldn't do all of these things while also talking to Ross. She could only handle so much. The moment was gone.

"Okay," Ross had said. "We'll be right here. I've got it under control."

She'd taken Lucas's sleep sack and bassinet sheet with her and thrown them in the wash. Ross did have it under control, she knew, but only because she'd set it all up for him. All he had to do was sit there and feed him with the milk she created. Ross didn't have to think about anything else.

That night, Ross had given Lucas a bath and put him down to bed. He made Brynn pasta—with butter and parmesan cheese, her favorite comfort meal. After dinner, he put his arms around her and held her. At first, Brynn resisted. She didn't want to be touched. She was touched all day long by Lucas and she felt suffocated. But then, she gave in and she hugged him back. He had shaved his face that morning, and his skin was soft and smelled like Irish soap. His embrace was strong and warm, his arms wrapped around her like a cocoon. When he held her, she was able to remember what it was like when it was just the two of them. She breathed him in and allowed her body to relax, to melt a little bit. They pulled back slowly and looked at each other. For a moment, Ross was still Ross to her. And she was still Brynn. They were still the perfect couple.

But that moment felt like a lifetime ago, now. There had been a slight shift in Ross's effort and behavior after that, but then it returned to how it was—distant, aloof, robotic—after a few days. It made her start to wonder if that was their new normal. If it was, she wasn't sure she could live that way. But she also wasn't sure if she deserved better.

Now, out of the shower, Brynn dressed herself in sweatpants and an old Amherst sweatshirt. She picked up the iPad that she'd thrown on the floor. Luckily, it was intact. She was about to put it back on his bedside table when she realized there was something she hadn't checked.

She opened it up again and searched for his WhatsApp. They had both downloaded the app during a trip to Mexico for a friend's wedding. Neither of them had used it since, at least Brynn hadn't. There were only a few open texts in the app, and most of them were old—from the wedding weekend a few years ago.

But there was one more recent message that Brynn noticed right away, and when she saw who it was from, her stomach dropped.

Ginny.

CHAPTER 8

Brynn picked up the phone to call Ginny and ask her what the *hell* she had been doing exchanging cryptic texts with her husband. There were only two texts between Ginny and Ross: one from last week asking him to meet her at the state forest parking lot on Barnes Road, to which Ross had replied "ok." Brynn had no idea what this meant, but her mind raced.

She tried not to, but she couldn't stop herself from imagining filthy scenes of the two of them together, just as she'd imagined Ross with Cecelia. She pictured Ross kissing Ginny's neck, Ginny reaching for his crotch, the two of them breathing heavily . . . except . . . Ginny was incredibly pregnant. Sure, Brynn remembered feeling very unexpected waves of . . . *desire* when she was pregnant, but she knew that Ginny had been supremely uncomfortable lately. She constantly complained to Brynn about her back pain and her incessant burping. The idea of Ginny and Ross having a torrid affair *now* just seemed . . . unbelievable. Still, what if Ross had been having affairs with multiple women right underneath Brynn's nose? What if he was some kind of sex-crazed psychopath, and she had no idea?

The only logical thing Brynn could think of was that Ginny

must have known something about the Nelson & Sons business—something like what Ross had whispered to her. But how bad could it be that she'd keep it from her best friend? What could she possibly have discovered that would make her go behind her best friend's back to her husband? Brynn recalled her recent interactions with Ginny. It all seemed pretty normal, but Ginny *had* been somewhat standoffish with her that morning. Maybe Ginny knew what the orange sun was. Brynn started to write a text to her, but before she sent it, her kitchen door opened and she heard Sawyer's voice. She'd forgotten that Sawyer, Margaux, and Henry were all coming over.

"Brynn?" Sawyer entered the kitchen with a pizza box in one hand and a six-pack of Offshore Ale East Chop beers in the other.

"Hi," Brynn said, taking the box from him.

"What a shitshow," Sawyer said.

"Yeah," Brynn said. "That's the only way to describe this."

"How are you holding up?" Sawyer sat down and cracked two beers, then handed her one.

"Not good. This is just . . . I guess I'm in shock." She remembered what Ross had told her about not trusting Henry. And Jacob, too. *Don't trust the Nelsons.* But it wasn't that simple for Brynn. She'd known Sawyer longer than she'd known Ross.

"Well, I'm pissed," Sawyer said. "This isn't right. I mean, obviously the police have *something* on Ross, but . . . I'm sorry, there's just no way he did this. It's *Ross* we're talking about. He's a fucking square!"

Brynn smiled and let out a little laugh, the first in a while.

"I know," she said. "I just don't understand how they could possibly think he did it. I . . . I went to the station. I talked to Pete. I needed some answers, you know? But he didn't tell me anything. Just that Mauricio isn't a suspect, even though I *saw him* there in one of the interrogation rooms, which makes no sense at all. And he said that they have evidence on Ross." Brynn sighed. "It was so crazy, Sawyer, sitting there and listening to this, not being able to do anything about it." She paused. "And honestly, not knowing what to believe."

Sawyer drank his beer. "I'm just so confused," he said.

Brynn wanted to tell Sawyer about the texts she'd discovered be-tween Ross and Ginny. She wanted to ask him about the orange sun. She had so many questions. But she held back.

"Sawyer," Brynn said, "do you think Ross has been acting different lately? Have you noticed anything off with him?"

Sawyer furrowed his brow. "Only that my dad's really been pushing him hard lately. And I think Ross has been pretty stressed about that. My dad's been . . . I don't know. *He's* been acting different, that's for sure."

Brynn nodded. Ross *had* been stressed about work lately, more than usual, and Henry had been particularly hard on him recently. Henry had always held high standards for Ross, but lately, those standards felt unattainable. He'd been pushing Ross to his limits, dangling his own retirement in front of him, just out of his reach, but within sight. He'd thrown him into tricky situations without any preparation, demanding that Ross find solutions to problems that Henry himself had created: promising a client a backordered slab of marble within a week, for-getting to budget in the cost of trucking hundreds of tons of unusable kaolin off-island during a pool dig, commencing the build of a beach-stone fireplace when the client wanted bluestone instead, promising building permits within days when they normally took months to get.

Ross didn't know how else to respond to Henry's demands other than doubling down on his hours, his efforts, his blood, sweat, and tears. Brynn could tell that no matter how hard Ross worked, it wouldn't ever be enough for Henry. But Ross refused to see it that way. He'd never stop.

There was something else that felt different with Henry, though, lately. It was something that had nothing to do with work. In the office and on the jobsites, Henry was tougher than ever. But at home, at the club, and at dinners, he was sentimental, effusively emotional about almost everything. He got teary-eyed whenever he held Lucas. He told the same stories again and again at family dinners—how he arrived on the island right after graduating from Durfee High for a summer gig painting houses and how he'd started his own construction company within just two years. How he'd built homes for a former president, several Fortune 500 CEOs, Pulitzer Prize–winning authors, and yet he was just a kid from Fall River. He talked as if his life was over and all he could do now was look back on it instead of looking forward, as if it were all slipping through his fingers. His emotion didn't seem to come from a place of joy. It seemed to come from a well of regret, a lifetime of remorse. For what, Brynn didn't know. But something was eating away at Henry from the inside out.

Brynn desperately wanted to tell Sawyer what Ross had whispered to her before his arrest—about not trusting Henry. But she couldn't. "I'm actually worried about Henry," she said. "And now with Cecelia dead, I just feel like he's . . ."

"Losing it?" Sawyer asked. "I know. Me too. I think we all see it but don't know how to deal with it." He had another sip of his beer. "Anyway, do *you* think Ross has been acting different lately?"

"No," Brynn said, maybe a little too fast. The truth was, he had been acting different, too. Not just Henry. Maybe it was just the pressure of work, or maybe it was something else. She wasn't sure now. "Nothing unusual," she added.

"Look, Brynn," Sawyer said. "Ross is innocent. This whole thing is a big, fucked-up mistake. He loves you. It's going to be okay."

Brynn smiled, though she wanted to crumple into Sawyer's arms and cry. Sawyer was nothing if not loyal, especially to his big brother. Brynn felt bad about not being more upfront with Sawyer, not telling him that she had to find *the orange sun,* or that Ginny and Ross had shared a suspicious text exchange. But she couldn't tell him. For his sake, she wanted to keep him out of it.

Brynn and Sawyer first met during Brynn's first summer working at the Galley, a burger and milkshake joint in the fishing village of Menemsha. She'd known who Sawyer was already, of course. They were both going to be seniors at the high school that fall. His older brother Ross was already off at college. The Nelson brothers were the kings of the island. They were natural athletes, playing on the varsity football, hockey, and baseball teams since freshman year. They excelled academically, too, especially Ross, who everyone knew would probably get into an Ivy (which he did—Cornell). They were kind and inclusive, known for bending the otherwise rigid social hierarchies of the high school, having friends in all different groups. And their family hosted epic parties. Brynn had never attended one, but she'd heard about them. The Nelsons had once hosted a fundraiser for Martha's Vineyard Community Services where James Taylor himself had appeared for a surprise performance.

Ross and Sawyer Nelson were island royalty, and Brynn knew all about them before she'd even met them. But it would be nearly a decade before Ross knew Brynn.

That summer, Sawyer was working as the unofficial first mate to a fishing charter captain who kept his boat at the docks right behind the Galley. Each day, when Brynn got in for her shift before lunch, she would see Sawyer cleaning the boat or fileting fish, already back in from the morning charter, hosing off fish blood and guts, scrubbing the crusted layer of salt off the center console, dumping out old ice and half-empty iced-tea bottles. At first, they only waved to each other, and she wondered if he knew her—an up-island theater kid, a writer, a bookworm. Not an athlete, not a party girl, not a *cool* girl.

Eventually, they started chatting, at first about fishing. Brynn impressed him with her fishing knowledge. Her dad had taught her to fish for bluefish and stripers on Lobsterville Beach right outside their house when she was as young as five. She knew how to rig her own fishing rod, she knew how to tie lures so that they wouldn't break. She knew how to hold striped bass by hooking her fingers inside of their mouths, and how to hold bluefish by the head and the gill plate, to avoid their sharp teeth. She could even handle herself on the Menemsha jetty during a crowded derby morning. Sawyer told her that he'd never met a girl who knew so much about fishing. "Are you an alien?" he'd asked her.

Their conversation evolved slowly into other topics—their love-hate relationship with tourists (hate the crowds and the attitudes, but love the hefty tips), their jobs (pros: close proximity to the beach; cons: blisters, long hours, and the occasional rude customer), school (whatever)—and eventually they just talked about themselves and whatever was going on in their lives. Sawyer opened up about the pressure he felt from his parents to succeed. To Brynn, it seemed like Sawyer was already perfect; how could they demand more from him? But Sawyer said his brother Ross was much more focused than him, much more ambitious, which was what his parents expected—or wanted—from him, too. But Sawyer just wanted to enjoy summer. He wanted to surf, fish, and hang out. He wasn't sure college was right for him at all, though his parents said he didn't have a choice.

"You're lucky to have parents who push you, though," Brynn had told him one afternoon as they sat with their legs dangling off of the dock, sipping milkshakes from the Galley. "They believe in you. I'm not sure my parents expect much from me. They just sort of let me . . . figure it out on my own. Sometimes, I wish they were harder on me, if that makes sense."

"Sounds like we'd have the perfect parents, combined," Sawyer had said. He'd turned to her then, suddenly, and planted a kiss on her lips. It was completely unexpected, but Brynn hadn't leaned away. She had wanted it to happen. Sawyer had tasted like the salt from the ocean and the sugar from the milkshake, warm and innocent.

But it had been the first and last kiss they ever shared. When school started again in the fall, they'd both returned to their designated social roles, which kept them apart. And the following summer, Brynn packed up her things and drove to UMass Amherst, and Sawyer headed to the University of Vermont. They'd planned to keep in touch, to see each other whenever they were home. But once Brynn started college, she was introduced to an entire world she hadn't known existed: people from the other coast, other countries, other religions, other belief systems. She wanted to absorb it all, she wanted to grow, and most of all, she wanted to redefine herself, on her own terms. She wanted to leave the island behind for a while, even if it meant turning her back on the person who had been the brightest spot in her life.

Brynn wondered if Sawyer had been angry at her that fall when she'd gone dark. He had never said so. But she had been the one to end things between them, not him. She hadn't even had the courage to break it off formally. There was nothing formal to break off anyway, she'd told herself. Even at that young age, Brynn was certain that the two of them could never actually make it together on the island. Sawyer and his brother were down-island royalty, and she wasn't part of that world.

So, she'd simply stopped returning his calls. She began answering his texts with single words and smiley faces instead of real responses. Time passed, and there was never an opportunity for him to confront her about it. Life went on. They grew up. She met Ross.

Though Brynn never asked him about it, she always thought it was funny that Sawyer had a job all the way up in Menemsha. He lived on the complete opposite side of the island, in Edgartown, his family's turf. Sawyer could have easily gotten a job in Edgartown on one of the charter boats there. But Brynn soon realized that the distance was exactly *why* Sawyer had chosen that job. At the time, he had wanted to be as far away from Edgartown—and from his family—as he could get.

"I think my parents will be here soon," Sawyer said. "Want another?" He lifted a beer bottle.

"Sure," Brynn said. She drank the rest of hers and then accepted the new one from Sawyer. *Fuck it,* she thought. She could pump and dump later.

While Sawyer put the pizza in the oven to keep it warm, Brynn defrosted a bag of breast milk for Lucas, whose murmurs she could hear on the monitor. He was waking up from his nap and was hungry.

She couldn't shake the question she herself had asked: *Had* Ross been acting different, and how so?

Ever since she'd known Ross, he'd always been humble. Never

flashy. He didn't care about having the fanciest car or the brand-name clothes, even though he could afford them. He preferred to keep a simple, low profile.

But recently, something had changed. She thought about the babymoon Ross had surprised her with last year to Turks and Caicos. They'd stayed at Amanyara, a resort so luxurious and expensive that she'd lied to her own parents about it because she was too embarrassed by its lavishness, telling them instead that they were staying at an all-inclusive resort using credit-card points. She thought about the outrageous new boat Ross had treated himself to: a twenty-eight-foot, pale blue Regulator with two 300-horsepower Yamaha outboard motors. (Sawyer had aptly called it a *fuck you* boat.) She thought about the new Volvo SUV he'd bought her in anticipation of Lucas's arrival, so that she wouldn't feel unsafe driving him around in her 2012 RAV4. She thought about the UPPAbaby stroller system, the Coterie diaper subscription, the Nanit baby monitor, the Artipoppe carrier—all the baby gear that was too expensive for her to even put on her registry. Ross had simply told her, "Bee, put it on the credit card. It's for our baby."

The credit card was a shared one, but one that Ross was responsible for paying. Brynn used it for groceries, household needs, and certain expenses for Lucas. She never used the card for herself, or even for Lucas's clothing. Those things, she paid for herself. The family card was for things that the family needed, and both Ross and Brynn felt it was fair for Ross to foot the bill, since he was currently making more money than she was. The card was not, however, for things that Brynn might want but that she didn't really need, even if they were for Lucas. She and Ross had agreed to be sensible when it came to spending; his recent looseness with it was uncharacteristic, she thought, though at the time she didn't object. She had just used the card, and now she felt foolish for relying on him so much. That was something she'd always told herself she wouldn't do.

Ross made good money, and Brynn's book deals weren't too shabby either, but neither one of them had exorbitant amounts of extra spending money. What if all this extravagance had been a red flag that she'd blindly ignored? What if Ross's behavior had told her everything she needed to know, and she'd just chosen to ignore it?

Everything that Ross had described to her—how Henry had been destroying the company for years—Ross himself could have done, too. Brynn felt sick thinking about the possibility, but she knew that he was capable of it. Maybe not morally capable of it, but he was certainly smart enough to pull it off. Ross was brilliant.

She thought back to so many of their arguments and debates: where to buy a house on the island, which preschools Lucas should be on the wait list for, even who Lucas's pediatrician should be. Sometimes, like with the pediatrician choice, she and Ross agreed. But with almost anything else, Brynn ended up deferring to Ross. She wondered if she'd ever really stood up to him about anything, *ever*.

"This is all just . . . too much," Brynn finally said. She stared out the window at their backyard. Ross had seeded the lawn himself last fall. It was now a vibrant green and surrounded by bright summer flowers that Brynn had carefully picked and planted herself just a few weeks ago. The beauty of it now somehow felt wrong and out of place. "And I can't believe Cecelia is dead. I mean, why Cecelia? How could she have been involved in *anything* that would make someone want to kill her?"

"I don't know," Sawyer said, shaking his head. "None of this makes sense. And I wish they would tell us how they even know it's a murder to begin with." He paused and looked down. "What went wrong?" he asked, looking up at her. "What happened? Between us, I mean."

Suddenly, there it was: the question she'd been hoping he would never ask, throughout all these years. She froze. She'd had half of her life to think of the answer, but she had nothing to say to him now.

"We grew up," Brynn said, looking away.

"Did we, though?" he asked. "Have things really changed?"

Brynn could feel Sawyer's eyes still on her. She turned toward him. She wasn't the girl at the Galley anymore. She was someone's mother, someone's *wife*, an author, someone who paid taxes and had medical insurance and took vitamins each morning. These things meant that she *had* grown up. And yet, Sawyer had a point. Just because time had passed, and her life had changed, and she'd created a human, had she herself actually changed all that much? What did it even mean to have grown up, when she still longed for the past?

Most days, since Lucas was born, Brynn yearned for her former self, the one that she felt had been erased. It was like no one saw her anymore as anything except a mother, a vessel and caretaker for someone else. Sawyer, though, saw her right now. He saw the old Brynn. And it felt so good to be seen, to be appreciated, to be remembered as something and someone more.

"Everything's changed, Sawyer," Brynn said, pulling herself away from him before something happened that she could never take back. They both heard a car outside pulling into the driveway. Margaux and Henry had arrived. "Or, at least, I have."

CHAPTER 9

The moment Margaux and Henry came into the house, Margaux burst into tears.

"Henry," she said, between sobs, "tell them what our lawyer just told us. I can't."

Henry sighed. He sat down at the kitchen island. Sawyer brought them both glasses of water. Brynn remembered what Ross said, about not trusting Henry, and she watched him closely as he spoke, trying to search his expression for some kind of evidence that he was lying, or keeping something from them. Anything.

"All she said was that the police shared their evidence with her and Ross," Henry said, "and . . . well, it just seems indisputable. I guess there's security camera footage."

Brynn thought she might vomit.

"Well, has anyone actually seen it?" she asked. "How do we know if it's even real?" She looked at Henry, trying to gauge his reactions.

"I don't know," Henry said.

"The footage could mean anything. It could be nothing. It could be a mistake," Margaux said. "Until we see it with our own eyes, we can't trust that it means anything."

Brynn nodded and swallowed, but she knew better than to agree. She felt a chill down her spine. Footage of *what,* she wondered. And if it was footage from the club, what would it show that linked Cecelia later washing up on shore on another part of the island, dead?

Brynn needed to call Ginny—*now.* She asked Margaux to watch Lucas while she went to the bathroom, then she ran upstairs and shut her bedroom door.

"Hey," Ginny answered. "How are you doing?"

"Ginny, stop," Brynn said. "I know about your messages with Ross. You need to be straight with me or I'm going to the police with it. There is way too much going on for you to lie to me right now, Ginny. Someone is *dead.* I just . . . Why does it seem as if whatever you're lying to me about has to do with Cecelia and Ross being arrested?" She felt like she was talking to a stranger, not her best friend.

Brynn could hear Ginny's kids in the background. It was their bedtime, an hour during which she'd normally never call Ginny, because she knew it was one of the most chaotic times of the day. But she didn't care. Not tonight.

"Okay," Ginny said, in a hushed voice. "I can explain. But it's better if I explain it in person. Tomorrow? I will tell you everything. But . . . I promise, Brynn, it's not what you think. Please, just trust me on that."

Brynn started to feel like she was losing her mind. She was tired of people telling her to simply *trust* them. And she was so tired that her grasp on reality was slipping through her fingers. Was she in a nightmare, or was this actually her life now? She couldn't think clearly. She didn't entirely trust *herself.*

She heard Lucas start to cry downstairs, and she knew she had to go to him.

"Fine," she said to Ginny. "Tomorrow."

Brynn looked at herself in the bathroom mirror before returning downstairs. All of Ross's things were still right there on the bathroom counter, as if he'd be home any moment. As if nothing had changed. His toothbrush, his deodorant, the face lotion Brynn got him that he

never opened, the bottle of Motrin that he'd been using a little too frequently lately to combat his back pain.

"What the *hell* is the orange sun?" Brynn whispered to her reflection as she gently touched all of Ross's things. The way Ross had said it to her made it seem like she *should* know what it was, like it was something the two of them shared. Something representative of their bond. Maybe she hadn't been paying attention to their relationship for all these years the way he had. She'd assumed it had been the other way around—that Ross had been the absent one. But maybe Brynn had been somewhere else in her mind, ignoring both the good and the bad.

She longed for the mundane routine of the lives they used to have, before today. She had grown to hate the mundane—the suburban domesticity of the life they'd created for themselves, the cycle of coffee and laundry and bills and baby spit-up and appointments and dirty dishes. But now she'd give anything to have it back.

When Brynn and Ross had first gotten together, it was because of a shared vision of their dream life. A partnership. A desire to take on the world together. A life far from the routine of brushing their teeth side by side in silence, peeing with the door open, making coffee.

Brynn had been living in New York, in a tiny walk-up in the West Village with two roommates from college, when she decided to move back to the island. She'd secured a deal for her second book—a good enough one to take the plunge into writing full-time and quit her editorial assistant job. Plus, she missed home, even though her parents had moved off-island. She wanted a change from New York, and a family friend had offered her coveted year-round housing in a basement apartment. The publishing world had burned her out even after just a few years. Every relationship she had in the city felt transactional. She needed to be somewhere where no one cared about celebrity book clubs and bestseller lists.

"Aren't you going to be *bored* there?" her friends asked her. But Brynn knew she wouldn't be. So many of her islander friends couldn't wait to leave the Vineyard, to move to big cities, to move *anywhere* else, but not her. The island called to her when she wasn't there. But just because she wanted to live there didn't mean she wanted her success to be inhibited. Brynn wanted to have a big life, even if she stayed on-island. She didn't know why she couldn't have both.

Ross was the only person she'd met who shared this specific ambition—this desire to stay on the island while also building something bigger for themselves. They ran into each other at a mutual friend's annual pig roast in Edgartown. She hadn't seen Ross in years, not since she and Sawyer had dated for one summer in high school. But even then, she wasn't sure he knew who she was.

"Hey, Brynn," he said to her at the beer cooler, with that smile.

It was almost immediate, what they recognized in each other. They both wanted the same life. They wanted to raise children on the island, they wanted to have a chicken coop and a garden, they wanted to spend summers out on the boat fishing, they wanted their kids to know how to dig for clams and fish for scup off the docks. But they also wanted big careers, too, and big success. They wanted to travel, to cook, to have great conversations, to make lots of different friends, to go on adventures and spend nights around a fire pit telling stories over a great bottle of red wine.

Meeting Ross again was like discovering a puzzle piece that Brynn had been missing her whole adult life. They spent the rest of the party just *talking,* getting lost in each other, ignoring everyone else there. Finally, the hostess had to politely ask them to leave. "Sorry, I've got to put the kids down," she had said, ushering them to the door. They'd completely lost track of time, but they didn't want to part, so they went into town for a late dinner in the cellar at Atria, and stayed there until the owner, Greer, turned the lights on and politely told them to leave.

That night, they shared their goals and dreams with each other, their fears, their regrets. They talked about their love for the island and their frustration with it, too, how they found comfort in its familiarity but also felt stifled by it. Suddenly, their previous lives without each other felt too small, too limiting, but together the future was wide open. From then on, they could never be without each other, as though the world they wanted to live in required their togetherness.

And the two of them had kept talking and talking and talking. Right up until Lucas was born. And then they had stopped.

Now, downstairs, Sawyer had taken the pizza out of the oven.

"Slice?" he asked. She nodded.

"I really think you and Lucas should just come stay with us, Brynn," Margaux said.

"Thank you," she responded, "but I think we're going to stay here. I don't want Lucas to feel disrupted." Brynn wanted to suggest that Margaux stay here with her instead, but she knew that Margaux wouldn't leave Henry alone.

"I spoke to Pete," Margaux said. "Just now, while you were upstairs. They're going to question Ross tomorrow, now that his lawyer is here. And I think they'll be questioning all of us, too." Brynn looked at Henry when Margaux said this, but his face was nonreactive. Frozen. "And I asked Pete about Mauricio," she continued. "And all he said was that Mauricio has been found, and that he is not a suspect. Which is very frustrating."

At least Brynn knew that Pete was giving them the same information. But it still didn't make sense.

Henry just sat in silence while they talked. Brynn watched and waited, hoping she could catch him doing *something*. But all she saw when she looked at him was a sad old man.

Margaux kept talking, even though no one else had anything to say. What was there *to* say? "I've had my doubts about Mauricio for years," she said. "I never really liked the way he treated the girls at the club. Henry, didn't I tell you this? I did. I always thought there was something unsavory about him."

"Yes," said Henry. "You're usually right about people. I should have listened."

"He was too hard on all of them. Worked them like dogs," Margaux said. "They're just college kids here for the summer. He was relentless."

It was clear that Margaux wasn't giving in to any belief that Ross could be guilty. She was remaining steadfast behind her son, no matter what new evidence came into the picture. Brynn felt guilty that she already couldn't quite say the same; she wasn't sure if she was one hundred percent behind Ross right now. Until she had more answers, she wasn't sure of anything.

When it came to protecting her sons—and her family in general—Margaux was fierce and unrelenting. So much so that it sometimes made Brynn feel self-conscious about her own ambivalence about being a mother. She knew that she was still in the early days of postpartum, and that her feelings would eventually change, but she didn't want Margaux to know that she lacked the fierce love for her son that Margaux clearly had for her own.

"Anyway," Margaux continued, "the police make mistakes, sometimes. Even Pete. They could have gotten something mixed up. Or they could be lying."

Brynn had the same thought, but she hadn't wanted to say it, at least not with Henry around. Even though Pete and Henry were close, if Pete had to choose to sacrifice his own son or Henry's, wasn't it obvious who he'd choose?

"You can't trust anyone to do their job these days," Margaux added.

Just then, Brynn's phone rang. She looked at her screen. It was an unknown number. She knew instantly that it was Ross. The room went silent as she answered.

"Hello?" she said, more like a statement than a question. Lucas gurgled. Margaux immediately went to pick him up. Brynn clutched the phone to her ear.

"It's me," she heard. Brynn nodded to everyone. They knew who it was, too. "You're probably with my family," he said. "I know you can't talk. Brynn, you cannot trust my dad. I . . . I don't know exactly what's going on yet, and I . . . I don't know that he is responsible for Cecelia's death, I mean, I can't imagine that he'd ever do something like that . . . but I know there's a connection. Maybe . . . maybe he hired someone.

Maybe Mauricio. Maybe Cecelia knew too much. I don't know yet, Brynn. But don't believe what he says. You need to make sure my mom stays out of whatever he's trying to do." Ross's voice was manic, shaky. He sounded like he hadn't slept in days even though he'd only been arrested that morning. He sounded unstable, as if the words coming out of his mouth were part of some hallucinogenic trip he was on. He didn't sound like Ross.

And Brynn was boiling. She couldn't confront Ross about the text with Ginny, not now, not in front of his family. She couldn't ask him about the orange sun. She couldn't ask him about the supposed security camera footage. She couldn't ask him *anything*! Not with Henry around. And even though she had so many questions, the only thing she really wanted to say to him was how angry she was. How indescribably mad at him she was. How she hated him now more than ever, and yet for some inexplicable reason, she still believed him. And she still loved him.

"I'm glad you're doing okay," Brynn said, too loudly, in an effort to sound normal. "We all miss you, Ross, and we're going to get this figured out."

"I have to go," Ross said, before Brynn could ask anything else. He hung up.

Brynn looked down at her phone for a moment, unsure if the call had been real or not. If anything was real.

"How did he sound? What did he say?" Margaux asked. "I can't stand the thought of him in there alone."

"He sounds okay," Brynn said. "He's being strong. All he said was that he doesn't know why he's being targeted but that they're going to figure this out."

Margaux started to clean up the kitchen. It was late. Brynn needed to feed Lucas, and bathe him, and try to get him down for the night.

When they all said goodbye, Brynn wanted to reach out to Margaux and tell her to stay. She wanted to keep her safe. She wanted to tell her what she knew, but she didn't know how. She couldn't right now. So, she let her go, with a pit in her stomach.

"We'll talk in the morning," Brynn said to them as they all walked out, into the night. She shut the door and exhaled in the silence of her house, alone now with Lucas.

She watched them out of the window of the kitchen. Henry went straight into the car and turned it on. Sawyer walked Margaux to the passenger side, and Brynn watched as they embraced each other. Sawyer was so much taller than Margaux that he practically enveloped her in his arms. Sometimes it was hard for Brynn to imagine Margaux as a new mother to her sons. She wondered often what those early years were like for Margaux, and whether she had been happy. In all the baby photos of Ross and Sawyer that Brynn had seen, Margaux was glowing, beaming with pride in her two beautiful sons. She looked healthy, rested, put together. She looked like it was the best time of her life, not the worst, like it had been for Brynn.

Once, she had tried to ask Margaux if she'd struggled as a new mom. If she'd found it as overwhelming as she had.

"Oh, of course," Margaux had said. Brynn had been surprised. "It's a lot of work, motherhood. It's exhausting. Nothing can prepare you for how difficult it is. Nothing!"

Brynn had sighed with relief, thinking that maybe she and Margaux were more alike than she'd realized.

"But that's why it's important to take care of ourselves. So that we can take care of our families, right? That's the most important thing we have, family."

"Right," Brynn had said, again feeling their divide. Maybe someday she'd feel that family was the most important thing. But in that moment, when Lucas was just a few weeks old, she felt like the most important thing in her life was her career and her independence, and she'd thrown it away to have a baby. She couldn't say that to anyone, not out loud, but it was the truth about how she felt. What did it even mean, she wondered, to be *family*? Everyone had told her that the love she'd feel for Lucas when he was born would be the most powerful love she'd ever felt in her whole life. Yet she felt . . . *nothing*.

Upstairs, in the bedroom, Brynn tapped the sound machine and night-light on, and sat down on the edge of the bed with Lucas. She held him like a football tucked on top of her forearm, a position she'd learned from one of the three lactation specialists she'd seen in her attempts to make breastfeeding work. He began eating with fervor, huffing through his nose, and she could feel his warm, tiny breaths on her skin. When he was done, she burped him, changed him, and tucked him into the bassinet. She'd skip his bath tonight. He dozed off instantly, finally giving Brynn a reprieve.

The house was suddenly too quiet. But she knew that tomorrow, nothing in her life would be quiet. Tomorrow would be full of noise. Tomorrow, she would have to talk to the police. Tomorrow, she'd confront Ginny about her meetup with Ross—she didn't have the bandwidth tonight; she was too tired. Tomorrow, she'd have to face questions from Annie and Marcus, whose calls and texts she'd been ignoring all day. Tomorrow, the island would begin speculating and hypothesizing, sharing tidbits of knowledge on the porches of Alley's and the Chilmark General Store, at spin class at the YMCA, in line for morning coffee at Rosewater and at Humphreys, at the dump's recycling station. Tomorrow, Brynn would try to find the orange sun. Tomorrow.

But for now, Brynn needed to rest. Still in her clothes, she collapsed on the bed and fell fast asleep.

CHAPTER 10

The silence of the house continued into the morning. Brynn woke naturally, at first with a relaxed ease, savoring the brief feeling of weightlessness that comes before the heaviness of the day. With her eyes still shut, it was as though the previous day had never happened. Everything was okay. Cecelia was alive, Ross was home, and the Nelsons had done nothing wrong. But then reality—and panic—set in. She opened her eyes. Why hadn't Lucas woken her with his usual cry? She felt her heart jump out of her body—the same feeling she'd had when she'd fallen asleep outside that day Ross found her. Just as quickly, her heart plummeted back inside her chest as she saw that Lucas was right there, in his bassinet, sleeping soundly, just as she'd left him. She looked at her phone; it was nearly seven in the morning. For the first time, Lucas had slept through the entire night!

Brynn instinctively turned toward Ross's side of the bed to share her excitement with him. But his side of the bed was empty, of course. For the first time, she felt his absence, and she missed him. Even though she'd been so mad at him lately, and so lonely when he was home, she longed to feel his body next to hers, to feel the calmness of his breath, the warmth of his skin on the sheets.

Brynn's phone was illuminated with messages and missed calls. She'd been ignoring her phone pretty much entirely since yesterday afternoon, aside from answering Ross's call. She knew that her friends were worried about her, but she wasn't ready to talk to them yet. She wasn't ready to talk to anyone. Except for Ginny.

She peeled off her clothes, which had left indentations on her skin from being slept in all night, and she crept into the bathroom before Lucas woke.

At this time yesterday, she had said goodbye to Ross as he set out for work. She'd felt sad but also angry as she had watched Ross pour himself coffee. She had felt a distance from him when he had kissed her forehead to say goodbye. As she brushed her teeth, she tried to remember if anything had seemed unusual yesterday. If he had been acting strange. If there had been clues. All she could remember, though, was her anger—toward Ross, toward Lucas, toward herself. Her anger had consumed her; she couldn't see anything outside of it. Now, she didn't feel angry, she felt lost and afraid. Lonely. Except it wasn't quite loneliness, it was something more—a profound disconnection from everything she thought she knew to be true, including herself.

"Hello?" she heard from downstairs as she finished washing her face. At first, she thought she was hearing things. It was still so early. "Brynn? Can we come in? It's *us*!" The voices were familiar: Annie, Marcus, and Ginny. "We know it's early, but we have been *so* worried about you!"

"Shit," Brynn said to herself. She peered down from the top of the stairs. "Be down in a minute."

She had wanted to talk to Ginny *alone,* not with their friends. But she couldn't wait; she'd have to confront her now. Whatever Ginny was hiding, she'd have to come clean about it to everyone, not just Brynn.

Lucas woke up and began to cry just as Brynn finished getting dressed.

"It's okay, you're okay," she said to him as she picked him up. His cry was different today, less agitated. "You slept through the night, you know that? You did such a good job." Lucas looked at her, and the corners of his lips just barely began to turn upward. But just as fast, they descended into an angry frown, and he began wailing. He was hungry.

She changed him and then brought him downstairs, where her friends had spread out an array of breakfast sandwiches, pastries, and iced coffee from the Scottish Bakehouse. They had let themselves in using the key under a flower pot, one that she'd told Ginny about long ago in case of emergencies. Ginny had already started to warm up a bottle of Brynn's breast milk that she kept in the fridge.

Brynn snapped the bottle out of Ginny's hands and gave her a scowl. Annie and Marcus didn't catch it. Brynn couldn't believe the nerve Ginny had to just show up here unannounced. She had to stop herself from slapping her across the face.

"Listen, Brynn," Annie said. "I speak for all of us here when I say that we love you and we are going to get through this *with* you."

"Yeah," Marcus added, "we're so sorry. We know you probably have to go to the station today and we thought we could help out, stay back with Lucas and watch him. Whatever you need."

Brynn had almost forgotten that she had to go in to the station to get questioned, as Pete had told her she would. It was starting to feel impossible to juggle it all.

"And I want to say too that none of us think Ross is guilty," Annie added.

"But . . . you do need to know what people are saying," Marcus said. "I mean, I'd want to know."

Ginny remained silent. Brynn could barely look at her.

"I want to know," Brynn said. "Tell me."

"Well," Marcus said, "everyone thinks that Cecelia and Ross were having an affair."

"*But* a lot of people are saying that Mauricio and the boyfriend aren't being looked into enough, too," Annie said.

"Some people are saying that maybe Cecelia was pregnant," Marcus said, in more of a whisper.

"Wait, stop," Brynn said, suddenly growing hot with rage. "Don't you understand that this whole thing is messed up? We're talking about my husband here. *Ross.* He didn't *murder* anyone. How can you even think that? Shouldn't we be talking about whatever went wrong in our police system that made them think he did it?" Brynn wondered if she was refusing to see the truth right in front of her, like so many of the women on the true crime podcasts she listened to while folding laundry or walking with Lucas. The ones who refused to see what was right in front of them, because if they did, it would mean that their entire lives would crumble. Could it be that she was one of those women, too? No, she decided. She was smarter than that. This was different. *She* was different.

No one said anything. Finally, Brynn turned to Ginny.

"Okay," she said. "You need to be straight with me. Explain yourself, Ginny. Right now."

Marcus and Annie shared a perplexed look.

"Are you guys okay?" Marcus asked.

"Not really," Brynn said. "I found texts between Ginny and Ross. Weird texts about meeting up."

Annie and Marcus were wide-eyed.

"I can explain. Sit down," said Ginny. "Please. It's complicated." Brynn didn't want to sit down. She wanted to run outside and scream. She wanted to turn back time. She wanted to get in the car and drive away from her entire life. But there was nowhere for her to go. She sat down, and she waited.

"Okay," Ginny began. "You know the big story I've been researching for a while now? The one on motherhood?"

Brynn nodded.

"Well, it's not on motherhood." Ginny looked down.

"Oh boy," Annie whispered to Marcus.

"I mean, I am writing that, too. But the story I've been spending time on is about something else. It's . . . it's about the Nelsons." Ginny looked up at Brynn now. Her eyes conveyed remorse. "I was *always* going to tell you, Brynn. Always."

"But what do you mean, it's *about* the Nelsons?" Brynn asked, her voice becoming shrill. "Like, a profile of them? What is going on, Ginny? I can't take any more secrets."

"No, not a profile," Ginny said. "More like . . . an exposé."

"An exposé? Are you kidding me? On *what*? What have they *done*?" If Ginny had ever considered Brynn a friend, she had to tell her everything. Now.

"Do you remember that little article I wrote earlier this year about post-pandemic development on the island and how construction companies are still struggling to get materials on time?" Ginny asked.

Brynn did remember, though only vaguely. The piece came out right before Lucas was born. Her mind had been on her baby registry and whether she was going to hire a doula. She'd barely read the article.

"Uh-huh," she said.

"Well, I did a little research into all the major builders on the island. Including Nelson & Sons. I truly wasn't looking for any dirt, I just wanted to get a handle on the types of projects these businesses were building and what kind of numbers they were working with." Ginny paused and nervously fiddled with her hands. "And I found . . . well, I found some things that just didn't add up."

"Like what?" Brynn snapped. She knew when Ginny was dragging out the truth. She couldn't wait anymore.

"At first, just some administrative stuff that didn't seem particularly egregious. There were a lot of permits missing that should have been filed. The timing of some projects didn't seem right either. Pools being built before property owners had been there for five years, things like that. No records of waste material being taken away by Keene's, no record of it being taken away by anyone."

Marcus spoke up. "I mean, not to be condescending here, but we're talking about a small island construction company, not, like *Meta*. How bad could things have been?"

"Yeah," Annie agreed, "I'm with Marcus on this. None of this sounds great but it also doesn't sound . . . *that* bad. I mean, it's not good, obviously. But it's not like Henry hurt anyone. It's not like he was stealing *millions* of dollars from like, the poor."

"Yeah, this is Martha's Vineyard we're talking about," Marcus said. "There's a lot of shady stuff going on that people get away with all the time. I mean, you're on *stolen Native land* for crying out loud."

None of them could disagree with that.

"That's what I thought at first, too," Ginny said. "I didn't think any of it sounded that bad. But I kept digging around. And I found a police report against Henry from almost twenty years ago."

"Well, what did it say?" Brynn was losing her patience.

"That's the thing," said Ginny. "It didn't say. It had all been crossed out. Like someone literally was covering up whatever happened."

"And so, what? You were going to confront Ross about it? If the police report was against Henry, why would you be going after Ross?"

"I wasn't going *after* him, Brynn. Even though this was a big story, my priority was always *you,* Brynn. You and your family. Lucas. Ross. But I still needed to find the truth. So, I thought I'd start with Ross. Give him the chance to share what he knew. I didn't want to drag you into this unless I had to. I know Ross. I know he's a good person. I wanted to tell him what I'd found. I figured it was possible that he didn't even know about any of it. But he needed to. Especially if he was going to be taking over the company. I thought about what could happen if he took the fall for everything. . . ."

Brynn softened. She felt guilty for imagining that anything might have been going on between Ross and Ginny.

"You still should have told me," Brynn said.

"I know," Ginny said. She looked sorry. "But Ross told me that he was already aware of all this, and that he was in the process of fixing it. Making it right. So, the morning we all found out about Cecelia, coincidentally, I messaged Ross and told him that I was dropping it for good. And that I would never tell a soul. I knew that there were bigger issues we had to focus on—like taking care of you, and Lucas. And I trusted that he was handling it. But I think he was still worried that the story was somehow going to get out there before he could protect you."

Brynn looked down. So Ginny didn't run a career-making story to protect her. *Brynn*. And everything with his family was what Ross had meant when he had texted *I can explain everything*. None of it had anything to do with an affair between Ginny and Ross. And none of it had to do with Cecelia. Ross had thought that the police had shown up for his father, not for him. None of this had made sense even to Ross. His shock had been genuine. It was all just truly terrible timing.

So then did that mean that Ross's arrest was something entirely separate? It was too much of a coincidence.

Now that Brynn had some of the answers she had been looking for, she was more confused than before.

"And," Ginny continued, "I didn't want to worry you. Neither did Ross. You've been so . . ."

"I've been so *what*, Ginny?" Brynn asked.

"You've been struggling," Ginny said. "Understandably. We didn't want to add to your plate. Not with your postpartum depression."

Brynn hadn't referred to her depression—or whatever it was she had been feeling since having Lucas—as postpartum depression. She hadn't referred to it as *anything*, really, except the acute sense that she was deeply unhappy, and that something was wrong. A bad case of the baby blues. To formalize it as anything more, to diagnose it, to give herself the time and attention that treating it might require would be too selfish, she thought. It would mean time and energy away from Lucas. And to label this feeling as something so clinical, so specific and severe, felt too serious, with consequences too grave for her to contemplate right now. It also felt like a defeat to acknowledge how much help she needed, how much she was struggling. She'd made the decision a long time ago to say nothing, and to just forge on.

"You still should have told me," Brynn said. "That's not an excuse."

"You're right," Ginny said. "And I'm sorry."

"Maybe none of this would have happened if you'd told me," Brynn added, twisting the knife. She wanted to make Ginny feel bad. She was still sore with the sting of betrayal.

"Maybe," Ginny said. "I obviously don't feel good about how I handled it."

"And, anyway," Brynn said, "I don't have postpartum *depression*. I just have the baby blues. It's . . . it's normal. It's fine. I'm *fine*." Brynn started crying as she spoke, which suddenly turned into a roaring laugh. Nothing about her current situation was funny. And yet here she was, more exhausted than she'd ever been in her life, with a newborn baby and a husband in jail for murder, and she was insisting that she was *fine*. It was the funniest thing she'd ever said, because it was so deeply untrue.

She wiped her eyes. "Seriously," she said, "I'm okay."

"Honey," Marcus said, "sorry to state the obvious, but, uh, you're obviously *not* okay." He gave her leg a loving squeeze.

"Yeah," Annie said, "and that's okay."

"You know," Ginny said, "I had postpartum depression with Sam, too. I've been on happy pills ever since."

"What?" asked Brynn. "You seemed so happy when Sam was born. Why didn't you tell me?"

Ginny was a sympathetic friend, but when it came to her own life and problems, she never complained. It wasn't that she pretended everything was fine, like Annie often did, it was that Ginny was exceedingly proactive. If she had a problem, she simply did something about it and made a change. She made it look easy. Brynn found it annoying, sometimes, especially when she herself wanted to vent and complain, to lament her choices and life decisions, but Ginny's response was always something sunshiny and simplistic, like, *Hey, you have a beautiful, healthy baby boy and a husband who loves you. It could be worse, right?* Once in a while, Brynn found some comfort in Ginny's positivity, but most of the time, it frustrated her and made her feel isolated, like her sadness was unwarranted, and within her control.

Brynn had once asked her how she stayed so positive all the time. *What other choice do we have?* Ginny had said. This had deflated Brynn; she couldn't relate to it at all. Her default, since having Lucas, was to assume the worst and expect it, too.

"I didn't tell you," Ginny said, "because I didn't want to plant the idea in your head that you needed the same treatment as me. Don't you remember when you were pregnant you told me that you hated all the negativity out there in the media about motherhood? The Instagrammers who warned you how hard it was going to be and how your life would be over when the baby came? You said you felt like all that stuff wasn't allowing you to be excited about becoming a mom.'"

Brynn did remember that. When she was pregnant and in full-on nesting mode, she'd noticed that so many articles and social media posts about motherhood only spoke of the *bad* parts of motherhood. It had started to make her feel unnecessarily anxious. She wanted to *celebrate* being a mom. She wanted more friends who would say *You're going to love being a mom!* Instead of saying *You'll never sleep again* or *Prepare to cry every day . . . but that's okay!* She wanted to read happy articles and encouraging essays. Brynn had made it a rule to ignore all the negativity. And she'd been very clear with her friends about this, too. Including Ginny.

"I took that to heart, Brynn," Ginny said. "I totally understood where you were coming from. I didn't want to prevent you from being excited about becoming a mom. So, I felt like if I told you about my own depression, you might resent me for it." She paused. "And as for everything else with the Nelsons . . . Yes, I should have told you right away, but I really did want to protect you. You had *just* had Lucas. I couldn't add more stress onto you, not until I at least knew what I was even talking about."

Brynn regretted how rigid she'd been about staying positive during her pregnancy, how she'd shut down any conversations that warned her of the terrors of the fourth trimester. Her own struggles and depression had hit her like a bus, head-on, with no warning, and she wondered if she might have been better prepared for it if she'd talked about it with Ginny beforehand.

"Well," Brynn said, her emotions still reeling, "I'm sorry I wasn't there for you more after you had Sam. Obviously, I didn't know. I had no idea." Brynn thought back to that time now. Her own future as a mother had felt light-years away back then. Babies were not on her mind. She was in the throes of finishing her second book and was on a big fitness kick, running six miles a day. Her life, at the time, was fabulous—and void of any real burdens.

She had gifted Ginny with ridiculous, impractical outfits for Sam and an expensive cashmere baby blanket. She had offered to babysit or take Sam out for ice cream once Olivia was born, but Ginny never accepted the help. Brynn's offers were always open-ended: *I'm here for you, anytime!* If a friend offered that to her now, Brynn thought, it wouldn't really occur to her to take them up on it.

Brynn realized that she'd never given a gift to Ginny *herself* after she'd given birth. She'd never offered to clean her house, cook her dinner, or simply let her nap while she watched the baby. Brynn hadn't known that those were things Ginny might have needed—far more than a silly baby headband with a big pink bow. But there was no way for her to have known it back then, not until she became a mother herself. She cringed now, thinking about all the friends who'd had kids, and how Brynn had basically only ever asked them, *How's the baby?* She'd rarely thought to ask, *How are you?*

Now, she thought, she would do it all differently, had she known what Ginny was going through. Had she known what *any* mother goes through.

"It's okay," Ginny said.

"Well," said Annie, "I've been on happy pills since long before I had my kids!" Brynn was grateful to laugh, even just a little bit.

Once the laughter faded out, Brynn sighed. "Guys, you don't have to be here. I don't want you to feel like you need to be involved in all this."

"Stop," Annie said. "We're your friends."

"Yeah," said Marcus. "We're here for you."

"There are just so many questions," Brynn said. "I feel like my brain is going to explode." She turned to Ginny. "And now with everything you've told me about the Nelsons . . . I need to figure out what it all means."

"I know," said Ginny. "I have so many questions too. Like, this police report. I couldn't quite tell if Ross knew what it was about and wasn't telling me, or if he didn't know. But then I never got to find out more. The next thing I knew, Cecelia had died, and Ross was taken away." She faced Brynn. "But there's no way that all of this happening at once was a coincidence. I just don't know what the connection is."

Brynn tried imagine what life was like twenty years ago, when that police report was filed. Ross and Sawyer were teenagers; she didn't really know the Nelsons then. But she remembered from her days at the Galley with Sawyer that he'd described his dad back then as working all the time. Hustling. At that time, Nelson & Sons was just taking off. Henry was still working on smaller jobs, not the big summer mansions just yet, and he was doing a lot of the hands-on construction himself. He had his contractor's license. Margaux was busy driving the boys to sports practices and running PTA meetings. If Henry had committed a crime twenty years ago, the rest of the family might not know anything about it. It still didn't explain what Cecelia would have to do with any of it. She'd only been a toddler then, and she wouldn't even set foot on the island for another twenty years. Besides, Henry might not be trustworthy, as Ross had warned, but it didn't make him a murderer.

But then Brynn had an idea.

"I know someone who can help us with the police report," Brynn said. "Jacob Hammers." Brynn had no reason to believe that Jacob would help her. But she remembered the way he looked outside the station when she saw him yesterday. She recognized that look. It was one of sincere grief. It was one of pain. He missed Cecelia. If Brynn could offer him a chance to possibly find some answers about what happened to Cecelia, he might be inclined to help.

"Oh," Annie chimed in. "That reminds me. I heard that Jacob was at his softball game the night Cecelia died. They all went to the Ritz afterward and then to Tony's house for late night. Basically, every dude on this island between the ages of twenty and thirty are his alibi."

Part of Brynn didn't believe it. The alibi was too convenient. *Too* solid. All the guys vouching for him were probably drunk, and never would have noticed if someone slipped away for a few hours over the course of the night. It wasn't his alibi that made Brynn believe he didn't kill Cecelia, it was the fact that she really did think he loved her.

"Apparently, there are pictures of him doing pickleback shots all night," Annie continued. "Poor kid. He must feel so guilty for not being with her."

"Can I just . . ." Marcus started to say. "Never mind." He looked away, avoiding eye contact with Brynn.

"What is it, Marcus? Just say it," Brynn said. She was burping Lucas, gently slapping him on his back.

"I just . . . Brynn, you know I love you; we all do. And we're here for you. So, please don't hate me for what I'm about to say. But . . . I feel like we're getting distracted from what's really going on here. People don't just get arrested for no good reason. I mean, I'm really sorry to be the one to say this out loud, but how do we know that Ross didn't do this?" Marcus shrugged his shoulders. "I just don't see what all this backstory has to do with Cecelia being dead and Ross being the prime suspect."

Brynn's initial instinct was to tell Marcus to leave. But nobody said anything. Because he wasn't wrong. Brynn *didn't* have any proof that Ross was innocent or any reason to believe he was. Not yet, anyway. She didn't blame Marcus for questioning Ross's innocence.

"I hear you," she said, even though Marcus hadn't explicitly said that. "And I totally understand why you'd ask that. None of this looks good. And I know I probably sound delusional. But . . . I know he's not guilty. I just know it. Plus, Ross told me . . ." She stopped herself. Brynn wasn't sure she could tell her friends what Ross had whispered to her before his arrest. She wasn't sure she *wanted* to. Wouldn't it be unfair to entangle them in all of this even more than they already were?

But she needed her friends. She couldn't do this alone.

"Ross told me to find a clue," Brynn said. "He said it would explain things."

"A clue?" Ginny asked.

"Yes," Brynn said. "He told me to find *the orange sun*. I have no idea what that means. I've been trying to figure it out . . . and I just don't know if I'll ever find it. But he said it would all make sense when I do."

The group was silent; no one knew what the orange sun was. Brynn worried that she might not ever know.

"Huh," said Marcus, finally. "The orange sun."

"That's why I'm not giving up on Ross. Not yet," said Brynn. "I need to find whatever he's talking about. I need to see it for myself. What if it really does explain this entire mess? What if it leads us to Cecelia's killer?"

Just then, Lucas released a guttural burp and spat up all over the back of Brynn's shirt. She felt the warm liquid seep into her skin.

"I'm going to go change," Brynn said. "And then I have to go to the station. I should get it over with."

After she saw Pete yesterday, Brynn had called her friend Izzy Melville, a local real estate lawyer that Brynn knew from hot yoga classes. She was whip-smart but had no experience whatsoever in this kind of case. Still, she was certainly better than not having a lawyer at all, in a pinch.

"This is really not my area of expertise," she had told Brynn yesterday. "You definitely should have a lawyer with you when you go in for questioning, though. The police will tell you they're just asking you standard questions, nothing to worry about. But you're the wife. They're going to be looking into you for keys to the puzzle. And there's *always* something to worry about. So, I'll help you. But you're going to need someone who's better equipped for this long-term."

"Let us help with Lucas," Marcus said. "That's why we're here. Just give us instructions and we'll make sure everything's okay. We have all day cleared."

Annie nodded in agreement. "Put us to work," she said.

"Thank you," Brynn said. "I'm going to change, and then we'll go. I guess we just need to find Jacob's number. If we can talk to him before I go in . . ."

"Already have it," Ginny said. "Let's call him from the car. 'Cause I'm coming with you."

CHAPTER 11

Marcus dutifully wrote down all of Brynn's instructions before she left, even though she gave him far too many details that he didn't need to know: the exact temperature Lucas's bottle needed to be, the right way to rock Lucas before his nap, the amount of Aquaphor to put on the little scratch on Lucas's cheek. Marcus knew that these details were Brynn's way of feeling secure leaving Lucas behind with him and Annie. So, he just nodded and wrote them all down.

"I'm missing something, I know it . . ." Brynn said. "Umm . . . Dr. Smith is his pediatrician. There's a thermometer and other medical stuff in a box under the sink."

"Brynn," Marcus said, his voice calm. He put his hand on her shoulder. "We got it. I promise. We'll take very good care of him."

"And we'll call you if we have *any* questions," Annie said.

For some reason, Brynn didn't want to leave Lucas. It was an unfamiliar pull, like a magnetic force. She wanted to hold him now more than ever. To smell his skin and feel the weight of his body in her arms. Normally, she couldn't wait to be free from the prison of motherhood in which she felt trapped. She'd usually jump at the chance to go somewhere without worrying about the car seat, the diaper bag, the spit-up.

But right now, she just wanted to be home with her son. She wanted to be with him and him alone, and to shut out the rest of the world.

"Okay," Brynn said. "We'll be quick, I think. Or, I hope. Thank you."

In the car, her body ached to be back home, in her bubble. She hated it there, and yet she never knew how to exist anymore outside of it.

Ginny drove; Brynn sat in the passenger seat. She rolled her window down. The air outside was cool; it was still early morning. It felt luxurious being driven by someone else, and not being the one responsible for everything. Even if it was just for a moment. She exhaled and let herself have the small indulgence. Then, she started to laugh. Not a real laugh, more like a cross between a laugh and a cry.

"I just can't believe this is my life, Ginny," Brynn said. "How did this *happen*?"

"I don't know," Ginny responded. "But you'll get through it. Now let's call Jacob."

Brynn called, and Jacob only answered after she tried him three times. He begrudgingly agreed to meet them on a trail in the state forest off West Tisbury Road.

"Do you feel safe doing this, Brynn? Maybe this is a bad idea," Ginny said.

Maybe it was stupid of her, but Brynn did feel safe. It was strange, but since she'd had Lucas, she felt like nothing could really scare her— except motherhood itself. Everything else seemed easy in comparison to what she'd been through giving birth, and what she was still going through as a new mom.

"I do," Brynn said. "I really don't think Jacob had anything to do with Cecelia's death. That said . . . I don't know if I can trust him. But I'm not afraid of him. And anyway, we have nowhere else to turn. If he can help us, we need to ask."

"Right," Ginny said. Then she put her hand on her belly and groaned. "Ah," she said, grimacing. "Just a cramp. I'm fine."

"Ginny, maybe you should just go home and rest. This is nuts. You're about to pop."

"*No,*" Ginny said. "I owe this to you. I shouldn't have talked to Ross behind your back, even if I was trying to protect you." She paused. "We are figuring this out together."

Brynn knew that she wouldn't win the fight with Ginny. Once they reached the entrance to the trail, Ginny parked alongside the road and Brynn got out.

"You still have my location tracking on your phone, right?" Brynn asked.

"Sure do," said Ginny. "I've got eyes on you."

"Okay. I won't be long, though." Brynn turned toward the trail. "Hey, Ginny. Thank you."

"Don't mention it, Brynn." Ginny smiled at her and then reclined her seat.

Jacob was waiting exactly where he said he'd be. He looked just as he'd looked to Brynn before—like a scared little boy. Brynn felt almost predatorial meeting him alone. She realized that *he* might be scared of *her,* and that he probably didn't trust her at all.

"Hi, Jacob," she said, and she swore she saw him jump.

"Hi," he responded.

On the phone, Brynn had told him that they had information on the Nelsons that he might want to know, in exchange for his help with the police report.

"Listen, let me start by saying that I know you didn't have anything to do with Cecelia's death. And I'm sorry for your loss. I really am. But I know that my husband is innocent, too. I don't know who did this to her, or why, but I know that it wasn't Ross."

Jacob scoffed and crossed his arms. "How do you know? And why should I trust you?"

"Well, I don't know, not for sure. Or, at least, I don't have proof." Brynn fidgeted with her hands. "But for some reason, I'm deciding to

trust you. And I think we can figure this out together. I have a feeling that Cecelia knew things about my family that she shouldn't have
known. And somehow . . . it got her in trouble. I tried asking your dad
about it, but . . ."

Jacob interrupted. "Don't bother asking my dad about anything
having to do with the Nelsons. He practically is one."

Brynn felt a shiver across her neck. "What do you mean?" she asked.

Jacob uncrossed his arms and paced around. "The only reason I'm
meeting with you is because . . . I don't trust the police. Well, no, it's not
that I don't trust the police. I mean, I *am* a police officer. I don't trust
my dad." He licked his lips, as if he'd said too much. "There's a lot of
things about the *Nelsons* that nobody is supposed to know. But my dad
knows all of it."

"Okay," Brynn said, "I want you to be able to trust me. And I know
you have *no* reason to. So let me prove it by telling you something that
no one else knows. Even though I don't owe you anything."

"I'm listening," Jacob said.

Brynn was bluffing slightly. She didn't really know *anything,* except
what Ross had whispered to her before being taken away by the police.
But she wanted to goad Jacob into telling her anything *he* knew.

"I think I know what you're referring to. About the Nelsons," she
said. "Right before he was arrested, Ross told me that Henry had been
doing bad things—*illegal* things—with the company. He said he'd been
doing it for years. And I don't know what the connection is, but he said
he knew why he was being arrested for Cecelia's murder and that it was
all related to what Henry had been doing. We need to find out. There
must be something big, Jacob, something that Henry did years ago that
got swept under the rug. And somehow, it's why Cecelia is dead."

Jacob looked off into the distance. Brynn couldn't tell if he was going to tell her she was crazy, or if he knew exactly what she was talking
about.

"You know, at the beginning," Jacob said, "Cecelia was really excited about the job at the club. She was excited by this whole island. Her

college roommate, Clarissa, had been a server there the summer before. She got her the job and convinced her to come. Cecelia had barely ever left Pottsville, Pennsylvania, you know, except for college at Middlebury. Her family had a small printing business, and I think that was all that was expected of her. To stay and work at her family's Main Street store. This island represented something bigger to her . . . something aspirational. Freedom. She wanted to impress people here, especially the members of Oyster Watcha. Even you."

Brynn felt queasy with guilt. She'd never considered herself someone that Cecelia had to impress. Now, when she thought about all of her interactions with Cecelia, she wondered how Cecelia had viewed her. And she realized, then, that she needed Jacob not only to find the police report but to learn about who Cecelia was. It was the question she had barely asked, but maybe it was the most important question of all.

"But that was in the beginning," Jacob continued. "She came in guns blazing, you know. She really wanted to be Mauricio's favorite. He's the one who assigns the girls the best tables, the best shifts, so she knew he had the power. And it worked. I think she was his favorite. But I think she was his favorite because he knew she could keep secrets."

"What do you mean?"

"Mauricio . . ." Jacob started to say.

"I knew it," Brynn interjected. "He did this to her. Where is he, Jacob?"

"No, no," he said. "You've got it wrong. Mauricio isn't a good guy, but he didn't do this to her. Or, I really don't think so, anyway. You see, Mauricio was sleeping with another waitress. Clarissa—Cecelia's friend. It's been going on for two summers now. And Cecelia knew all about it."

"Oh my God," Brynn said. "Well, maybe he wanted to get rid of Cecelia to keep her quiet. That would make a lot of sense, right?"

"Maybe," Jacob said. "Except that Mauricio was with Clarissa that night. Everyone knows it. Well, everyone knew it, except Mauricio's wife. And now she definitely knows."

Brynn deflated. "So, Mauricio couldn't have hurt Cecelia that night. He wasn't anywhere near her, is what you're saying?"

"Yup," said Jacob.

"It still feels weird that he disappeared right after she was found," Brynn said. "Why would he have done that?"

"I don't know," Jacob said. "But . . . for better or for worse, Mauricio liked Cecelia. He respected her work ethic. I mean, he's a slimeball, but he didn't treat Cecelia badly, at least as her boss." He paused. "After a while, Cecelia became . . . obsessed with the wealth on the island. She'd never seen anything like it before. You and I . . . we're not part of it, but we've lived in it, or beside it, our whole lives, so we're used to it. I think she got, like, spellbound by it."

"Well, so? I can understand that," Brynn said.

"It eventually made her angry, though," Jacob said. "The whole reason she took the job at the club was because she hoped it would get her connections, a career opportunity, something to get her foot in the door. It's not like the staff at the club are making money in tips. They're not allowed to accept tips—you know that. It's not about that. It's about the potential relationships they can make there. A babysitting job for a family with a seat on the board of whatever museum, things like that."

"But three summers went by and nothing came about, right?" Brynn asked.

"Exactly. By the third summer, when we were dating, she was pretty jaded about it all. She didn't make the same effort as before. I know that Mauricio still had high expectations for her, and assumed she'd be available to work all the time, doing a better job than anyone, but she just didn't care as much." Jacob sighed. "The only person who seemed to have a real interest in her was Henry."

Brynn paused, unsure of what to say. But she had to say the truth. "I think he genuinely cared about her, Jacob. I do. He spoke so highly of her. I guess it was weird, but he seemed to truly enjoy her company."

"I know," Jacob said. "I believe that. But that's the problem. I think she resented him, in a way. Once she realized that Henry *wasn't* from

New York or whatever, that he was a local guy who worked in a blue-collar industry, she didn't see what he could offer her. I mean, he's wealthy, sure, but he's not part of the world that she wanted to be in. Even if he thinks he is."

Brynn nodded. Jacob had Henry pegged. Henry and Margaux both were somewhat anomalous on the Vineyard. They could keep up with the summer folks, but they weren't summer folks themselves. They were members of the same clubs and supported the same charities, but they hadn't attended Ivy League colleges—or any colleges. Their paths to success had been earned through grit and scrappiness, not through pedigrees. And somewhere deep down, Brynn heard her mother's voice in her head—*They think they're better than us. They're ashamed to be locals.* Maybe she had been right.

"So why did Cecelia keep making such an effort with Henry, then? She always went out of her way with him. It seemed so sincere," Brynn said.

Jacob looked down at his feet. "I'm not proud to say this. It was wrong. But she was in a dark place, I think, by the end." Jacob looked back up at Brynn. "Henry started telling her all this stuff . . . confessing stuff. Bad things he'd done, crimes he'd committed. He said he felt pressured to make more and more money for his family. He didn't know how to stop." He paused. "She told me all of this."

"And you didn't do anything about it? Even though you're a police officer?" Brynn started to question whether or not she could trust Jacob after all.

"No, I *did*. Of course I did. Or, I tried, anyway. I went straight to my father. But he shot me down. Told me I didn't know what I was talking about. That I had no proof. That I was wasting my time. And he told me never to mention this to anyone again. Ever."

Brynn didn't know yet whether Jacob had any awareness of the police report. She started to open her mouth to ask, but Jacob kept talking.

"So, I was going to go around him. I swear I was. But then . . . right before Cecelia died . . . she said that Henry had told her something else.

Something far worse than the other things. Something that really scared her. But she wouldn't tell me what."

"And you have no idea?"

"No," Jacob said. "But she made me promise not to look into it or go to the state police or the FBI. She made me promise to do nothing about it. To just forget about it. That's what she asked me to do."

"Wait," Brynn said. "I need to know something first. Whatever this thing was, did she ever say that Ross was involved? As far as she knew?"

"No," said Jacob. "And I have to say, I wish I had a different answer. Things would be a lot easier if the answer was yes. I wish that Cecelia had told me bad things about Ross. Then I wouldn't be conflicted. I wouldn't be talking to you at all about this. But in all my research and in everything that she told me, I never found anything that directly implicated Ross in any wrongdoing. It was all Henry."

Brynn let this sink in. She wasn't crazy. She still didn't have all the answers, but she at least had one other person now who agreed with her. Mostly.

"But," Jacob continued, "the thing is, how could Ross *not* have known? How could he not have been a part of it? He was going to take over the company, right? And what about his brother, Sawyer. How could neither of them really not know about any of it?"

"Well," Brynn said, "this might be why Ross is being blamed for Cecelia's murder. He *did* know, Jacob. At least, he had just learned about it. He hadn't been part of it, but he discovered it. And I know for sure that he was trying to make it right. He was going to make Henry come clean."

Jacob looked skeptical. "What about Sawyer, then?"

"Sawyer is involved in the business much less than Ross," she said. "Everyone always knew that Ross would be Henry's successor, not Sawyer. I really don't think he knows anything. Plus," she continued, "I think both Ross and Sawyer really *trusted* their father. Ross did, anyway, until he found out what had been going on."

It was clear that Jacob didn't totally believe her yet, and Brynn could understand why. "Jacob," she said, "you know there's a police report filed against Henry twenty years ago. In Edgartown. It just got . . . blacked out, or something. Do you know about this?"

Jacob laughed. "Of course I know," he said. "Obviously, I looked into the report myself. But my *dad* was the one who blacked that out. Don't you get it?" He stared at Brynn. "They were in on it together. Pete and Henry. For years."

Brynn remembered the way Henry had *screamed* at Pete when they came to arrest Ross. Henry's response had been so fierce, so visceral. It had seemed like the only appropriate response from a father who loved his son and wanted to protect him. A father who knew his son was innocent. And, perhaps, now in retrospect, a father who was guilty himself. Whatever Pete and Henry had been doing together, it didn't seem like arresting Ross had been part of the plan.

"So," Brynn said, "how do you know your father didn't . . ."

"Kill Cecelia?" Jacob asked, bluntly. "Unfortunately, I know that he didn't. I don't love to admit this to everyone, but I still live with my parents. Not sure if you're aware of real estate prices on the island lately, but I don't really have a better option at the moment. I know my dad was home that whole evening. There's no way."

"But you must know what evidence they have against Ross. Or what evidence they *say* they have, right? Something about . . . security camera footage?" Brynn thought that her conversation with Jacob was going to help clarify everything, but she was starting to feel more confused than before.

"I don't. Honestly," he said. "But whatever they have, it's not good. Whether it's true or not."

Brynn checked the time. She had to get down to the station to meet Izzy and prep for questioning.

"Jacob," she said. "Thank you for meeting me. I . . . Just one question. This might seem really out of the blue, but does *the orange sun* mean anything to you?"

"Huh?" Jacob gave her a confused look. "No, sorry. I don't know what you're talking about."

"Yeah," Brynn said. "Me neither. I have to go. But . . . let's keep in touch. There has to be a way to find out what that police report is about. And what Henry told Cecelia."

"Hey, by the way," Jacob said, eyeing her, "no one's actually accounted for *Henry's* whereabouts that night yet, you know."

"Margaux has," Brynn said.

Jacob raised his eyebrows at her.

"All in the family," he said.

CHAPTER 12

Ginny was asleep in the car when Brynn returned. A string of drool slid down the side of her chin. She jumped upright when Brynn opened the door.

"Tell me everything," she said. "Argh." She rubbed her belly as she stretched. She shot Brynn a look before she could say anything. "I'm *fine*. Just some little cramps."

Brynn knew that Ginny downplayed her pain all the time, just as she often downplayed her emotional pain or stress. She also knew that until Ginny's baby was out of her belly and in her own hands, and she could hear the baby's breath and heartbeat, she would be nervous. She would be terrified. And if anything went wrong, she'd blame herself.

When Brynn and Ginny had first met, Ginny told her that she wanted to have what she described as a *big, chaotic family*. She and her husband tried for years. But before she had her son Sam, Ginny had endured a series of painful, relentless miscarriages. Brynn had been by her side during one of those times, holding Ginny's hand as she sat on the toilet and watched the red cluster of cells fall into the water, leaving a bloody swirl on the surface, like an oil spill. Ginny had abruptly reached for the handle to flush it away, and then it was gone. The immediate days and hours after, Ginny told her, were the hardest for her because she felt like she was grieving someone she had known intimately, someone she'd loved, and yet someone she'd never actually known. *An invisible death,* she'd said. Brynn always felt that part of the mourning Ginny experienced was also the mourning of herself. The perceived loss of her ability to do the thing she wanted to do most in life.

Each time Ginny got pregnant and then became unpregnant, she told Brynn that she felt less and less entitled to be sad. *Take the pressure off yourself,* people would tell her, *stress is the worst thing for pregnancy.* As if that would make her less stressed. She confided in Brynn that she thought all the miscarriages were somehow her fault.

"There's nothing wrong with you," Brynn would tell her each time. "You're *going* to have a baby. A perfect, healthy baby."

And Brynn had been right. Just before Ginny almost gave up entirely, she became pregnant with Sam. And then with Olivia. Both had been surprisingly uncomplicated pregnancies. And now, she was due to have another baby in just a few weeks. But Brynn knew that Ginny was still on pins and needles, waiting for something terrible to happen, waiting to be told that there was, in fact, something wrong with her. It didn't help that Ginny's two experiences giving birth hadn't exactly been positive. Brynn's birth story was also traumatic for her, but she hesitated to divulge it to Ginny, who she knew had suffered more.

"Doctors don't believe me when I tell them I'm in pain because I'm black," she had told Brynn once, bluntly. "Seriously. The racism is so real. It's why black moms are three times more likely to die in childbirth than white moms."

"Jesus," Brynn had said. She knew that her response was wildly insufficient. But she didn't know what else to say. "I'm so sorry."

"I just have to advocate for myself a lot more than you would," Ginny had said. "If I don't educate myself and then ask the right questions, no one will tell me anything. Trust me, after two kids, I know. But," she'd added, "we *all* have to advocate for ourselves. As mothers, I mean. The system is designed to put us on the back burner."

Ginny had told Brynn this before Brynn herself had become a mother. At the time, Brynn had secretly rolled her eyes at this, just a little bit. Not at Ginny's personal experience, facing entrenched racism—that was all too real—but at what Ginny had said about the *system*. Brynn knew plenty of mothers who'd had great birth experiences, and she'd wanted to look forward to giving birth. It was only once she experienced it herself that she learned just how right Ginny had been. There was more medical follow-up for a sprained wrist than for birthing a human. Mothers were expected to *suffer* and to simply *carry on*. Mothers were expected to *sacrifice*. And if mothers spoke up, or objected, or questioned, they were often silenced.

After one of her miscarriages a few years ago, Ginny had told Brynn that she'd had an abortion right after college. She didn't regret it, she said, but sometimes she wondered if her miscarriages were some kind of punishment.

"Don't get me wrong," she'd said to Brynn, "An abortion was the right choice for me. But . . . what if . . . I don't know. What if I threw off the entire course of my life, or something."

"I had one, too, you know," Brynn had told her. She'd gotten one during her sophomore year of college after a night with a lacrosse player named Brian who had been so sweet and affectionate that Brynn had thought *fuck it* when they searched his dorm room for a condom but couldn't find one. It was exam week; a bad idea to be making important decisions. She was so distracted that she'd forgotten to go get the morning-after pill the next day, and the day after that. And then, suddenly, a week had passed, and it was too late. And just as she'd feared, a month later, her period didn't arrive when it was supposed to.

Brynn hadn't wanted to go to the school clinic, so she took the train into Boston and went to a Planned Parenthood. She went alone. An exceedingly friendly nurse with a Jamaican accent explained her options to her, and when Brynn said that she knew she wanted an abortion, the nurse then walked her through what the process would be like. She would take a series of pills at home, some vaginal and some oral, and she'd experience cramping, fatigue, and possible nausea, but she could put this all behind her very soon.

Brynn had felt such overwhelming relief when she'd left and returned to her dorm. Even in the throes of the abortion, when she was curled up in the fetal position, suffering through the worst cramps of her life—far more pain than she'd been warned of—she was grateful.

"Your abortion has nothing to do with this, Ginny," she'd assured her.

As they sat in the car together, Brynn knew that Ginny was thinking about her abortion. Thinking about the choices she'd made that led her to where she was now. It was something Brynn wouldn't let herself do lately. She couldn't. Otherwise, she'd be filled with regret and longing—which was all she'd been feeling lately.

And so, Brynn didn't push Ginny on how much pain she was actually in right now, and what kind of cramps she was having, and if she should go to the doctor. Ginny would just shush her and tell her again that she was *fine*.

Instead, Brynn told her everything that she and Jacob had discussed. How Mauricio had been sleeping with another waitress, and she was his alibi. How Jacob knew about the blacked-out police report but didn't know what was in it. How Pete had been protecting Henry for decades, and how he might still be protecting him today. But what kind of a person would throw his best friend's son under the bus for a crime unless he was certain he committed it?

As Ginny drove toward the police station in Edgartown, Brynn started to cry.

"Sorry," she said, wiping away her tears. "I just keep thinking that if I had actually tried to talk to Ross, or tried to listen, then none of this would have happened. Cecelia might still be alive, somehow."

"Come on," Ginny said. "We still don't know if anyone in your family actually has *anything* to do with Cecelia's death. Let's not forget that.

This could all be a big mistake. We don't even know for sure that it wasn't a drowning."

"Well, maybe, but Jacob seemed to think that there was some solid evidence to prove otherwise." She looked out the window as they drove by Morning Glory Farm. Next weekend was their Strawberry Festival, not that Brynn would be going. That life seemed so far removed from her already. "I just feel like I had tuned everyone and everything out the past few months, and maybe if I hadn't, Ross could have talked to me. We could have figured all of this out together."

Brynn had stopped asking Ross about work months ago, even before Lucas was born. She had stopped caring. Though she admired Ross's work ethic and loved his passion for what he did, she found the work itself boring. Another mansion, another pool, another greedy client, another hearing with the zoning board, another feature in *Martha's Vineyard* magazine. If she thought about it too much, which she tried not to do, she actually *hated* the work that Ross did because of what it stood for. On an island with a housing crisis, where local residents were forced to do the seasonal shuffle of finding housing in the winter and separate housing in the summer, Ross's business of building multimillion-dollar homes for wealthy summer residents epitomized everything that Brynn hated about the island and how it had changed since she was a kid. So, she had stopped asking him about work, and if Ross did talk about it, she had stopped listening. Maybe, she realized in a panic, she had tuned him out entirely. Maybe he had tried to tell her about whatever was going on and she hadn't listened. Maybe she'd shut him out too much.

"You can't blame yourself, Brynn," said Ginny, as she turned right into the Edgartown library entrance. She drove behind the school and past the graveyard, to the police station.

They could see Izzy standing outside the station, looking the part of an island lawyer in cropped white jeans and a blue button-down blouse. She was maniacally typing on her phone. She looked up and waved excitedly when she saw Brynn, as if they were meeting for cocktails. "Oh God," Brynn said. "What am I even doing?"

"It will be fine. Izzy will know how to respond for now. Basically, I think you'll want to just say . . . nothing," Ginny said. "And, Brynn. I know you don't totally trust me right now, and that's okay. But I promise you, I'm not doing anything with this story anymore. Just in case that wasn't obvious. You are more important to me than anything I'll ever write."

Brynn looked at her friend. She knew she could believe her, even though part of her was still mad. She nodded.

"And remember," Ginny said as Brynn started to get out of the car. "Do *not* trust the police. Especially not Pete."

"Yup," Brynn said.

"I'll wait here," said Ginny, reclining the seat back again and rubbing her belly. "Don't worry, I already took two pee breaks in the woods when you were with Jacob."

Brynn smiled. "Thanks," she said. "For the ride, I mean."

CHAPTER 13

"I think our strategy should be *exhausted new mom, doesn't know any-thing*," Izzy said, as if she were about to pitch a reality show to a Hollywood network. She smoothed a hair out of Brynn's face. They stood on the police station steps together. "What do you think?"

"Well, that *is* the truth," Brynn said. "I really don't know anything, Izzy. This is all a mistake, like I told you. There's no way Ross did this." She had decided she wouldn't tell Izzy everything she'd learned from Ginny, or the clue Ross had told her to find.

"Uh-huh," Izzy said. It was clear to Brynn that Izzy didn't believe her. "Well, the priority right now is *you*, not Ross."

"Right, but I want to defend my husband. I mean, he's not perfect, but I know he's not a *murderer*."

"Do you remember when Ross got home that night?" Izzy asked. "I just know they're going to ask you that right away. So, we should prepare."

Brynn had been going over it in her mind all morning. When she'd hired a sleep coach a week ago, the coach had advised her to write down when Lucas fell asleep and when he woke for night feedings, so that she could keep track of his progress. That night, she'd written in the

Notes app on her phone: *10pm. Dream feed 4 ounces, spat up and had to change onesie, changed diaper, back asleep by 10:25.* She remembered that after that feeding, she'd gone to the kitchen to wash the bottle and run the dishwasher for the night. Ross still wasn't home. Then, she went to sleep.

Ross had told her that he'd come home, and they'd talked in bed. But she couldn't remember. It sounded familiar, but in the way a dream sounds familiar. She wasn't sure if it had really happened or if she just had the *sense* of it happening.

The next note she'd written was a couple of hours later. *12:30am. BF ten minutes right side.* At that feed, she remembered for sure, Ross was home and asleep next to her. She'd gone back down to the kitchen again to pump her left breast and store the milk away. Even in her nocturnal daze, she'd noticed with resentment the empty water glass that Ross had left on the counter for her to clean up.

"I know he was home that night, asleep in bed with me," Brynn said.

"Okay, that's good. You have nothing to hide, Brynn. But still, say nothing. Okay? Let me do the talking."

Brynn could feel her insides shifting around. She'd made the bad choice of wearing the one pair of jeans that fit her and a gray T-shirt, but now she felt claustrophobic and sweaty, and she wished that she'd worn something flowy and loose.

She reminded herself, as they walked in, that Izzy was right: she had nothing to hide. Even the knowledge she had about the Nelsons didn't implicate her in anything, and it didn't yet implicate Ross, either. Still, she felt like all the eyes were on her when she opened the door. She felt like *she* was the prime suspect.

Inside the station, the air was mercifully cold, and it smelled of day-old, microwaved coffee—the same as yesterday.

"Come on," Izzy said.

Pete emerged instantly from a hallway, and greeted Brynn again as if she were a wife in mourning. As if everyone knew that Ross was guilty, and that he'd never see the light of day again. As if Brynn were just the dumb wife who never saw it coming.

"Chief, hello. I'm Izzy Melville," Izzy said before Pete or Brynn could say anything. She extended her hand. "I'm Brynn's attorney. I don't think we've ever met."

"Nice to meet you," Pete said, with what Brynn detected as a stifled laugh. "Nice to see you again, Brynn. Why don't you ladies come with me? This won't take long. We just have a few questions we need to ask and then you'll be on your way. Promise."

They followed him into a gray conference room with metal chairs and a white plastic table.

"Well," Pete said as they sat down, "I don't usually get in the weeds like this anymore. But in this case, to respect the family, I felt I owed it to you all to personally see this through, and to handle it with the most delicate of gloves, and the most discretion."

"Thank you," Brynn said, though his words sounded slippery and made her feel queasy. She wished she'd had some water before this. She felt dizzy and tired; her exhaustion from weeks of sleepless nights suddenly hitting her.

Pete cleared his throat. "Now, there's a couple puzzle pieces I'm trying to put together that I'm hoping you can help me with. But it's nothing to worry about. Basic stuff, to just clear it off the decks, so that you can go on your way, and we don't have to do this again. Okay?" *Just get to it,* Brynn thought to herself.

Brynn nodded. Pete cleared his throat.

"Would you say that you and Ross were happy together? Or had you been struggling, you know, as a couple?" Pete's forearms were crossed and resting on the table, and he looked at her as if he knew the answer to the question already: that they *weren't* entirely happy.

"Brynn doesn't have to answer that," Izzy snapped. "Furthermore, it's irrelevant."

"I know that might seem like a personal question," Pete said. "We're just trying to figure everything out, and, well, sorry to be so blunt, but we have reason to believe that your husband, Ross, and the victim, Cecelia, had some kind of relationship. Were you aware of this?"

Izzy chimed in again. "She doesn't need to answer that, either."

This time, though, Brynn spoke up.

"No," she said. "They did not have any kind of relationship other than knowing one another through the club. Ross and Cecelia were not close. Your son was her boyfriend, as I'm sure you know. Henry, however, was particularly close with Cecelia, but not in an inappropriate way." Brynn swallowed. Maybe she shouldn't have said Henry's name like that. It might turn Pete on her. But it was the truth. Ross *wasn't* close with Cecelia. Henry was. And everyone knew that. "I mean, all of us in the family knew Cecelia and cared about her," she added, "but not in an abnormal way."

"What do you mean, you *all* were close with her?" Pete asked.

"Brynn," Izzy said, turning toward her, "you don't have to say anything else."

Brynn knew that she should take Izzy's advice and just zip it, but she *had* to say the truth, which was that no one in the Nelson family had an inappropriate relationship with Cecelia. Or, at least Ross didn't. She couldn't just sit there and not defend what she knew to be true. What if she didn't have this opportunity again? "I just mean, we all thought Cecelia was great. We all liked her very much. All the members at the club did. But Ross was not *sleeping* with her, if that's what you're getting at. Ross and I are happy." She regretted her last sentence the moment she said it; she knew she sounded like she was overcompensating. Because she was. She and Ross weren't happy. Not really.

"I never said that," Pete said, leaning back in his chair. "I just said they had a relationship. Why would you suggest that they were sleeping together?" He wrote something down on a legal pad.

"I'm not suggesting it," Brynn stammered. "You said they were having an affair, I just . . ."

"I didn't say affair, Brynn," Pete responded. He was too calm, too serene. He seemed to be enjoying this too much.

"Please," Izzy interrupted. "Let's focus on whatever you need to ask Brynn outside of her personal life."

"Okay," he said. "Okay. Do you remember what time Ross came home the night of June twenty-fourth? Anything unusual happen that night, or the next morning?"

Brynn took a breath. Pete knew very well that she had already told him yesterday that Ross had been home with her. She was going to stick to that story, even if she wasn't entirely sure. She had to. "He was home with me that night, asleep in bed. And the next morning, he went to work like normal. Everything was like it always was."

"But what time did he get home? Do you remember? I know this is hard."

Izzy nodded at her, confident.

"He came home around eleven, which is very typical on a night when he's gone for dinner and drinks with clients. I know this for sure because I write notes on my phone to keep track of our son's schedule and feedings." She showed Pete the notes on her phone that she'd shown Izzy just before. "He was home and sound asleep by the second night feed, so he probably got back around eleven."

"Got it," Pete said, writing something else down. "This is really helpful, thanks Brynn."

Brynn nodded. Surely, this *would* be a key in clearing everything up. There's no way that Ross would have had time to leave the club after dinner and drinks, drive all the way out to the end of Norton Point on the beach, and then come all the way back home. There simply wouldn't be enough time, especially considering that he'd have to stop to deflate his tires to go out onto the beach and then fill them back up again on the way home.

"So, does that clear everything up?" Izzy asked.

"It does, yes," Pete said. "But . . . maybe not how you think. I'm sorry to tell you this, Brynn, but . . . you see, the security footage from the club that I mentioned to you, well, it shows Ross during that window of time when he wasn't home yet. It shows Ross with Cecelia."

Brynn felt nauseous and dizzy. She'd only tried to help by telling Pete that Ross got home around eleven. "Your timetable actually *secures* our evidence."

"*What?*" Brynn felt her voice begin to growl. She took a breath. "I need to see that footage." She knew she sounded defensive. But she *had* to see it. She wouldn't believe it until she did.

"I thought you'd say that," Pete said, tapping an iPad that he'd had on the table. "Let me just pull it up here." He fiddled with the screen. "I'm an old guy. Never quite know how to work this stuff." He smiled at them. "Here you go. See for yourselves."

Brynn and Izzy looked, wide-eyed. The video started. It was grainy, but clearly showed the back door of the club basement, which led out to the staff parking lot. It was date- and time-stamped: June 24, 10:05 P.M.

At first, Brynn thought the tape was frozen. All it showed was the still image of the dark entryway. Nothing was happening. But then Cecelia burst out into the frame, running, *sprinting* away. And seconds later, Ross ran out behind her. They both disappeared from the frame, and the stillness continued on as before.

"Can I see it again?" Brynn asked.

Pete nodded and played it again. Brynn looked closer this time.

The video showed them both from behind. She could only see a sliver of the side of his face, but not fully.

"But you can't see his face," Brynn said. "This could be anyone. This doesn't prove anything."

"Well, not really," Pete said. "It is a private club, after all. There are only so many people that could be in this video."

It was true. Even though she couldn't see Ross's face, it looked just like him. It certainly wasn't Sawyer, or Henry. She tried to picture Mauricio; it could be him, maybe. It might even be Jacob, if he had only about five extra layers of clothing. Brynn felt sick; whoever was in the video was either Ross or his clone.

"Still, you can't be one hundred percent sure that it's him," Brynn persisted.

Pete lifted a paper bag from his lap and put it on the table. He reached inside and pulled out a baseball hat.

"Is this not Ross's hat?" Pete asked, holding the hat out for Brynn to examine.

Brynn knew the hat instantly: it was Ross's lucky fishing derby hat from the year he won first place for the bonito he caught from shore. It was indisputably his: on the side of it was his derby pin with his lucky number 16, turned upside down to indicate that he'd caught a weighable fish.

"We found it on the ground outside the club. Right where he would have been chasing after her." Pete paused to look at Brynn more closely. "Do you recognize it?"

"This doesn't prove anything," Izzy said before Brynn could respond. But Izzy's voice practically croaked. Brynn could tell that Izzy wanted to get herself out of here almost more than she did. "Are we done here?"

"Look," Pete said, "I'm not trying to paint you as the enemy here, Brynn. I want to help you. I don't think you had anything to do with this. So, you need to think about how to help yourself. And how to help your baby."

Brynn wanted to scream. She suddenly wished she were younger, a child, before the weight of adulthood and parenthood had come crashing down on her. She wished she were back at her parents' old home on Lobsterville Beach. She could smell the woodstove, hear the crackling of logs burning on a cold winter day, feel the bristle of their old rug on the living room floor, taste the sugary sweetness of her mother's blueberry scones. She had felt so trapped there, so suffocated by her parents' simple lifestyle and by the four walls of that small house, but now she'd give anything to be back there in the warmth of her mother's quiet strength and her father's reliable routines. She didn't belong here in Edgartown. She was in over her head.

Someone had told her once that when two people get married, they make a silent decision to choose one person's family as their touchstone, but never both. Brynn and Ross had chosen his family. It was never a conversation. But it was also never an option, Brynn thought, to do otherwise. Her parents didn't create the opportunity for her to choose them. They didn't go out for family meals, they didn't travel on family vacations, they didn't throw neighborhood parties. And then they left the island altogether. Maybe Brynn should have tried harder with them. Maybe she should have at least *asked* them to be more involved. Or asked Ross to help her reconnect. Or maybe she and Ross should have discussed choosing *neither* of their families, and just starting their *own* life together, somewhere else entirely. Would Ross have joined her, though, or had he picked Brynn because he knew that she would always adapt to *his* life, and not the other way around? Would he have chosen her over his family? Would he now?

Brynn mustered a goodbye to the chief. "Thank you," she said. It was all she could manage.

The station went silent once more as Brynn and Izzy walked through the main room.

Outside, Izzy grabbed Brynn by the shoulders.

"Brynn," she said. "You need to smarten up."

"Excuse me?"

"I'm sorry, I know that sounds tough. But this is way more serious than I thought. You need to protect yourself, like he said. And protect Lucas. I'll text you some names of other lawyers. You don't want to get implicated in this in any way. Trust me." Brynn had never seen Izzy look so serious.

"Yeah," Brynn said. "Thank you, Izzy. I really owe you for being here."

"Don't mention it. I'll see you on the mat soon." Izzy gave her a weak hug, patting her on the back.

Brynn nodded, even though yoga class existed in another galaxy now for her.

Ginny was digging into a family-size bag of peanut M&M's when Brynn climbed back into the car.

"Go," Brynn said. "Drive."

Ginny put down the candy and backed the car out of the lot.

"Actually, can you go out to Katama?" Brynn asked. "Right fork. I need to do something. I need to clear my head."

"Sure," Ginny said.

"Ginny, it's bad. They showed me the security camera footage," Brynn said after a few minutes. "It shows Ross running after Cecelia. Like they're in a fucking *horror* movie." She sighed. "And they found his hat outside. His lucky hat. It's bad, Ginny. It's so bad. I think I've been blind this whole time. There's no other explanation for it."

Ginny didn't say anything. There was nothing *to* say. She pulled the car into the bumpy dirty parking lot of South Beach's right fork. The car bounced through mud puddles and then came to a stop facing the dunes, which hid the roaring waves just beyond. The lot wasn't too crowded for a summer day. Normally, it was packed, cars stuffed into the lot like sardines in a can, and beachgoers jockeying for the best spot to set up their tents, their volleyball nets, their grills.

When Ginny turned the car off, Brynn jumped out and took her jeans off right there in the parking lot. Underneath, she had on black, full-coverage underwear. She needed to go for a swim, somewhere where the waters were rough, dangerous, and loud. Somewhere close to where Cecelia was found. Somewhere that might drown her, too, if she swam out far enough.

She walked out to the beach, Ginny following behind silently. Brynn could feel the eyes of sunbathers on her as she marched into the sea with her T-shirt and underpants on. She didn't care. She dove under a crashing wave and swam, swam, swam out to sea. When she couldn't swim any farther, she took a big inhale and ducked under the surface. Her ears filled with water, and the sound of the ocean consumed her.

Underwater, Brynn opened her mouth and screamed. She screamed for Cecelia, she screamed for Lucas, she screamed for Ross, but most of all she screamed for herself. She screamed for the self she used to have, the one she was scared she'd never get back, the one she'd let disappear, the one she'd given up on, the one she needed now more than ever. She screamed and screamed until she had to push herself back up for more air. But as much as she breathed, it didn't feel like enough.

Her life was collapsing, she thought, and now she had to figure out what to do. She and Ross had to be over. There was too much evidence against him. She wasn't going to bother looking for his fucking *clue,* the orange sun. Whatever that was! He'd been fooling her all along, but she was done.

She hated that she knew how much easier her future would be if Lucas didn't exist. She felt guilty for thinking about it. But if she and Ross only shared memories and a marriage license, then she could just extract herself from his family and never look back. But with Lucas, she and Ross were forever connected. Forever intertwined.

How could Ross have done this to her? How could she have been so stupid? Why hadn't she picked Sawyer? Or, why hadn't she picked neither of them, and instead thought about what *she* wanted in life?

She considered what one of her heroines would do. While she didn't live in a world of the romance genre, she still tried to make her female protagonists strong, capable, modern women. Surely, none of them would stand by their husband in a situation like this. They'd go off on their own. They'd raise their child alone. They'd stand up for the victim, not the accused. They'd leave this island and never look back, not for a second. The right decision seemed so easy when she was only writing it, not doing it.

But Brynn wasn't one of her protagonists. She wished she were but she knew she wasn't. She was real, and flawed, and complicated, and this was her actual life, not one that she was making up for herself. As much as she wanted to walk away from Ross—from all the Nelsons, from her own life—she couldn't just yet. Even if Ross *had* killed Cecelia, it didn't make Henry innocent. Brynn had to find a way to help Margaux and Sawyer now, too. She couldn't turn her back on them.

And yet . . . she still *wanted* to find the clue. She needed to. Whatever *the orange sun* was, she knew that she wouldn't be able to put anything behind her until she found it.

She was so furious with Ross for not telling her what he knew. And she was furious with him for telling her what he did know, too, just before he was taken away. She was furious because as much as she couldn't argue against the evidence the police had on him, she still, deep down, believed him. She *fucking believed him,* and she hated him for that.

Brynn floated on her back. The sky was cloudless, and the water so clear that she couldn't quite tell where the ocean ended and the air began.

She wondered if this was how Cecelia felt in the last moments of her life.

CHAPTER 14

Lucas was sound asleep in his own crib upstairs when Brynn and Ginny returned.

Marcus and Annie were lounging on the living room sofa, finishing their iced coffees and watching him on the monitor.

"We knew you'd been wanting to transition naps to his nursery instead of your room, so we figured we'd try it. I hope that's okay," Annie said to Brynn when she and Ginny came inside. Normally, Brynn would be annoyed. As much as motherhood challenged her, she inexplicably wanted the burden of it to be hers and hers alone, as though she could find some solace in wearing her suffering as a badge. Help was something she couldn't naturally accept. If she wasn't struggling, she didn't feel like she was being a good mom. But now, today, she was grateful.

Marcus and Annie had closed all the blinds and curtains in the house; outside, cars drove by slowly, as if they were trying to get a glimpse inside. By now, everyone on the island was buzzing with the news of Ross being arrested. It was the biggest story the island had experienced in years. Brynn could barely bring herself to check her phone; she had hundreds of missed calls and messages. Izzy had advised her to

speak to no one. Not that she wanted to, anyway. She was barely capable
of talking to her own friends.

The island felt like it was in mourning, too. There were shrines
already set up all over the island for Cecelia at her favorite spots: Mocha
Mott's in Vineyard Haven, Nomans, Among the Flowers, and the Chilmark Tavern, where she'd done a few waitressing shifts on nights off
from the club. Everyone on the island suddenly seemed to be Cecelia's
former best friend; everyone knew her, everyone was grieving her death,
and no one could believe that such a bright star had been taken from
this world so soon.

A police cruiser was parked across the street from Brynn's house.
Pete had told her that they'd be keeping an eye on her and the house.

"Since you're alone there, with the baby," he had said, "we want to
make sure you're safe." Brynn hadn't feared for her own safety until he
had said it like that. Seeing the police car right outside made her feel
even more on edge than she already was. She couldn't trust them, and
now they were watching her.

She sat down to pump. The machine hummed and Brynn felt an
instant relief.

"Well, it's worse than I thought," she said to her friends. She no
longer had the energy to hide things from them, or to care if they'd
already made up their minds. She told them about Ross's lucky hat and
the security camera footage, how Ross was caught running after Cecelia
like he had something to lose, like he'd do anything to catch her, like
whatever she was running off with was worth sacrificing his entire life
for. But she also told them what Jacob had said about Henry confiding
in Cecelia. How whatever she knew, she shouldn't have known. And it
might have been what got her killed.

They sat in silence for a moment, absorbing it all.

"Well," said Marcus, "the footage thing doesn't sound good at all."

"No," added Annie.

"But maybe there's another explanation for it. I mean, we obviously
can't trust the police," said Marcus.

"And do you still have no idea what the orange sun thing is all about?" Annie asked.

"No," said Brynn. "Jacob didn't know either. And honestly, I don't know if I even care anymore about finding the clue. I want to give up. It's getting really, *really* hard to believe Ross at this point. And . . . I'm *mad* at him. Why should I be the one to pick up the pieces for whatever he was hiding from me? Even if he is innocent."

Annie and Marcus both looked to Ginny.

"So, we stop looking for the orange sun clue for a bit," Ginny suggested. "Maybe it'll come to us."

Brynn rubbed her eyes. "I'll ask him about it again when I get to talk to him, but who knows when that will even be. He hasn't called yet. And I don't know if he'll even be able to answer me, with the police around him, I mean."

"Well," Annie said, "we want to help you, Brynn."

"Yeah," Marcus said, "we're with you every step of the way."

Lucas began to wake, and Brynn knew that she had to let her friends go home, to return to their own families, their own lives, which all seemed so much easier and simpler than hers.

The perfect couple, indeed.

By the time her friends left, it was somehow only midday, but Brynn felt like she'd been awake for five days straight. Lucas woke, and she went to feed him. It took a few minutes for him to latch on; Brynn had to take several deep breaths so that he wouldn't feel the tension radiating from her body. Finally, he started to feed. But then he lost his grip and she had to readjust him again. Over and over, the cycle continued.

Brynn desperately wanted to stop breastfeeding, especially now that she was so distracted and having a hard time sitting still. She'd hated doing it from the first moment in the hospital when a nurse pushed Lucas's head onto her breast, while she was still somewhat shaking from the anesthesia. She'd hated it even then, but she felt some need to keep trying. Most of the other moms she knew on the island breastfed their babies for almost an entire year—or longer—and the hospital had pressured her to stick with it.

"Breastfed babies are not only less likely to be obese," one nurse had told her the day after Lucas was born, "but they also have a deeper bond with their mother." Brynn didn't necessarily agree. For her, breastfeeding only made her feel detached from Lucas. When he fed, it was as if they were strangers, meeting for the very first time, fumbling their way through basic communications and getting nowhere. Brynn's nipples were raw, and her breasts were often lopsided from Lucas feeding from one breast but not the other, forcing her to immediately pump after each feed. By the time she finished that, she only had a few moments before Lucas was ready for his next feed. The cycle continued relentlessly, over and over, with only a few minutes' reprieve in between each session.

The worst part of breastfeeding, though, was how deeply lonely the feeding sessions were, filled with tears of regret and longing and frustration, a physical state of actual paralysis that made her feel emotionally paralyzed as well.

There was so much that Brynn needed to do right now, but she sat there with Lucas for as long as he needed. She'd missed him, that day, but now that she was home with him, the fear of the dark, looming hours ahead of her started to creep in. She remembered something one of the lactation consultants had said to her during an appointment at the hospital during the first few weeks of Lucas's life. She'd been crying nonstop that morning and hadn't showered or slept in days. She had held Lucas to her breast with shaky hands, waiting for the woman to give her some direction, some piece of advice that might finally make everything easier.

"Oh, sweetie," the woman had said. "Remember: the days are long, but the years are short."

In that moment, Brynn had never heard truer words. Sometimes, the minutes in each day crept by so slowly that Brynn truly wasn't sure she'd make it to nightfall. She felt terrible that she would count down to each of Lucas's naps, when she'd have a moment of silence, a moment to herself. And yet time had a way of flying by too fast, as well. Brynn would stare at the same pile of unfolded laundry for hours, sometimes days, before managing to address it. Somehow, there wasn't *enough* time to accomplish anything, even though there was too much of it. In her mind, she could see where she wanted to go—where she *needed* to go—physically and emotionally—she could *see* the version of her she wanted to work toward, and yet she was totally trapped, unable to move forward. The problem was, she had plenty of time, but not a minute for herself.

Once she finished feeding Lucas, and burped him, and changed him, she brought him down to the living room and placed him in a bouncer chair.

She had to check her phone. She'd been avoiding it all day.

She called Margaux back first.

"Brynn, I've been so worried. How did it go at the station?" Margaux asked right away.

"Not great," Brynn said. "Margaux . . . they showed me the security footage. From the club. And . . . it shows Ross running after Cecelia, out the back door. I mean, you can't see their faces, but it doesn't look good. It's getting really hard to . . . believe him."

Brynn heard silence on the other end. Finally, Margaux spoke.

"It doesn't make sense, Brynn. It just doesn't," she said. "I just don't see how my baby boy would do this. No matter what the footage shows."

"I know," said Brynn. "But . . . there's more." Brynn hesitated. "Margaux, are you alone?"

"Yes," she said. "Henry went in to the office. He didn't know what else to do with himself today."

"I . . . I really don't know how this all fits together yet, but I'm worried that Cecelia's death has something to do with . . . Henry. Or, I mean, with Henry's business. With mistakes he made in the past. Things he might have accidentally told Cecelia about." Brynn wanted to delicately hint at what she'd learned, to see if Margaux might have something to add, or if it might unlock something. Maybe Margaux knew what the orange sun was.

But the silence that followed indicated the opposite: that Margaux knew nothing, and Brynn had just suggested that Margaux could have been completely left out of her husband's business for decades. She hadn't meant to offend her, but Brynn knew that she had. "Never mind," said Brynn, before Margaux could respond. "It's just a weird hunch I had. That maybe things at work had become really stressful."

"Maybe," said Margaux. "But if there was something going on at work, I'd like to think that I would know, Brynn. Henry and I have been married for almost forty years. We can't exactly hide things from one another anymore."

Brynn felt bad, but she also was angry on Margaux's behalf. Margaux was smart, capable, and creative. She was an amazing mother. She could have had a career of her own, but that wasn't the deal that she and Henry had made when they started a family. Margaux had taken care of the boys and the home full-time. That *was* her career, her commitment, her entire life. And as Brynn had recently learned, that was a relentlessly demanding job in and of itself. Maybe the *most* demanding. How could Henry have hidden things from the mother of his children when she had worked tirelessly to give him the life he'd always wanted?

"Right," said Brynn, regretting her choice to have said anything at all. The last thing she wanted to do was make Margaux feel cast side. "Sorry."

"Are you sure you don't want to come and stay with us for a while, Brynn?" Margaux asked. "I can get everything all set up for Lucas."

"I'll be okay here. I promise," she said.

"Well, if you change your mind, just call."

When Brynn hung up, she wasn't sure how she felt. She wanted to ask Margaux if she was certain that Henry had come home that night. But she couldn't risk alienating her.

If Henry really had kept Margaux in the dark for *decades,* though, then who knew what else he was hiding from her—from all of them.

What if Margaux wasn't safe there with him now? The thought that Henry was some kind of predator didn't seem entirely plausible, but Brynn couldn't shake the feeling that whatever twisted secrets Henry was hiding were the key to all of this, and to Cecelia's death.

It occurred to her then that she simply might not ever find the answers. She might not *ever* find the orange sun. What if Ross had too much faith in her, too much confidence in her ability to understand his clue and find the truth? Or what if there was no clue, after all?

Brynn picked up the phone to call Margaux back. She had to tell her the truth about what she'd learned from Ginny and Jacob—all the horrible things that Henry had done. The mystery police report. Because if Henry *was* guilty of something even more sinister than what Ross had said—if Henry was guilty of *murder*—then how could Brynn *not* tell her? How could she not protect her? If anything happened to Margaux, it would be Brynn's fault.

But before she could do anything, her phone rang.

This time, she answered.

CHAPTER 15

"Brynn, I only have a few minutes. Maybe not even that," Ross said. His voice was coarse and raspy. His breaths were short and hurried.

Brynn instinctively looked around, nervous, as if she were being watched.

"I miss you," he said. "So much. Are you okay? How's Lucas?"

Brynn started to cry immediately. She hated that hearing Ross's voice was both a relief and a trigger. She hated that she felt like she wanted him with her now, more than ever. She hated that she believed that he was innocent, even though all she could picture when she shut her eyes was Ross running after Cecelia at the club. And she hated that he needed her help, when he knew she was already drowning as it was. Everything would be so much easier if she could hate Ross. But despite everything, Brynn loved him. And that was enough for her to keep believing him. She sobbed.

"Brynn," he said, "are you alone?"

"Yes," she said, between cries. "But why does that matter? I'm so *mad,* Ross. And I'm so confused. You've kept me in the dark about everything. Everything! And now someone is dead. I still don't understand it. But . . .

I saw the security footage. I saw you running after Cecelia that night at the club. I saw it!"

"What? What are you talking about?"

"Don't lie to me!" Brynn yelled.

"Brynn, seriously. I don't know what you're talking about. What did the video show exactly?"

"It showed you and Cecelia. Running out the back door of the club, to the staff parking lot. You're . . . running after her. Like you're trying to catch her. Pete showed me." Brynn wiped her eyes. Lucas started crying.

"I don't know what that is," Ross stammered. "That makes no sense. Brynn, that's not me. I've never even been down there. Whatever that is, I *didn't do this.*"

"But they found your *hat,* Ross. Your lucky derby hat," Brynn yelled back. "How do you explain that?"

"My derby hat? You're sure?"

"Yes. With your pin on it. Pete showed it to me. I'm sure it's yours."

"Brynn," Ross said, his voice steadying. "Think about it. I only keep that hat on my boat. It should be on my boat, nowhere else." His voice rose. "I'm telling you: this is all a *setup.*"

There was an intensity to Ross's voice that she had only heard once before. Normally, Ross's voice was steady and soft, strong but even-keeled. He almost never yelled. The only time Brynn had heard Ross yell with that same voice, she'd been in labor with Lucas and things had taken a turn for the worse. Had Ross not been in the room with her, she and Lucas might not have made it through.

"Brynn," Ross had said a few hours after Lucas was born, and she was recovering in the hospital bed. "You don't have to do everything alone. I'm here for you. You can trust me, you know."

Brynn had never wanted—or needed—protection from Ross. That wasn't what she had looked for in a partner. In fact, what she'd always loved about her relationship with Ross was that they felt like a team.

They were equals. And she assumed that her independence was something he loved about her. For her entire life, Brynn had taken care of herself—that was all she knew, and so she thought that was all she was entitled to.

But if she let Ross take care of her, if she let Ross fight for her, she worried that she'd forget how to do it herself. The thought scared her.

What Ross had said to her that day had seemed so heavy at the time, and such an impossible thing to ask. Because what Brynn had gone through delivering their baby was something *only* she had experienced. Ross would never understand what it was like, and he would never know what it had been like since then, either. But she'd allowed herself to let those words sink in, that one time, and when they left the hospital to return home with the baby, she had been buoyed by the hopefulness of this new partnership, one where she let herself be vulnerable to Ross's support.

Thinking about that now only made her angrier and more confused. Because once the novelty of the birth had worn off, once the pot pies and chili stopped being dropped off by friends, once *normal life* resumed, Brynn felt like Ross's perception of her had returned to what it was before: he knew she could take care of herself. She'd opened herself up to him because of the promise he'd made her—that he'd take care of her—and then he'd left her hanging. When she'd needed him the most.

"Well then why would they have the hat, Ross?" she yelled. "It's getting really hard to just keep believing you."

Brynn could hear a man telling Ross to wrap it up.

"I have to go," he said. "But please, Brynn, you *need* to find the orange sun. I can't say anything more specific about it. It's not safe. But please. Don't stop looking."

"Ross, I don't know what this means! I have no idea what the orange sun is. Why can't you be more specific? I don't know where to look. Please!" She could feel her face redden with frustration.

"Brynn, someone is always listening. Just . . . you'll find it. Think about *us*. Focus on *us*. You and me. That's what matters," he said. "Don't give up on me. Don't give up on us."

He hung up, and the line went dead. Brynn's tears continued to fall down her cheeks. The setting sun outside cast shadows across the living room floor. She felt like she was on the stage of a play, a one-woman tragedy, except there would be no applause. No lights up. No ending.

It was true, she thought, that Ross didn't actually wear that hat. At least, she couldn't remember seeing him wearing it recently. But . . . he'd been on the boat just last week, fishing for fluke. Maybe he'd worn the hat off of the boat and forgotten. It wasn't implausible at all.

Us. You and me. That's what matters. Brynn changed Lucas's diaper and sat down to feed him again, wondering what Ross had meant by that. Once Lucas was latched, she shut her eyes. She tried to imagine the best times that she and Ross had shared, when they felt happiest, and most connected. But all she could see was the basement of the club, and the heavy metal door leading to the back. All she could hear was Ross's pounding footsteps as he ran after Cecelia. All she could smell was the musky wetness of the basement corridor. She didn't see how focusing on her and Ross would help anything, let alone help her find the orange sun.

By the time she finished feeding Lucas, it was early evening.

She decided to give Lucas a bath. Bath time was one of the rare activities during which Brynn truly enjoyed being with Lucas and felt like she was doing something right as a mother. Lucas loved the water, and never protested when Brynn gently poured it over his head or lathered up his little fingers with baby soap. He was fascinated by the gurgling sound of the drain, the way bubbles floated on the surface of the water, the way light reflected off his wet skin.

But despite the joy Brynn felt in seeing Lucas so carefree in the tub, so happy, she couldn't shake the feeling that he was so vulnerable during bath time, too. It was an incredible weight on her, knowing how dependent he was, how fragile, how powerless. What if she slipped and fell, and couldn't get him out? What if she made the water too hot? Even in the moments with her son where all she wanted was to simply feel *happy,* she was crippled by the overwhelming responsibility of it all, and the voice in the back of her head insisting that something was going to go horribly wrong.

And it was.

CHAPTER 16

Brynn wasn't optimistic that Lucas would sleep through the night as he had before, but just in case, she tried to replicate everything she could remember having done: the same onesie, the same swaddle, the same amount of breast milk, the same volume level on the sound machine, the same whispery rendition of "Twinkle, Twinkle, Little Star." She tiptoed out of the room and barely breathed until she had completely shut the door.

Her breasts ached. She went to the kitchen to pump. She sat like a zombie and ate half a box of Wheat Thins while the machine worked away at her. And after about fifteen minutes, she'd produced several ounces from each breast. It was a relief, since she'd been running low on her supply after being too tired to pump regularly enough during the last few nights. She wouldn't freeze these; she'd keep them in the fridge, she decided, and use them the next day to save herself some time.

She turned the pump off, but as she removed the flanges from her bra, the bottles slipped through her fingers and dropped to the floor, spilling everything she'd made all over the kitchen tiles, and all over her. A complete waste. Brynn wanted to burst into tears. There were so many parts of motherhood that went unseen; so many invisible efforts, so many internal struggles that were never expressed or acknowledged. The milk pooled around Brynn's feet, and she stood there for a moment, feeling the liquid between her toes, the physical product of yet another failure in her day, in her life.

"Hello?" she heard from the kitchen door. She nearly screamed she was so startled. But to her relief, it was Sawyer.

"Uh, hi," Brynn said, on her knees, where she was cleaning up. "You scared me." She'd closed her pumping bra and pulled her shirt back on, barely. She looked up at Sawyer, and then down at the mess.

"Sorry to just show up unannounced," he said, immediately lunging for some paper towels and getting down on the floor to help clean up. "But you weren't responding to me, and I got worried about you. You know, I spilled my breast milk earlier today, too." Brynn couldn't help but laugh. "Seriously though, sorry to scare you. I just didn't think you should be alone. I can go, though, if you want."

"Sawyer," she said, standing up, "I'm *fine*."

"I know," he said. "I know you're fine. But still. I'm here."

"Thanks," she said. "But honestly, I was going to go to bed soon. I'm so tired."

"I figured," he said. "I won't stay long. My mom told me what you said. About the security camera footage from the club."

"Yeah," Brynn said, realizing that she hadn't told Margaux about the hat. She'd forgotten. "It was shocking. I'm still in shock."

"I couldn't believe it, either," Sawyer said. "I mean, I just can't. You're *sure* it's him?"

Brynn nodded. "I mean, it looks like him, at least from behind. You can't really see his face. But . . . I don't see who else it would be. Maybe the video is edited, I guess. I really don't know what to think."

"I wouldn't put it past the police to have messed with it, somehow," Sawyer said. The thought had obviously crossed Brynn's mind. She also wondered if Mauricio might have edited the footage, somehow, and gotten access to it before the police did. He could have planted Ross's hat there, too, but how would he have gotten it in the first place? Even though Jacob had told her Mauricio had an alibi with Clarissa, he was still too conveniently embedded in the club to not further consider.

Brynn wanted to tell Sawyer everything else she knew, but she held back again. It wouldn't do any good to drag him into the mess she herself didn't yet understand. For now, Sawyer didn't really know *anything*. She felt sorry for him, in a way. He was never first, and yet he was always loyal.

The dishwasher chimed and Brynn snapped out of her memory. Without saying anything, Sawyer opened it and began putting the clean dishes away. The last time Ross had done that, it had nearly set off the biggest fight they'd ever had.

"I unloaded the dishwasher for you," Ross had said that day. Lucas was just a few weeks old then, but Ross was fully back at work. He had uncharacteristically unloaded the dishwasher that morning before he left for the day.

"For me?" Brynn had growled back at him. "You unloaded the dishwasher *for me?"*

She was so enraged that hot, angry tears immediately sprang from her eyes.

"Sorry," he said, "I just meant . . . never mind. I unloaded the dishwasher, okay?"

Brynn had been too exhausted to let the fight escalate. But her resentment built up inside of her over the course of that day. When Ross came home from work that night, he kissed her on the cheek, and she shuddered and pushed him off. The thought of being touched by him repulsed her. Not only was she annoyed with him—actually, *annoyed* didn't really begin to describe how she felt—but she also felt disgusting in her own skin. Even when weeks had passed, and her doctor gave her the green light to have sex again, the thought still revolted her. Before Lucas was born, Brynn and Ross never struggled to find a sexual connection with each other. Their attraction had been instant and strong, even when Brynn was pregnant. But after . . . Brynn didn't understand how she could go back to being sexual with Ross—or with anyone—when her own body had become a complete stranger. Plus, after a day of breastfeeding Lucas, she felt entirely touched out. She wanted space, she wanted air. She wanted to break free from herself.

Sawyer put the last of the dishes away.

"What?" he said. Brynn didn't realize that she'd been staring at him.

"Nothing," she said. "Thanks."

What happened next happened so quickly that Brynn wasn't sure she had even been aware of it until it was too late.

Sawyer moved closer to her, and they were face-to-face. At the same time, they both leaned forward, into each other. Naturally, neither by accident nor a conscious intention, and before Brynn could tell herself not to go any further, their lips were touching. She felt Sawyer's hand on her lower back, his palm and fingers stretching out as though to absorb as much of her as possible. His lips were rough and still tasted of salty ocean water, and long-lost summer afternoons, just like their first kiss. She felt his breath, and then his tongue. His other hand moved to her neck and her chest. She did not pull away, but instead she let herself melt into it, and she descended into what she knew was an irreparable fracture of her own making. But it was a fracture that made her feel better than she'd felt in a long time. It made her feel like someone else.

"Holy shit," Brynn said a second later. She pulled herself back and sprang up, stepping away. "I can't believe we just did that. That was a mistake."

It hadn't *felt* like a mistake, though, and Brynn knew it. It had felt warm and natural and comforting, like hearing a familiar song, or like sitting by a fire on a cold winter day, or like the smell of the first rainfall of spring.

Sawyer hung his head and looked down at his feet.

"I'm sorry, Brynn," he said. "That was my fault."

She didn't say anything. Kissing Sawyer had been the most exciting thing Brynn had done in the past year. And it might have been the most dangerous thing she'd *ever* done. It was the kind of kiss that she imagined her characters having, the kind she wrote about, using words like *electric* and *fervor*. It was the kind of kiss that started a complete, utter downward spiral, the kind that unraveled someone's entire life. It was the thread pulled on a sweater that would tear it all to shreds.

Brynn wondered, though, if the kiss was so powerful because of how she felt about Sawyer (what *did* she feel for Sawyer?), or because it was the only thing that she'd done in the past year that was entirely . . . *selfish*.

Her life revolved around Lucas, Ross, and their home. Her career was secondary. Her needs were secondary. Each moment of her time, including when she slept, was devoted to *their* well-being, particularly Lucas's. Even the shadowy, hidden layers of her psyche, the place where she kept secrets and dreams, private memories, and regrets, had become overpowered by the omnipresence of her son. And her body, of course, she had surrendered long ago to him, and it now existed as a malleable feeding vessel marred with stretch marks and scars like the body of a fallen soldier. She had nothing left that truly belonged to her, and only to her.

But that kiss had belonged to her, and only her. That kiss had been for no one else.

"I don't regret it," Sawyer added, before Brynn could say anything. "I mean, I know we shouldn't have. I know it's wrong. But, fuck it, these feelings are real. I know they're real for you, too."

Again, Brynn felt like she was in one of her novels, not in her own life. She was still in recovery from having a child. She hadn't showered, her skin was greasy, her breasts were sore, her nipples were cracked, and the bags under her eyes gave away the fact that she hadn't gotten a decent night's sleep in months. Was Sawyer really professing his love to her? *Now?*

"Sawyer," she said, forcing the words out. "We can't."

"You're beautiful, you know," he told her.

Ross used to tell her she was beautiful all the time. Every single day.

"My wife is *hot*," he would say when she climbed into the shower. Or "I'm so lucky," he'd say when he kissed her good night before dozing off to sleep. Sometimes he'd even interrupt her, midsentence, while they ate dinner, just to tell her that she was the most beautiful woman he'd ever seen in his life. Brynn didn't need the validation from him, that was never what it was about. It was about feeling wanted by him, feeling desired, and feeling seen. It wasn't about her appearance. It was about their connection. It was about their love for each other. But now, Brynn couldn't even remember how it felt to be told that by Ross. It had been so long.

"Stop," she said to Sawyer now. As good as it felt, she refused to hear more. She wouldn't allow herself to be someone who would bend so easily just from hearing a few nice words. She'd made her decision years ago, when she chose to make a life with Ross, and to leave behind whatever she'd had with Sawyer. She'd told herself that their romance was the stuff of kids, fueled by light beers and too much sun, the rush of driving in a Bronco with the top down, but when she really examined it in its core, there was nothing between them that could sustain her in the long term. That's what she'd told herself, anyway.

Sawyer cleared his throat, and they both heard Lucas cry, an unusual welcome for Brynn now, to break the moment.

"You should go," she said to him. "I need to be alone."

Sawyer nodded.

"Call me if you need anything," he said, heading for the door. He turned back toward her. "And Brynn, think about what I said. About Ross. I know it seems crazy . . . but you have to look at the facts."

"Goodbye, Sawyer." Brynn watched him get into his car and drive off.

Almost the moment Sawyer was gone, Lucas stopped crying, before Brynn even had a chance to go to him. For the first time, Brynn wished that Lucas were awake. Because then, she wouldn't have to be alone.

She wouldn't have to be alone with her thoughts.

She felt an unexpected stab of longing for Lucas to remain a baby forever, even though she hated this time and couldn't wait for him to be older, to be talking, running, and playing with her. She desperately wanted to wish the time away, and yet she also wanted to hold on to the way he was right now, because she knew that at this age, she could keep him safe. She could hold him and protect him. She knew there would come a time when he would be on his own, with people she didn't know, making his own choices, his own mistakes, creating experiences and secrets that he might never share with her. One day, if they made it far enough, she thought, he might find himself on a beach in the middle of the night, too, like Cecelia had.

And she wondered if she would be missing him then, and if he would be missing her, too.

CHAPTER 17

At midnight, Lucas woke up screaming. By now, Brynn could differentiate his various cries and identify what they signified. When Lucas cried in a low-pitched moan, it usually meant that he'd woken up but was trying to go back to sleep. If it was more of a shriek, Brynn knew that he wanted to get out of his swaddle and move around. The thumping percussion cry of repeated *wah*s indicated hunger. She didn't equate her understanding of his cries with some inherent motherly instinct; it had simply become a pattern that she'd learned to follow.

But this time, Lucas's cry was all of these things, and none of them, too. He howled, like his voice was coming from the depths of his belly and burning his throat on the way out. Brynn went to him. His forehead was hot, and his skin was moist with sweat. He had been so peaceful and happy just a few hours ago, but she knew immediately that he'd spiked a fever.

She'd managed to sleep for two hours already, but it had somehow made her more tired, and she now felt delirious and weak. She took Lucas out of his swaddle to change him and take his temperature. He screamed at her, swatting her away. His entire body radiated heat, like he was a tiny egg she'd taken out of boiling water, his shell ready to burst.

"I know, I know," she whispered to him, lifting his legs once she'd taken off his diaper. She braced herself as she inserted the thermometer and held it steady. The first time she'd tried to take his temperature, when he was just a few weeks old, Margaux had been at the house and Brynn had needed her help to do it.

"Won't it hurt him?" she'd asked, tensing up as she watched Margaux skillfully proceed.

"No," Margaux had said, "he won't feel a thing."

Now, Brynn did it just as Margaux had shown her, knowing she had to. The numbers climbed and finally stopped at 102.4. She quickly put him in a new diaper and a short-sleeve onesie.

She pressed the sound machine to turn the night-light on as well. With the soft glow of the light, Brynn could see that Lucas's skin was red and angry. His cries continued, and now he was gasping for air in between his sobs. She felt her own body growing hot with panic, the reality sinking in that she was home alone in the middle of the night with a sick newborn, while her husband sat in jail, accused of murder.

Brynn didn't know what to do. She hadn't ever given Lucas any medicine like Tylenol—he hadn't been old enough, or sick enough. She wasn't even sure how to administer it to him. She carried him to the bathroom and took out a bottle from the medicine cabinet. She scanned the label for instructions. *Under two years: ask a doctor.*

Balancing Lucas on her lap, she looked up the number for the after-hours line of the hospital's pediatrics department. The number she thankfully hadn't had to use yet. She lifted her shirt to see if Lucas would feed, but he only cried harder.

"Pediatrics?" a tired female voice answered. Brynn held the phone between her ear and shoulder.

"Um, hi," Brynn said, suddenly feeling embarrassed for calling so quickly, for immediately outsourcing her own duties as a mother. Didn't babies spike fevers all the time? What did the other moms do when this happened to their kids? Why was she so incapable of handling anything by herself? Maybe she should hang up, she thought. But she didn't. "Um, my son is a patient of Dr. Smith, and uh, he has a fever of 102.4, and I'm just . . . I'm not sure what to do." Brynn heard the sound of typing.

"What's your son's full name?" the woman asked.

"Lucas Henry Nelson," Brynn said.

Brynn swore there was a heavy pause on the other end of the phone. By now, the entire island knew what had happened to Cecelia and knew that Ross was the prime suspect. Could the nurses refuse to help her? What if this nurse had known Cecelia? She heard more typing. Suddenly, her own bladder felt impossibly full. She carried Lucas to the toilet with her and held him while she went, cradling the phone under her ear. Lucas continued to cry, though now his cries were more like hiccups, defeated by his fatigue.

"Shhh," she whispered to him. "It's okay."

Finally, the nurse responded.

"A hundred and two point four you said?"

"Yes. He was fine when he went to sleep, um, a few hours ago. Now he's just really hot and irritated."

"Well," she said, "there's not much you can do besides comfort care."

"Comfort care?" Brynn asked.

"Comfort care, right," she said again.

"So, just . . . nothing?"

"Well, no," the nurse said. "You can give him Tylenol or Motrin. Make sure it's *infants'*, not children's, though. There's a difference. Give him 1.25 milliliters. Keep him hydrated. Is he feeding? Is he crying actual tears? Is he making wet diapers?"

"Yes, lots of tears. And I just changed his diaper. He wouldn't nurse, but I'll try again."

"Okay, good. Try to get him to nurse or try a bottle, and just keep him cool, maybe a cold washcloth on the back of his neck, that sort of thing. The medicine should help. Call us again if the fever doesn't go down or gets worse."

"Um, okay." Brynn didn't want to hang up. She felt safe on the phone with the nurse, even if she felt somewhat judged. She knew that the moment she hung up, she'd forget what the nurse had told her, and she'd feel the same wave of panic and desperation she felt when she first called. "Wait, um, sorry, so, 1.25 milliliters and . . . just, just hold him? What if he doesn't get worse but he doesn't get better?" She racked her brain; there must be more questions she had to ask. There must be more advice she needed. The solution couldn't just be to basically wait it out!

She heard the nurse breathe.

"It's going to be okay," the nurse said. "I know it's scary the first time your baby gets a fever. Just remember that it usually passes quickly. And don't worry about calling again. That's what we're here for."

Brynn could feel her own tears falling down her face, once again.

"Okay. Thank you," she said, and hung up.

She took the Tylenol into Lucas's room and filled the syringe while Lucas waited on the soft rug on the floor. He squirmed.

By some stroke of luck, he sucked the medicine right down. Brynn waited, holding him upright, worried that he might vomit it back up. But he didn't. He latched on to her for a feed and stopped crying. At last, they both sat in silence.

She held him until he fell asleep, and she was so tired that she wasn't sure if it had taken five minutes or two hours, but eventually she swaddled him back up and put him in his bassinet. She curled up on the bed. Her body felt dry and frail, wobbly, as if she were made of paper, an origami person masquerading as a real one.

She imagined the times that she'd been sick as a baby, and what her own mother had done, in their simple house back in the early nineties, without a sound machine, without Velcro swaddles, probably even without Tylenol. Brynn had been a colicky baby.

"Oh, you cried *constantly*," Brynn's mother had once told her. "Absolutely constantly."

But her mother had told her this with a smile, as though in retrospect, it had been the best time of her life, as though the sleepless nights had been a harmless joke, a funny memory. That was the thing about those early days—mothers were so tired that they forgot the messy and painful details quickly. They forgot how hard it all was. And when they looked at baby photos, they only felt affection and nostalgia.

"That's why humans have multiple kids, you know," Annie had once told her, another fact she'd taken from one of the many *momfluencers* she followed. "Because we forget how bad it is. We literally *forget*. We rewrite our own histories. After a year or two, we look back and just think, *Oh, newborns are so snuggly, I want another one, it was such a cozy time.* Our bodies refuse to remember, and then they fuck us over by making us go back to hell!"

She couldn't believe that Annie was right. How could she *ever* forget the difficulties of this time? All she could think about, all she wanted to talk about with anyone who would listen, was the trauma of Lucas's birth, the struggle of getting him to eat, to sleep, the absolute insanity of becoming a parent. She'd remember this forever. It had changed her permanently, in her soul. She'd have to carry it with her for the rest of her life.

Brynn's eyelids were heavy, and she yearned for sleep, but her mind wouldn't let her. There were too many what-ifs. She worried now that she hadn't taken Lucas's temperature properly. What if his fever was even higher? What if she needed to take him to the emergency room? What if she fell asleep too hard, and woke up hours later to find Lucas dead? The thought had crossed her mind before, more than a few times. Not as something she wanted—not ever—but as one that made her feel, just for the faintest, fastest flicker, a terrible sense of relief, followed by the awful pain of guilt. She'd never hurt Lucas, but she still wondered what life would be like if he died, though she'd never vocalize the thought to anyone. What if, she wondered, there was a terrible accident, out of her control? What if he died of SIDS? She imagined how people would feel sorry for her, how she'd live in silence, how she could sleep and be left alone.

And then she'd buried the thought away and told herself that there was something wrong with her, something rotten. What kind of a mother had those thoughts? What kind of a mother longed for the kind of silence that only exists without children?

Brynn realized that she had barely thought about her kiss with Sawyer, she'd been so distracted by Lucas's fever. It seemed irrelevant now, compared to having a sick baby. A reckless mistake, that's all it was. It didn't count. She could forget about it. No one would ever know. And yet, Brynn knew that wasn't true. Even if they never told Ross, she would always know that it happened. And she would always wonder.

At some point in the middle of the night, Brynn drifted off to sleep. She dreamed about Cecelia. She could see her working at the club the night she died, gliding among tables, smiling and chatting, balancing a tray on the palm of her hand. She could see her texting with Jacob on her break, making plans to meet later. She could see her carrying out a final round of drinks before the club closed for the night. But she couldn't picture Ross at all. He wasn't there. She knew he wasn't there.

Brynn's eyes opened. She awoke with a sudden thought. It hadn't occurred to her before that Cecelia's body had been found *washed ashore* at Norton. She'd been in the water, perhaps far out at sea, but she hadn't necessarily started her journey to sea from the beach. Maybe she'd never actually gone to Norton at all, but rather ended up there after being thrown overboard offshore. Maybe she had been in a boat—the kind of boat that had enough horsepower to charge through the rough waters off the south shore of the island. A boat like Ross's. The one where he kept his lucky hat. His stupid, lucky fishing hat.

Brynn's stomach was empty, but she could feel her intestines and throat clenching as if she was about to be sick. She looked at her phone and remembered the app that was connected to the satellite phone that she'd insisted Ross buy last summer when he got his boat. She knew that he'd lose cell service when he went offshore tuna fishing, sometimes more than a hundred miles away to a spot called the Canyons, where the continental divide began and the ocean floor plummeted thousands of meters deep. A satellite phone kept on the boat was the only way to track his location.

Ross took care of the boat with an intensity only matched by the way he took care of Lucas when he was on *daddy duty*. He scrubbed it clean after each use. He was methodical in his organization of the gear he kept on board. He kept his lucky derby hat and favorite beer koozies safely in the center console, along with an extra set of fishing pliers and a first aid kit. The boat keys, attached to a neon-green inflatable key fob, always hung on the hook in the mudroom. Everything was accounted for, as if the boat was the most important thing in Ross's life.

The Regulator was a far cry from the patched-up aluminum boat with a 10-horsepower motor that Brynn's father had kept trailered in their backyard, occasionally launching it in Lobsterville in search of stripers or bluefish.

Ross had promised endless family boat outings all summer. He'd even bought an infant-size life preserver, a navy and yellow marshmallow of a jacket that engulfed Lucas. But, so far, Brynn had only been aboard a handful of times last summer for a few sunset cruises after Ross finished work.

She opened up the app. She considered closing it before she looked at location history. Wouldn't all of this be easier, she thought, if she just removed herself from it? Wouldn't it be easier, in a way, to accept that maybe Ross *had* done the unthinkable? She could potentially wrap her mind around it if the situation were black-and-white. He was guilty or he wasn't. But now she wasn't sure. She wanted to believe that he was still her husband that she knew, and loved, and still the dad that Lucas adored. But she also knew what the app would say. Somewhere, inside of her, she just knew.

And there it was.

The night Cecelia died: a round trip from Eel Pond in Edgartown, where Ross kept the boat, out to the waters off Chappaquiddick, past Cape Poge, past East Beach, past Wasque, all the way to the south side of the island, where she was found on Norton Point Beach. Fast, direct, and precise. There was no way to misinterpret it.

Before Brynn could process anything, Lucas woke up, screaming.

CHAPTER 18

By morning, Lucas's fever had dropped down to 99, and his body now felt warm and sticky but not aflame. Brynn had managed to catch a few accumulative hours of sleep, even though Lucas had returned to his ninety-minute howl-and-feed schedule.

Her head throbbed; she was back to feeling hungover, bone-tired, lightheaded and on the verge of manic. Before yesterday, Brynn thought that her life had unraveled. But then she had kissed Sawyer. And she'd discovered the location tracking history of Ross's boat. Her definition of *unraveled* had changed. Now, her life hadn't just unraveled, it had combusted, and she was stuck on the ground, watching the embers of it all float off into space.

The only silver lining of being up all night with a sick Lucas was that she hadn't really had time to think about anything. She had been able to block out the memory of Sawyer's lips on hers. But in the morning light, everything came flooding back. She felt sick. Sick with guilt, sick with regret, but also sick with the fact that she *didn't* totally regret it. Not entirely.

Whenever Brynn was struggling to make progress with her novels, she forced herself to just *write*. Anything. She called it the *vomit draft*. As long as she wrote something, even if it was garbage, she knew that it would evolve into something better, something closer to what she wanted it to be. Now, the only thing she could think to do was to write.

She started with what she remembered from the day Cecelia died. Saying goodbye to Ross that morning. Crying on the couch with Lucas. Watching Bravo. More crying. Reorganizing Lucas's clothes. She wrote down the feeding times she'd recorded on her phone—the same ones she'd shown Pete in the station. She wrote down the times that the satellite tracking app said Ross's boat had been taken out and then returned to its mooring.

And then she realized: it couldn't have been Ross who took the boat out. Even if he hadn't yet been home during the time of the security camera footage, he *was* home when the boat was taken out. She was sure of it. She remembered that he'd been sleeping soundly (it infuriated her) next to her at the same time that the boat was rounding the corner of Wasque.

Given those facts, Brynn concluded that someone else must have taken his boat out at that time. It couldn't have been him.

She called Ginny, her hands shaking.

"Brynn," Ginny said, "how are you holding up?"

Brynn couldn't get the words out fast enough. Once she had laid it all out to Ginny, she released a deep breath.

"Okay," Ginny responded. She sounded weary. "But . . . the video footage. I mean, do we still not have any idea how to explain that?"

"Don't you get it, Ginny?" Brynn snapped. "Someone took Ross's boat. They took Cecelia out in his boat, and she fell overboard. Or, or they pushed her overboard. I don't know. But it wasn't Ross."

"And you're sure that he was home then? You wrote it down?" Ginny asked.

"Well, no," Brynn said, defensive, "I mean I didn't write down what time he got home. But I remember him being home for one of the late-night feedings. And I did write down the feeding time."

"Right . . ." There was a pause. "I just know how hazy things get with the night feeds. I remember those days. It's hard to keep track," Ginny said.

Something had changed in the past twenty-four hours between them. Brynn could feel it. It was the undeniable presence of doubt. Ginny no longer believed her. Or, rather, she no longer believed what Brynn believed.

"Forget it," Brynn said. "Forget I said anything."

"Wait," Ginny pleaded. "Brynn, come on. I'm sorry. I'm on your side. I'm just trying to be rational. Do you think maybe Henry took the boat? Is that what you're saying?"

"Maybe," Brynn said. "I don't know. Henry isn't a water guy. I don't know that he even knows how to use the boat. Especially not at night. But I just know it wasn't Ross."

"Well, you don't know for sure," Ginny said. "I mean, you know because . . . it's Ross," she said quickly. "But, I just want you to be careful. And I want you to try to rest. Do you want me to come over?"

"No, but thanks," Brynn said. "*You* need to rest, Ginny. I'm going to ask Margaux to come. Lucas is sick. Perfect timing, right?"

Brynn was planning to ask Margaux to come over, but she wasn't planning to rest. She was too fueled on adrenaline by her discovery now. She needed to keep going. She needed to find the orange sun. She said goodbye to Ginny and got dressed.

Once Lucas fell asleep in his swing in the living room, Brynn made herself some coffee. She pulled the curtains on the kitchen window aside. A police cruiser still sat across the street. Brynn picked up her phone and went to the *Vineyard Gazette* website.

UNANSWERED QUESTIONS LOOM OVER CECELIA BUCKLEY INVESTIGATION, the headline read.

The article didn't mention Ross by name, but it did say that a suspect was being held in custody.

"New evidence has led police to believe that the murder might have been premeditated," the article said, "though police have yet to release that evidence to the public."

Shit, Brynn thought. The new evidence had to be Ross's boat. There were cameras along the banks of the harbor that would catch anyone coming in or out, she knew that for sure. But there weren't cameras, she didn't think, on the drive out to Norton Point Beach, which was the way she'd assumed Cecelia was taken. *By car.* She knew that what she'd just discovered on the satellite phone app was critical evidence, and she was withholding it from the police. It was a crime. But she couldn't hand it over. All she had to prove that it wasn't Ross on the boat was her own fuzzy memory. No one would believe her.

Smarten up, she remembered Izzy telling her. She knew that Izzy was right. Brynn was acting like a fool! She'd never let her characters be such idiots. And yet . . . she couldn't tell anyone what she'd found. Not until she found the orange sun. She'd decided, overnight, that there was one place she needed to go for answers, but it might get her into trouble.

Brynn spat her coffee out into the sink. It tasted bitter. Ross was the one who usually made the morning coffee, not her. It was one of Ross's few day-to-day contributions that she desperately relied on. She couldn't drink it, though, even if she'd made it right. She felt nauseous. Coffee was the last thing she needed, even though she was exhausted.

She stepped onto the porch, which faced the backyard. There was a breeze whistling through the trees. She heard birds—robins, cardinals, bluebirds, a woodpecker. Some of them stopped to feed at the birdhouse she had hung from the magnolia tree that Sawyer had given her. She watched them as they sang, and ate, and flew. She wondered where they'd each go next, and what it felt like to fly from place to place, to look down on the world instead of feeling trapped inside of it.

Sawyer texted her: *Let me know if I can swing by today.*

She started to respond, but then deleted it. Seeing Sawyer would just confuse her more today. She needed to have blinders on.

Instead, she called Margaux.

"I was about to call *you,*" Margaux said. "How are you holding up?"

"I'm okay," Brynn said. "But I could use a break. Lucas was up all night with a fever. I think he's better now, but I . . ."

"Say no more," Margaux said. "I'm coming right over. You're going to go straight to sleep."

"Well, actually, I was hoping to get out of the house. Go for a walk. Clear my head."

"That's a great idea. Some fresh air always makes things better. I'll see you soon."

Brynn wiped down the counters and swept the floor, tidying up as much as she could. It seemed silly, cleaning the house in the midst of everything that was going on. But she still had to carry out the daily tasks of her life. Everything would fall apart if she didn't. She prepared a bottle and left it in the fridge with a note reminding Margaux to warm it in a mug of hot water for just a minute.

When Margaux arrived, Brynn felt an immediate sense of relief. Not just because she'd become more comfortable with Margaux taking care of Lucas, but because she knew that she was doing something good for Margaux by having her here. Letting Margaux take care of Lucas right now gave her a sense of purpose. And it allowed her to be away from Henry, away from everything.

"Thank you for coming," Brynn said as Margaux settled in, taking off her cardigan and placing her purse on the kitchen counter.

"Please," Margaux said. "You know I love seeing my Lucas. And you. I can stay with you for a while, if you like. How is he doing? Is his fever still down?"

"Well, he's asleep now," Brynn said, "but when I checked an hour ago it was down to ninety-nine."

"Good," Margaux said. "I always say if it's under one hundred, it's not a real fever. Sounds like he's just fine."

"I think so. I put a bottle in the fridge," Brynn told her. "And . . . well, you know the rest."

"Warm water for forty-five seconds. I remember," Margaux said with a smile.

"Yes," Brynn said. "Exactly."

She put on her sneakers and grabbed her headphones. She wore her usual outfit of bike shorts and a big T-shirt.

"I think I'm going to drive to the bike path and walk the three-mile loop in the state forest," she told Margaux as she headed for the door. "So just call me if you need anything, and I'll head right back. Thank you for coming."

"Don't worry about a thing," Margaux said. "Take your time. Do whatever you need to do. This is a hard time, Brynn, and we need to take care of ourselves." Unlike the past two days, where all they could focus on and talk about was Ross, neither Margaux nor Brynn mentioned him today. What else was there to say at this point? "And, Brynn, I'm always going to be your mother-in-law, you know. We're always going to be family." Margaux said this as if Ross were gone for good. But it was starting to feel that way, just a little bit.

"I know," Brynn forced herself to say. "Thanks, Margaux." Brynn realized then that she really wanted to hear those words from her own mother, who had been texting Brynn daily and even called a few times. But she'd only offered to come to the island once, and the offer had felt hollow. Brynn felt like her mother was holding herself back from saying *I told you so*. She never liked Ross. Maybe there was a part of her that was glad this had happened, in a way. She could say that she was *right*. Not just about Ross, but about all the Nelsons, about all the rich islanders, all the summer people and the year-rounders who serviced them.

Brynn left the house and got in her car. She turned the ignition and wondered for a moment if she even remembered how to drive, she felt like it had been so long. She rolled down the windows, unclenched her jaw, and drove off.

But she didn't drive to the bike path. She drove up State Road and then turned right onto North Road, slowing down at the entrance to sprawling Seven Gates Farm, where she pulled in. She headed down the winding road, looking out onto the pristine, expansive field, bordered by a thick wood. She drove and drove until the road became tighter and the woods became denser, until finally the horizon broke free and the ocean and sky were revealed. She reached a newly restored farmhouse surrounded by a lichen-covered stone wall. She shut off the engine and took a deep breath.

Brynn had remembered Henry saying that a member of Oyster Watcha had offered his family's home to Cecelia's parents while they came to the island to pick up the pieces their daughter left behind. That morning, Brynn had looked up the member's address in the club directory, and decided that she'd go there, looking for answers. Looking for *something*.

She stepped out of the car and straightened her shirt. There were several other cars there, too, indicating visitors. She knocked on the front door and waited.

A moment later, a woman in her fifties opened the door. She looked like she'd been crying, and she wore a baby-blue sweater and khaki pants.

"Can I help you?" the woman said.

"Mrs. Buckley?" Brynn asked. Her voice was on the verge of shaking.

"Yes?"

"I'm . . . I was a friend of Cecelia's," Brynn said.

Mrs. Buckley gave her a confused look, just for a moment. Brynn realized that she no longer looked the same age as Cecelia, but they weren't *that* far apart in age. It wasn't entirely unplausible that they might have been actual friends. But then Mrs. Buckley's face softened.

"Come on in," she said. "It's nice to meet a friend of Cece's from the island."

Brynn nodded and stepped through the door, following Mrs. Buckley.

She wasn't sure why she was there, or exactly what she was going to say, but she knew she'd come to the right place.

CHAPTER 19

She didn't recognize anyone else there, not at first. There were several people around the same age as Mrs. Buckley, presumably her husband and maybe her sisters or friends. There was a preteen boy who looked just like Cecelia, and Brynn remembered Cecelia mentioning that she *did* have a much younger brother. There were a few young women and men about Cecelia's age milling around, though Brynn had never seen them before. Someone was bustling around the kitchen, organizing containers of food and arrangements of flowers.

"I don't want to impose," Brynn said to Mrs. Buckley. "I just wanted to pay my respects and tell you what a wonderful daughter you had."

"How did you know Cece?" she asked Brynn. Her eyes were off somewhere else, vacant, detached. She wasn't really listening. She wasn't really there.

"Just from around the island," Brynn said.

Mrs. Buckley nodded and smiled. She rested her hand on Brynn's arm. Her hand was cold and bony, and her fingers trembled slightly. Brynn had an impulse to ask her what her birth experience was like. How long had she been in labor? Did Cece arrive early? How big was she? Did she get an epidural? What were the first few months of motherhood like for *her*? But she didn't ask. Mrs. Buckley glided off to the kitchen.

Brynn slipped into a hallway off the living room, away from the crowds, but her eyes kept scanning the room. A man in an awkward-fitting blue blazer, which felt far too formal for the setting, was sipping a drink alone in the corner. It took Brynn a second to realize who it was, but once she realized it was Mauricio, she stepped back so he wouldn't see her. She'd never seen him outside of the club; it felt like seeing a teacher outside of school. Out of place and strange. She peered around the corner again to take another look.

Then she felt a tap on her shoulder. She nearly screamed. She turned around to see Jacob standing in front of her.

"What are you *doing* here?" he whispered under his breath, his voice quiet but tense.

"I . . . I honestly am not sure," Brynn said. "I just wanted to try to understand more about Cecelia. Find out . . . who she was. What her plan was."

"You can't be here," he said. He looked around. "If anyone here finds out who you are . . . who your *husband* is . . . Just, come with me."

Brynn looked back to the living room where Mauricio had been sitting, but he was gone.

Acting calm, Jacob walked through the living room and out two French doors leading to a porch, and then down a stone staircase to the lawn. Brynn followed.

"Keep walking," he said to her, without turning back.

Only once they were across the lawn, all the way out on the bluff overlooking the sea, did Jacob face her. The sky was completely clear; Brynn could easily see all the way to Naushon and Woods Hole.

"Seriously, Brynn, what are you doing here?" he asked. Brynn was sure she could smell beer on his breath.

"Look, I'm sorry," Brynn said. "I am so sorry. I'm just . . . I'm trying to find this clue. Something Ross told me. Remember, I asked you if an orange sun meant anything to you?"

"Jesus," Jacob said. "I don't know what you're talking about. But you're not going to find it here."

"Well, I've been thinking, what if the footage from the club was edited—"

Jacob interrupted her before she could say more.

"Stop, just stop," he said. "You seriously still think your husband is innocent?"

Brynn wasn't sure what had changed since yesterday. She thought that she and Jacob were in alignment and that he might have more information on the old police report.

"Is this about the boat?" she asked. She regretted it the moment she said it. Jacob gave her a confused look.

"Boat? No," he said. "It's about the golf club. You really don't know?"

Brynn swallowed. "No! What golf club?"

Jacob shook his head and looked off toward the water. "I probably shouldn't tell you this. Maybe I've had one too many beers because I don't know how else to cope today. But, screw it, it's about to become public information anyway. They just got new evidence today. This is it, Brynn. It's over. I'm sorry. I was on your side until now, I really was. I didn't think Ross could do this."

Brynn felt like all the air was being sucked out of her body.

"They finished the autopsy," Jacob continued. "We already know that Cecelia died of blunt force trauma to the head." His eyes watered. "And, well, they searched Ross's golf locker. One of his clubs has her blood on it. Like I said, it's over. Just stop."

"But . . ." Brynn struggled to speak. She'd gotten so close to what she thought was the truth. And now she was ten steps behind. "But what about everything with your dad, covering up Henry's crimes, and, and . . ." Anything she said now, she knew, sounded irrelevant, silly.

"Yeah, I don't know," he said. "I just don't know what that has to do with anything. All I know is that Cecelia is gone. And your husband killed her. Listen, you need to leave. I don't want to see another Nelson as long as I live."

"I'm not a Nelson," Brynn said. She'd changed her name to Nelson the moment she and Ross got married. She'd been proud to be a Nelson at first. The name meant something on the Vineyard. "I mean, I am," she continued, "but I'm not." Her words sounded weak. She began to question why she had come there at all. It had been a mistake.

"For all I know," Jacob snapped, "*you* could have told Ross to kill Cecelia. *You* could have been part of this, too." He looked away for a moment. "That's not so far-fetched, you know. To think that you had something to do with it. Makes a lot of sense . . . let's say your husband has an affair with a young woman, you get jealous, and you want to take care of it. Crazier things have happened."

Brynn understood that from an uninformed perspective, it could appear as though Ross and Cecelia were having an affair. And maybe she, the tired, neglected, depressed wife, found out and told him to *handle it*. Or maybe she did it herself. Jacob was right; that theory *wasn't* totally far-fetched. Murders happened all the time for less compelling motives than that. Had Brynn been completely blind to the possibility that people might not feel sorry for her at all, but rather, that people might think *she* was an accomplice?

But no, this wasn't one of her novels, this wasn't a movie. How could anyone think something so absurd about her? She was a *mother*, after all.

"I'm going to leave," she said, "and I'm sorry. I shouldn't have shown up like this. But . . . Jacob. You and I both know that there was nothing going on between Ross and Cecelia. And Ross is a smart guy. Do you really think that if he did kill Cecelia with one of his golf clubs, he'd just put it right back in his locker? I mean, seriously?" Brynn had been thinking out loud when she said this. But now that she had, she realized that there was no way Ross would ever do that. Not even an idiot would.

"I'd be lying if I said I hadn't had the same thought," Jacob whispered. "But it still doesn't look good."

"I know," she said. "But it's possible that the golf club was planted, right?"

Jacob waited before answering.

"It's possible," he said after a few seconds. "But that's a huge accusation. To say that the police planted it."

"But what if it wasn't the police?" Brynn asked. "What if it was someone else?"

"You mean what if someone framed him?" he asked.

"Obviously that's what I'm saying. Or maybe they had someone else plant it. Like Mauricio. Look, I have proof that someone took Ross's boat out during the time Cecelia was killed. And it wasn't him. I know it wasn't. He was home, with me." She paused. "I'm pretty sure he was."

"You're *pretty sure*?" Jacob let out a laugh, a little too loud. It was clear that he was tipsy, but was he blind *drunk*? "We're way past being *pretty sure* about things, Brynn. You either know or you don't."

"I *know*," she yelled. "Sorry . . . but can't you see it's Henry behind all this? It's so *obvious*!" She hadn't meant to yell at Jacob. But she was so tired, so frustrated from going around and around in circles. Every time she thought she might have a handle on the truth, it slipped between her fingers. "This is just such a mess. I'm sorry. But I'm going to find the clue. There's just no *way* Ross did this."

Jacob laughed a little bit again.

"What?" Brynn asked. "You think this is funny?"

"No," he said, "sorry. I just . . . when you said *obvious,* you sounded just like Cece. She used to say that a lot. It was actually pretty annoying." He laughed again and wiped his eyes.

"What was she like?" Brynn asked. "What was Cecelia *really* like?"

Jacob cracked his knuckles.

"She was so smart," he said. "Not like, normal smart. She was brilliant. She was always asking questions."

"She was curious," Brynn said.

"Well, yes, but more than that. She had to understand why everything was the way it was. And if something didn't make sense, or if it wasn't fair, she couldn't let it go. In a way, it ended up being to her detriment. Like, she could never just let things *be*."

Brynn considered this. It was possible that Cecelia had dug into the Nelsons more than she should have. Maybe she got herself in too deep.

"What do you mean?" she asked.

"Well, with Henry," he continued, "she should have just let it go." Jacob looked back toward the house.

"What do you mean let it go? You wish she hadn't told you about the things Henry had done?"

"No, that's not it. I'm glad she told me, even though I couldn't do anything about it, in the end," he said, casting his eyes down in shame. Cecelia had confided in him, and he'd been rendered useless by his own father. "There's more to it," he said. "I didn't tell you yesterday, because . . . well, because I guess I didn't want to say anything bad about her. It feels wrong now, you know, to criticize her in any way. Because I'm not saying that what happened was her fault, not at all . . . but . . ."

"But what?"

"When I told her that my father said to shut it down, she refused. She said she was going to go back to Henry herself and tell him that she would take it public, unless . . ."

"Unless what?"

Jacob exhaled and puffed his cheeks out, and she noticed how young he looked, his face soft and his eyes wide.

"She was trying to extort Henry," he finally stammered. "Listen, I didn't tell you before because . . . It doesn't really matter. She didn't deserve to be killed. I didn't want to admit to something that she shouldn't have done. She should be alive today, and it's not fucking fair. Whoever did this to her, I swear to God, I could kill them myself. But . . . but she wasn't perfect, you know. She got herself into trouble. She *willingly* got herself into trouble, like she sought it out. And that's the truth. It's not her fault, what happened to her. I just wish that she would have minded her own business more. I told her not to, but she wouldn't listen."

Even before Cecelia's death, Brynn thought of Cecelia as exceptionally decent. Not necessarily perfect, but good. Virtuous. Hardworking. Honest. But maybe these were just the things that she—and perhaps her entire family, maybe even all the members of Oyster Watcha—had projected onto her. Did it make it easier for them to be waited on by someone if they convinced themselves that that person *wanted* to be serving drinks? That they enjoyed it? That they found meaning and satisfaction in that work? The truth was, Brynn and her family knew nothing about Cecelia. They never did. They'd invented a palatable version of her that fit neatly into their own world and refused to see anything different.

"So, what do you mean by *extort?* Was Henry paying for her silence?"

"The last thing she told me about it was that he refused. He was hurt that she'd even suggest that. He said that if she needed money, she could just ask him. She said it wasn't about that. It was about justice. But I don't know if it really was."

Jacob cracked his knuckles again.

"It's this place," Jacob said. "That's what did it. That's what killed her."

"The club?" Brynn asked.

"Not just the club," Jacob said. "The island. It changed her. I love this place. Obviously, this is my home. But it's not easy to be here. I think Cece felt like she loved this island too, but it didn't love her back. She wanted a future here, but she couldn't see one for herself, if that makes sense. Like, a future here wasn't possible. I mean, there's not a single home on this island listed for less than a million dollars. The only reason I can live here is because I live on my parents' property and they bought their house forty years ago, you know? And the more time she spent here, as the summers went on, the angrier about it she got. I told her that's just the reality here. It's how it is. But she wouldn't accept it. It's like she wanted to be part of it, but she resented it, too." Brynn thought of her mother when Jacob said that. She thought of how this island sometimes pulled people in and then turned on them. Or turned them into something bad. Jacob continued: "Henry, to her, eventually represented everything she thought was wrong with this place. She figured that she could use him."

"But why Henry?" Brynn asked, though she could hear her own mother's words ringing in her ears. "Did she actually hate him?"

"Well, she had dirt on him. It was easy to go after Henry. He chose to trust her, and she knew that she could use that. But . . . it was more than that. She thought he was a hypocrite. I mean, he's a year-rounder, he raised kids here, and yet he is the single most successful builder for the wealthiest residents on the island. He's literally an integral part of the problem with this place. It's because of his clients that most people *can't* afford to live here."

Brynn's stomach churned. It was an argument she'd heard so many times before, one that was part of the island's core identity crisis: it needed its seasonal residents just as much as it was hurt by them.

"Cece had started to feel that way about Henry even *before* he told her what was going on behind the scenes. She'd started to think he was just another island snob who wasn't willing to help a newcomer," Jacob continued.

"But do you really think Henry would *kill her* because she knew he was—what—embezzling some money, cutting corners? I'm not saying what he did with his business was right, but you think he'd *kill* someone over that? I don't know. And plus, I saw the footage myself. Unless that footage is fake, it's *not* Henry in the video. It's just not."

"I never said I thought Henry killed her," Jacob said. Brynn had to remind herself that Jacob still thought it was Ross who did it. "But you're right," he said. "And I told you—just before she died, Henry told her something else. Something way, way worse. Whatever is in that police report."

Brynn knew that she needed to talk to Henry alone. Without Margaux. Ross had told her not to trust Henry, specifically, but that was exactly why she needed to get to him. Maybe Henry himself was the missing clue. Maybe he would just up and confess to killing Cecelia. To *everything*.

"Let me ask you, Jacob," Brynn said. "What do you *think* happened?

I mean, really, what do you think? What does your gut tell you? Do you really think Ross did it?"

Jacob looked away, out toward the water, and shuffled his feet. His face tightened as if he was fighting off memories he didn't want to see.

"I don't know, Brynn," he finally said. "Ross as the killer is the only logical conclusion. He had motive. He had the physical ability. He had the golf club. He's on the fucking security camera. It honestly doesn't get more airtight than that. So, logically, yeah, I do think he did it. I do. But . . . putting all logic aside . . . what does my gut think? No, I *don't* think Ross did it. The Ross I know could never do something like this." He looked Brynn in the eyes. "But I guess we never really know who someone is."

CHAPTER 20

Brynn had gotten what she'd needed from her visit to the Buckleys, even though it didn't change anything. As she headed to her car, she heard a voice from behind.

"Ms. Nelson. Wait." She knew immediately who it was—because only one person ever called her *Ms. Nelson,* and it was Mauricio.

She turned to face him.

"This is my fault," he said. "I should have protected her from your husband."

"What?" Brynn said. "Mauricio, stop, I can't be talking to you."

"Did he ever hurt you, too?" Mauricio asked. "Brynn, don't let him brainwash you. Don't let any of them. I've done some bad things, but I'd never hurt someone like he did."

Brynn turned her back on him and got in her car. What was he even doing here, paying his respects to Cecelia's family when he'd been forcing her to keep his shameful secret to herself? Then again, what was *she* doing here? Brynn was no better.

She could see Mauricio standing there, watching her go, as she backed out of her spot and left. She was disgusted with him. But maybe she was disgusted with him for saying something to her that might be true—the thing she hadn't been able to admit to herself. The possibility that Ross could be guilty after all. The possibility that Brynn had been the woman she'd written about in her books, who was brilliant and full of potential but was completely blind when it came to the person she loved. No, she thought. That wasn't her.

Once she was out of there and safely back on State Road, she called Ginny. She knew that Ginny would berate her for being so reckless by showing up to meet Cecelia's parents. It *had* been reckless, Brynn knew. But she didn't regret it. Seeing Cecelia's mother made Brynn realize that she had to find the truth, not just for Ross, but for Cecelia. Because even though she didn't know Cecelia well, she knew that she was someone's child. She was someone's everything. And now she was gone.

"You *what*?" Ginny screamed through the phone at Brynn. "Are you fucking *nuts*? What the hell were you thinking, going to see Cecelia's *parents*?"

"I just needed to," Brynn stammered. "I can't explain it."

"Brynn, I'm worried about you, I really am," Ginny said. Something about Ginny's tone felt accusatory to Brynn, like Ginny was saying she couldn't trust her. Like Brynn was some kind of liability.

"You need to be careful," Ginny added. "Seriously. That could have been bad. Really bad." Brynn could hear Sam in the background crying. "Look, I have to go, but do you want me to come over later?"

"Sure," Brynn said. "Only if you can. I'm heading home now."

"Okay, keep me posted," Ginny said. When they both hung up, Brynn realized she hadn't asked Ginny how she was feeling, or how her most recent doctor's appointment was. Ginny was at the stage where she was going to the doctor every few days. It was almost go time.

When Brynn pulled into her driveway, she saw that Sawyer's car was there, parked behind Margaux's. Her cheeks flushed instantly, remembering the feeling of his lips on hers, the way his hands eagerly grabbed at her waist, the warmth of his skin. She thought about pulling out, driving somewhere else to let time pass. She could go see Henry, she thought, and talk to him alone. But she decided against it.

She wasn't ready. He'd tell Margaux and then everything would get confusing.

She'd been gone almost two hours; she had to get back to Lucas, anyway. Her guilt was already consuming her.

When she entered the house, she heard Lucas screaming. It was the fever scream from last night—the shrill, barbed-wire scream that Brynn knew meant he was in pain.

"Shh, shh," Margaux whispered to him, cradling him in her arms. "Mommy's back," she said, looking up at Brynn, who washed her hands in the kitchen sink.

"What happened?" Brynn asked. Sawyer sat at the kitchen island, but Brynn couldn't look at him. She was too focused on Lucas, now. She instantly became determined to fix him, to heal him, to make him feel better. That was all that mattered.

"His fever spiked again," Margaux said. "Right after you left, when he woke from his nap. I did get him to drink a few ounces, and he's made a wet diaper, so he's staying hydrated. He's just hot and bothered."

Margaux had done everything right, Brynn thought, but she was still mad that she hadn't let her know. She was Lucas's mother, after all, and even if she hadn't done a single thing differently, she should have been the one to make the decisions about how to handle it.

"I wish you'd called me," Brynn said, her voice sharp. She felt bad the moment she said it, knowing she sounded ungrateful and controlling. "Sorry," she quickly added, "I just meant that I would have come right back."

"I know," Margaux said, "but I wanted you to have your alone time. And I didn't realize at first that he was actually still sick. Not until he woke up. You said his fever had gone away."

"Well, I said it was down to ninety-nine," Brynn quipped. She was angry, now. Maybe she was being overly sensitive, but she heard in Margaux's voice the accusation that it was *her* fault that Lucas was sick, like she'd downplayed his fever and ignored the signs, that she never should have taken time away from him for herself.

"Well, babies get fevers. He's going to be okay. He's a tough little guy, Brynn," Margaux said, handing him to her. Brynn hoped that he'd stop crying once he was in her arms, but he continued to wail, and she felt self-conscious of her deficiencies as a mother. If her own son couldn't find comfort in her arms, she must be doing it all wrong.

"I, uh, I'm going to call his doctor again," Brynn said, looking for her phone. She bounced Lucas in her arms, hyperaware of her actions in front of Margaux—how she was holding Lucas, how her bike shorts were riding up on her thighs, how she was the type of mom who was okay leaving her sick child at home for a few hours with someone else. And why was Sawyer still there? she wondered. Why was he there at all? What *was it* with this family? she thought suddenly. What was it with Sawyer and Margaux being so close? She wanted them to leave, she needed to be alone with her son, as though she was certain that his discomfort was because of *her* discomfort in their presence, and that once they left, everything would be fine.

Sawyer spotted her phone on the kitchen counter and handed it to her.

"Brynn," he said, "don't worry. He's going to be fine."

She nodded. She could tell from Lucas's cry that he was hungry. She wanted to ask Margaux when she fed him, and exactly how much, whether or not she burped him, if he spat up, and if so, how much and what it looked like. But she didn't bother asking. Margaux wouldn't have the answers. Because even though Brynn didn't even *like* being a mother most of the time, she still somehow automatically needed to have this information seared into her brain at all times. These were the details that ran through her mind twenty-four hours a day, forcing her to constantly evolve and adapt to whatever Lucas needed. No one else would understand. No one else would care as much as her. They never would. And even when Brynn didn't want to care, she couldn't help it; she always would.

She carried Lucas to the living room with her and sat down to breastfeed. Both Sawyer and Margaux looked away. Lucas struggled for a minute and Brynn could feel sweat forming beneath her breasts, but after a while, he latched on, and then the only sounds were the grunts of contentment from him as he ate.

"Sorry, Margaux," Brynn finally said. "I didn't mean to snap at you, I really didn't. I just get so worried about him. I shouldn't have left."

"Don't apologize," Margaux said. "I should have called you. But you needed some time for yourself, Brynn, and I wanted to make sure you got that. You're going through a really tough time. It's not healthy for you to be alone with Lucas all day, every day. You need help."

Brynn knew that she was right. But she needed help even *before* all this happened. She'd needed help from day one, but she hadn't known how much she would need it, and then she didn't know how to ask for it, and then she didn't think she deserved it. She still didn't think she deserved it. Why had she become a mother at all if she couldn't handle being one? As her own mother would say, she'd buttered her bread, and now she not only had to eat it, but she also had to say a prayer of gratitude for it, too.

"I know," she said. "I've never been good at asking for help."

"Well, most women aren't," Margaux said. "And usually, it's because we know that we can do everything better than anyone else, right?" She smiled at Brynn. "But asking for help doesn't make you a bad mom. Actually, it makes you an ever better one."

Brynn wanted to cry, but she resisted.

"I know," she said again. It was all she could say.

"Anyway," Margaux said, "we're going to be in this for a long time. I'm here for you."

"Uh-huh," Brynn said.

Brynn wanted to tell Margaux how she really felt: that she didn't think Ross did it, that none of it made sense, that there were still unanswered questions, and that it had to be Henry behind it all, somehow. But something in Margaux had shifted and she no longer seemed to be saddened by Ross's absence, only saddened by the acceptance of it. He was her first *son*! Brynn wondered if she'd stand by Lucas if he was ever accused of something terrible, and if all the signs pointed to him doing it. Would she believe him if he said he hadn't done it? Would she have his back? She'd like to think she would. But she didn't know for sure.

"Uh, Brynn," Sawyer said from the kitchen, where he still sat, away from her while she fed Lucas. "I fixed the fridge. I remember you'd said it was leaking a little bit. Shouldn't be a problem anymore. That's why I came by. I'm gonna head out, now."

Now, Brynn felt even worse. She'd been angry at both Margaux and Sawyer for butting in, for overstepping, but all they'd tried to do was help.

The person she needed to be angry with was the one person she hadn't really talked to yet: Henry. The one person who was hiding behind his supposed grief, his increasingly feeble mind, his untouchable place in the community. She needed to talk to him. She needed to find a way through to him. It might lead her to whatever Ross had told her to find—to the truth.

"Thank you," Brynn said to Sawyer. "And thank you, Margaux. I truly don't know what I'd do without you both."

"We're family," Margaux said. "We always will be."

CHAPTER 21

By the time Brynn got Dr. Smith on the phone, Lucas was asleep in his bassinet, and his fever had gone back down to 99.

"Brynn," Dr. Smith said, "there's unfortunately not much you can do. Most likely, he's got a virus that his body is just trying to fight off. That's what fevers are. They indicate the body working in overdrive to fight something off. You just have to let it run its course and monitor it closely. Hydration and rest are the best tools you have right now."

"But how do I know it's not something more?" Brynn asked. "Something else, I mean? Could it be Covid? Or some kind of infection?"

"You can give him a Covid test, if you're comfortable administering it," he said, "but even if it is Covid, the care would pretty much be the same right now, considering his symptoms at this point. Just keep an eye on him. If his temperature rises or if he stops drinking, or gets a rash, anything like that, let us know. Otherwise, just hang in there, kiddo. You're tough as nails, like I always say. Lucas will be okay, and you will, too."

By now, Dr. Smith surely knew about Cecelia's death and Ross's arrest. Everyone did. Even everyone *off-island* knew. Brynn waited for Dr. Smith to say something about it—to imply that he was on her side, that he believed her, that he felt sorry for her, that when he said she would be okay, he wasn't just talking about getting through the night with a sick newborn.

"Thanks, Dr. Smith," Brynn said when it became clear that Dr. Smith was done. "I really appreciate it."

"Don't mention it, Brynn. Call if anything changes."

When Brynn hung up, the house was silent. She waited, as though suddenly, somehow, she'd hear Ross come clamoring through the door, asking where his jacket was, or his keys, or whether they had any more of their favorite pinot noir. All the noises he made that had angered her. All the requests that had made her feel like he'd stopped seeing her and instead only needed her for logistics, for domestic things, for function. But not for love, not for partnership. When had she started hearing his words this way? When had it all changed? When and where had it all gone wrong?

In retrospect, it seemed that the chasm between Brynn and Ross had only formed once Lucas was born; before that, Brynn and Ross had been a team. Their bond had only grown stronger with excitement as their due date approached. They stayed up late writing down possible baby names, reading chapters out loud from a book for expecting parents. They'd babyproofed the house together, they'd taken a birthing class together, Ross gave her nightly foot rubs and rested his head on her belly, eagerly awaiting Lucas's next kick.

Before Lucas, everyone in Brynn's life told her that she would be such a good mom. The *best* mom. She was always the first one to play with the little kids at a family barbecue, the one who showed up with the cutest baby gifts when her friends became moms, toting bags of organic cotton onesies with matching booties, hand-knitted hats with kitten ears, books about unicorns. She volunteered to babysit for friends whenever they needed it—even for some coworkers now and then in New York—and she loved it. She could calm even the fussiest baby or the most manic toddler. But she dreamed of having her *own* child. A chunky little boy, she had said, was what she always wanted.

That person she used to be—the babysitter, the energetic friend who loved kids, the woman who couldn't help but coo at a stranger's baby across a restaurant—was a stranger to Brynn now. She'd been warned about the change in hormones, the baby blues, and the effects of sleep deprivation. But she had assumed that wouldn't be her. It just wouldn't. She had been a joyful pregnant woman. She'd loved building her baby registry, having her shower, getting Lucas's nursery ready, picking out little onesies. She and Ross had even done a two-month-long birth class together to prepare for the aftermath: life with a baby. She'd gone through it all with joy and gratitude and genuine happiness for what was to come.

But once Lucas was born, her old self had been replaced with this new one. One who mostly looked the same, but who sometimes felt nothing for her child, who missed her old life, who often regretted her choice to become a mother, who was *sure* that this life was not the one she was meant to be living. And, above all, who knew that her son would be better off without her. She knew that in her core. She knew that even when he drank milk from her own breast and was comforted by the smell of her skin. This new version of her, she thought, was not only incapable of loving her son, but incapable of being loved by anyone in return.

But, she wondered, when exactly had it all changed? Was she destined for this change or had something gone irreparably wrong that day when Lucas came into the world?

Her water had broken a week early. It was a raw, bitter day in March, one that teased the threat of late spring snow with near-freezing temperatures. The air was wet and icy. Ross was at work; spring was the busiest time of year for him by far. Summer was jammed, too, of course, but spring was when homeowners started to grow impatient. As summer loomed nearer and nearer, demands grew higher, deadlines got closer, and workloads became less manageable.

Brynn had just finished assembling a new cordless vacuum when she felt a damp trickle inside her stretch pants. Her hospital bag was already packed—it had been for weeks—but nothing could have prepared her for that moment. She called Ross.

"I think it's happening," she said.

She heard a scuffle and a thud.

"Brynn? Brynn?" Ross yelled into the phone. "Sorry, I dropped my phone, I . . . Oh my God! Okay, should I come get you?"

"Yeah," she said. She wasn't having contractions yet. She felt completely fine. "I don't think you need to rush just yet. Come get me. I'll let the hospital know we're coming."

"Okay, see you soon. Okay. Wait, are you okay? What do you need? Do you feel okay?"

Brynn laughed. She wasn't nervous, she wasn't in pain. Not yet. She was just excited. It was finally happening. She was *happy*.

"I'm great. We're having a baby, Ross! See you soon."

Ross sped into the driveway only minutes later. He raced inside.

"Brynn?" he yelled. "I'm here!"

She waddled into the kitchen, her bag over her shoulder.

"Ross, take a second," she said. "Take a deep breath. We've got some time. You should pack a bag, too. They're still not letting us leave the hospital once we're there, because of Covid. Remember?"

"Right, right. Shit. Okay, uh, let me throw some things together really quick." He ran upstairs to their room. Brynn had told him to pack a bag for weeks now, but he hadn't.

Ross's nervousness had been soothing to Brynn, somehow. It made her laugh. He cared so much. He was so eager to become a dad, and to support Brynn becoming a mom. He was almost more excited than she was.

He emerged with a boat bag stuffed with clothing and a toiletry kit, and then he hastily threw some snacks from the kitchen cabinet in it.

"We can't leave, right?" he said. "I want to make sure you have food you like."

"Thanks," Brynn said.

An hour later, after being examined by a nurse and a midwife, they were told to leave the hospital and come back in three hours. It was entirely anticlimactic. Brynn hadn't started dilating or having contractions yet, and there wasn't an available birthing room yet, anyway. It was a small island with a relatively small hospital, after all.

"Come *back*?" Brynn had asked.

"Well, you'd just be waiting around here," the midwife said. "Go enjoy the last few hours you have with just the two of you. Trust me."

Brynn and Ross walked out to the parking lot.

"Do you want to go home?" Ross asked. It was early evening now. "Or we could go out to dinner?"

Brynn wasn't sure going out to eat was a good idea. But she *was* hungry, and she wasn't sure when she'd be able to eat once they came back. Going home felt strange; what would she do? Refold laundry? Reorganize the diaper station? She was as ready as she'd be.

"Let's get dinner. The last one with just the two of us," she said.

They went to dinner at Beach Road. It was quiet; they had just re-opened after winter. They were seated right away at a table overlooking the pond in back.

"We're celebrating," Ross told the waitress. "My wife is in labor."

The waitress's eyes went wide and she looked at Brynn, confused.

"Not really," Brynn said. "Well, sort of. We're going to the hospital after this."

"Well, you better order then," the waitress said. "No time to waste!"

And they did: a glimmering seafood tower with all the raw crusta-ceans and shellfish that Brynn had painfully avoided over the last nine months, a feathery light shrimp tempura, a fusilli pasta with bursting tomatoes and buttery lobster, and, the restaurant's secret star, a plate of piping-hot, extra-crispy fried chicken.

They ate, and they laughed, and they celebrated what they knew would probably be the last meal between the two of them before their lives changed forever, before it would never just be the two of them again, not really.

Brynn had felt so lucky at that table, so loved, and content, so cer-tain that she'd chosen the right person. She'd found someone who un-derstood her, and loved her, and wanted her to be happy. She knew, in that moment, that whatever happened to them and whatever life hit them with, they would be okay if they were together. She and Ross, she thought, could weather any storm.

But Lucas's birth hadn't gone according to plan. It had all gone wrong. When they'd returned to the hospital, they were set up in a spacious birthing suite. Brynn started to have contractions. She bounced on a ball. She took a hot shower. She walked around the room. She wasn't dilating fast enough. Contractions started to become painful and intense. Eventually, they gave her Pitocin over the course of twelve hours. The midwife reached into her vagina with what looked like a knitting needle so she could fully break her water; the pain was acute and intrusive. When the Pitocin didn't work, they gave her Cytotec over the course of another twelve hours. But that didn't work, either. Brynn knew that she wasn't going to deliver the baby vaginally. She could tell. Her body was fighting it. She felt like her body was locking itself down, as if to say *I'm not meant for this. I'm not doing this. I'm not ready.* But she had to. The baby was coming, one way or another.

By then, the contractions were so painful that Brynn started to become sick, shaking, sweating, and vomiting. At some point, she'd bent over and received an epidural from a visiting doctor in from New York, who assured her the epidural would make everything better. But it hadn't. She continued to be sick. And every time she had a contraction, the baby's heart rate would plummet. She was hooked up to a large monitor that showed the baby's heart rate, so every minute when she writhed in pain with another wave of a contraction, she'd be reminded by the large, beeping neon machine that things were going south. That she had already—even before she'd become a mother—done something wrong.

At that point, Ross demanded that the doctor come in and take a closer look. Brynn hadn't been able to say what he said for her.

"Something is *wrong*," he had said when the nurse arrived. "We need the doctor."

"Ross, let them do their jobs," Brynn had told him, embarrassed to be asking for any extra attention. "I'll be fine."

"Brynn," Ross had said, sternly. "Let me take care of you. For *once*, let me help. Please. I got this." He rested his hand on her forehead. His palm felt cool and comforting.

When the doctor came in, Ross stood up.

"My wife is sick," he said. "She's in pain. Something isn't right." His voice was unyielding and stoic, resounding but not shrill.

"It's probably the reaction to the epidural," the doctor said. "But let's take a look."

"It's not just that," Ross said. "My wife is *sick*. You need to listen to how she's feeling."

As soon as the doctor put her hands on Brynn's belly, she turned to Ross. "You're right," she said. "We need to do an emergency C-section right away. Let's go."

Even in the midst of her pain, Brynn hadn't felt entitled to advocate for herself. It was exactly what Ginny had told her. Brynn had *known* that she'd have to speak up, and she never thought that it would be a problem for her. She'd always been able to ask for what she wanted. But when she had actually been in the moment, she'd been too overwhelmed to even know what to ask for, or how to describe what she was feeling. After all, labor and delivery were *supposed* to be painful, she told herself. Birth was *supposed* to be scary and difficult. She had signed up for the pain when she'd decided to have a baby, right? This was what every mother on the planet had endured; Brynn didn't think she was allowed to act as though it was harder for her than it had been for any of them. The person she was before the baby—a champion of herself—had gone into hiding beneath the scratchy hospital sheets, and she'd remained silent.

If Ross hadn't been there, and if he hadn't spoken up for her, Brynn might have lost the baby. She might have lost herself.

And by the time the doctor came in and felt Brynn's stomach, she said they had to do a C-section, and fast.

Fetal intolerance, prolonged labor, cephalopelvic disproportion, and *failure to progress.* Brynn would learn later that those were the things that were happening to her and the baby at the time. But she hadn't known to ask, and nobody had told her. While she was being poked and prodded and observed, Brynn had silently assumed that whatever was happening was simply her fault. She wasn't equipped to be a mother. It was that simple.

Brynn was wheeled down the hall, and Ross had to stay in the birthing suite. Covid rules. She continued to vomit throughout the operation. No one asked her if she wanted the curtain to be up or if she wanted to see the baby emerge from inside of her. If they'd asked, she would have said that she wanted to see it. But she didn't think to ask for it, it all happened so fast. So, she just stared up at the lights on the ceiling, occasionally turning her head to vomit in a bag held by a nurse. And then, suddenly, a few minutes later, someone held up a crying baby, and presented it to her as her son. Brynn hadn't felt him come out of her, and she hadn't seen him come out, either. She looked at the baby and didn't know for sure that he was hers. He could be anyone's baby, she thought. She stared at him. His eyes were black, his skin red and somewhat loose around his small limbs, as though he hadn't finished growing into himself yet. There was nothing about him, she thought, that made him hers. There was nothing about him that connected him to her. He was a baby, but she didn't feel that he was hers. She felt nothing.

They stitched her back up while they cleaned the baby. She glanced over and saw a black, tar-like substance being wiped from his bottom. His testicles were engorged. A nurse told her that was normal. She continued to be sick while they closed her stomach back up, turning her head every few seconds to vomit bile or gag. The nurse who had been holding the bag had stepped away to help with the baby, so Brynn heaved and retched into the air like a sick dog.

She couldn't hold him, not for almost half an hour. She was still shaking from the epidural. The baby cries started to hurt her head. She wanted to cover her ears, but she could barely lift her arms. She was desperate for water. She was thirstier than she'd ever been in her entire life. But when she asked for water, she was told she'd have to wait. *We don't want you to get sick again,* they said.

These first few moments with the baby are the most important. It's when you'll bond. This is the golden hour. The what? The golden hour. The first hour of your baby's life. It's the most important time for you to bond with your child. To have skin-to-skin contact, for your child to imprint on you, and you on him. The bond you make right now is the bond you'll have for life.

It seemed like a lot of pressure to put on a mother who had just endured a trauma and could barely hold the cup of ice chips they had finally given her. She didn't want to hold the baby. She wanted to go to sleep.

Someone took the cup of ice chips from her and handed her the baby. *I'm not ready,* she started to say, but no one heard. She held the baby in her arms like a glass vase. The backs of her knees were sweaty and itchy. She wanted to scratch them, but she couldn't do anything with the baby in her arms. It was so small, so fragile. It was not cozy and soft, it was an uncomfortable nest of bones, an angry creature who seemed to be offended by the arms of the person who had just housed him inside their own body for almost a year.

When they wheeled Brynn back up, Ross was still there, just as before. Except now, they had a baby. Now, it was the three of them. Everything had changed in an instant.

Upon the advice of the nurses, Ross removed his shirt. A nurse took the baby from Brynn's arms and gave him to Ross. He stared at the baby with something in his eyes she had seen before: true love, true adoration, true devotion. She'd seen him look at her that way before.

"He's amazing!" Ross said to her. "He's perfect!" He was crying.

Brynn had heard that sometimes fathers struggled with the lack of attention on them after the birth of a baby. Suddenly, all the love from their partner went to the baby, and not to them. But Brynn felt that way herself. Why was this baby getting all the praise, when all it had to do was show up? She was the one who had done all the work. She was the one who had just experienced the most terrifying moment of her life. She was the one in pain. She was the one who was bleeding. And she was the one whose life would be changed the most by this. She was the one who had to now say goodbye to who she was. She'd left that person on the operating table. Did Ross not see that? Did Ross not see that she was the one who needed to be looked at the way he was looking at the baby?

"And you're amazing, honey," he said, like an afterthought. He didn't look up from the baby. That baby had become his whole world.

The next few days in the hospital only solidified Brynn's feelings of isolation. The priority of everyone around her was getting the baby to breastfeed. Brynn sat in bed, propped up by pillows, while the nurses hovered over her, adjusting her breasts, squeezing her nipples, demonstrating different feeding positions. Nothing seemed to work. Nothing felt comfortable or sustainable. The baby latched on, but with a weak grasp, not enough for Brynn to feel like he was really connecting to her and filling up. *Try the football hold, like this,* one nurse said. Brynn stuffed the baby onto her forearm as if she were a waitress with an extra tray, and he tried to clamp onto her nipple from the side. *Hold him more horizontal, like that,* another nurse said, and Brynn readjusted again. *Lie on your side with him next to you,* another suggested. *Just make sure you don't fall asleep like that, of course.*

Later, a nurse showed Brynn how to massage her breasts to avoid mastitis. Already, her breasts had turned into giant iron lumps, completely unfamiliar to her, as though someone had sewn boulders into her body while she was in surgery. Brynn asked about bottle feeding, but the nurses shook their heads. "Breastfeeding will work for you if you keep trying," they said.

Brynn wanted to sleep. She was so tired. But someone came into the room every hour or so to check the baby's vitals, to help her breastfeed, to poke and prod. The hospital policy was to keep the baby in the room with the mother twenty-four hours a day. There was no nursery option. This was for *optimal bonding,* they'd said. The brief moments when Brynn could sleep were narrated by the noises of the hospital—the swishing of the privacy curtain opening and closing, the beeping of machines, the cries and moans of other mothers in other rooms, the urgent pounding of sneakers in the hallways. Ross slept soundly on the couch by the window, with an eye pillow that a nurse had provided him wrapped around his head. He remained asleep even when a nurse came in and turned the lights on. He just stayed asleep.

Her body ached. Her insides had been taken out and put back in, but that wasn't what hurt. Her body hurt from exhaustion. Her bones needed sleep. Her skin needed sleep. Her heart needed sleep. Every cell in her body was begging her to shut down. Could it be possible, she wondered, to fall asleep, in the deepest sleep imaginable, and wake up in another life? A life where things had happened as planned. Where she was actually happy to have become a mother. Where she was anywhere else besides this cold room with a baby she didn't know and an oblivious, sleeping husband. Somewhere where someone could hold her hand, look her in the eyes, and say *You just did something incredible. I'm proud of you.* Somewhere where that was said before anything at all was said to the baby.

She told the nurses how much her body hurt. They gave her Tylenol and stool softeners. She couldn't eat anything until she released a big fart, they said.

"*What?*" Ross blurted when he heard this. He had woken up for the hospital breakfast.

"The body has a lot of trapped gas after the surgery," the nurse said, unfazed. "You need to release it before ingesting anything." Everything about the recovery process was designed to humiliate her, Brynn felt. Every private part of herself was no longer hers. It now belonged to the baby, and was therefore open to the hospital to investigate, to manipulate, to use for experiments. The fact that she herself had just endured surgery was irrelevant. It was no longer about her. Or maybe it never was.

When she felt ready to walk around and move, she could only circle the floor of her room, like a fish in a tank.

"Can't go out into the hallways," the nurse instructed. "Covid rules."

Brynn gingerly stepped around the room, her insides feeling like a lava lamp, squishy and out of place, ready to collapse at any moment. She went into the bathroom and shut the door. She looked for a window; there wasn't one. In the mirror was a stranger—a washed-out woman, bloated but empty, silent but screaming. She splashed her face with water. Even the way the water washed down her skin felt new and different. She'd transformed into someone she didn't know and didn't want to know.

Back in the room, Ross was watching TV. *Naked and Afraid.* A woman battling severe bug bites was trying to keep a fire going despite the impending jungle rain.

I don't want to be here, the woman said, hanging her head in her hands, crunching her gnawed body into a ball. *I just don't think I can handle it. I want to go home.*

Brynn had looked at the hospital bag she'd packed for herself, realizing how stupid and unnecessary it all was. It was stuffed with brand-new items she'd put on her registry—a cashmere bathrobe, a floral-print nursing wrap, a bamboo-cotton onesie with matching hat for the baby, organic nipple cream, a travel sound machine. Items that she'd imagined herself wearing and using back when she thought she knew what having a baby would be like. Back when she thought she would be ready. The bag sat on the floor by the bed, untouched.

She'd give anything, she had thought in that moment, to trade places with the woman in the jungle. To hear nothing but the sound of rain and the static of other creatures not reliant on her, to be able to hear her own breath, her own heartbeat, simply existing within the world.

CHAPTER 22

Ginny, Annie, and Marcus showed up the next morning, just as *The Vine-yard Gazette* and *The MV Times* were publishing stories about the golf club. Brynn's entire world was crumbling down around her.

Outside of the house, it looked like a traveling circus had come to town. There were local and off-island reporters milling around, two police cruisers, and lots of people who happened to be going for walks right on Brynn's street. She'd kept all the curtains and blinds shut since the night before, but she still felt exposed and ashamed.

Her friends burst in through the door together, Ginny groaning as she held her stomach.

"You guys," Brynn said, "you didn't have to come. I'm sure you want nothing to do with any of us. With me. It's probably a bad idea for you to be here. Go home."

"Stop it," Marcus said. "We know who you are. We love you. We're always going to be here for you."

"Where are the kids?" Brynn asked them all.

Marcus's son was at home with his grandmother, Ginny's kids were at the Farm Institute for a two-week day camp, and Annie's twins were with their dad.

"Why is it always like he's *babysitting* when they're just his children?" Annie asked, rolling her eyes. "I come home and it's like, do you want a fucking prize for taking care of your own kids?"

"Seriously," they all said, collectively.

Brynn put on a pot of coffee. She was so tired. Lucas had woken four times throughout the night, and Brynn had fed him, burped him, changed him, taken his temperature, and put him back to sleep each time. She'd fallen into a rhythm, a muscle memory. *Maybe,* she thought in her exhausted delirium, *being a good mother is just about going through with the motions, until you believe that you're doing it right. Maybe everyone else is pretending.*

Throughout the night, Brynn could tell from feeling Lucas's skin that his temperature had gone down, but he still woke in discomfort, pleading with her for something. She wished she knew what. He was only comforted when she held him in a particular crook of her arm and sank her hips down into squats, over and over again, Lucas's body rising and falling with her movements until he was lulled to sleep.

But even once Lucas was asleep, Brynn had trouble dozing off herself. The thing was, even on nights when Lucas wasn't sick, Brynn felt an intense fear of letting herself fall truly, deeply asleep. Instead, she fell into a sort of half-resting state. She was asleep enough to let her mind give in to fears and fantastical nightmares, but not asleep enough to gain any kind of restoration from it. The fears were too consuming, too vivid. She pictured Lucas turning over, pushing himself into the mesh sides of the bassinet until the flat of his face gave way to the mattress, suffocating him, while his arms were held prisoner in his swaddle. She imagined him choking on his own saliva, coughing desperately, his baby eyes bursting in despair. Sometimes, his noises wove into the narrative of her dream, and she wasn't sure if she was awake or asleep. Sometimes, she wasn't sure what was real. But then again, she wasn't sure it really mattered. The same fears permeated both her waking and her sleeping hours.

The truth of her fear wasn't just that something terrible might happen to Lucas. That was Ross's fear, and it was why he got so mad at her when he found her asleep outside while Lucas wailed away, alone. But Brynn's real fear was not that something bad might happen, but that she might *let* it happen. What if she waited ten seconds too long to go get him, to pick him up, to fix him, simply because she was too tired to move? What if she used those ten seconds for herself, to just lie horizontal with her eyes closed, holding on to the moments before she would be needed again? What if those ten seconds were the ten seconds that made it all too late?

Sometimes, Brynn just watched Lucas while he slept. She had to see him to know that he was real, to remind herself that this was her life now, and that she wasn't dreaming. She felt the need to see and touch the normal items surrounding her that had existed before him: the stack of unread books on her bedside table looking back at her with neglect, the half-empty water bottle that she needed to wash. And, in the drawers of her bedside table, the hibernating remnants of her former life: a pink vibrator, condoms, a jade roller, an expensive body oil. When she saw these things, she returned herself to a sense of normalcy and stability. This was where she was, this was real.

"How's Lucas feeling?" Ginny asked as she sat down.

"He's fine," Brynn said. "How are *you* feeling?"

"Big," Ginny said. "Very big. They're going to induce me in three days if my water doesn't break before that."

"Oh my God," Brynn said. "I can't believe it."

Ginny put her feet up on another chair. "I can."

"Brynn," Marcus said, pouring everyone coffee. "We were thinking. You know, a spot just opened up in that daycare program that I'm sending Liam to in the fall. Have you thought more about it, for Lucas?"

"Uh, I hadn't really thought about it at all," Brynn said.

"We just thought maybe it was a good time to consider options. In case you're going to be on your own for a while," Annie said.

"It's not going to be like this forever," Brynn said. "We're fine." She wasn't sure why she was getting so defensive at her friends all of a sudden.

But somehow the suggestion of daycare stung. It felt like a jab at her, like they were saying that they knew she couldn't handle all this on her own. That she wasn't capable.

The funny thing was, just a few weeks ago, she'd suggested the same thing to Ross. She'd had a long few days with Lucas, and when she told Ross that she needed more time to herself to write, he instantly suggested they call Margaux more.

"Maybe we can have my mom come over on a more regular schedule," he said. "I'm sure she'd love that."

Brynn nodded. "Well, I was thinking about daycare, too, maybe," she said. "The place where Marcus's son is going looks really nice." She braced herself for Ross's response. Daycare was a hot topic for them, something they'd completely ruled out from the start because Brynn herself had decided they didn't need it or want it for Lucas. She was the one who'd been insistent with Ross that she wanted to stay home with Lucas full-time, while also continuing to write. Not only had it been what Brynn had wanted, but she'd thought it would be totally doable. She'd almost demonized daycare in her previous conversations with Ross—telling him that Lucas would get sick all the time, or that she'd miss out on all his milestones, or that he wouldn't feel as bonded to her as he would be if he stayed home.

Except that was the *old* Brynn who had those ideas. The version of her who had no clue how hard motherhood would actually be. She hadn't known that she would be incapable of maintaining her own mental sanity while constantly hearing her baby cry. She hadn't known that all day long she'd either be washing pump parts, or doing laundry, or vacuuming, or sorting through baby clothes, or setting up a new gadget that promised a calmer newborn, and that there'd be no time whatsoever for herself or her own work. She hadn't known that if she *did* have a window of free time, she'd be so wiped out that the only thing she could do was sleep. She hadn't known that one trip to the grocery store or the pediatrician would exhaust her for the rest of the day. She hadn't known that her body would still feel like one big open wound. She hadn't known that it would be impossible to do it all at once.

"I didn't think you wanted to do daycare," he said. "And remember how many kids in daycare were getting respiratory viruses? It just seems like if we don't have to do it, why would we, right? Plus, it's so expensive now."

Brynn deflated. She hadn't expected a different response from Ross, but she had hoped for one, anyway. Initially, when they'd discussed childcare options back when she was pregnant, Ross's attitude was open. He had insisted that *she* make the decision that she thought was best for both her and Lucas. She'd planted these ideas in his head about why daycare didn't make sense for them. Maybe she'd been trying to justify her decision to herself, but whatever the reason, she'd completely convinced Ross that daycare wasn't the right choice for Lucas. She had also gotten the sense that when she told him firmly that she wanted to stay home with their son, Ross had been thrilled. She felt like she was mirroring his own perfect childhood and re-creating it for his son. Even if he didn't admit it, she knew that Ross loved the idea of her being at home with Lucas while he went off to work. Just like his own mother, he wanted Brynn to devote all of herself to Lucas—and to him.

Because Ross had brought Lucas's health into the conversation, she couldn't argue with him. The Covid pandemic had only just been declared over, but everyone was still more conscious of germs than before. She knew that sending Lucas to daycare would put him at a greater risk of getting sick, but she also wasn't sure that was an entirely bad thing. He needed to build up his immune system. But if she tried to explain this to Ross, it would only sound like an excuse, a selfish reason for her to put him in harm's way.

"I just thought we could talk about it. As an option," she said.

"We can, of course," Ross said. "I just want to do what's best for Lucas."

"Obviously, I do, too," Brynn responded. "I just feel like I need more time for myself. To write."

"Maybe I can do bath and bed every night?" Ross suggested.

"It's hard for me to write at the end of the day when I'm tired," she said. "At that point, it's like, I'll just do bath and bed myself, you know?" She knew she sounded defensive, but it felt like such a useless offer. What could she possibly do for herself that was productive or beneficial after she'd been taking care of Lucas all day long? She was practically brain-dead at that point.

"I'm trying to be helpful, here, Brynn," Ross had said.

"I know, I appreciate it. I just . . . I don't know if helping in the evenings is what I need. I mean, it would be nice for you to do it, yes, for sure, I just don't think I'd be able to get work done then."

"Well, why don't you think about what I can do to be more helpful, and tell me, okay?"

"Okay," Brynn said. "Thank you. For now, I just think I need more time for myself during the day."

"Great, then we'll get my mom over here more. Would that work?"

The conversation circled right back to how it had started. Brynn nodded.

"That would work great," she said.

She was mad at herself in that moment for not defending her career more, though that was something she'd always struggled with. She had never felt justified to prioritize her writing or entitled to take the time she needed to write successfully. Most people, but especially Ross and his family, didn't understand that just because Brynn didn't report to an office or attend staff meetings didn't mean she was excluded from having deadlines, obligations, and professional challenges. To them, it seemed ridiculous to send Lucas to daycare when she could write at the kitchen table in the comfort of a bathrobe. She kicked herself for never really explaining to Ross that she needed actual, physical space and solitude to write. Or that sometimes, a productive day for her did not actually include much writing at all, but instead consisted of taking a long walk to think, to ponder, to crack a writing roadblock.

She knew that Ross was proud of her. He made a big fuss out of both of her books being published, taking her out to dinner at The Sweet Life Cafe to celebrate the first and State Road for the second, going up to strangers and telling them that they would *love* his wife's books. But Brynn still got the itching sense that he thought of her writing as being *cute*. Not a real career.

Perhaps what irked Brynn most, though, was that she knew, deep down, that *she* was the one who wasn't taking herself seriously. Her lack of certainty in herself had nothing to do with Ross. The reason she wasn't writing lately wasn't just that she'd been busy with Lucas. It was that she'd completely lost the belief that she *could* write. At least not while being a mother at the same time.

Except nobody had warned her of this. Brynn had only ever been told the opposite for her whole life. She'd grown up in the age of feminism, working moms, and the notion that women could indeed *have it all*. Or maybe that's just what she'd chosen to hear.

"And I'm here to help," Ross had added. "You just need to ask me more. I can't always read your mind, you know."

Her friends waited now for Brynn to say something else.

"It's just . . . it's hard to see when this is going to go away," Annie said.

"And we just want to help you plan for the future." Marcus put his hand on hers.

"Especially because you need to be taking care of yourself, Brynn," Ginny added. "Have you thought more about asking your doctor about antidepressants? Do you want me to make an appointment with that therapist if you haven't yet? Postpartum depression is real, Brynn. But there are so many good solutions now."

"I was practically hallucinating for five months straight with the twins," Annie said. "We don't think clearly when we're so tired and depressed, you know?"

"And you've been under so much stress trying to write your book, too," Marcus added.

Brynn knew she was tired, and not herself, but she still trusted her intuition. She still could tell right from wrong. Except . . . she *had been* particularly forgetful lately, and absentminded, and anxious—well before Cecelia had died. Last week, she put her cell phone away in the refrigerator and then panicked for three hours when she couldn't find it. Another day, she brought Lucas to music class at the library but on the wrong day. And most recently, she and Lucas went to Cronig's for groceries, but Brynn found herself driving in the completely opposite direction, all the way to her parents' old house in Lobsterville. She reached the Orange Peel Bakery before she realized she had been zoned out the entire time. She pulled in and bought herself a cranberry scone, her hands shaking with the fear of what might have happened if she hadn't snapped back to reality.

What if she'd been wrong this entire time? Not just in the past few days, but the past few months, the past few years? What if Ross had been the bad guy since the beginning and she'd never seen it? Had she been so distracted, so in another world, that she'd completely ignored something right in front of her?

"*I know,*" Brynn said. "*Obviously.*" She felt tears dripping down her cheeks. She'd cried so much in the past few days—and in the past few months—that she marveled she had any tears left at all. They came on so fast, so urgently. There was no stopping them. "I'm doing my best, okay?"

"Brynn," Marcus said, "we're not criticizing you."

"Not at *all,*" Annie said. "We just want to help you."

"I'm *fine.*" Brynn didn't have time for this. She didn't need their pity. She didn't need their sympathy. She needed to be proactive. She needed to get answers. She needed to talk to Henry. And, as pissed off as she was, she still wanted to find the orange sun, whatever the hell it was. "There's just . . . a lot I have to figure out. The orange sun . . ."

"Brynn, maybe it's time to stop being a detective," Marcus said. "I thought you said you'd hit pause on that."

"Yeah, this doesn't have to be all on you," Annie said.

"You don't understand. There are answers that I need to find.

And . . . I mean, I still don't know that Jacob's innocent, not really. Or Mauricio. Why am I the only one who thinks it's strange that Ross is the *only* suspect? I saw Mauricio, you know, and he seemed . . . he definitely seemed suspicious." As Brynn spoke, she heard her words and how hollow they sounded, how uninformed, how futile. She herself didn't even believe what she was saying. "I just need answers."

"We know," Ginny said. "But you also need to take care of yourself."

The group eyed one another, as if they were waiting for someone to say something else.

"Seriously," Brynn said, "I'm fine. We're going to Margaux and Henry's. I told Margaux we'd come over. I need to go. Thanks for coming, but . . . I'm okay. Really." She couldn't look her friends in the eyes. She knew she sounded crazy. She knew that they had no logical reason to believe that Ross was innocent anymore, or that any of her missions made any sense.

"Okay," Ginny said, "we're here if you need us."

Once her friends left, Brynn took a shower while Lucas was still napping. Their shower had glass doors and faced the mirror above their sink. She let the hot water scald her back, and she cried. She washed herself, feeling like a stranger in her own skin, like some kind of malleable, floating entity, so far from what she'd been before.

The fancy bath products gifted to her from well-meaning friends only worsened her mood. No body scrub would erase the trauma of Lucas's birth. No conditioner would instantly bring back all her hair that had broken off. No soap would make her feel like herself again. And yet she knew she was so lucky to have a shower, to have soap, to have a body to wash at all. That knowledge, too, made her feel worse.

Out of the shower, she rubbed lotion on her skin. Her C-section scar was still purple and fresh, dotted with pubic hair that she was told never to shave during the healing process. She threw on her usual outfit. Her old clothes stared at her as if she'd abandoned them by choice. She wasn't sure she could ever wear them again, as much as she wanted to. It wasn't just the weight gain from pregnancy, it was the way her body had completely changed shape, too. Her hips had expanded, her stomach had softened, leaving her belly button a wrinkled canyon, and her breasts had become entirely foreign beings to her, like they no longer belonged on her body at all.

She was embarrassed to admit it to anyone, but sometimes, when she ran errands with Lucas, at Cronig's or Granite, Brynn secretly hoped that a stranger might assume she was Lucas's nanny or babysitter, rather than his mom. Even though she was the same age as many other moms she knew, she felt like she was younger than them, somehow. Yes, she had a child, but no, she didn't feel like a mother.

But no one ever mistook her for a babysitter. It was obvious, she knew, that she was Lucas's mom, not just because they shared certain distinct features, with dark eyes, porcelain skin, and chestnut hair, but because she looked exhausted. She looked like her definition of a *mom*. When the teenage cashiers checked her out, she always wanted to tell them *I was young once, too. I wasn't always like this. I used to be like you.* But she never did. She was invisible.

Lucas woke soon after. Brynn quickly restocked his diaper bag.

She went to get him out of the bassinet. He stared up at her. He looked *just* like Ross, the spitting image of him. It was so unfair, she felt, how newborns almost always looked like their fathers, and less like their mothers.

Brynn had read somewhere once that babies looked more like their fathers at first so that the fathers would feel more of an attachment to them and wouldn't abandon them. Brynn had shared this with her friends at the playground, and Marcus had shot her a disapproving look.

"That sounds like a bunch of crap," he'd said. "Obviously Liam isn't my biological child, and we look nothing alike. But I couldn't love him more." Liam's biological mother was a fourteen-year-old in Texas. Liam's hair and skin were both pale white, and his eyes were sparkling blue. Marcus had the dark skin and structured cheekbones of his Wampanoag ancestors. "I mean, seriously," he added, "that's ridiculous."

"I just read it somewhere," Brynn said. "I'm not saying it's true."

Brynn agreed that it was probably bullshit, but in Lucas's case, he really did look just like his father. Sometimes Brynn wondered if she'd ever find a sign of herself in her son. Maybe once he started talking, he'd sound like her, or maybe he'd have the same vehement aversion to peas, or maybe he'd love swimming, like she did. For now, though, all she saw when she looked at him was her husband.

"Come on," she said to Lucas, hoisting him up. "We're going to see Grandma and Grandpa."

CHAPTER 23

Henry and Margaux's house felt heavy with grief, like they were properly mourning the death of Cecelia. The house was quiet. When Brynn stepped inside, clutching Lucas to her chest, it was as if she were stepping into an igloo. The air conditioner was on high, the lights were off, and the shades were drawn.

"Hello?" she said. She'd texted Margaux before she left, letting her know they were stopping by.

She heard voices coming from the living room. She put down Lucas's diaper bag and slowly walked toward them. Her phone buzzed. Annie was calling. Brynn ignored it. She'd have to call her later. She couldn't deal with hearing—or giving—another apology right now.

Henry and Margaux sat in the living room's club chairs, which flanked the stone fireplace. Margaux was dressed in her usual slim white jeans and crisp button-down, but Henry was still in his pajamas. For a moment, he looked like a little boy, home from school with a stomach bug. Something about the way he sat in the chair, with the light cotton of his pajamas draping over his body, made Brynn feel like she'd intruded on them. The sight felt far too intimate.

"Brynn," Margaux said. "Good morning. How are you doing?"

Without waiting for a response, Margaux moved toward her to take Lucas from her arms. Brynn did not object; she handed Lucas over, and he happily nestled into his grandmother's embrace.

"Okay. Very tired," she said. "Exhausted, actually. How are you both?"

Henry didn't answer; he stared into his coffee mug. His eyes were blank.

"We're doing the best we can," Margaux said. "We're just in shock, really. We still haven't processed what's happened. How Ross could . . . do something like this."

Brynn realized that the house was not full of grief for Cecelia. Henry and Margaux were grieving Ross. It was as though *he* had died. Whoever their son was, it seemed that they'd made up their minds that he no longer existed, and now they mourned the son they used to have. And really, Brynn couldn't blame them. There was so much evidence stacked against Ross. It felt insurmountable.

Lucas began to cry.

"I have a bottle," Brynn began to say.

"Why don't you let me?" Margaux asked. "I've got the guest room all set up with the crib, still, so how about I feed him and put him down?"

"That would be great, thank you, Margaux," she said.

"And you just sit down, relax," Margaux said. "Maybe even take a nap yourself." She smiled at her and then disappeared down the hallway with Lucas.

Brynn waited until she heard the guest room door upstairs close.

"Henry," she said, trying to seize her moment alone with him, "how are you really doing? I haven't had a chance to talk to you."

He turned to her.

"I'm sad," he said. "This is just a terrible mess. What happened to Cecelia was just awful. Awful. But there's got to be an explanation for it. An accident. I just don't think our Ross would . . . he could never. Could he?"

Henry's voice wasn't weak. It was strong and clear. Brynn could hear in his voice what she perceived to be genuine concern and confusion. He sounded just like she did. It was almost as if Henry had been waiting to talk to her alone just as much as she had been waiting to talk to him.

"No," she said. "I mean, I certainly don't think Ross could ever do this. But, you know, there's so much evidence against him. It's hard to know what to think right now."

"Mmm," Henry said. "Right."

"I'm wondering," Brynn asked, picking her words carefully, "about that last night. You were there, at the club, right? Do you remember anything . . . that stood out? With Cecelia? Or Ross?"

Henry looked up at her. His expression had changed. Just for a second, his eyes were no longer blank. They sparked with recognition and awareness. They lit up with fear.

"What do you mean?" he asked.

"I'm just trying to figure out how all this . . . unraveled," she said.

"I . . . We spoke that night. But we always talked. I enjoyed talking to her very much," Henry said.

"What did you talk about?" Henry couldn't be pushed, she knew that. She had to be careful.

"Oh," he said, rubbing his eyes, "I told her too much. I don't know. It was nice to be around someone who wanted to listen. Who cared what I had to say. . . . She listened to my stories . . . she . . ." His voice trailed off, as if he was trying to remember.

This was exactly the kind of thing Henry had said lately that made his family feel like he was . . . well, *losing it,* as Sawyer had said. It was a vague sentimentalism, as if he was trying to conjure memories from long ago but couldn't quite articulate it.

"Why do you think you told her too much, Henry?"

"I just . . . I burdened her. She didn't need to know all of my mistakes. And God knows I've made plenty."

"Like what?" Brynn asked, her voice coming out as a whisper. She cleared her throat. "Was it something that happened a long time ago?"

Henry didn't say anything. He looked down at his hands, which were balled into fists.

"No one else would listen to me," he said, still looking down. "Margaux wouldn't. I had to tell someone."

Brynn heard the guest room door upstairs open and close. Margaux's footsteps echoed down the stairs.

"What *happened,* Henry?" Brynn asked. "Please."

Henry only shook his head. Brynn opened her mouth to ask him more, but Margaux stepped in, a burp cloth slung over her shoulder and an empty bottle in her hand.

"He's down," she said, holding up the bottle. "He drank all six ounces, too. He was hungry." Even with everything going on, Brynn still managed to feel like an inadequate mother at the suggestion that Lucas had been hungry.

Brynn had lost the moment with Henry. But it had given her enough to get the wheels in her mind turning. Henry *must* have been the one to kill Cecelia; she knew it before but now she knew for certain. Or maybe he asked Mauricio to do it for him, and that's why Mauricio had been such a wreck and gone into hiding at first. The only logical explanation for everything was that Henry had been behind it all, one way or another. And for some reason, he'd let Ross take the fall for it.

But that was the part that Brynn couldn't understand.

Unless Ross was in on it, too.

"I think it's time for *you* to take a nap, now," Margaux said to Henry, placing her hand on his shoulder.

Something had shifted in the air since Margaux had gone to put Lucas down. Brynn suddenly felt that she was an intruder in the family, that her presence wasn't wanted. But now Lucas was asleep; she couldn't just wake him up now and leave. It would look too alarming, too suspicious.

"That's a good idea, honey," Henry said. "I think I'll do that." He rose from the couch, pushing his palms onto his thighs. He plodded up the stairs. Brynn wanted to yell out to him, to find some reason for him to come back, for him to finish telling her what he'd started to say. But he was gone.

"Thank you," Brynn said to Margaux, "for putting Lucas down."

"You know I love nothing more," Margaux said. "Brynn, why don't we both sit down and talk. Let's take a break. You deserve to just relax. If that's even possible right now."

Brynn could feel her throat tightening. Her breasts felt sore; she needed to pump, but she hadn't come prepared for that.

"Okay," Brynn said, sitting down.

Margaux sat across from her and folded her legs. She held the burp cloth in her hands and twisted it. Brynn could see the whites of her knuckles.

"Sometimes we don't want to see what's right in front of us," Margaux said. "A lot of this is my fault, you know. I blame myself, I really do."

"What do you mean?" Brynn asked.

"I tried to raise my boys to be good men. To do the right thing. But I put too much pressure on Ross, I think. He had this drive to be perfect. You know what I'm talking about. He would do anything to achieve the things he wanted."

Brynn nodded but didn't say anything.

"I think we all had this vision of who Ross was," Margaux continued. "He was my perfect little boy. Except . . . maybe he wasn't. And I refused to see it, because I always loved him so much. He was my baby. But it was all right in front of me. How could I not have seen the signs?"

"He's still your son," Brynn said, her words startling her. "Have you completely given up on him? What about his side of the story?"

"Brynn, what could his story possibly be?" Margaux asked. "I feel like a terrible mother saying this, but all the evidence is right there. It's just undebatable." She shook her head. "I planned on fighting for Ross this whole time, believe me, I did. But with everything that's come out . . . I don't see how there's any other version of the truth."

"Maybe," Brynn said. "Except for one thing."

"What's that?" Margaux asked.

"The fact that you and I both know, deep down, no matter *what* the evidence says, that Ross just wouldn't do this. You *know* him. You *know* he couldn't do this. Margaux, you have to believe that. Right?"

Margaux looked away. She started to fold the burp cloth into squares, over and over, until it became a compact little cube.

"I'd like to believe that, yes," she said. "I didn't think he was capable of this. But I have to believe it now. What's the alternative? At what point do we just let go?"

Brynn sighed. She felt her phone buzz and checked it. Annie had called her again.

Brynn texted her: *Can't talk now. Call you soon.*

"I'm going to make us some tea," Margaux said, retreating to the kitchen.

Margaux's abandonment of Ross had surprised Brynn. She thought that Margaux would believe Ross's innocence until the very end, maybe even more so than Brynn. But perhaps Margaux's change of heart was a survival mechanism. Maybe it was too painful to keep fighting for something that she might not ever win. After all, Margaux wasn't used to that.

While Brynn waited, she scrolled through her phone. Her photos app alerted her to a collection of memories from the first summer that she and Ross dated. She usually ignored these alerts. Lately, while she was trapped on the couch breastfeeding, they only made her sad and nostalgic for her old life. But she clicked the album anyway.

A series of photos of Brynn and Ross swirled across the screen: fishing on the Menemsha jetty, an after-dinner selfie at Atria, drinking dirty bananas at Donovan's Reef, hiking to the Brickyard. She paused on a photo of the two of them at the Hot Tin Roof. It was the last year before it closed, right when she and Ross had started dating. They were so young. Back then, the Hot Tin Roof was the coolest place to go at night on the island. They had the best bands and musicians—legendary acts from all over the world. The venue had a way of bringing together people from all parts of the island, too. Down-island royalty like Ross, and up-island free spirits like Brynn.

The night the photo was taken, they'd gone to see Toots and the Maytals. The show was epic and electric, the air full of energy and joy. They'd danced for hours, shouting out the words to "Country Road" and "Pressure Drop," jumping and swaying their hips until they were drenched in sweat. Someone had taken a picture of the two of them on the dance floor, Brynn standing in front of Ross, his arms around her from behind. They were both tan, happy, in love.

She looked closer. Behind them, she could see the bar, the side exit out to the patio, and the iconic Margot Datz mural on the wall, a pair of lovers dancing by the sea, the bright tangerine glow of the setting sun illuminating the clouds and water behind them.

Brynn suddenly gasped.

That was it: the orange sun.

It *had* to be. The photo represented exactly what Ross had told her to focus on: *Us. You and me.* The very thing she'd disconnected from months ago, before Cecelia's death.

And still—it didn't make sense. The Hot Tin Roof had closed years ago. It was now a gourmet food store and a fish market. The murals had been relocated to the Martha's Vineyard Museum. But what could the mural itself contain that would unlock anything? Brynn bit her lip. She'd go to the museum after this, she decided. The answer must be there. It had to be.

But then she remembered: Ross had this photo framed in his office at work. She'd seen the photo a million times. She'd seen it just a few days ago when she went there to look around. It had been right in front of her the whole time.

Her phone buzzed with a text from Annie: *Call me ASAP.* Brynn tucked her phone away; she couldn't deal with being reprimanded by her friends for *playing detective* right now. She had to stay focused.

Margaux returned with two cups of tea.

"Thank you," Brynn said to her. She took a deep breath. She knew that she couldn't give herself away to Margaux—she didn't want to drag her into this, especially not when Margaux was clearly in the midst of her own emotional response to everything. But she was itching to get out of there as fast as she could and run to Ross's office.

"I think you and Lucas should stay with us for a while," Margaux said. "We've got room. And it's not healthy for you to be alone with the baby right now."

"That sounds nice," Brynn said, going along with it. "I'll think about it tonight. It's hard being alone."

"Well, it's important for us to all stay close, now." Margaux took a sip of her tea. "We have to stick together and, well, just keep going. We have to keep looking to the future."

Brynn nodded. "It's hard for me to do that right now," she said.

"Well," Margaux said, "life must go on. Someday, Lucas can take over Nelson & Sons."

Brynn had to stop herself from laughing. She'd never thought that far ahead about Lucas's career. He was a newborn baby! And in a way, part of her had always hoped that Lucas would leave the Vineyard. Even though she'd made the decision to come back, and she wouldn't want to raise him anywhere else, she hoped that he'd find his way off-island someday, in the bigger world.

"After all," Margaux continued, "that's why we've done everything we've done. Why Henry and I have worked so hard. For our family. Our legacy. What's the point of building something if you don't have children to pass it down to?"

"Right," Brynn said. She felt a surprising swell of gratitude—and guilt—for her own parents just then. They hadn't been the most involved, or even the most supportive, but one thing they'd never prevented Brynn from doing was pursuing her own path. They'd always encouraged her to be whoever she wanted to be. Maybe their push for her to be independent wasn't rooted in a lack of love but a desire for her to be the architect of her own life.

"Lucas is very lucky to have you and Henry," Brynn said. "So am I." She pursed her lips and blew onto the surface of her tea.

"And we're lucky to have you, too, Brynn. I know how hard this has been. A nightmare. None of us saw this coming. How could we?" She shook her head. "I just keep wondering what I did wrong, as a mother."

"Margaux, you are literally the best mother I know." Brynn meant it; Margaux was the most devoted mother she'd ever met. She'd truly do *anything* for her boys, for her family. "You can't think that way."

"Well, I've made my mistakes. Just like anyone else," she said. "But you're right. I shouldn't think that way. I guess I need to find a way to just . . . accept this new reality."

Brynn wanted to reach out and hug Margaux, to tell her that none of this was her fault, and that she was going to find the truth.

"I know" was all Brynn could say.

"I'm just glad I still have my sweet Sawyer," Margaux said. "He's going to really need to step up. But I think he's ready."

Brynn heard Lucas cry from the other room. It was one of the first times that the sound of his cry made her feel intense relief rather than panic. She was so glad he was awake. She sprang from her chair; she had to get to the office as fast as she could and find that photo.

"I've got it," she said, and she bolted up the stairs. Lucas stopped crying when she came in the room and picked him up. She changed him as fast as she could and brought him downstairs.

Margaux had started prepping dinner in the kitchen, chopping onions, carrots, and celery.

"I'm making my Bolognese for dinner," she said. "Do you want to come back tonight?"

How Margaux could focus on what to make for dinner and act like everything was okay was something Brynn couldn't understand. But that was how Margaux coped, she'd learned—by finding comfort in the ordinary and the mundane, the return to the routines. It was how she found control.

"Sounds delicious," Brynn said. "But I think we're going to stay home tonight. Get organized for next steps." She had no intention of moving in with Margaux and Henry, but she wanted Margaux to think that she did.

"Okay. We'll talk later," Margaux said. She gave Brynn a stiff hug, her arms tightly gripping Brynn's shoulders and back. Brynn opened her mouth to tell Margaux what she knew—what she suspected—but she didn't. She was so close to finding the truth, she couldn't tell her more until she knew what she was dealing with. She didn't want to put Margaux in any more danger.

She pulled out of the driveway and headed toward the Nelson & Sons office. She gripped the steering wheel, her hands shaky. Her phone rang again. *Annie.* She'd forgotten to call her back.

"Sorry, sorry!" Brynn blurted when she answered. "I got caught up at Henry and Margaux's, but I think I figured out what . . ."

"*Stop,*" Annie said. "Stop, Brynn. Something's happened."

"What? What do you mean?" Brynn felt her heart jump. She looked in the rearview mirror and breathed a sigh of relief when she saw Lucas safely strapped into his car seat, sucking on his thumb.

"It's Ginny," Annie said. "She's in the hospital."

"Oh my God," Brynn said. "She's in labor?"

"Not exactly," Annie said. "She's in Boston. At Mass General. They medevacked her about an hour ago. We've been trying to reach you."

Brynn's heart sank. She couldn't even remember the last time she'd asked Ginny how *she* was feeling. She hadn't even thought about it. She'd only been thinking about herself. About whether she knew who her husband really was, whether she should have chosen Sawyer instead, whether she was a good mom, whether she was meant to be a mom at all, what the orange sun meant, what crimes Henry had committed, what Jacob knew or didn't know, where Mauricio had been. She hadn't thought enough about Cecelia, or Ginny, or anyone else. And for *what*? She still didn't have the answers. She might never have them.

Ginny had needed her, and Brynn hadn't been there.

"We can't go to Boston yet," Annie said. "The best thing for us to do is stay here. The kids are at Ginny's mom's house. They're all fine. Obviously, Trey is with her. And Marcus is driving up now to drop off a bag of her things."

"But," Brynn stammered, "but what happened? Is she okay? Is . . . is the baby okay?"

"I honestly don't know right now. We have to wait. We're getting updates from Trey."

Brynn could feel the air slipping out of her lungs. She tried to inhale but couldn't catch her breath. She'd reached the Nelson & Sons office. The parking lot was empty. She pulled in and turned off the ignition.

"I'm sorry, Annie," Brynn said. "I'm so sorry."

"You don't have anything to apologize for," Annie said. "And our girl is going to be okay. And she has the best medical care in the world. We've made sure of it."

Brynn was crying. Somehow, even though she knew it wasn't logical, she felt that this was all her fault. She'd been so mad at Ginny for looking into the Nelsons behind her back and talking to Ross about it. Maybe she'd been too hard on her. And what had Brynn been thinking, dragging Ginny deeper into her own family's drama? She never should have put her stress onto Ginny—onto all of her friends. Maybe if she'd let Ginny stay out of it, then Ginny and her baby would be okay.

But now Ginny's worst fear, the one that had loomed over her during all of her pregnancies, the one that Brynn had told her not to worry about, had come to life. And there was nothing Brynn could do.

"I'll keep you posted," Annie said.

"Thanks," Brynn told her. "I'll be here."

When she hung up, she looked back at Lucas. He was awake, but just silently watching her. His eyes were wide and curious.

"I'm sorry to you, too," Brynn said to him. "I'm sorry about all of it. Let's go grab something inside really quick and then we're out of here, okay?" She wiped her eyes. She felt like a failure in every way.

She used the key under the doormat to open the front door, and pushed it open with one arm, carrying Lucas in his car seat in the other. The office was dark and empty, almost as if it had been deserted.

Ross's office had the familiar smell of him—pine and juniper berries.

She spotted the framed photo of the two of them at the Hot Tin Roof immediately. She picked it up. The metal frame was cold in her hands.

"Got it. Now let's get out of here," she said to Lucas, taking the photo with her.

CHAPTER 24

Ginny's house did not look like it belonged to a family in distress. It was so full of life that when Brynn stepped inside, she swore she heard the patter of little footsteps, the bouncing of rubber balls, the splashing of water in a bathtub, the monotonous but joyful tune of "The Wheels on the Bus." But it was empty; no one was home.

"Hello?" she said, as she walked in, knowing that she wouldn't get a response, but checking anyway.

She lugged Lucas inside with her and sat down to feed him. She'd been in Ginny's house countless times over the years, but never when Ginny or anyone else wasn't there. It felt strange, being in her house without her or Trey or the kids. But she knew it was the right place for her to be. It had been unlocked.

After she fed and burped Lucas, and did some tummy time with him, and bounced him around in her arms, she put him down for a nap on a baby pouf that Ginny kept in the living room for when she and Lucas visited.

She took the framed photo of her and Ross out of her bag and held it. There was a slight bulge protruding from the back side of it.

She started to disassemble the frame but stopped. She put it down on the kitchen desk instead, not ready. The desk was scattered with mail, books, birthday party invitations, some receipts. The chaos of a busy family. The photo looked right there, among the mess. Except it didn't belong there at all.

Brynn rolled up her sleeves.

She cleaned the kitchen first. She scrubbed the inside of the oven, she wiped away grease from the fan above the stove, she soaked and washed each of the burners. She took apart the fridge and cleaned each shelf. She threw out moldy fruit and some wilted lettuce. She vacuumed and mopped the floors, getting down on her knees to scrub the baseboard moldings. She did the same in the bathrooms, and she scoured the toilet until it was pure white. She stripped all the beds, gathered up all the used towels, and ran everything through the washing machine. She dusted the bookshelves, she disinfected the kids' toys, she lifted couch cushions to vacuum away crumbs and hairs. She sprayed and wiped every window until she could see her reflection clearly in each pane.

Brynn knew that what she was doing wouldn't make up for the pain that Ginny was in. She knew that what she was doing might not even be wanted. But she had to do something. She had to give her friend *something*, even if it was as menial as giving her a clean house to come back to. Maybe, deep down, the work was for herself, more than it was for Ginny, but Brynn needed to do something that brought her back to reality, that brought her back to the day-to-day tasks of life that she'd felt prisoner to but that now felt comforting in their simplicity, their structure of beginning, middle, and end. Cleaning Ginny's house was something she could control, something she could offer, in a situation when no one could control anything. There was nothing else Brynn could do while she waited for her friend. Nothing else she could say to her that would make her friend's fear lessen, nothing she could give her that would replace the child she so desperately wanted to have.

When she finished, she was sweating, and thirsty. She poured herself a glass of water and drank, then had another. There was just one load of laundry left to dry, and one bed to make, and she would be completely done. She sat down. Lucas was still sleeping. Brynn had been cleaning nonstop for two hours.

She picked up the photo. She was ready. She peeled back the little metal tabs of the frame and lifted the cardboard out. A square of tightly folded paper fell out.

Brynn held it in her hands. It seemed to be two pieces of paper condensed into something smaller than a playing card. But it felt heavy in her hands, impossibly heavy. She knew it contained the answers she'd been looking for. She knew that once she unfolded those papers, she could never fold them back up. She could never unsee whatever they held.

She suddenly wished she'd never found them at all. She wished she hadn't been able to figure out what Ross meant by *the orange sun*. Life would be easier if she could have let herself believe that he was innocent. Life would be easier if she could turn her back on him. But she had to face the truth now, even if it meant fighting for a husband who she felt hadn't been fighting for her in months.

Brynn sat down. Before she opened the paper, she picked up her phone and she called Ross. His phone was with the police, and she knew that. It had been taken as evidence right away. It went straight to voicemail, as she knew it would. But she still wanted to say something to him. Even if he might never hear it. She needed to.

"Ross. It's me," she said. "I know this is crazy. You're not here. I'm here . . . I'm . . . lost. And I'm trying to figure out how we got here. Where things went wrong. I'm trying to find answers." She took a breath. She thought about the vows they shared during their wedding. They wrote their own. *I promise to let you have the last word,* Ross had said, laughing. *And I promise to listen.*

"All I ever wanted was to be a family with you," she continued. "We wanted the same things. Remember? Do you remember? We wanted the same things because we shared something, you and me. We had the same . . . *spark*. But then, when Lucas was born, I felt like I lost that spark. And you should have helped me get it back. You should have tried harder for me, Ross. I got lost, and you never tried to find me. I know you think I'm so strong all the time. You think I can handle anything. But I can't. And I need you to admit that. I need you to admit that I'm not perfect all the time. That *life* isn't perfect all the time. I've been so afraid of letting you down. But I'm not afraid anymore. The fact is, Ross, you've let *me* down. You haven't been there for me. I need help. I'm not happy. I can't do this alone, and right now, I feel alone. More alone than I've ever felt in my life." Brynn felt relief. She had more to say—so much more—but this was a start. "I want to believe you. I really do. But it's getting hard, Ross. I still don't understand. I just . . . I don't know what to believe. I still love you. But I just don't know. Things need to change."

She hung up, feeling uneasy now that her voicemail was out there, out of her reach. Permanent.

She was ready to open the letter now. She sat down and unfolded the paper carefully, as if it might explode.

It was a handwritten note, signed by Henry.

Brynn began to devour it.

The letter explained everything . . . and yet, nothing at all. If the letter was real—if what Henry had *confessed to* in the letter was true—then Brynn finally understood what Ross had been trying to tell her all along: that Henry's crimes went far beyond Cecelia's murder and were much darker than anything he'd done with his company. And it wasn't just what the letter revealed, it was the fact that Henry had kept it so well hidden for decades. Not only did no one suspect Henry of anything, but he was highly esteemed, respected, *revered*. He was a leader. He was a devoted father. He'd held Brynn's own child with tenderness and care. She didn't understand how the person who wrote the letter and the person she thought she knew could be the same. But they were. They had been all along. And that's what Ross had been trying to keep her from.

The letter was dated just a few days before Cecelia was killed.

To My Beloved Family,

In the summer of 2008, I hired a promising young man named Gabriel Barbosa. I hired him right off the steamship. He was living somewhere on the Cape, though I never knew where. I think he had friends on the island who'd told him there was good work here. He was from Sao Paolo, Brazil, and he wanted to make money to send back to his family. Told me he could run any machine and would work longer and harder than anyone. So, I hired him.

Back then, we were all hiring guys under the table. My company had been doing well, though we were just getting started. I had two boys to provide for now, and a wife. We wanted things. But then, the recession hit. All the jobs got halted. Everything stopped. The jobs we still had, we had to finish—fast, and cheap. We were all cutting corners to make it work. We were all hiring illegals right off the boat, paying them nothing, paying them under the table. It's just how it was done back then.

I was stressed that summer. At my limit. This one job, in particular . . . it was like it was cursed. We hit a water line, we hit the electric line, the foundation was set too high, everything kept getting messed up. It was way out by Edgartown Great Pond. Dozens of acres, this property. No one around. So, we worked late into the night most days. One night, I'm out there with Gabriel, just the two of us. I was really riding him hard. Too hard. But we had to get it done.

I was in the excavator. I didn't usually work in the machines, not anymore. I didn't even have my hoisting license anymore. By then, I was overseeing the jobs. But I was doing whatever I could to finish. Something went wrong. Something with the excavator tracks. Gabriel, he was good with machines. So, I told him to go down there and check it out, see what was wrong. I thought I'd put the machine in park. I really did. I could have sworn I did. But when he was down there, I let my foot off the pedal and I ran right over him. It happened fast. I don't think he suffered.

At that point, though she wasn't done, Brynn had to put the letter down. She needed a break. *I don't think he suffered.* Brynn imagined Henry writing these words out, telling himself that this man didn't suffer—for what? To make himself feel better about what he'd done? She pictured all the happy times she'd shared with Henry over the years: the graduations, her wedding, anniversaries, summer barbecues, Lucas's birth. How had Henry been able to enjoy life—or pretend to enjoy life—when he'd committed such a despicable crime? How had he been able to look his family in the eyes, expect their trust, expect their love, when he had taken someone's life? Who *was* Henry? Brynn wasn't sure she could even keep reading. Her head was throbbing, and she felt her coffee start to rise up in her throat. She took a deep breath and continued to read. She had to.

That night, I took Gabriel's body, and I buried him deep in the woods of that property. No one would ever go back there, I knew. I used the same excavator that killed him to dig his grave. And then I poured concrete over him. Covered it up with a few tons of fill. And drove home.

When I went back the next day, I checked the spot. It looked exactly as it had before. Like nothing had ever happened.

And, after a while, that's how I felt. Or I guess I convinced myself that nothing had happened. Life went on. I got busier. Kids got older. I shut the door on the past.

But then, when I found out I was becoming a grandfather, something changed. I couldn't pretend anymore. I tried to find Gabriel's family. But I couldn't. I didn't know anything about the kid. I confessed it all to Pete Hammers. I was ready for him to put me behind bars. But . . . Jesus, it's gotten so complicated. He wouldn't do anything about it, because he and I . . . we'd been working together for a long time already. I'd built the success of my business by cutting corners that Pete allowed me to cut. In exchange for cash. We barely ever even spoke of the agreement, but over the years it just kept esca-

lating. Anything I wanted that I wasn't supposed to have, I could get, as long as he got a share, too. At one point, someone called the police to say that Gabriel was missing, and they thought I had something to do with it, because I was his employer and basically his only island contact. Another Brazilian guy, probably another worker he'd become buddies with on the ferry every morning. But Pete shut it down. Took the report and blocked it.

Brynn gasped. The police report was about Gabriel, this whole time. Gabriel *did* have at least one person who was looking for him, who cared about him, and who took the time to call the police to say something. But Pete had just silenced them, and it was never mentioned again. Gabriel disappeared.

And eventually, Margaux and I built a new house, we'd sent both the boys to college. I wasn't about to throw it all away. But something about becoming a grandfather changed that. I'm ashamed of what I've done. I'm remorseful.

I tried to tell anyone that would listen. The last person I told tried to use it against me. She wanted money from me in exchange for her silence. I told her I didn't want her silence; I wanted her help. I wanted her to make it right. But it's like nobody cared.

So, I'm telling you. I'm telling you because I can't take it anymore. And because I'm sorry. I'm so sorry for what I've done. But I can't undo it.

I can't live like this anymore. Please. Forgive me.

Brynn put the letter down. Henry had planned to take his own life. That must have been why he'd been acting so out of sorts, so distant, so aloof. He wasn't *losing it,* he was just consumed with guilt and remorse. Ross must have convinced him not to go through with it. He wouldn't let him do that to himself, to his family, even after discovering what he'd done to Gabriel all those years ago.

The pieces were starting to fit together. Henry must have confessed all of this to Cecelia in an attempt to tell someone outside of the family—someone with high morals, who he knew would turn him in. But even she had let him down. Even she hadn't cared. Like Jacob had said, Cecelia wanted to extort him. She didn't care about justice for Gabriel. So Henry had nowhere else to turn. Maybe Cecelia's indifference and callousness had set something off inside of him that made him take her life, too. Or maybe he changed his mind and regretted telling Cecelia the truth. It would have left him with no choice other than to kill her. The security footage, Brynn thought, must have been doctored and planted by Pete, in order to protect Henry.

Brynn ran to the kitchen sink that she had just thoroughly cleaned, and she vomited. When she was done, she wiped her eyes and drank some water from the tap.

She felt sick thinking about Margaux going to bed every night with Henry, and how she'd cared for his sons, nursed them, loved them, made a home for them, carried the mental load of motherhood and partnership for decades. Margaux had devoted her entire *life* to Henry, and yet Brynn wondered if Margaux knew the real him at all. And if Brynn told her what she'd found, would Margaux even believe her? Would she *want* to believe her?

Margaux had spent her whole life protecting her family. But now, it was Brynn's turn. She picked up her phone and called her mother-in-law.

"Margaux?" she said, packing up her things and turning off the lights of Ginny's house. "We need to meet. I found something. I found a clue that Ross told me to find. A letter that Henry wrote. I still don't know how Ross had it. It . . . it explains a lot. But I need you to come alone. Where's Henry? Are you safe?"

Margaux didn't say anything, but Brynn could hear her breathing, thinking, waiting to respond. What if Henry was there with her, listening? What if Margaux needed her help right now? Brynn started to panic. Maybe she should go there, she thought. But do what? How would she protect Margaux? Would she be too late?

"Henry has been lying to you," Brynn continued, her voice hushed. "You need to leave. *Now.* Meet me at my house. And where's Sawyer? He needs to come, too." Brynn didn't want to see Sawyer. She couldn't handle that right now, but she knew that the three of them had to talk together.

It was the only way they'd figure out what to do—as a family. Without Henry.

CHAPTER 25

When Brynn had gone into labor with Lucas, her parents had rushed back to the island right away to be there for her. They stayed with some old friends in Vineyard Haven who had a guesthouse. Nobody except Ross could be in the hospital with Brynn, because of Covid, but they waited, on standby.

"Do you want me to come clean your house? Do some laundry? Get groceries?" her mother had asked when Brynn was first admitted to the hospital and was circling her room, occasionally bouncing on a ball to increase dilation.

"Thanks, but we're okay," Brynn had said. She didn't tell her that Margaux had already stocked their fridge and sent over her longtime house cleaner that very day, the moment Brynn and Ross left for the hospital.

"Don't even mention it, Brynn," Margaux had said to her, "it's nothing."

In all of Brynn's life, her parents only had professional cleaners come to the house one time, after a horde of cousins visiting from Colorado had stayed with them over Fourth of July weekend and subsequently trashed the place. Brynn's uncle had insisted on paying for cleaners, and Brynn's parents begrudgingly accepted. When Brynn had returned home after the cleaners were finished, she felt like she was stepping into a palace. Everything felt brand-new and lighter, the years of smudge marks and neglect lifted away. For days after that, Brynn had tried to make her bed exactly the same way the cleaners had done it, with tight, precise corners. She wiped down the bathroom sink after each time she brushed her teeth. She even tried to refold the end of the toilet paper roll into the same origami-like triangle that they'd left behind, but she never was quite able to get it right. And then, a week or so later, the house silently shifted back to how it was before, collecting dust and crumbs, and giving off that sticky, slightly moldy smell that Brynn could almost taste during the hot summer months. It was as if the cleaners had never come at all.

After Lucas was born, her doctor advised Brynn and Ross to limit visitors during the first few weeks. They were still in the pandemic and had to be careful about who held Lucas, who kissed him, who breathed on him.

"Mom," Brynn had told her mother on the phone from the hospital, "we should probably wait a few days before you guys see the baby." Brynn could feel her insides shifting around as she spoke. "The doctors say we have to limit exposure, even with family. I didn't really think about it before. I don't want to hurt your feelings, but . . . we just want to be safe."

"Oh," her mother had said. "I understand."

The truth was, Brynn *had* thought about it already. Margaux and Henry were already planning on being at their house when they left the hospital, waiting for them with open arms. Brynn had always planned on having her family and Ross's family *both* come see the baby and be around as much as possible during those first few days. But once the baby was born, she suddenly didn't want to see her parents, especially her mother. She *couldn't* see her. Margaux was so good at taking charge and at initiating help. Her instinct was to lead. She would bring food and supplies without being asked. She would buy whatever swaddle or onesies she'd read online were the best. Brynn felt comfortable sitting back and following Margaux's instructions. She didn't know what she was doing, but Margaux did.

Brynn's own mother, however, was deferential to Brynn, and that scared her. After the first few days had passed, and Brynn's parents came over, she started to feel aggravated by her mother's submission to her.

"Brynn, honey," her mother would say, "I think Lucas is constipated. What do you want me to do?" She'd look to Brynn for answers, but Brynn had none. How, she wondered, had her own mother raised her during those first few months? What had her mother done in rural Aquinnah, without internet and a cell phone, when Brynn had gotten sick as a newborn? Who did she talk to about the struggles of breastfeeding? How did she ever get Brynn to sleep through the night?

"Um," Brynn would usually respond, "I'll do bicycle legs with him. That usually helps."

Brynn put Lucas down on his back on the living room floor and held his legs, moving them in circular, bicycle pedal motions. Though Brynn didn't say so out loud, Margaux had taught her this trick to relieve Lucas's gas. But Brynn didn't want her own mother to know how heavily she was relying on her mother-in-law.

When she asked her mother how she managed during those newborn days, her mother simply shrugged.

"Things were different then. I just breastfed, and that was that. I mean, it was hard at first, but that's what I did. And you slept when you slept. There was no schedule, no blackout curtains, no sound machine. None of that nonsense." She looked at Brynn, realizing how she might have sounded, dismissing all of the gear Brynn had bought for Lucas, all of the toys and tools and gadgets meant to soothe and calm him. "I just mean that it was a different time."

"Right," Brynn said.

Brynn pushed her mother away during those first few weeks. Things were easier without her around to force her to question herself.

Even though no one ever asked her to do so, or made her do so, Brynn started to lean on Margaux more and more, and on her own mother less and less.

Brynn realized that her closeness with Margaux was probably the reason her mother had become distant. She'd tried her best to shield her mother from the deepening relationship she had developed with Margaux, but Brynn knew that her mother still saw it. The truth was, Brynn had pulled away from her mother, not the other way around. It wasn't Margaux's fault, either—she hadn't made Brynn choose. Brynn was the one who had abandoned her parents, her old life, her old self. She'd made it clear to her mother not just that she no longer needed her, but that she no longer wanted her.

Only now, Brynn yearned for the musty smell of her parents' old house, the creaky wood floors and the antique bathroom sink that was always brown around the drain, no matter how clean it was. She yearned for the comfort of that place, and the comfort of her own mother's ease with herself, her sunburned hands, the way she didn't try to be anything she wasn't, the way Brynn knew she was there for her even though she wasn't the type of mother she'd perhaps wanted her to be. Her stomach twisted in knots of guilt as she thought about the years she'd separated herself from the woman who had given her life, the woman who had raised her.

She thought back to the time when her mother told her they were selling their house and moving off-island. Brynn had just gotten engaged to Ross.

"Why would you move now?" Brynn had asked.

"Brynn, we can't afford to live here anymore," her mother had said. "What we can get for our house, it would be crazy not to take it. We can save that money, put it away, leave something for you when we die."

"Mom, stop," Brynn had said. "I thought we could plan my wedding together. And I thought you'd be around to see your grandkids. We've been talking about that, you know, having kids." Brynn remembered the way she used to talk about having children—like getting a dog, buying a new sofa, something fun and exciting but not necessarily life-altering or permanent.

"I'll always be around, Brynn. But we're barely getting by here. If we move off-island, we can actually afford to retire sometime soon." She had sighed and looked away from Brynn, as though it was too painful to make eye contact. "And, anyway," she added, "you have the Nelsons. You have Margaux. They're such a close family. I know they'll always support you."

Brynn's mother had hardly ever said a kind word about the Nelsons before this. Once she and Ross got engaged, though, it was as if her mother had submitted to them. As if she'd said to them, and to Margaux specifically, *You win. If this makes you happy, if this is what you want, then you win.*

As Brynn pulled into her driveway, she saw Sawyer's car parked in front. He sat on the steps, waiting for her. He looked relaxed, with his elbows propped behind him like kickstands. He stood up and waved. Margaux wasn't there yet.

Sawyer was so tall that his body swayed like a willow tree when he stood, his limbs dangling by his sides. He moved so fluidly, his stride consistent and calming but loose. Brynn thought about the way Ross's body looked on the security camera footage she'd seen—again and again in her mind. How his legs rotated with tightness and urgency, his body like an efficient machine, his feet pounding the ground beneath him.

The letter had explained so much, and yet it still didn't explain everything, and Brynn felt like she could scream because she knew she was so close but not there yet. It didn't explain the footage. It didn't explain the boat's satellite phone tracking. It didn't explain the hat. It didn't explain the golf club. It only explained what Cecelia must have known that got her killed. But after all this, it *still* wasn't enough.

Brynn was getting tired of trying to convince herself of things. She'd done enough of that for a lifetime. She wasn't ready to admit it yet, but maybe Ross had steered her toward the letter so that she'd divert her attention away from Ross and onto Henry. So that she'd somehow overlook all the clues attached to him, that were still, somehow, undeniable. So that she'd choose him again instead of Sawyer.

Sawyer opened the back door and started unclipping Lucas's car seat. Brynn's mind flashed to the image of them kissing—the feeling of their bodies so close together, the wetness of their mouths intertwined. She felt her face redden. Now was not the time to think about that, she told herself. But even now, she craved that feeling. The feeling of escape she got from the kiss, the way it transported her into another life, another body, another time. She was awful, she told herself, for liking it. She was awful for wanting it, and she was awful for thinking about it right now, when everything around her was imploding. When there were so many other, bigger things to worry about.

"Hi," Sawyer said. "How are you holding up?"

"I don't know," Brynn said. "My friend Ginny, she had to go to Mass General. I don't know if the baby's okay. I don't know if she's okay. And now . . . I . . . I have so much to tell you. So much to tell Margaux."

Sawyer put his hand on her back as they walked into the house. She was grateful he was there. She needed his support. She needed his trust.

As soon as they stepped in the house, Brynn felt her exhaustion kick in, and tears welled up.

"I'm so worried about Ginny. She's been through so much, and I haven't been there for her. I haven't been paying attention, Sawyer. And now Cecelia is gone, and it's not fair, and I just know, somehow, it's all my fault." She was sobbing heavily now, her body shaking with her cries.

"Brynn," Sawyer said, "none of this is your fault. You've been taking care of everyone—Lucas, Ross. You've been doing an amazing job throughout all of it. And you must be so tired. You just need to rest."

Brynn nodded. Sawyer was right. Her exhaustion had caught up with her. She wasn't thinking clearly. Maybe she wasn't thinking at all. Sawyer leaned in and wrapped his arms around her.

"It's going to be all right," he said. She inhaled his warm, salty smell.

It was so familiar to her, even after all these years. Time stood still with his arms around her. She felt safe.

"I'm going to go put Lucas down," Brynn said, wanting to remove herself from the situation before things went any further. "I'll be right back."

Her body relaxed when she stepped away and went into her room with Lucas. She thought about what Ross might be doing in that moment, and her heart hurt imagining him alone, while she was in their shared home with his brother, who had just told her he had *feelings* for her. Ross was still her husband; and she still believed him. Or she wanted to, anyway. She knew that what she and Sawyer had done was wrong, and she hated herself for having done it. But she hated herself more for having liked it.

When she came downstairs, Sawyer was leaning against the kitchen counter. He smiled when she walked in. Without saying anything, he began to lean toward her. So much of Brynn's physical being wanted to pull him close to her, to feel him on her mouth again, to connect with him. And so much of her didn't. But before their bodies touched, something caught her eye.

It was something small, almost entirely hidden, and certainly *meant* to be hidden from her. But she saw it, nevertheless. Poking out of the top of Sawyer's front jeans pocket was the tip of a neon-green key fob.

It was the key to Ross's boat.

CHAPTER 26

"Thanks, Sawyer. I . . . I don't know what I'd do without you," Brynn said as she released herself from his embrace. "I, um, I need to move some laundry along. I'll be right back." She could feel her voice quivering, her throat going dry. But Sawyer just nodded at her.

Brynn went into the mudroom and opened the washing machine. She grabbed some dirty clothes from the hamper and threw them in, just to make some noise to cover up the sound of her own shortened breaths. Her fingers trembled as she pushed the buttons to start the machine. She had to remind herself to breathe. She peered out of the mudroom to make sure Sawyer was still where she'd left him. He sat at the kitchen island, scrolling through his phone.

She needed a moment to think. She needed a moment to process what she'd just seen: Ross's boat keys. Brynn looked up at the spot on the wall where Ross always hung them. It was empty. How long had they been missing? She hadn't even noticed before. She silently screamed at herself for not having checked sooner. She *knew* that Ross kept his keys there. How could she *not* have checked? Had they been missing this whole time? She felt a wave of dizziness wash over her, as though her feet were leaving the floor and she was hovering above the ground, about to crash down at any moment.

If Ross had been the one to take his boat out that night, as the satellite phone had indicated, Brynn had no doubt that he would have brought the keys back and returned them to their spot. Ross would *never* misplace them. It just wouldn't be something he'd do. *Ever.*

And then she remembered too that as Ross had said, he never would have taken his lucky derby hat off the boat. But if Sawyer had been on Ross's boat, he would have been able to get his hat, and then plant it—or give it to Pete to plant instead. Or to Mauricio.

The video footage of Ross was too dark to see exactly what hat he had been wearing—that could have been *any* hat. But the one that had been sealed up in a plastic *evidence* bag that she'd held in her hands at the police station—that one must have been taken off the boat. Brynn was so mad at herself for not having been smart enough to realize this then, when Pete had first shown it to her. How could she have missed it! She could have spoken up and unraveled the lie then and there. But now, it was too late.

Brynn took her phone from her back pocket and hastily typed a message to Jacob: *Get here ASAP. It was Sawyer. He's here.*

"Need some help?" Sawyer asked, peering into the mudroom, startling her, just as she was putting her phone away.

"Oh, thanks, no, sorry." Brynn slammed the machine door shut and turned it on. She brushed past Sawyer into the living room and swept Lucas up in her arms.

"I, uh," she said, fumbling her words, "isn't your mom coming?"

"Brynn, do you need to sit down?" Sawyer asked. He got up from kitchen stool. "You seem sort of out of it. I think you should have some water, maybe rest."

"I'm fine," she said. "Just tired, like you said." She looked at Sawyer closely. She always saw him as the Sawyer she used to know: the boy on the docks in Menemsha. The black sheep of his family. Good, but misunderstood. Fumbling, free-spirited, but endlessly kind and sweet.

Even when she'd made her decision to be with Ross, and to turn her back on the past, she couldn't help but see Sawyer and feel something. But now, all she could see was a man she didn't know. Someone she might not have ever known. Had she always been blind to who he really was? Or had he changed somewhere along the way? The boy on the docks—did he exist the way she'd seen him, or was he something she'd conjured up because she'd needed him at the time? Or had he changed into this person because of *her*?

Brynn suddenly wished she could call Margaux and tell her not to come. She had to protect her now, even if it meant keeping her from her own son. There was no time, though, because just then, the door opened, and Margaux burst in.

"Hello?"

Brynn and Sawyer looked at each other. Brynn wasn't sure, but it felt like Sawyer knew that something had shifted between them just in the last few moments. She ran to the door to see Margaux, and to look at the hook on the wall where Ross hung the keys. They were now back in the spot, as if they'd always been there. For a moment, Brynn wondered if they *had* always been there. Was she sure she'd only seen them moments ago in Sawyer's pocket? She was so tired—was it possible that she'd imagined the whole thing?

Her mind reeled with what to say to Margaux, with how to get her alone to explain. It all fit together now, she thought: It was Sawyer who had killed Cecelia. It was Sawyer who had dumped her body out to sea. It was Sawyer who had plotted and planned this, having stolen one of Ross's golf clubs so that he could then plant it as the first major piece of evidence against his brother. And he'd done it all for Henry. He'd done it all *because* of Henry, to cover up all the horrible things he'd done so many years ago, because Henry was too much of a coward to truly come forward, and too much of a coward to take his own life. Sawyer had done it so that Henry would finally approve of him the way he'd always approved of Ross. He'd done it to hide the secret contained in the letter. And—perhaps—he'd done it so that he could rob Ross of the life he'd had and take it for himself. He'd done it, somewhat, for Brynn.

"Margaux," Brynn said. Her voice was shaky. She wasn't sure what her plan was—should she blurt out the truth to Margaux right now, in front of Sawyer? Or should she pretend that she knew nothing? She couldn't go to the police; she knew that much. Maybe she could call the FBI. She hadn't heard anything from Jacob. And what would Jacob be able to do, anyway? Even though Brynn had found the orange sun, and the letter, it still—after all this time—wasn't enough to prove Ross's innocence. All she really had was her own theories.

The only thing Brynn knew for sure was that she had to protect Lucas and Margaux. She couldn't let Margaux be implicated in anything. Ross had told her to keep her out of it all, and she owed that to him.

"Margaux, will you help me with something in the nursery?" Brynn asked. "I want to take Lucas's temperature, and you know how much he squirms around."

"Oh, sure," Margaux said, unloading her purse and washing her hands in the kitchen sink. "You said though that you wanted to talk to both of us. Brynn, what's going on?"

"I, uh, I just wanted to make sure you were both okay," Brynn said, almost stuttering. Margaux and Sawyer shared a look. "Really, the truth is that I just didn't want to be alone. I'm having a hard time." Brynn saw them both soften at the lie.

"Brynn, you are not alone. We're here for you. We're going to get through this together, remember?" Margaux held her by the shoulders. Brynn nodded. "Now, let's go take that baby's temperature."

Brynn looked back at Sawyer as she and Margaux headed upstairs to the nursery. She couldn't see the key fob poking out of his pocket anymore. Once upstairs, Brynn gently directed Margaux into the bathroom instead of the nursery.

"Margaux," Brynn whispered as soon as she shut the door. "I . . . I need to tell you something."

"Okay . . . what is it, Brynn?" Margaux looked concerned. Brynn was used to this look from people by now—it was a look of both pity and perplexity.

"I think I know what happened. To Cecelia. I think it was Sawyer. I . . . Basically, Henry told Cecelia something that he did a long time ago. He . . . well, I know this is going to sound crazy, Margaux, but he killed someone—a man, someone working for him—twenty years ago. It was an accident on the job, but he covered it up. And then, for some reason, he told Cecelia about it. I think he felt like no one would listen to him. He obviously regretted telling her, and had Sawyer kill her."

Margaux frowned. "Okay, this is . . . a lot. But, Brynn . . . then how do you explain the security camera footage? Or the golf club?"

"I . . . I don't know. But someone took Ross's boat out that night. And Sawyer has the keys. I saw them. He must have forgotten to put them back right away. And the hat—the hat they found at the club—it was from Ross's boat. He wouldn't have taken it off the boat." Brynn was talking so fast that she was nearly breathless. "I know this sounds . . . Well, it's a lot to take in."

"It is," Margaux said. "It's a lot. I'm just . . . I'm not sure I understand. What do you mean, Henry killed a man twenty years ago? And kept it from me all this time? You think he'd be capable of that?"

"Yes, Margaux, I do," Brynn said. "I now think he'd be capable of killing someone."

"That's not what I mean," Margaux said. "I meant, do you really think he'd be capable of keeping something like that from me for all this time?"

It was subtle, and sudden, but Brynn felt it. It was an unmistakable change in the air between them. Out of everything Brynn had just said, all Margaux had heard was that Brynn was still underestimating her role in the family.

"No, I mean . . ." Brynn wasn't sure what to say, or what Margaux was getting at. "I didn't mean to imply that you've been kept in the dark."

"Like some fool?" Margaux asked. "Like a woman whose husband has committed crimes that she had no idea about?"

Brynn knew that the comment was directed at her. *She* was the one with a husband behind bars right now, not Margaux. Until Ross was proven innocent, *she* was the fool, if anyone.

"Margaux," Brynn said, "not like a fool. Like a loving and trusting wife and mother who was blindsided by a manipulative husband."

"Well . . . why don't we just ask Sawyer, then?" Margaux suggested. Brynn was surprised. She wasn't *scared* of Sawyer; she felt, perhaps stupidly so, like he would never hurt her, or his mother. But she was scared of what he might say. "Come on."

They walked back downstairs. Sawyer was in the kitchen right where they'd left him, drinking a seltzer.

"Sawyer," Margaux said, "Brynn wants to ask you something." Brynn had never felt this kind of chill from Margaux before. Margaux was obviously mad at her, and letting her feel the brunt of it now.

"I . . . Did Henry force you to do something, Sawyer? To Cecelia? I won't think it's your fault. Just . . . tell me the truth. Did he make you do it?"

Lucas cried; Brynn was holding him tightly to her chest. He could feel how hot she was getting, how anxious. She needed to stay calm for him, but how could she right now? How could she do anything right now besides panic? She bounced him gently as she walked, trying to stay close to the door, deciding whether she could run out of there, and how.

"Brynn," Sawyer said, looking at her straight on. "Henry didn't make me do anything. No one did."

"Sawyer," Margaux interjected, "let's explain some things to Brynn. I think it's time."

"What? What things?" Brynn could feel her heart beating faster.

"There's a lot you don't know," Margaux continued. "You're right about some of it. I want to tell you the truth, I do. But I need to know that I can trust you. I need to know that you are going to stay committed to this family."

"I'm just trying to find the truth. Figure out who killed Cecelia, and why. If Ross really did this . . . then I won't stand by him. But if he didn't . . . if there's a chance that he's innocent, like he told me he is, then I need to see that through." Her own words were starting to sound like meaningless noise.

She glanced over to the mudroom to check again that the boat keys were there.

Brynn blinked. Could she be *certain* that she'd seen the keys in Sawyer's pocket just moments ago? Why hadn't she bothered before to check the hook and see if the keys were there or not? There were so many details she realized she'd probably been missing along the way, but she'd been so tired, so distracted. So busy being a *mom*.

"Okay, then," Margaux said. "Sawyer knows all this already. He's really been my rock throughout all this." She smiled at her son in a way that Brynn had never seen her smile at him before: with approval. Validation. Recognition. What he'd always wanted from *her,* and from Henry. The things that had usually only been reserved for Ross.

"Years ago," Margaux continued, "we had an accident on one of our jobs. It was tragic. Just terrible. A young man was working with an excavator and there was a machine malfunction. Something none of us could have predicted or prevented. Just one of those . . . *accidents.*"

So Margaux knew. She knew all of it, all along. Brynn nodded, acting as though this was new information to her.

"It was no one's fault," she said. "We take on risks in construction. That's what you sign up for. We must accept the consequences of those risks. And that's what happened to this man. He knew that getting hurt was a possibility."

But he didn't just get hurt, Brynn thought to herself. *He died. He was murdered.*

"The thing was, no one else would see it that way," Margaux said. "To anyone else, we knew that it would look like it was our fault, somehow. Like we could have prevented it."

"But if it was just an accident . . . Henry could have called the police," Brynn said.

"Yes," Margaux responded, a little too loud. "But there was nothing we could have done. The man was dead. It was involuntary manslaughter. Operating heavy machinery without an up-to-date license. We thought about going to the police, of course. But think about what would have happened if we'd done that. Think about what would have happened to our family, Brynn. The boys were just coming into their roles in the business, things were coming together for all of us. We couldn't just give that up. Throw it all away. And besides, it wouldn't have changed things. It wouldn't have brought that man back. We had to accept what had happened and move on."

Brynn couldn't believe what she was hearing. But what was more remarkable was the *way* Margaux was telling her this. Margaux spoke as if she truly didn't care, as if she felt no remorse whatsoever, as if another human's life meant nothing to her. Only moments before, she'd called Margaux to *protect* her, to help her. There was no way, she thought, that Margaux—a *mother*—could have known what Henry had done and stood by him.

"This man," Brynn said. "Who was he? Did he have a family?" She imagined what Gabriel might have thought when he first got hired by Nelson & Sons. Henry had surely shared with him his own stories of arriving on the island with little to nothing. The man had probably looked at him and thought, *I want that life. Someday, I can have that, too.* But they stole that from him.

Margaux gave her a confused look.

"We don't know," she said. It was clear to Brynn that Margaux had never wanted to know. It didn't even matter to her. To Margaux, Gabriel meant nothing. To her, he didn't have a name. He never even existed.

"So you chose to protect your family," Brynn said.

"Exactly, Brynn," Margaux said. "We made a pact that no one could ever know. Even the boys. We wanted to protect them—and you—by keeping it from you. The only reason Sawyer knows now is because Henry . . . well, Henry broke that pact."

"He told you?" Brynn asked Sawyer.

"No," he said. "He told *Cecelia.* And then Ross and I found out because she was going to blackmail him."

"I'll never understand why he told that girl so much," Margaux said, with anger in her voice. "I don't know why he always talked to *her* instead of me. I'm his wife. She was just some girl."

Brynn couldn't believe how inhumane Margaux sounded—how detached from all human emotion. *That girl* . . . Margaux had known Cecelia just as long as any of them, and now Cecelia was dead. Her language scared Brynn. But at the same time, there was a tiny part of Brynn that understood what Margaux was saying. How hurtful it must have been to have had her longtime husband turn toward someone else for compassion and comfort instead of her.

"I gave everything to Henry," Margaux said. "I *sacrificed* things for him. My body, my time, a chance at my own career. I suppose that's what all mothers do, in a way. Men will never understand the sacrifices we make to give them children. And this is what he did for me in return? He betrayed me, our entire *family.* And for what? To get something off of his chest? To share our deepest secret with some girl who was practically still a teenager?" She paced around, her arms crossed. "You know, Brynn, Henry really *is* losing it." Margaux's anger was palpable. It radiated from her.

And the truth was, Brynn knew that Margaux *had* given her entire life to Henry and his plan. She'd worked tirelessly for him, and with him, and without him, to build a life for their family that he'd always wanted. And Henry had chosen to betray her, whether or not his intentions were good. Whether or not *she* was good. He'd still turned his back on her.

But Margaux's coldness and her utter lack of humanity frightened Brynn to her core.

"I know that you would have done anything to protect this family, Margaux," Brynn said. "But why did Cecelia have to die, too?"

"I've had to make choices that . . . that might be hard to understand,

Brynn. But you must know that it was all for you, right?" Margaux smiled at her—a smile that felt so misplaced that Brynn actually grimaced in return. "I did what was best for us. I only wanted to keep the family together and for everyone to have what they need. I wanted my children to have the best life possible. What mother wouldn't do anything to make that happen? That's what mothers do, right?"

Brynn nodded.

"You'd do the same thing, Brynn. Now that you're a mother."

Brynn wanted to scream that she'd *never* do what Margaux did, but she knew that she had to keep her talking. There was still so much more she needed to know.

"So," Brynn said, gently, "what happened with Cecelia, then? What was she going to do?"

"She was going to destroy us, Brynn," Margaux said. "She was. I had to stop her."

"What did you do?"

"Henry came home that night," Margaux said. "I knew right away that he'd done something terrible. That he'd made a mistake. I can always tell. He started *crying*. He said he'd let it all slip. He'd told Cecelia *everything*. To clear his conscience? It was entirely selfish of him. Reckless and selfish."

Margaux paused and looked out the window; then she turned back toward Brynn.

"But he did say that there might be a chance to salvage things," she said. "He thought that we might be able to pay her to stay quiet. It seemed that Cecelia wasn't as well-intentioned as we all thought. She wanted to take advantage of Henry's vulnerability. So, I went to talk to her myself. To make a deal."

"That night? You were going to pay for her silence?" Brynn asked.

"Yes," Margaux said. "And if she'd just taken it, we'd all be fine right now. I offered her money—quite a lot of money. I thought that's what she wanted, after all. That's the whole reason she was at the club in the first place. She wanted *in*. But I was wrong. She said she didn't want a penny from us. She said she wanted nothing to do with us, that we were *disgusting* to her. Can you imagine her telling me that?"

Margaux's voice was shaking, and Brynn could see the vein on her forehead protruding.

"It was very hurtful, what she said," Margaux continued.

Brynn remembered what Jacob had told her about Cecelia planning to extort Henry, to take the awful truth and use it to her advantage. Turns out, he'd been wrong. Cecelia had changed her mind. In the end, she was going to do the right thing. This island might have killed her, but it hadn't destroyed who she was at her core. It hadn't ruined her. Cecelia had been good. But it had been too late.

"I understand," Brynn said, trying to keep Margaux engaged, "and so . . . what happened? Was it Mauricio who did it? Did you pay him to help you?" Brynn was still trying to figure out who was on the security footage. She was desperate for Margaux to say that it was *anyone* but Ross. But at this point, there was simply no other explanation.

"Mauricio?" Margaux asked, confused. "He wasn't involved."

"So, then, it was Ross? Just tell me! Were you all in on it together?" Brynn felt like she was back at square one.

"You have to understand something else," Margaux said. "Before all this, before Henry spilled his guts to Cecelia, we learned that Ross was building a case against us. Our own son. He had told Henry that he *had* to come clean, and if Henry didn't do it himself, Ross would do it for him. He'd been collecting evidence against us—his *family*! The people who gave him everything."

"How long had this been going on?" Brynn asked. "What do you mean collecting evidence?"

"Oh, come on, Brynn, you know," Margaux said. "Ross was digging up anything he could on his father and anything he'd done wrong in his business. And then, Ross found out about the man, from twenty years ago. I think . . . I think that was too much for Henry."

"What do you mean, too much?" Brynn asked.

"Henry couldn't handle facing that again. When Ross brought it up and told him that he had to turn himself in . . . Henry was no longer willing to choose his family over the truth. You've seen it yourself . . . he's been losing it."

"Or maybe he's just been feeling guilty," Brynn said. "Maybe he wanted to confess. He wanted the truth to come out. He couldn't live with the lie anymore."

"Well, I obviously couldn't let that happen," Margaux said. "You know, it's always the women who are strong enough to make the tough decisions. The ones no one wants to make. But they're the decisions that keep families together."

"So, what did you do?" Brynn had been bouncing Lucas up and down to try to keep him calm. It wasn't going to work much longer; she could feel him starting to claw at her chest for milk. "Did you make Ross kill Cecelia?"

Margaux stared into her eyes, assessing her, probing her. Brynn knew that the one thing Margaux truly *would* fight for was her family, especially Lucas. Margaux couldn't lose him, which meant that she couldn't lose Brynn. She had to let Brynn in, finally. She had to tell her the truth.

"Brynn," Margaux said. "I thought you'd have figured it out by now. No. Ross didn't kill Cecelia. But my own son who I birthed, and fed, and took care of, and who I gave *everything* to . . . he was ready to turn his back on all of us. He was ready to throw us to the wolves. He was ready to do something even worse."

"But then . . . I still don't understand," Brynn stammered. "If Ross didn't kill her, then who did? What happened? Is the security footage from the club fake? Did Pete doctor it to frame Ross?"

Brynn felt the vibration of her phone in her back pocket. She couldn't look at it now, as much as she wanted to. She had to keep Margaux on track. But her stomach dropped as she imagined the possibilities. What if it was Jacob, telling her that Pete had intercepted him and was on his way instead? Or—the worst of all—what if something had happened to Ginny and her baby?

"I just wanted to have a civilized conversation with Cecelia, I really did," Margaux said. "But she was being *crazy*. Unhinged. Irrational. Even after I offered her a very, very generous deal. The girl should have taken it. She was foolish. I couldn't talk sense into her. I could feel things just . . . slipping out of my control. You know how that feels, right?"

Brynn did know how that felt. She knew *exactly* how that felt—to have everything you thought you knew to be true ripped apart, to not know where to turn or what to do. That's how she'd felt since Lucas was born. But it made Brynn sick to hear Cecelia being talked about this way, while her lifeless body was underground and while her family still mourned.

The kitchen sink faucet had been dripping. Margaux turned her back to Brynn and went to turn it off. As Brynn watched her go, she noticed the way her legs moved and the way her shoulders remained squared off, the way the flat of her foot hit the floor with each step. She and Ross really did have the same build and the same gait.

And then, it hit her.

"Oh my God," Brynn whispered. "The security footage isn't fake. It was *you*. It's not even Ross on the camera at all. It's *you*." Brynn had always thought that Ross and his mother looked strikingly similar and had the same build. Sometimes she even felt strange looking at Margaux; it was as if she were looking at an alternate version of her husband. But she'd never, ever considered *this* a possibility.

Margaux turned around slowly and faced Brynn.

"You killed Cecelia," Brynn said.

"It's not what you think," Margaux said, calmly. "I never planned to kill her. And I never planned to frame my son. But this girl, well, she was being so irrational. She was scaring me, Brynn. I happened to be standing right next to Ross's locker. I took a golf club out just to . . . protect myself. And it was cold, so I put on a jacket and a hat."

Margaux paused, the holes in her story becoming more and more visible. She looked at Brynn closely, as though to ensure their bond before she said anything more.

Brynn imagined this—Margaux making the conscious decision to reach into her son's locker, to disguise herself with his clothes, to arm herself for battle. She wondered if in that moment, Margaux had remembered Ross as a baby. She wondered if she remembered when and where he took his first steps, or when he first said *mama,* or when he broke his arm in the fourth grade, or when he was six and he insisted on her reading *Where the Wild Things Are* over and over again until he fell asleep. All the things that Brynn could picture unfolding in the future for Lucas—the good and the bad—that she'd be there for. Or, at least, that she hoped she would.

"But . . . how did things escalate?" Brynn asked. Even now, there was a part of her that was hoping Margaux would say *This is all a misunderstanding. We had nothing to do with Cecelia's terrible death.* Brynn didn't want to believe that Margaux was capable of doing what she knew she was about to admit. She didn't want to believe that *anyone* was.

"I swear, Brynn, I thought that Cecelia was going to hurt me. She started to come at me, and I . . . I didn't know what she was going to do. I swung at her. Just once. Only once." Brynn thought she detected remorse from Margaux, a moment in which she thought Margaux might break down and cry. Maybe the first moment in which she realized the gravity of what she'd done, the permanence of it. But instead, Margaux stiffened and pushed her shoulders back. "It was self-defense," she said. "Nothing more."

Brynn could hear the thud of the golf club against Cecelia's skull, the cracking of her bone, the ripping of her flesh, the sticky dripping of her blood. The vision of Ross running toward her came to life now, in her mind, but this time, he slowed down and paused, and he craned his head to the side, and then turned his body back toward the security camera. It wasn't Ross. It never was. It was Margaux. Margaux, in her own son's jacket. Margaux, with the same build and the same gait, the sturdy and confident physique that she'd passed down to him. Margaux, who had spent countless hours caring for Lucas, soothing him, loving him, while Brynn had been somewhere else, asleep, her trust entirely placed in Margaux's bloodstained hands.

"We didn't plan to do it," Sawyer chimed in. "It was an accident, Brynn."

"What do you mean *we*?" Brynn asked. Sawyer had remained unusually quiet while Margaux had spoken.

"Well, I wasn't going to leave my own mother all alone with this," Sawyer said, as if that were the most normal response in the world. "She needed my help. It was an *accident*."

"You didn't even think to call the police?" Brynn asked. "Sawyer, we *knew* Cecelia. She was a human being. She was . . . she was . . . How *could* you?"

"Come on, Brynn," Sawyer said. "It really was an accident. Self-defense. My mom is not a murderer. But the police would never believe us. It looked bad."

"How could we ever have explained it?" Margaux asked. "Everything would unravel."

Even now, it seemed like Margaux had confidence that her plan would work, that she'd get away with it all, and that she and Henry could continue on with their perfect family and reputations intact. Ross would be the only one to bear any consequences.

"But . . . Ross," Brynn said, "how could you let him just take the blame when he had *nothing* to do with this?"

"How many times do I have to explain this?" Margaux was frustrated now. Brynn had never seen this side of her—flustered, angry, the bitter, blunt end of her emotional fuse gnawed down to nothing. "Ross was plotting against us. And all the while, everything he had was because of our hard work. Why can't you see that, Brynn?"

Brynn wished that Ross had gone straight to the police once he'd found the letter. Everything could have been different. Cecelia would still be alive. Except, maybe not. The police might *not* have believed him. And a body might not ever be found.

Margaux continued. "He was going to take Lucas—and you—away from us. I don't know why he hadn't yet. But he was planning to."

"We couldn't let him destroy everything, Brynn," Sawyer said. "And you were having such a hard time. We were also thinking about what was best for you. Ross hadn't been there for you like he should have. We all know that. You needed more support than he was giving you."

"Don't even try to involve me in this," Brynn said. Sawyer might have been right, that Ross certainly hadn't been there for her when she'd needed him most, but that didn't mean he should be in jail for something he didn't do.

"It just made sense," Sawyer said.

Made sense? Brynn thought. The way he said it was so nonchalant, as if he were talking about picking a convenient spot for a coffee date. Not putting his own brother away for a murder that he didn't commit.

"So, you . . . you came here, to *my house,* to steal Ross's boat keys, and then you went and took Cecelia and dumped her off of Norton?"

"I'm not saying that I did or didn't," Sawyer said. "But that would be a heck of a plan, wouldn't it?" He smiled at her. The same smile he'd always given her. She only noticed now how crooked it was, how sinister.

Brynn was starting to piece it all together. She couldn't believe that she hadn't seen it before. It all made sense now. It was all so clear. Sawyer and Margaux weren't geniuses. They'd just planted the right evidence in the right spots and spun the perfect narrative. *Almost* perfect.

"And the hat you planted at the club," Brynn said, "the one Pete showed me at the station? I know you got that off the boat. And that makes no sense. Because Ross *only* kept that on the boat. Why would he ever go *back* to the club and drop that hat there?" Brynn knew what she was saying made sense, and yet it was such a small glitch in all the evidence they had compiled against Ross. She still didn't have enough solid ground for anyone else to believe that Ross was innocent and that his own family had orchestrated this against him.

"Maybe so," Sawyer said, "but I don't think anyone's going to worry about that now."

Brynn's phone rang again, but she couldn't answer it. Her heart sank. She pictured Ginny in the operating room, crying, trying to reach her. Brynn had to get out of here, away from these people.

"Listen," Margaux said, "Ross was going to take us down anyway. He had already decided a long time ago to betray his family. Do you think you two would have this house if not for my hard work? I gave him the life he has—the life *you* have—and he was ready to throw us to the wolves."

"But we didn't *plan* to set him up, Brynn," Sawyer added. "Ross had been digging through all of our dad's stuff. He was onto him. And whatever he found, he was going to use it to take us all down. And now . . . maybe this is how things were meant to be. Maybe we can all move on from this together."

"Sawyer is going to take over for Henry," Margaux said, matter-of-fact. "He's always been better suited for the job. And Ross . . . he's not innocent, you know. He might not have killed someone, but like Sawyer said, he was going to betray his own blood."

"You really came up with the perfect plan," Brynn stammered. "You silenced Cecelia forever and then you silenced Ross by putting him in jail. And now . . . what? You're just going to act like everything is okay? Take over the business? Act *normal*? Pretend to be *happy*?"

"Yes. And you are, too, Brynn," Margaux said. "I know this is hard to accept. It's a lot to take in. It's painful. I know you might not understand all the decisions I've made. The actions I've taken in the best interest of my family. But you will. You're a mother, too, Brynn. This is what mothers do."

Brynn had a decision to make, except she'd already made it. Long ago.

"No, Margaux," she said. "It's not what mothers do. It's what killers do."

CHAPTER 27

The screen door to Brynn's kitchen didn't burst open, but it creaked open slowly, as if a gentle gust of wind had pushed it.

"Don't move," Jacob said, so quiet it almost came out as a whisper. Brynn wasn't even sure she heard him at first. She was so used to hearing noises coming from the monitor. But then she looked and saw him there, holding his gun out in front of him with such fragility that it almost seemed too heavy for him. His face was stony, but Brynn could tell that he was terrified.

Brynn had been eyeing the door to plot her exit, clutching Lucas tightly to her. She could run to a neighbor's house, she thought. Or run into the woods behind the house. She'd tried to pretend with Margaux and Sawyer that she was on their side, to protect herself until she was away from them. She'd tried to not let on that *she* was the one who had been searching for the truth. But she couldn't pretend anymore. Something inside of her had snapped. She had to get away from them and never look back.

"Backup is on the way right now," Jacob said. "Don't move."

"Is your father coming?" Margaux asked, not skipping a beat. She seemed relaxed. Even now, Brynn thought, Margaux appeared completely confident. She was so used to getting her way, she didn't know how to accept that this time, it might not work out for her.

"Actually, no. He's too busy down at the station," Jacob said. "Being arrested."

Margaux and Sawyer shared a brief glance, and Brynn thought she detected a small crack in Margaux's steeliness. If Pete, the chief of police himself, was being arrested, then things weren't looking good for them.

"Cecelia knew about my dad's involvement in everything you and Henry were doing," Jacob explained, still holding his gun out. "And I knew all about it, too."

"Well, if you actually *knew* anything and had any proof, you would have brought charges against us a long time ago, Jacob," Margaux said. She said *Jacob* as if he were a child she was reprimanding, one step away from slapping his wrist.

"You're right," Jacob said. "I didn't have enough evidence before. I tried, but I couldn't do anything about the way you were cutting corners, stealing from clients, exploiting your workers. I failed. And I let it go. I started to think that that was just the way things were on this island. I started to think that bad people just got away with bad stuff. Especially on this island." Jacob hung his head, and for a moment Brynn thought he might drop the gun, realize that he was in over his head, and let it all go. "But not anymore. I won't let that happen again. I won't let you get away with what you did to Cecelia."

"What *we* did? Jacob, you're confused," Margaux said. "You know as well as I do that Ross killed her."

"Oh, you didn't know?" Jacob asked, suddenly seeming much more self-assured. "I've been here this whole time. Brynn texted me. I happened to be nearby. I've been right outside the door this whole time. I heard everything you said."

"You didn't hear anything," Margaux scoffed. She glared at Brynn. "It proves nothing."

"Jake, buddy," Sawyer said, inching closer to Jacob, his hands held up. "You just lost your girlfriend. You're in shock. But we're all on the same team here. Let's put the gun down, man. Let's talk about this. You don't want to make a mistake here that you can't take back, right?"

"Step back," Jacob said. "You're done talking."

"Jacob, whatever you think you heard," Margaux said, "it still doesn't prove anything. All the evidence goes to Ross. I'm devastated, of course. He's my *son*, for God's sake. I feel *awful*. We loved Cecelia like a daughter."

"Don't even say her name," Jacob growled. "You don't get to do that."

"You have no proof of anything," Margaux said, definitive.

"Actually," Jacob said, confidently, "I have the original police report filed against Henry when Gabriel went missing twenty years ago. I tracked down the officer who filed it. He'd left the force and moved off-island years ago, but I found him. He remembered it, clear as day."

"An old police report that went nowhere?" Margaux asked. "That's not proof."

"Well, I have proof," Brynn blurted out. "I have something else."

Jacob raised his eyebrows and looked at her, as if to ask, *What are you doing?*

"I have proof," she said again. "I have the letter from Henry."

Sawyer looked surprised, but Margaux just looked disappointed, like she'd been waiting for Brynn to get one step ahead of her.

"A letter saying *what*?" Margaux asked.

"A letter confessing to the murder of Gabriel Barbosa," Brynn said. She pulled the letter out of her pocket and unfolded it for everyone to see. Margaux's face dropped, and Brynn thought she might lunge at her for the letter, but she stayed still. Sawyer looked to his mother, seemingly for guidance. They were almost at the edge of the cliff, and they both knew it.

"Well, a letter doesn't prove anything, either. Where's the body then?" Margaux scoffed.

"We're going to find it. The letter says where it is. The property, anyway." Brynn tried to sound brave, but she was worried that Margaux was right. What if they *never* found his body? What if the letter proved nothing?

Jacob shuffled his feet, and Brynn thought he might drop his gun he still seemed so nervous.

"The thing is," Jacob said, "we don't even need the letter. Because Henry is telling us everything right now. You see, Henry was picked up and brought down to the station. We're just waiting on the FBI. They're flying in from Boston right now to take over the case. But apparently Henry's already spilled his guts to the local police that are holding him. He's confessed everything. And he told them what you did to Cecelia as well, Margaux. That, combined with what I just overheard myself . . . well, as they say, things have sort of taken a bad turn for you, haven't they?"

Brynn was impressed. Jacob had scrambled and actually come through. He'd done it for Cecelia. He'd fought to get her the justice she'd always tried to find herself.

"Well, we're happy to clear up any confusion. You know, Jacob, Henry really isn't *there* mentally anymore. He's lost it. You know that. You really can't believe a word he says." Margaux shook her head.

"We thought you'd say that," Jacob said. "Henry warned us that you'd say *exactly* that, in fact. From what I've heard today, Henry is as sharp as a tack. I think he just had to get some heavy stuff off his chest."

"Brynn," Sawyer said to her, pleading. "Are you really going to do this to us?"

"Sawyer," Brynn said, "you did all of this to yourself."

Margaux looked down at the floor. It finally seemed to be dawning on her that it was all crashing down, that it was over. She looked up at Brynn.

"Does it not mean anything to you that we're family, Brynn?" she asked. "Lucas needs his grandmother."

"We're not family," Brynn said. "I don't think we ever were."

This time, Margaux and Sawyer had no response. There was nothing left to say. They both seemed to shrink, their shoulders caving in, as if the air in the room were crushing them.

The sound of sirens grew louder, and then there were police flooding the house. Margaux and Sawyer didn't even try to resist.

"Don't say anything," Margaux said to Sawyer. "Not a word."

Brynn looked at Sawyer as the police escorted him out. Suddenly, her great what-if was gone. It was sad, in a way, that the years she'd felt a certain way about him now felt like they existed in another lifetime, a movie, a dream. She wondered if he'd always been who he was today, or if he'd changed along the way. If he'd grown angry with the world and his place in it. Or if he'd been complacent, too scared to do what he knew was right, too cowardly to say no to his own parents' wrongdoings.

"Please tell me you weren't bluffing," Jacob said to Brynn once everyone had moved outside. "About the letter. Because, uh, we could definitely use it."

"Nope," she said. "I wasn't bluffing. This is what Ross wanted me to find." She handed it to him.

"A few agents are heading out to the site where Henry said the body is. I guess it's way out in a hundred-acre property on Great Pond. Want to go for a drive?"

"Are you kidding? No," Brynn said. "But I hope they find him. I hope Gabriel's family can finally have some peace."

"They will," Jacob said. "I'm going to make sure of it."

Brynn nodded. "And Ross? When can I see him? When can he get out?"

"They're working on dropping the charges now. It's in motion. And my dad . . . he's at the station, too. Awaiting questioning by the FBI."

Brynn knew how hard that must have been for Jacob. How this would alter his life forever. How he'd already been through a trauma losing Cecelia, and now he'd have to mourn the loss of his father, too, in a way.

"Well, I'll let you know what we find out there," he said to her. "Thank you, Brynn. I doubted you at first, and I'm sorry for that."

"I doubted myself, too. It's okay," she said.

"And I doubted Cecelia, too. I really thought she wanted to get money out of this situation, and I thought she'd put herself in danger because of it. I'm not proud of it, but that's what I thought." Jacob looked down at his feet.

"You didn't doubt her, Jacob. Sometimes it's easier to blame the people we love when something bad happens. It's a lot easier to be angry at someone you love than it is to miss them." Brynn thought about how angry she'd been at Ross for the past few months, how distant they'd felt from each other, and how she hadn't been able to admit that her anger might have actually been the pain and longing for the love they used to have. The love that she hoped they could have together again.

"Thank you," Jacob said, nodding. "We'll be in touch, Brynn. This isn't going to be a fast process, you know. Or an easy one. But we will get justice for Cecelia. And whoever else they hurt before her. We will. I owe it to her."

Once everyone had gone, Brynn was alone with Lucas. She was grateful that he was still a baby, and he'd never remember what had just transpired. He wouldn't carry the weight of this trauma with him. There was still time for him to grow up happy, without worry, only feeling loved and safe.

She sat down to feed him. They were both hot and sticky with sweat. She hadn't realized how hard she'd been holding him to her for the past hour, and how overheated she'd become. She needed water.

She shut her eyes, just for a moment. But then there was a knock on the door.

"Brynn?" she heard. "Are you home? Brynn?"

The moment she heard the voice on the other side of the door, she began crying. She cried tears of relief. It was finally the voice of the one person who could help her, who could take care of her, who could tell her that everything was going to be okay, that she was doing a great job as a mom, that things would get easier, that none of this was her fault.

She put Lucas down in his swing and ran to the person who'd come through the door, burying her face in their chest, breathing them in, feeling sorrow and comfort and gratitude all at once. She hadn't known until that moment that this was the only person in the world she needed to see right now. The only person who could make things better.

"Mom." Brynn sighed. "Mom."

CHAPTER 28

It seemed ludicrous to go to sleep when there was so much going on, when there were so many things that could happen at any moment, but Brynn's mother insisted.

"I'm here now," she told her. "Go rest. I know what to do."

It had been Brynn's mother calling her, when Margaux and Sawyer had been over. She'd gotten a sixth sense, she'd told Brynn, that her daughter needed her. And when Brynn didn't answer, she decided that she'd just show up on her doorstep.

And this time, Brynn welcomed her. This time, Brynn agreed that her mother *did* know what to do. She'd known all along, but Brynn hadn't wanted to accept her help. Now, she was ready. Now, she needed it. They'd talk later, Brynn knew. She'd apologize to her mother later. And her mother would apologize to her, too. But right now, Brynn needed to sleep. She texted Annie and Marcus before she dozed off, asking for an update.

Nothing yet, Annie said.

When Brynn woke, three hours later, the house was quiet. Peaceful. She looked outside. The sun was just making its descent, and the air seemed to have cooled. A breeze blew through the trees. Brynn went downstairs to the living room.

Her mother was working on a needlepoint pillow—she always was—and had made herself a cup of tea. Lucas looked content, asleep in his swing.

"Thank you, Mom," Brynn said. "For coming."

Her mother looked up from her work and smiled.

"I'm going to stay as long as you need me," she said. "As long as you like."

"I'd really like that," Brynn said. "I need your help. I'm sorry I didn't ask for it before. I didn't know how. I didn't know I really needed it." She sat down next to her. "It's just been so hard. I mean, even before all this. Motherhood, I mean. I just . . . I wasn't prepared."

"Brynn, *no one* is prepared for motherhood. You can't prepare. Not really."

"But I just never expected to feel this way. I never expected to . . ."

"To not like being a mom?" her mother interjected. "No one loves being a mom all the time, you know."

"But I feel guilty," Brynn said. "I feel guilty for missing my old life. Obviously, I love Lucas, but . . . sometimes I look at him and I just . . . *resent* him. For ruining things. For making life so much harder. Sometimes I think *What have I done?*"

"I think every mother in the world has felt that way, even if they don't admit it," Brynn's mother said.

"I'm a bad mom," Brynn said.

"No, you're not. You're an amazing mom," she responded. "But you're also a human being."

Brynn felt a feeling of homesickness—not for her old home, necessarily, but for the time she'd lost with her mother, the time she'd lost with herself. There were so many things that had permanently changed since she'd had Lucas—even since she'd become pregnant. There were so many facets of her life that had morphed into something else, or been replaced, or simply disappeared. She'd never be able to be as spontaneous as she was before, deciding at the last minute to go on a trip or have that extra drink at the bar. She'd never be able to hole herself up in her room for a week straight and subsist only on ramen noodles and popcorn while she poured herself into a novel. She'd never be able to move someplace where no one knew her and start over as someone mysterious, someone free, someone with no ties to anyone or anything. She'd never not feel a tight tingling in her lower abdomen where her C-section scar was. She'd never not have stretch marks running down the tops of her breasts like water lines after a flood. She'd never not hear a child scream and panic, thinking, *Where's Lucas?*

None of those things seemed important, when she really thought about them. And yet, they *were* important, and Brynn knew that she needed to give herself permission to acknowledge that. She needed to grieve. She needed to accept the loss of things in her life as much as she'd accepted the new changes. She was not who she used to be, and she would never be her again.

"I'm sorry I pushed you away," Brynn said.

"Stop apologizing," her mother said. "We both should have done things differently, I suppose. But I'm here now. We're here together." She rose and went to the kitchen to prepare a bottle for Lucas, who was beginning to wake up. "You know," she said from the kitchen, "a mother's job is not just to take care of her children. It's also to take care of herself. And I should have told you that, Brynn."

Her mother emerged from the kitchen, bottle in hand. She suddenly saw her mother as someone other than her mother, for the first time. She saw her as a woman, as *a* mother, not just hers, someone who had an entire life before giving birth to her, someone whom Brynn had never really gotten to know aside from the way she knew her as her daughter.

"I know you're right," Brynn said. "And I haven't been taking care of myself. But I . . . I haven't been ready to admit what I'm feeling. But, Mom, I know that I don't want to feel this way. I don't want to be this depressed. I want to love Lucas more. I want to love *being* with him.

Maybe not all the time, but most of the time. And I want to love Ross again. I want to love my life again."

"What about you?"

"What do you mean?" asked Brynn.

"The first thing you need to do is love *yourself* again," her mother said.

"Yeah, I know, but . . ."

"No, really, Brynn. I know that sounds a little hippy-dippy, and I'm just your mom, but trust me, you've got to start by acknowledging how far you've come, what an incredible job you're doing. You've got to love *you* before you can love your boys."

Brynn nodded. "Easier said than done, though."

"Yes," her mother said. "But you will get there. We're going to get you into therapy. You can talk to your doctor about medications. We should find you some scheduled help, or daycare. So that you have time for *you*."

"Will you help me?" Brynn asked. "I don't know where to start. I can't do all that alone."

"Honey," her mom replied, "that's why I'm here. To help."

Her mother picked Lucas up and began to feed him. Lucas was comfortable in his grandmother's arms, as if he knew her deeply, as if he knew he was connected to her.

"Thanks, Mom," Brynn said as she watched them.

Her mother looked at her but didn't say anything; she didn't need to. Brynn knew that her mother had done her best. She had tried to be a good mother, in the ways that she knew how, with the limited resources she'd had. She'd kept Brynn safe and healthy, she'd gotten her to college, she'd driven her to the library or the Boys & Girls Club whenever she'd needed to go. Maybe she hadn't fit the mold that Brynn had wanted in a mother, but when she thought about what that meant to her now, it all seemed irrelevant. Margaux had been the archetype of the good mother Brynn had wanted her own mother to be: someone who knew how to use a baby monitor, who understood sleep training, who showed up with homemade pots of white bean chili and fruit salad, who bought herself a brand-new car seat when her grandson was born so she could shuttle him around, who converted their guest room into a nursery just for him. But what Margaux lacked, her mother had, or, at least, she had the potential to give, even if she hadn't given it all before. Brynn's own mother had integrity. She had decency. Her love for Brynn—and for Lucas—might not be perfect, but it was honest, and it was unconditional. Brynn's mother lived her life by an ethical code that was selfish, at times, but was well intentioned. Brynn decided then and there that she'd take all that over the perfect cookie-baking grandmother any day.

Lucas finished the bottle and Brynn watched as her mother burped him. It wasn't how she usually did it—with one or two full palm slaps to the back. Her mother patted his back gently, like rain pattering on a roof. Brynn opened her mouth to correct her but then decided not to say anything. Lucas would be fine whether her mom burped him *right* or not. It was okay to take a step back.

"God," Brynn said, "Lucas looks bigger than he did yesterday. It's like he changes overnight."

"That's what babies do," her mother said. "They remind us how fleeting everything is. Each moment unfolds into the next. Sometimes, you just want to stand still. But you can't. That's sort of the joy of it, too, though. Going along for that ride."

Her mother was right. Everything was changing, Brynn thought. And changing so *fast,* all the time. She'd been trying to fight the momentum. She'd been holding on to the past, clinging to it the way you'd cling to a tree in a tornado. She hadn't let herself be present for the ride. She hadn't let herself move forward. Now, she needed to let go.

Brynn's phone rang. Her mother nodded to her as if to say *I've got Lucas, go.*

Ginny's name flashed across Brynn's phone screen; she frantically reached for it to answer.

"Ginny!" she yelled. "Ginny, I've been so worried."

"Hi," Ginny said. Her voice sounded tired and weak. Brynn's stomach dropped instantly. It was the weight of this whole mess that had put Ginny in such distress. She just knew it.

"Oh, Ginny, I'm so sorry," Brynn started to say.

"Brynn," Ginny said, interrupting her. "We have a baby girl," Ginny said. "She's perfect, Brynn. Totally perfect."

Tears sprang from Brynn's eyes. Her whole body seemed to exhale in relief.

"Brynn? Are you there?"

"Sorry," Brynn said, wiping her tears away with the palms of her hands. "I'm just so happy for you. I'm so happy."

"She was so brave, Brynn. She's a fighter."

"Just like her mom," Brynn said. "I can't wait to meet her. And I can't wait to see you. How are you feeling? I want to hear everything. When you're ready."

"I will be okay. It was scary, for a while. And I'll tell you the whole story when we're home. But the point is, we made it out okay." Brynn heard the cry of Ginny's baby girl in the background. It was that distinct, newborn screech that can only come from a brand-new life, screaming out to be heard in a terrifying, overwhelming, brand-new world. And then Brynn heard the cry begin to abate and transform into a pattern of tiny breaths. "Shh," Brynn heard Ginny tell her daughter. "I'm right here."

Brynn continued to wipe her tears away. She felt a surge of gratitude that Lucas was healthy, and so was she. Her own birth experience had been traumatic, but they'd survived it. And for that, she was lucky. She was thankful. She would learn later, once Ginny was home, that Ginny had suddenly felt a lack of movement in her belly. Her instincts told her to go to the hospital immediately. She knew that something was wrong. And she'd been correct. Her umbilical cord had become wrapped around her daughter's neck and was cutting off her oxygen. They'd done the C-section immediately in the Martha's Vineyard Hospital, but they'd had to medevac them both to Mass General to restore the baby's oxygen levels and get her into the NICU. Ginny had almost lost her daughter after she'd birthed her. But she hadn't. They'd both survived.

"The real question," Ginny said, "is how are *you* doing? I heard what happened."

"Of course you already heard," Brynn said. "Even in the hospital. It's the Vineyard."

They both laughed a little.

"Well," Ginny said, "seriously, though, are you okay?"

"I will be," Brynn said. "Ross will be home soon, hopefully. I don't know what we're going to do, or if we'll stay here, or what will happen, there's a lot to figure out . . ." Brynn was rambling. "And two people are dead. Because of my family."

"Brynn," Ginny said. "None of this is your fault. You know that, right?"

She shook her head silently. Brynn *didn't* know that. Somehow, it *all* felt like it was her fault.

"I know," she lied. "I just don't even know where to start picking the pieces up."

"One day at a time," Ginny said. "That's how you start. Today, you focus on today. Tomorrow, you focus on tomorrow."

"One day at a time," Brynn said. "Okay."

CHAPTER 29

A few days later, Ross was home, while his mother, father, and brother sat in jail, awaiting their arraignments. Along with the disgraced former police chief.

The reunion between Brynn and Ross had not been one of fervor and longing. It had been awkward and clunky, uncertain, and new. Brynn went to pick him up at the jail, with Lucas in tow.

Ross looked different when he came outside. Though it had only been a few days, he'd grown a scruffy beard. He looked exhausted. But he also, somehow, seemed lighter, and younger, and more at ease. He seemed more like the Ross that Brynn had fallen in love with.

She wasn't sure whether she should hug him or not. Neither was he. She wasn't sure she *wanted* to hug him. But they did embrace. It was a strange meeting of their bodies; at first, they held back, but after a second, their muscles seemed to soften, and they leaned on each other, finally. His embrace felt different from Sawyer's. Being with Ross felt comfortable. It felt right.

Lucas was in his car seat. He gurgled with a smile when he saw Ross, who opened the back door and stuck his head up against Lucas's. He breathed in the scent of his son. Brynn could see Ross' body relax.

"I've missed you both so much," Ross said, closing Lucas's door. He opened the front passenger door and climbed in.

"We've missed you, too," Brynn said.

She backed out of the jail parking lot and turned up Edgartown–Vineyard Haven Road. Lucas was quiet. The radio was off. The three of them sat in silence as she drove. They passed by the Stop & Shop, its renovation just completed within the last week. They drove past Donaroma's, whose June flower beds of peonies and poppies were now replaced by midsummer hydrangeas and dahlias. Everything looked different, and yet, it was all the same as before, too.

"Brynn," Ross said. "I want to start from the beginning. I want to explain everything. If you will listen. And . . . I understand if you won't. You have every right to be angry with me."

Brynn was angry with him. Not just for the secrets he'd kept from her, even if he had been trying to protect her. She'd been angry with him *before* all this. She'd been angry with him from the day Lucas was born. And she was angry with herself for not telling him. But she'd tell him now.

"I am angry," she said, "but not just because of what's happened. I'm angry because you haven't been there for me like I've needed you to be. It hasn't felt like we're *partners,* Ross. And that's what we always were before, right? I should have told you how I felt more, and I didn't, but I didn't really know what I was feeling. Or I didn't think I was allowed to feel it. Either way, I'm telling you now that we need to change things. We need to be in this *together,* as parents, and as partners. I'm drowning, Ross, and I can't do this alone."

"I know," he said. "There's no excuse. This isn't how I wanted our life to be, either. I never wanted you to feel like you were in this alone, Brynn, ever. I'd do anything for you. *Anything.* I promise, whatever you need from here on out, I will do it."

Brynn took a deep breath. "I want to believe you, but you've lied to me already. It's going to be hard for me to just . . . trust you again."

"I know," he said. He looked down at his hands.

Brynn drove through the rotary past the high school and turned onto Barnes Road to avoid the Vineyard Haven traffic.

"Well," she said. "Start from the beginning, then."

"Okay," Ross said. "I guess it actually starts when we first moved back to the island. When we decided to make our life here."

Lucas had fallen asleep. Brynn and Ross agreed to keep driving, all the way to the Aquinnah cliffs, so that Lucas could sleep, and they could talk. She put the travel sound machine on so they wouldn't wake him.

When they first moved back to the island, Ross told her, the future looked so bright. Everything was falling into place. Brynn was working on her second book, feeling motivated and inspired, and Ross was learning the ropes from his father, ready to take over in just a few years. Business was booming, Ross and Brynn were in love, and everything seemed . . . *perfect*.

And then, Brynn became pregnant. The Nelsons were *elated*. Margaux wasted no time getting their house ready to be the best grandparents they could be. Henry was excited, too, but the news of becoming a grandparent suddenly made him more nostalgic and sentimental. He started telling Ross that he wasn't sure it was a good idea for Ross to take over the company—that Ross could do something better with his life, something more important. He started turning down high-profile jobs, the ones the Nelsons had worked so hard to become known for.

"He just wasn't himself. It was like he didn't care about anything anymore," Ross said. "I didn't think that much of it, though, until I found the letter." He looked at Brynn.

"Was it meant to be a suicide note?" Brynn asked.

"I don't know," Ross said. "And I don't think I'll ever know. I'm not sure I want to. Whatever it was, I wasn't meant to see it. But I did."

Ross explained that Henry sent him back to the office from a jobsite one day to get a work order he'd left on his desk. The letter had just been sitting there, in the light of day, right next to his now-cold cup of morning coffee. No one, not even Loretta, went into Henry's office without his permission. But Henry had *asked* Ross to go. It was almost as if he'd wanted Ross to see the letter. Ross had sped back to the jobsite, certain that his father would have taken off, and that it might be too late. But Henry was right there, just as before, directing a carpenter to replace a slightly warped two-by-four with a straight one.

"I waited for him to say something," Ross said, "but he didn't. So, I didn't say anything, either. Not at first."

"But how could you *not*?" Brynn asked. "That letter revealed something horrible. How did you not go to the police right away?"

"Brynn," Ross said, "this is my dad we're talking about. I've idolized him my whole life. To me, my dad was like . . . this god. Someone I aspired to be like. All I've ever tried to do is get his approval. His validation. So, the idea that he could have done something like this was just so . . . so . . ."

"You didn't even believe it, did you?" Brynn asked.

"I couldn't believe it at first," Ross said. "I couldn't let myself believe that it was true. I started telling myself lies about it, making excuses. Maybe he was writing a story. You know, he said he'd always wanted to write a book. Or I thought, maybe he really was developing dementia, and this was some bizarre memory he'd created."

"Wow." Brynn wondered what might have happened if Ross had gone straight to the police instead of waiting. Cecelia would probably be alive.

"I'm not proud of it," Ross said. "But I didn't ignore it completely. I decided that I had to find real proof. The letter wasn't enough. So, I started digging around."

"What do you mean, digging around?"

"I went through all the old project files and records. I had to find out what jobsites they were working on when this happened. I started snooping around my dad's office at night. That's why I'd come home late so often, Brynn. I was trying to find answers. That's when I found out about how dirty my father's business had been. For years. I wanted nothing to do with my family. And I wanted to get you out, too."

"So, when did you confront your dad and tell him that you knew?" Brynn asked.

"I didn't," Ross said. "My mom found out before I could. She confronted me."

Brynn realized that even in the final moments when Margaux had told Brynn what happened with Cecelia, she'd been lying to her. She'd never told Brynn that she had confronted Ross.

There was nothing Henry did that Margaux wasn't aware of, Ross told Brynn. The day Ross found the letter, Henry told Margaux that it was all over, that he had to confess. That nothing was worth carrying the guilt he had been carrying, and that he didn't want to pass down a legacy of filth to his sons. But Margaux wouldn't have it. When Henry told her that he'd written a confessional letter and that it had disappeared from his desk, she immediately went to Ross, knowing that he'd found it.

"My mom came at me," Ross said, "as if I was the enemy. It was so surreal, Brynn, she acted like I was some stranger coming into *her* life, trying to destroy her. But she and my dad . . . she helped him cover up a *murder*. There was no way I was going to just . . . keep it a secret. That's what she wanted me to do. She wanted me to pretend like I'd never read it. Like the letter wasn't real, it was just some nonsense that Henry had dreamt up."

Brynn shook her head. "You were wrong not to go to the police," she said.

"I couldn't," Ross said. "My mom told me that Pete would just squash it. And . . . she said that if I told *anyone,* she'd find a way to make it seem like I had been in on everything the whole time. All the business stuff. And that would ruin everything for you and Lucas."

"I just can't believe . . . your own *mother* would do this to you." Brynn had pulled into a parking spot outside Aquila. The café's deck was packed with smiling visitors sipping iced mochas.

"I know," Ross said. "But she kept saying that she was doing it for our family. That if I came forward, I would be destroying all of us. Including you and Lucas. And I guess . . . I sort of believed her for a while."

"But why didn't you tell *me?*"

"I couldn't *put* that on you, Brynn. At this point, Lucas was about to be born, and I only wanted you to focus on being happy and healthy. I couldn't burden you with my . . . my own family's fucked-up stuff. And then, after Lucas was born, I knew that something was wrong. I knew that you were unhappy. I just thought that if I acted like everything was normal, and everything was okay, then maybe it would be."

Brynn imagined what might have happened if Ross had come to her. Would they have moved off-island together, gone to the Boston police, changed their last name, started over? Or would Margaux have found a way to implicate Brynn in everything, too? Or, worse, would Brynn have believed Ross, or would she have thought that maybe he was trying to cover up his role in everything, too?

"I started to compile all my evidence secretly," Ross said. "I told Margaux that I destroyed the letter. I told her that I was all in with the family. That I wouldn't betray the Nelson name. But clearly, she didn't believe me, in the end. She must have known that I was planning to turn them in, at the right time. I was just . . . too late."

"But what about Cecelia? I just don't understand how she got caught in everything."

"Brynn," Ross said. "Henry was desperate to tell someone who he knew would turn him in. As crazy as it sounds, he felt trapped. I think he expected *me* to be that person. And then when I wasn't, or he didn't think I was, he went to Cecelia. He had to tell someone he knew was *good.*"

Brynn focused her eyes on a couple on the observation deck looking through the spyglass viewers. All at once, she remembered a moment she'd shared with Henry, just a few days after Lucas was born.

Ross had gone out to pick up dinner. Henry and Margaux had come by for a visit. Margaux was upstairs folding and organizing piles of new baby clothes that she'd just laundered. Brynn and Henry were in the kitchen, while Lucas slept in his bassinet.

"Brynn," Henry had said. "I'm so glad you're part of this family. You're such a good person. You always . . . do the right thing."

"I try," said Brynn. She wasn't really thinking about his words. She'd just given birth four days ago. She wasn't seeing clearly. She wasn't even there.

"I want to tell you something," Henry said. "It's important."

"Okay," Brynn responded.

But just then, Lucas started to cry. Brynn hoisted herself up from the kitchen stool with a heavy sigh. "I'll be right back," she told Henry. She took a bottle out first and popped it in the bottle-warmer machine.

When she returned with Lucas, she sat back down and started to feed him, but Lucas continued to cry, refusing to latch on to the bottle. Brynn had wanted to breastfeed, but she felt uncomfortable doing it right there, alone in the kitchen with Henry.

"We're still getting the hang of things," Brynn muttered, as she continued to try to feed Lucas.

"You're doing a great job," Henry said.

"Sorry, Henry, what did you want to tell me?" Brynn asked him. Lucas turned his head toward Henry just then, away from the bottle.

"Nothing," Henry had said. "Never mind."

And that was all he had said. Brynn had completely forgotten that he'd wanted to tell her something, that he'd tried to. But now, she remembered.

"Ross," she said now, "I think he tried to tell me, too."

"Well, I'm glad he didn't," Ross said. "Who knows what might have happened."

Brynn wondered about that. She might have been able to prevent Cecelia's senseless death if she'd listened to Henry that day. If Lucas had started crying just a minute later. If she hadn't been in such a post-traumatic daze after giving birth. But that wasn't how things had unfolded, and there was nothing she could do about it now.

"It's not your fault," Ross added. "If anything, it's my fault. I should have come forward sooner. I was planning to. I just hadn't yet. And then . . . he told everything to Cecelia. He knew that she would turn him in. He knew that she was smart. He knew that she'd do the right thing."

Brynn felt her stomach churn. She thought about all the things in life that Cecelia would never get to do. All the experiences she'd never have, the joy she'd never feel, the people she'd never love. Brynn had all the freedom to do all of that. She'd never take it for granted again.

"But of course, my mom found out . . . and at that point, she knew that I had made up my mind to turn on her, on all of them. So, she just figured she'd blame it all on me."

"And Sawyer . . . when did he find out everything?" Brynn wasn't ready to tell Ross what had happened between them. She might never tell him. She didn't have to. It had been a mistake. The woman who'd kissed Sawyer wasn't who she was today. And, anyway, Brynn was allowed to have her secrets, too.

"Once my mom knew that I wasn't going to go along with their lies, she started leaning on Sawyer more. He replaced me. And I think it's what he'd always wanted. Not just with work. But with you, too. . . ." Ross let out a sigh. "I know that he picked up the ball sometimes when I dropped it, Brynn. And that's one of my biggest regrets."

Brynn nodded.

"I don't think I'll ever see them again," Ross said. "My own family."

Brynn knew that he was probably right. Once Jacob had arrested them all, he'd quickly organized a team to find Gabriel's body that same day. Everything came crashing down at once, and Henry, Margaux, and Sawyer were taken to jail.

"But we're a family, now," Brynn said. "The three of us."

"Yes," Ross said. "*This* is our family. Do you think we can start over? Just us?"

Brynn and Ross looked at each other. Now, Ross shared her exhaustion. He shared her anxiety. He shared her fears. They were finally in it all together.

They looked at Lucas. He was still sleeping soundly.

"I think we have to," she said.

EPILOGUE

"Mama!" Lucas yelled as he ran across the lawn to the small garden where Brynn was putting a new basil plant in the ground.

Lucas fell on his belly as he ran, splaying his arms out in front of him to catch his fall. Brynn dropped her spade and ran to him, but he got up on his own, laughing. He'd started wobbling on his feet at eleven months, and now, at eighteen months, he was so fast that Brynn could barely keep up with him.

"You're so tough," she said to him, scooping him up in her arms and giving him a kiss on the cheek.

"Mama," he said again.

The soil in Maine was different from the soil on the Vineyard. It was darker, richer, and denser. It was still unfamiliar to Brynn. Even her hearty herbs were struggling this summer. But she knew she'd get the hang of it, soon. Or eventually, anyway.

She and Ross had sold their home almost immediately after he'd been released from jail. They'd decided that the only way to move forward was to get away from the island. If they stayed there, they could never start over. They could never be who they wanted to be. They could never give Lucas the life that he deserved. Nelson & Sons shut down, and a local real estate firm bought the offices to use for their rental business. The family had all but been erased, with only the mansions they'd built left behind as their legacy. Brynn and Ross knew that the island needed to be free from the Nelson family, just as much as they needed to be free from it, too.

Maine seemed like a safe choice for their next chapter. They found a small two-bedroom home to rent just outside of Portland, which had some of the familiarity of the Vineyard but was big and different enough to allow them a fresh start. The house was all they needed. It had a little backyard and a porch with enough space for three chairs.

Brynn and Ross had both testified at the trials of Henry, Margaux, and Sawyer, which were carried out quickly. And they never spoke to any of them directly again. They couldn't. For Ross, it was a reckoning. A re-imagining of his entire childhood, his entire identity. Without his family, he could be himself, though he had to figure out who that was. He had to start over. Brynn got to know him all over again, and slowly, she started to fall in love with him again. But this time, it was different. They were equals, and they trusted each other. They'd been through something that they were certain would break them, but it hadn't.

Now, Ross came home from work every day around five, tired but happy. He was working as an independent carpenter, doing small jobs, mostly custom cabinetry, but he was content. He found meaning in the work. It was honest. It was his own.

During the trials, Brynn had locked eyes with Cecelia's mother at one point. She was certain that Mrs. Buckley recognized her from her visit right after Cecelia's death, when she had pretended to just be one of Cecelia's friends. But Mrs. Buckley had just nodded at her. Nothing would bring Cecelia back. Nothing would ever fill the void that Mrs. Buckley and her family would have forever. Brynn knew, as a mother herself, that Mrs. Buckley would have traded places with Cecelia in a heartbeat if she could have. But she'd never get to do that. Cecelia was gone. Once the trials ended, and all three of the Nelsons were sentenced to life in prison, Brynn knew that at least Cecelia's family could take comfort in knowing that the people who hurt their daughter would never see the light of day again. But all Brynn could do was try to be grateful that she had her own son with her, alive and healthy, and that she'd love him every day as much as she could, since Mrs. Buckley could never do the same.

The transition into their new life hadn't been easy for Brynn and Ross. At first, Brynn was resentful of the potential move. *Why should I have to uproot my life,* she had thought. *Ross should go, not me.* After all, she thought, it was Ross's family that created this whole mess, not hers. But the truth was, she didn't *want* Ross to go anywhere without her. She still wanted to be with him. She still wanted to make it work. Leaving together was the only chance they had.

Before they'd left, Brynn's mother had found her a therapist in Vineyard Haven named Dr. Wanda Lee, or just Wanda, as she liked to be called. Brynn had to pay out of pocket for each session, but it was worth every penny—and it still was. She still saw her virtually every two weeks. Wanda helped Brynn realize that part of her depression was chemical, and there were prescriptions that could help with that. But part of her depression, Brynn learned, was also due to a lack of support, a lack of sleep, a lack of feeling adequate. And those things, Brynn and Ross worked on together, as a team. They still fought, and it wasn't easy, but they were communicating more than ever before. Brynn felt entitled, for the first time, to vocalize her needs, her expectations, and her desires. And this time, Ross listened.

In fact, it was Ross's idea to find a daycare for Lucas. "Maybe just a few days a week?" he had suggested. "I could do drop-off in the mornings." They'd lucked out and snagged a spot at a daycare just a few minutes away. She and Ross had dropped Lucas off together for his first day. She'd sobbed the moment he ran off from them and joined a group of kids gathered around a water table in the fenced-in yard. She had to turn away so he wouldn't see, but Lucas wasn't looking at her, anyway. Ross had put his arm around her as they walked back to the car. She felt like her heart had been ripped right out of her chest. She desperately wanted to run back into the school and grab her son, hold him close, breathe him in, and never let him go. And she told herself that she could, if she really had to. But she didn't. She let him go. And he was happy. Pretty soon, so was she.

And during the time that Lucas was at daycare, Brynn wrote. She poured herself into her third book, feeling much more liberated as a writer this time around. She felt confident in her writing in a way she'd never felt before. Because even when a blank page stared her down, making her question her ability and her ideas, she knew that writing a book would never be as much of a challenge as motherhood was. She knew that she could finish it, and she did.

Her editor told her it was her best yet. "It feels so *authentic,*" her editor had said. It just so happened to be about a dynastic family in a rich summer community whose empire eventually crumbles. With, of course, some juicy sex scenes thrown in.

And Lucas . . . somewhere along the way, Lucas had grown into a young toddler. A real boy. He'd made friends, he'd started babbling, he laughed. Sometimes, after he went to sleep for the night, Brynn collapsed onto the couch and scrolled through newborn photos of him. She wanted to squeeze his chubby newborn thighs, to smell his sweet, sticky skin, to nuzzle his chunky arms and his full cheeks. When she looked at those photos, she felt a longing for a time that she'd missed. She had been there, but she hadn't been present. Even just a little over a year later, she could barely remember those days. Not really. All the things she was certain she'd remember forever had somehow evaporated. Those days seemed so far away now. Or maybe Brynn had blocked it all out from her memory on purpose. Maybe the forgetting was how she'd survived.

But she didn't want to be absent anymore. She didn't want to forget anymore. She didn't want to look back at photos of Lucas a year from now and think *Where was I?* So, she tried to be present with him as much as she could. She tried to put her deadlines and the laundry and the chores on hold when she spent time with him. Sometimes, she couldn't. Sometimes, she had to turn on the television for him so she could get something done—and that was okay. But just as her mother had told her, she knew that each moment with Lucas would just keep unfolding into the next, and she tried to hang on as best she could.

"Are you ready?" Ross asked, rounding the corner from the garage where he'd gone to get his drill. He was reinforcing one of Brynn's raised cedar garden beds, which he'd made for her when they first moved into the house. "Ready to see your friends, I mean."

Ginny, Annie, and Marcus were all coming for a visit that weekend with their kids. Brynn found an Airbnb for them to stay at just down the road, and she had the whole weekend planned out: lobster rolls, wine, laughter, and maybe even a visit to her new local playground, for old times' sake.

Ginny's baby daughter was healthy and thriving. Sam and Olivia had taken her under their wings immediately. Ginny somehow still found the time to write, and she'd finally published the big story on island maternal care. Her piece garnered so much positive momentum that the hospital changed some of their policies to provide more post-partum support. Almost every day, a different mother reached out to her to say one thing: *thank you.*

Annie's business had exploded because of a mention in *The New York Times,* which described her as "the *it* wedding planner of coastal New England." She'd hired several new staff members and rented a bigger office space in downtown Edgartown. Her twins, now in kindergarten, knew the difference between a veil and a train.

And Marcus and his husband were still totally in love, and had managed to fit weekly date nights into their busy schedules. But every now and then, a stranger still assumed that Annie and Marcus were a married couple, and it made them laugh. Their son Liam was starting preschool in the fall.

Her friends were what Brynn missed most about the island, but she knew that they'd all be there for one another in a heartbeat if anything happened. Even though she couldn't see them every day like she used to, she knew they were there.

When Lucas had turned one, they had all FaceTimed her from Ginny's house.

"Happy birthday to Lucas, obviously," Annie had said, "but really happy *birth* day to you, Brynn."

"Yeah," Marcus had said. "You made it."

Ginny had nodded in agreement, her three kids climbing on top of her. "You survived the first year of motherhood, Brynn. You can do *anything.*"

It was true, Brynn thought. She'd been through so much during that past year. She'd helped bring justice to *two* murder victims, she'd walked away from a dangerous family, she'd uprooted her own family's entire life, and she'd written another book. But despite all of that, what Brynn was most proud of was surviving that first year of motherhood. It had been the hardest year of her life, and she was no longer afraid to admit that. She no longer believed that acknowledging her struggles made her a bad mom. There were so many times during that year when she didn't think she'd make it. There were times when she didn't know who she was. There were times when she was certain that she was lost forever, and that she'd never find herself again. There were times when she thought she'd never love Lucas the way she was supposed to.

And yet, she loved him now in such a deeper way than she had known was even possible. She just had to give herself permission to get there on her own time. And, maybe more importantly, she was starting to love *herself* again, as her own mother had told her to.

"I can't wait," Brynn said to Ross.

She picked up Lucas and gave him a raspberry on his belly. He howled in delight.

"Brynn," Ross said, looking at her with a smile, "you're such a good mom."

She laughed.

"You're right," Brynn said. "I am."

ACKNOWLEDGMENTS

Thank you to my agent, Cait Hoyt, the true shepherd of this book from day one. Thank you to the rest of my team: Alex Rice, for guiding this book into the right hands. Michelle Weiner and Alexandra Trustman— thank you for the magic you bring to everything. Thank you to my brilliant editor, Madeline Houpt, for pulling out the best parts of this story and making it shine in a way that I never could on my own. Thank you to the endlessly talented team at Minotaur Books: Omar Chapa, David Roststein, Alisa Trager, Allison Ziegler, Paul Hochman, Michael Clark, Diane Dilluvio, Kayla Janas, Katie Holt, Drew Kilman, Maria Snelling, Esther de Araujo, Terry McGarry, Maddi Bruining, and Megha Jain. After working with all of you, I am certain that there is nothing you can't figure out—and make fabulous.

Thank you to my boys at home, Casey and Winston. Thank you to my parents, Vivian and Lionel, and my sisters, Becca and Laura. Thank you to the Ellistons. Thank you to my local work wife, Emma Brodie. Thank you to my friends and community on Martha's Vineyard, especially my spin class family.

It really does take a village: Thank you to Caroline Davey Hannah for taking such incredible care of Winston so that I could work. This book is for—and because of—you! Thank you to Ariana Binney for loving and caring for him as well. Thank you to Marcy Klapper, too, for always being there with a smile. Thank you to Whitney Januszewski for Saturday mornings. Thank you to Cassie Courtney for being my unofficial co-mother from day one.

Thank you to my local public libraries and their amazing staff, especially the Chilmark Public Library, the West Tisbury Public Library, and the Edgartown Public Library. Thank you to my magical local bookstores, Bunch of Grapes (thank you, Molly!) and Edgartown Books (thank you, Mathew!), for always supporting me.

Last but certainly not least, thank you to you: my readers, especially the parents. You are the heroes.

ABOUT THE AUTHOR

Chandler Cook

Julia Spiro lives year-round on Martha's Vineyard with her partner, their son, and their two rescue dogs. *Such a Good Mom* is her third book.